Other books by Liza Cody

Anna Lee series

DUPE
BAD COMPANY
STALKER
HEADCASE
UNDER CONTRACT
BACKHAND

Bucket Nut Trilogy

BUCKET NUT
MONKEY WRENCH
MUSCLEBOUND

Other novels

RIFT
GIMME MORE
BALLAD OF A DEAD NOBODY
MISS TERRY
LADY BAG
CROCODILES AND GOOD INTENTIONS
GIFT OR THEFT

Anthologies of Short stories

LUCKY DIP and Other Stories
MY PEOPLE and Other Crime Stories

The Short-Order Detective

Liza Cody

gatekeeper press™
Tampa, Florida

Copyright page

LIZA CODY © 2024
The moral right of the author has been asserted.

Cover design © Sam Camden-Smith

The Short-Order Detective

Published by Gatekeeper Press
7853 Gunn Hwy., Suite 209
Tampa, FL 33626
www.GatekeeperPress.com

ISBN (paperback): 9781662950629
eISBN: 9781662950612

For all my friends and family.

The Short-Order Detective

1

I am not built to sit still. The calf muscle in my left leg was jumping, warning of a lurking cramp. My nasty old Toyota smelled stale. But here I was on a Sunday night hanging around outside a block of flats in Streatham. I knew which flat 'that bitch blonde' lived in. It was on the second floor, and a light showed through the front room curtains.

'Easy-peasy, Hannah Abram,' I murmured, just to prove I was still alive and hadn't died of boredom. But I wished I was still a smoker. There's nothing like a cigarette or two for getting you through tedious hours of surveillance when you've eaten all your sandwiches, a banana, and half a packet of chocolate Hobnobs.

The only comforts were that it was not cold or rainy and Ryan Reynolds rarely stayed away overnight. Or so Mrs Reynolds assured me. Ryan was 'having a drink with his team mates after their snooker match'. Or so he told the Missus. Snooker, my boring bum!

So, here's a question for a hard-up private detective: am I following a lying, cheating twat for a bewildered, tearful client, or am I working for someone who's known for ages that her marriage is a rotting corpse but who wants the goods on the lying, cheating twat that will allow her to keep the house and most of the communal property?

Do I care?

I do not. But it helps to have something to think about during the dark hours when the twat and the blonde are undoubtedly having more fun than I am.

Ryan Reynolds left the flat at eleven forty-seven, so I texted the missus: 'He should be home in 20 minutes.' Missus R texted back; 'Ok thanks for previous information. Talk tomorrow.'

I'd checked land registry and the electoral roll and discovered the name of the flat's owner, which was different to the occupier's. I'd also added that Ryan, the cheat, had a key of his own. This spoke volumes about the duration of the relationship. This I didn't mention to Mrs Reynolds. There are some speculations a client has to work out for herself. Or pay me quite a bundle extra.

Mrs Reynolds paid me by the day. The tailing, waiting and goofing around on my iPad had taken a day and a half. She was already complaining about the half day so this gig wasn't going to do much for my overdraft or my reputation as a canny investigator who's worth every penny.

I followed Mr R's black compact Mercedes back to his street, more because it was on my way than out of diligence. Then I went home to bed, creeping up creaky stairs so as not to disturb Eleanor and Olive.

I used to have a flat of my own. I used to have a steady job with the Metropolitan Police. But I lost the job when I pushed my Sergeant into the canal, and the flat went when the sickness reduced my options to working part-time at Digby's Sandwich Shack. This plummet down the career ladder means that even though nowadays I only have an attic room (no smokers, drinkers, meat or men) I must scramble like a hungry rat to make the rent. My landladies, Eleanor and Olive are nursery-school teachers, and Digby is a double-dyed bigot-boss.

2

The Sandwich Shack squats like an ugly toad at the edge of the Common. After five hours sleep I was there, in my cleanest surgical mask, making and serving breakfast to bright-eyed dog-walkers, recreational runners, cyclists and early workers. The griddle spat bacon fat on my arms, sausages had to be saved from rolling onto the floor, the toaster had its usual mid-morning breakdown and Digby strutted in two hours late. The expression on his face said, 'I may not be as tall as the average ten-year-old, but I got lucky last night – put that in your drawers and sit on it.'

Five minutes after that Dulcie, the new Shack employee, sidled in looking deeply embarrassed. I could've stuffed my greasy apron down both their throats and shoved their heads in the dishwasher.

Instead, with great restraint, I handed Dulcie the spatula, a hairnet, apron and mask. I made myself a hot chocolate with whipped cream and sprinkles, took a warm croissant, and went to an empty table outside in the smoking area.

Unwisely, Digby followed and snapped, 'Who said you could take a break?'

My calm demeanour shattered. I said, 'I hope you get haemorrhoids up your nose as well as up your fat arse.' I dunked the pastry into the hot chocolate, took a luxurious bite and waited while he framed his response.

Eventually he yapped with laughter, said, 'Nice one,' and strutted back inside. For which, I suppose, I should thank Dulcie. He's fired me for less – several times.

I was just swallowing the last crumb of croissant when my client, Mrs Ryan Reynolds, turned up without an appointment. Normally I meet clients in the office behind the kitchen when I have time off. But I couldn't negotiate office time with Digby after mentioning his nose and his haemorrhoids in the same sentence. So I waved my hand at the empty chair.

She sat. She was carefully dressed and made up. She did not look heartbroken.

'This is unexpected,' I said in the voice of a professional who's been taken advantage of – a hard act to pull off with half a mug of hot chocolate and a plateful of crumbs in front of me.

'I'm on my way to see my solicitor,' she said, ignoring me. 'I'll need the photos you took last night.'

'Okay,' I said taking my phone out of my pocket. Then I hesitated. 'And of course,' I added sweetly, 'I'll need the fee we agreed on.'

'The job isn't finished,' she said. 'My solicitor told me he'd probably need a deposition.'

'You asked me to find out where your husband went, who he was with and to take pictures to prove what I saw. Which I have done. We agreed a fee for that job. You did not mention a deposition, therefore a deposition was not factored into my estimated price.'

Her chin jutted. The ice pink of her lip gloss glistened. I sighed. It's so difficult to make a decent living these days.

'Tell you what,' I said, 'your solicitor probably has a fixed fee for depositions. If he needs one from me, why not leave it up to him to ask?' I had a strong feeling now that she'd already known everything she'd wanted me to confirm. And she was busy convincing herself that since she hadn't needed me there was no point in paying me. She was fiddling with the clasp of her handbag. I wanted to snatch it out of her hand and yell, 'If you're that effing mean-minded, put a padlock on it.' But I held my tongue and waited instead. I can do that. It makes my jaw ache but I'm learning that, where money is concerned, them that's got it make the rules that them who want it

4

must abide by. Recent events have taught me that beating a woman over the head with her own handbag will not turn out well for me.

The woman clenched her teeth and said, 'No deposition, no money.'

No class, see? It's the sickness and isolation from the rest of the world. Everyone thinks everyone else is out to rob them. Including me.

I clenched my fist and said pleasantly, 'No money, no photos.'

She looked at the fist. 'Show me the photos.'

I thumbed my album icon, picked a picture of Ryan leaving a door clearly marked 137, and tapped it to full screen. I held my phone so that she could see. 'Is that your husband?'

'Yes.'

I tapped the screen again to enlarge the number. 'Is that the same house number I told you about last night?'

She nodded.

I switched the phone off. I didn't have to say anything else. Reluctantly she said, 'Give me your bank details. I'll transfer the money as soon as I get home.'

I bared my teeth in what, after dark, might just be taken for a smile, and said, 'Things being how they are, I think I'd prefer cash. There's an ATM on the High Street. I can wait.'

Later, with next week's rent tucked securely in my pocket, Digby said, 'You have the body language of a debt collector. Don't you trust your own clients?'

'Do *you?*' I replied.

'Fair point,' he muttered and turned to tug a large ham out of the fridge. It was time to make the lunchtime sandwiches.

3

Before I worked there I used to like the Sandwich Shack. And I still like the Common.

The first time I came here was as a rookie member of a huge group of police officers and volunteers searching the ground for a seven-year-old girl who'd been missing for two days. It was a mile from her home but some boys reported having seen her with a man. The man was white, black, fat, thin, tall short, old and young. But they all agreed the little girl was blonde, blue-eyed and wearing a bottle-green school blazer. 'That,' said the old copper who was supervising me, 'is because that's what the picture in the local rag looked like.' He was very experienced and very cynical. 'Now go and get us an Americano and a sausage sarny from that crappy caff over there.'

That was my first encounter with Digby, who didn't like uniformed police officers. It was a while before I realised he didn't like anyone, so I took it personally.

I was on another coffee run when the shout went up and everyone surged towards a thicket where they found the little girl's body. I didn't see it because I was immediately pressed into crowd control. It was my first experience of how quickly a dead girl's body attracts a large audience.

It turned out that the perpetrator was the young bloke who 'discovered' the body. He was a hero for all of two hours before he confessed.

I was astonished, but the old copper said, 'Oh yeah. It's a type. *They* know what everyone *wants* to know. They feel omnipotent because having valuable information no one but them has gives them such a buzz. Then they can't help themselves taking the credit for the "find" as well.'

Not unlike my current boyfriend, I remember thinking at the time. He was a guy who used information like a weapon – giving me hints but withholding the nitty-gritty to suit himself – like where he was and who with.

I didn't have a boyfriend now, and Digby still didn't like me. Some things change; others don't.

While his back was turned I made two extra sandwiches – one chicken mayo, one ham, cheese and pickle –wrapped them and hid them in my apron pocket. BZee likes meat fillings but these days Digby is far more vigilant about how much filling we put into sandwiches and what happens to leftovers. Everyone's feeling the pinch, what with the sickness, inflation, and supply chain disruption. Take those factors along with the undeniable truth that Digby has always been a mean sod and you find a situation where it's getting more and more difficult to keep BZee onside.

I need to keep BZee onside because he's a wizard at finding lost or stolen dogs. It's another feature of hard times that dognapping is epidemic too. Now, I can't swear that BZee is always a dog*finder* rather than a dog*napper* but my relationship with him is symbiotic. There are many dog walkers on the common, more than there were before the sickness. That's when people bought up the world supply of puppies.

Because all the Shack's customers knew I was an ex cop and a PI, more and more bereft pet owners have come to my door.

Amazing, isn't it, that nearly all the missing dogs are pedigree? For some odd reason the average refuge-sourced mongrel isn't anything like as popular. But either way, a dog isn't just a dog. When a dog goes missing, for the owner, it's like losing a member of the family. That's where BZee and I come in. And our success rate is way better than the cops' – which is next to nil. Our success rate is suspiciously high. But I can't afford to be suspicious. I have a living to make.

BZee is a skinny, neglected kid who, like many others, doesn't get enough to eat. I feed him; he helps me find 'lost' dogs. Our common enemy is Digby.

At the moment BZee is lurking inside the tree line, beyond the running track, keeping his sharp eyes on the Shack, waiting for Digby to rush out to the bank with the breakfast and lunchtime cash. Cash is becoming a problem. Since the sickness most customers want to use credit cards and not risk their precious lives on the dirty notes and coins sick people might have touched. Digby agreed with them. And for a while we only did takeout food and refused to handle cash. Then Digby and I had a fight about it because most children don't have credit cards, a lot of old people don't either and nor do rough sleepers.

'So what?' said Digby. 'Those aren't the big spenders.'

'Nobody's a big spender at the moment,' I retorted. 'Or haven't you noticed? What's worse, no one leaves a tip anymore and you haven't added a service charge.'

'So what?' he said again. I could tell he was waiting for me to lose my temper.

'If you're going to deprive me of tips,' I said, 'I want a raise.'

'Hah!' Digby crowed. 'So much for the poor little kiddie-winkies and the unwashed homeless – this is all about you wanting more of my money.'

'Okay, you mean midget miser,' I yelled, even though I knew it would give him satisfaction. *'I quit.'* And I flung the hated apron on the floor and stormed out.

Of course, he couldn't replace me and I couldn't find another job. So four days later he shoved a handwritten note through my letterbox telling me we could re-instate cash provided I cleaned it. But he couldn't afford to add more than one stingy pound an hour to my pitiful wages.

So now we keep an antiviral alcohol spray next to the cash register and tip jar, and I guess we have the cleanest cash in South London. Laundered money.

Now BZee and I were waiting impatiently for tiny Digby to smother himself in his enormous coat and go to the bank. All because BZee and I share a belief that it's unfair for a dog, even though it's pedigree, to be worth more than a hungry teenager, though his morals are questionable.

Digby of course is not a member of our club and he was taking his time. At last he turned to me and said, 'I've done you a good turn, Hannah. It's against my religion as you well know, so you can wipe that ape-like look off your ugly mug and listen up.'

My jaw had indeed dropped. But I was suspicious. Digby's idea and mine about what constitutes a good turn are as far apart as London and New York. On very rare occasions we have cooperated, but it has never brought us closer. We are forced to work together at the Shack because, although he is the shittiest employer in the catering business, I am otherwise unemployable. I was sacked from the Met. I have an undeserved reputation as a violent man-hater. And a deserved reputation for bad manners, which *I* prefer to call intolerance for bullshit. If bullshit was an athletic event Digby would hold the world record.

He said, 'A friend of mine…'

'You have friends?' I couldn't help myself.

'More than you, *sociopath*,' he snarled. 'Are you going to listen for a change? I've got a client for you. A friend of mine has a godson who needs help. He will be here at six-thirty after you close up.'

'I get off at *four*-thirty today,' I said. 'You and Dulcie are supposed to close up.'

'I'm giving Dulcie a couple of hours off this afternoon,' Digby said with a leery smile, 'to visit her sick grandmother. I thought you needed the extra bunce. Take it or leave it.' And he swanned off without answering any of the basic questions like, who, what, where, why.

'Bum fluff!' I yelled after him. But he didn't even turn round. He left Dulcie, blushing like a July strawberry and twiddling her apron strings. I gave her such an evil glare that she started clearing tables without being asked.

Then I saw BZee making his way across the grass. And it began to rain. 'Effing perfect,' I said, and turned towards Dulcie.

She stopped what she was doing and cowered as if I was going to decapitate her. 'It's not my fault,' she muttered. She was plump and slightly spotty, prettyish but vacant.

I said, with as much forbearance as I could muster, 'We all make mistakes. But right now I need you to bugger off.'

'What?' she asked, so meekly that though she was in her twenties I could see the mistreated child in her eyes. I wanted to dance on Digby's face in tap shoes even more urgently than usual.

'Oh crap,' I said. 'Go to the office, shut the door, tidy the place and don't come out till I tell you.'

'Okay,' she said, looking up at me like I was an enemy general. 'But if you're sending me away so you can give that kid who's too scared to come in those sarnies you stole for him, don't bother. I'll use the token and get him some free crisps to go with them.'

Sometimes, *very* occasionally, I'm forced to admit that I'm not a hundred percent accurate in my judgement of character. I stared at her.

She said, 'He goes to my old school. He sleeps on the pavement outside his mum's block when she's got company. I wish I could feed him meself. Okay?'

'Okay,' I said, and beckoned BZee in out of the rain.

''Sup?' he said.

'You know Dulcie?' I asked.

'Seen her,' he said, watching while she got the vending machine token out of the cash register. He stood next to her and pointed. She extracted three packets of smoky bacon flavoured crisps and a can of Coke.

She and I busied ourselves wiping tables, carefully not noticing how ravenously he ate. When he'd finished she cut him a wedge of chocolate cheesecake and started to load the dishwasher. She was way more tactful then me. I would've sat down and started talking business straight away. And I'm pretty sure I would've forgotten the cheesecake.

BZee was suddenly so sleepy that he folded his arms on the tabletop, put his head down and closed his eyes. I was about to kick his chair when Dulcie fetched my padded jacket and laid it gently over his shoulders. She looked at the clock and said, 'I gotta go. He told me to be in the car park at four-thirty, sharp.'

'About Digby…'

She cut me off, 'I won't tell, honest.'

I started again, 'Okay, but about Digby…'

'Don't,' she said, and left the Shack.

The heavy rain emptied the Common. Except for a few shivering customers begging for hot drinks at the takeout window no one came. It was a typical late summer afternoon in South London.

I woke BZee an hour later when the rain stopped and grudgingly gave him the two unsold slices of pizza I'd reserved for my own supper. See, everyone I know calls me Hard-hearted Hannah, but here I am, feeding the hungry and sheltering him from the rain. No one knows me at all.

He said, 'Got a line on that golden retriever.'

This was Moira Lancer's dog, Gus, missing for three days. She loved him more tenderly than she loved her kids.

'Yeah?' I said. I brewed us both a cup of tea – milk and four sugars for him.

'Yeah,' he said, knuckling his crusty eyes and yawning. 'They want a hundred cash, no questions. Swing it?'

Moira owned one of the beautifully preserved Victorian villas that border the Common. Of course I could swing it. I also knew that because Gus had been neutered he couldn't be sold on for breeding purposes. Therefore this was a ransom situation. The low asking price told me that BZee's mates were probably responsible.

I paused for a moment giving him the hard stare. In fact I was setting what I ought to do against what I'd done in the past and would do again. It isn't my business to redistribute wealth, nor to encourage delinquent entrepreneurs. But these are hard times and the government doesn't seem to be doing anything to make BZee's life more bearable. Nor is Moira Lancer.

Look at it this way: I'm giving her the opportunity to act like a mensch whether she knows it or not. And I'm getting her dog back unhurt.

I took out my phone and called her. When she answered I said, 'If you can lay your hands on a hundred and fifty pounds cash right now, you can have Gus home tonight.' A hundred for the dognappers and fifty for the middle-woman, me, seemed fair.

BZee watched over the rim of his cup. A day-old chick couldn't have looked more innocent.

'Oh my god!' Moira yelled. 'You *found* him! Is he alright? Is he hurt? Does he miss me?'

I almost couldn't answer for fear of laughing. I had to remind myself that in spite of being an idiot she really did love and grieve for her dog.

I said, 'I haven't seen him. I'm negotiating. This is a cash deal; no questions asked. If things go wrong it's the dog that suffers. Know what I mean?'

'I just want Gus back safe.' She began to cry. 'I'll pay whatever they say and do whatever they ask.'

'Then bring a hundred and fifty pounds in used notes to me now. I'll be here till six.'

When I cut the call, I looked at BZee. I said, 'She's coming. Get the damn dog. Wait in the trees. The usual place. I'll wave when I have the money in my hand. Fuck me around and that's the end. Okay?'

'You always say that,' he complained.

'I always mean it,' I told him unnecessarily. 'Now bugger off and do what you have to.'

*

'Can't you stop them?' Moira asked. 'Why can't you involve the police? What was the point of my paying the vet to put a chip in his ear?'

I sighed. Now that she had her arms tight around Gus she felt free to criticise. 'The cops aren't interested. Also the last time the police got involved, the dog was found floating in a sack in The Drain. And after that, the next two dogs who were returned had their ears cut off. One of them died of septicaemia.'

'That's awful,' she cried. 'Can't you do anything about it?'

'I have no authority. You came to me cos you know I've been successful. I have contacts and I keep my ear to the ground. But recovering Gus is *all* I'm willing to do. You want to upset the status quo? Well good luck with that – the next terrified owners won't thank you.'

'But it's wrong,' she said stubbornly. 'It's a crime.'

'No argument.' I looked at my watch. It was almost time for me to close the Shack and wait for my next client – whoever he was. Another small misery, I expected; another symptom of things falling apart. Things *were* falling apart. If they weren't I would be safely in the Metropolitan Police Force, not scratching a living in Digby's Sandwich Shack and pretending to be a PI.

*

Myles Emerson was a surprise. He wore a mask, had a handful of anti-bacterial wipes, and an anti-viral spray which he used liberally on the table and chair. Then, in spite of having decontaminated the chair till the paint bubbled, he took a sheet of polythene from his backpack and covered it before sitting down. His hair had been parted with a ruler, he wore surgical gloves and paper socks over his shoes.

I watched him rearrange the table so that the salt, pepper, sugar and napkin holder were exactly central and equidistant apart. All this took time. I said, 'I was going to offer you a hot drink but I imagine you'd refuse.'

'I brought my own,' he said.

So I made strong tea for myself and he poured what looked like plain hot water from a space age thermos into a stainless steel cup. To save more time I placed my chair exactly opposite his and at least two metres away. I couldn't stop myself: I said, 'Is being you tiring?'

I thought, in spite of the mask, that he was smiling. He said, 'Thanks for noticing. Most people simply show their irritation.'

'Oh, I expect I'll show mine too,' I told him. 'I've been told my manners are shite. Shall I apologise in advance?'

'Don't bother; I'm used to it. I've been like this since puberty. The sickness of course has made it worse.' He looked down at his hands which were folded precisely in his lap. I noticed he was breathing the way people do when they've practiced meditation.

I wanted to sigh loudly and say, 'Get the fuck on with it,' but managed, this time, to control myself. If I thought of his behaviour as a symptom of extreme anxiety I could silently congratulate him for coping very well. Or at least congratulate myself for keeping my mouth shut. I did wonder however if this was one of Digby's attempts to drive me crazy.

He looked up and began: 'I've been getting fraud phone calls. Lots of them. I expect you have too – it's a consequence of poverty, I believe.'

I nodded. It was true that threats and attempts to steal bank details had multiplied over the last few years. People had to be way more vigilant at a time when they were also way more vulnerable.

He went on, 'But there's a handful of recent calls that I'm particularly worried about.' From an inside pocket of his coat he brought out a phone. He cleaned it and his gloved hands with an antibac wipe and fingered the screen.

A woman began to speak. She said, 'This is a debit card fraud alert: the sum of two thousand, eight hundred pounds has been debited from your account on a single purchase abroad. If this unusual activity is an unauthorised transaction, not made by you, press one on your keypad... ' He switched off the recording and looked at me.

I looked back, disappointed. This was not something I could deal with. If the Fraud Squad, the Office of Fair Trading or any fraud protection agencies can't deal with international fraud crimes, nor can I.

He caught my expression. 'Don't worry,' he said. 'I'm not sending you off to an unknown destination to bring down an international ring of fraudsters.'

'Why on earth not?' I asked, batting my eyelashes. 'Don't I look like 007?'

'Of course you do,' he said gravely. 'And I'm sure your egg salad sandwiches are shaken, not stirred.'

That's a relief, I thought. He may look bloody barmy, but he isn't. 'So what can I do for you?' I asked. 'I take it you pressed one on your keypad just to see what would happen?'

'I did. And I was answered, on a very bad line, by someone for whom English was far from a first language. The background sounds were of some crowded room, maybe even a railway station. "Sorry," I said. "Wrong number." I rang off. It was clearly a scam. So... ' He paused.

'So?'

'So, how would you, personally, describe the voice on the message I played for you? Just tell me what kind of woman you picture when you hear a voice like that.'

I revised my previous complimentary opinion of his sanity and just stared at him.

'Humour me – I have a reason for asking,' he said, again reading my mind. Perhaps he was accustomed to people thinking of him as nut-house fodder.

'Oka-ay,' I said cautiously. 'Well, she sounded educated, middle class, English; not young – perhaps in her mid-thirties; quite warm and friendly while also professional. Is that the kind of answer you're looking for?'

'Yes,' he said, 'I agree. Now why would a woman such as you describe be working for a gang who wants to frighten people into giving away bank details that would lead to them losing absolutely everything?'

'Out of work actor?' I said without even thinking. 'Desperate for any kind of work.' I was, as I usually am, thinking of myself. Then catching the glint in his eyes, 'You think you recognise the voice, don't you?'

4

Myles said, 'This is a modern dysfunctional family story.'

I held up my hand. 'I get relationships wrong even with old-fashioned functional families. May I record this?'

He nodded and waited while I set the recorder. Then he said, 'It's not that bad. My mother married Gina's father when I was seven and she, Gina, was twenty. I'm afraid it's Gina's voice warning of an "unauthorised transaction." She's my step-sister. She would be forty-three now.'

'Okay,' I said. 'Not a blood relation.' I was thinking, so he's thirty, only a couple of years ahead of me. He seemed younger; his skin was pale and unlined as if he'd been living underground. His eyes were candid blue, but there was something indefinably weird about him. I couldn't put my finger on it, but if he'd been a teacher the kids would've given him a very hard time.

'Correct,' he said, 'not a blood relative. But she was kind to me when her brother and sister were not. They resented my mother in all the conventional ways and took their resentment out on me.'

I stopped him again. 'Is Emerson *your* family or your step-family's name?'

'Mine. I reverted to it when I turned eighteen. So yes, Gina was Gina Margaret Turner.'

'Gina as in Georgina?'

'No. Just Gina. And you're right; I think I want you to find her. So yes, that's the name on her birth certificate.'

Where to start? I said, 'What's the difficulty?'

'My step-father's dead, my mother has Alzheimer's, step-sister Emma Turner is in New Zealand and step-brother Gordon Turner's a hostile dolt.' He paused and wiped his gloved fingers again. 'This is the first time I've been out of my house for nearly five years and it's bloody stressful. So if you don't mind, just let me explain myself my own way. We won't meet in person again. Will WhatsApp be okay with you?'

'Yes. But before you start there are a couple of practical details we need to sort.' I meant money of course. He *looked* top-end high street well-dressed and his mask was about the most expensive one on the market, but that doesn't mean a geezer's going to pay on the nail – especially if I fail. This could be a bog-standard missing person, or it could be a complicated and time consuming search.

'I charge by eight hour periods,' I told him. 'I keep a record of my hours. I'm not a lawyer, so an hour means sixty minutes. And I want a cash advance.'

'I was told you were a founder member of the awkward squad.' He sounded as if he was grinning. 'But no one said you were dishonest with money. Even your boss, Digby, didn't hint there was a discrepancy in the takings here.'

'That's only cos he never caught me.' I made it sound like a joke and he laughed. But feeding BZee only a couple of hours ago was an act of thievery.

He said, 'I haven't met Digby and I don't intend to. He didn't give you a stellar reference. But my godmother thinks he doesn't want you working for anyone but him. She said he was a "peculiar little person". But he mentioned that no one tried to cheat him since he got an ex cop on the pay-roll. And he said the ex cop worked part time on "piddly little cases the fuzz wouldn't touch."'

I glared at him. 'The "piddly little cases" are the small miseries that drive ordinary people crazy. The successes don't go to court but they often give comfort to people with nowhere else to take their problems.' I sounded like a pious, pompous twat even to myself so I added, 'And I still want a cash advance.'

He or his godmother had checked me out pretty thoroughly and he'd come cash in hand. I donned surgical gloves, sanitised a pen and signed a receipt for the pristine white envelope filled with twenty-five spanking new twenty-pound notes.

'So now,' I said, 'what won't the cops do for you?'

'Unless you call 999 it's practically impossible to speak to a real person. But when, finally, I did get through to my local station I overheard the man who answered the phone yelling, "Oy Sarge, it's a nut job with another sodding missing person." So I hung up.' He gave me an old fashioned look and added, 'Unsurprisingly, I'm sensitive about being called a nut job.'

'I'll try to remember that,' I said. He wasn't paying me for my famed tact and diplomacy and I thought I'd better begin as I meant to go on.

He paused, eying the envelope as if he could rectify a mistake. I tucked it firmly into the back pocket of my less than hygienic jeans.

'To save time I've prepared a sheet with known facts about Gina. I've included her brother and sister's addresses, my contact details, those of my godmother, and all I can remember about her friends et cetera.' He passed another envelope across the table.

'Good,' I said, accepting it. 'Now tell me why you're "afraid" it might be Gina's voice on the phone message.'

'Because if it's her, she's worked, at least once, for some very nasty people. The gangs who perpetrate this kind of financial fraud are not philanthropists who treat their employees fairly. Exploitation is the name of the game.'

I nodded.

'I want to know if she's in trouble. My life has not been so full of generosity that I can afford to overlook someone who was kind to me in difficult circumstances.'

'Go on.'

'My first day at a new school after Mother and I moved in with the Turners: I was in the Junior school; Emma and Gordon were in the Upper school on the same street. They were supposed to take me there. But when the bus came and the three of us got on, at the last moment Gordon pushed me off. Emma just waved goodbye, laughing, as the bus moved away. I'd fallen into a puddle in the gutter and sat there, crying, wet through, not knowing what to do.

'I was saved by Gina on her way to college. She cleaned me up, calmed me down and took me to school herself. She deposited me in the right classroom, apologised charmingly for being late, explained about "an accident" and promised to meet me at the gate to take me home. Which she did. She warned me never to mention the incident to any other member of the family – Mother included – and to pretend I'd sorted everything out myself. She said that the only way to cope with bullying was to deny it had any power.' He paused, waiting for my comment.

I managed not to say, 'Aw, poor baby', in my sarkiest tone of voice and he went on, 'It was the only advice I was given. My mother and Mr Turner were, I think, in denial that their attempt to combine two families was failing. But in the end, my mother caved and sent me to boarding school.'

He paused and then went on, 'Sorry, this was supposed to be about Gina; not about why she meant so much to me.

'So, when I was seven, she was twenty and beginning her second year at drama school. Even her father, who always strongly opposed her career choice, had to admit she was gifted. Her brother and sister, toadies both, made fun of her for "play-acting", "dramatising" and "attention-seeking". My mother, as always, supported her husband in whatever small-minded opinion he had about the profession. Gina must've felt abandoned by her birth family. I, of course, worshipped her.

'The first show she took me to was a Christmas panto, Cinderella, and although she only had a small part, I couldn't believe how wonderful and funny she was. Afterwards, backstage, she introduced me to everyone; and it all seemed larger than life – men

22

in women's clothing, women in tights and sequins, everyone in a frantic state of bonhomie, lapping up praise even from a little boy. I made up my mind to become an actor too. Which did not endear either Gina or me to her family and my mother.'

He must've caught the sceptical expression on my face because he said, 'Yes, absurd. When I was about twelve, after a severe bout of flu, all my hair fell out and I became obsessed with germs and started washing my hands compulsively – a somewhat limiting state of affairs for anyone dreaming of an ensemble future.' Catching my glance at his sleek dark head, he added, 'It grew back; this isn't a rug.'

He was a little too quick for my liking. I'd been taught listening skills by an old cop who said, 'Ears open, mouth shut, poker face, and for fuck's sake don't argue or laugh at a witness.' Keeping my mouth shut, as almost everyone will tell you, was the hardest part. I thought I'd been doing pretty well.

I said, 'Okay smart-arse, you're describing how Gina became alienated from a family that also had trouble accepting you – creating a bond, I suppose?'

'Correct. But I'm also telling you why she and I lost touch. I was sent to boarding school and later to "special needs" schools which supposedly could cope with my condition.'

'No cure?' I asked.

'Plenty of anti-anxiety medications to choose from combined with behaviour changing therapies. It's controllable under normal, calm conditions. But a pandemic?' He snorted derisively. 'And the stress and anxiety that attends economic meltdown? No chance.'

'So you're stuck with it for now?'

'I'm actually having a good day,' he remarked, looking as though he was surprising himself. 'I'm here, aren't I? And I'm surviving *you*. You aren't the most sympathetic un-pressurising person I've ever met.'

'Thanks,' I said. 'I do my best.' I was tired and not at my most mannerly. I'd been at the Shack for over twelve straight hours. Babying the disabled isn't top of my skill-set.

5

I had to admit though that OCD Myles had used his disability well. He'd supplied me with a detailed, typed fact sheet. As far as this ignoramus was concerned there was not even a comma out of place. *And* he'd even used a couple of semicolons. That, I thought, was showing off.

I had Myles' five hundred quid in my pocket nestling up to the fee Moira Lancer paid me for 'finding' Gus, so I treated myself to an Indian takeout on my way home. Spicy Indian food is the only way I can smuggle meat past my vegan landladies. Believe me, they could smell a cheeseburger from half a mile – as I found out when I was nearly evicted in my first week of residence.

Licking Jalfrezi sauce off my fingers I decided that the first person I'd ring was my tidy client's godmother. She was the only one on the list I wouldn't have to explain myself to, and I was tired. So I punched in Sophia Smithson's number, and this is what I heard: 'If you're scamming me or selling anything be advised – I have no money whatsoever. So go away and bother someone else.' It wasn't a voice message.

When I'd finished laughing, I said, 'Nice to talk to you too, Ms Smithson. Myles Emerson gave me your number. I'm Hannah Abram, the…'

'Oh, right,' she said. 'I know who you are. What can I do for you?' She sounded as if she'd rather do something *to* me than for me.

'Well, most of what Myles told me first hand about his stepsister stops when he was nearly sixteen. Everything else comes from the

Turners and seems to be them justifying themselves for why they excluded her from the family. "Dead to me," I think the father said.'

'Gina was an idiot,' Sophia Smithson said impatiently. 'What did she expect? She married a gay Cuban ballet dancer, simultaneously got work with a soft porn film producer in Paris and expected that bourgeois nest of vipers to approve and support her. They cut her loose.'

Before I could comment I heard the tap as the phone was put down on a hard surface. Then there was the gurgle of a drink being poured. I sighed and waited.

Sophia sighed too, and said, 'But she was sweet to Myles – I'll say that for her. Possibly only to annoy the others. I haven't the faintest idea why Irma, his mother, married into a family like that, and subjected a bright kid like Myles to the Turner's spite and small-mindedness. Perhaps she couldn't face life without a husband, however controlling and mean spirited he was. There are women like that.

'Well, the horrid little man's dead now and good riddance. The girl followed a commodities trader to the antipodes. Grim Gordon is still fighting me for what he calls his "inheritance", which he says is being wasted on Irma's care. Irma fortunately, when she realised she was going slowly do-lally, assigned Power of Attorney to me. She'd be out on the streets now if her care had been left to Gordon.'

Sophia sounded like a lecturer, impossible to interrupt. She took a breath and I jumped in. 'Did Irma stay in touch with Gina after the family cut her off?'

'Irma was deluded,' Sophia said. 'She thought she could be a peace-maker and bring those back-stabbers together. Whereas anyone could see they delighted in having a black sheep to tear strips off. No one listened to her; she wasn't a "proper Turner", you see. So yes, she tried to stay in touch with Gina after the Turners made it clear there would be no *rapprochement*. I think she knew a lot more about his mistreatment at Turner hands than she ever admitted to. I…'

'Why on earth didn't she leave and take Myles with her?' I butted in. It was the only way to have a two-way conversation with this autocratic old bird.

'I told you,' she said impatiently. 'You should listen. She wanted to be *married* – however uncomfortably for herself and Myles.

'And, while we're on the subject of discomfort, I should admit that I'm somewhat uneasy about the action Myles is taking now. You should know that he can become obsessive when he has a project. What do you intend to do if, after you've exhausted all reasonable avenues, he still presses you to continue?'

'Jump straight to the end, why don't you?' I snapped. 'I haven't hardly begun. And I'm sure, with you watching his back, if there's even a hint of me taking advantage, you'll take me out and shoot me.'

She cackled suddenly, but didn't deny it. 'Irma stayed in fairly regular touch with Gina until she went to Cuba. She only married Alessandro so that he could get a temporary resident's visa. I think she thought it would work the other way round. I don't know what happened, but when Irma next heard she was in Miami.'

She paused. I heard ice cubes tinkle, so I asked quickly, 'Was there a divorce?'

'Not that I heard of. So, yes, that might be worth following up. She couldn't remarry unless she divorced Alessandro. She might still be Gina Ruiz officially. Or she might have reverted to Turner without divorcing. Or she might have re-married and have any damn name at all. Good luck with that.'

While jotting down something approximating Ruiz, I cut in, 'Myles didn't tell me about this.'

'Irma didn't tell him anything she thought might upset him. In his teens and early twenties his condition was unstable. She told me he needed to avoid stress or excitement.'

'How's Irma now?' I asked. 'Might I be able to visit her?'

'She has good days and bad days as you might expect. But no, I won't allow you to just swan in to see her with a list of questions whenever it pleases you. I would insist that you apply to me to make arrangements for you, and that I should be present at any visit. Would that be acceptable?'

'Am I talking to the same Sophia Smithson who criticised Irma's late husband for being controlling?' I said before I could stop myself.

'You certainly are,' she said. 'And you'd better remember it.' With that she rang off leaving me with a mouthful of unspoken insults.

I must stop letting other people get the last word, even if they're clients, I thought, slouching back on my narrow bed with my feet up. What else do I want? I want a car that would make my ex sick with jealousy. I want a partner who won't secretly take pictures of me in the shower and then sell them for laughs to the people I work with. I want a proper job with insurance or enough money so I can get my impacted wisdom tooth fixed. I want…

6

Next morning I waited till Eleanor and Olive left before getting up and having a long luxurious shower. I would not go in to work till after ten. I'd had it up to my ponytail with early shifts. Digby could eat maggots before I lost any more sleep on account of his unimaginable sex life. Digby and Dulcie – he was twice her age and half her height.

It's amazing how brave I am when there's a thick wedge of cash in my pocket.

I was in the middle of online searching Gina Turner, Gina Margaret Turner, Gina Ruiz, Gina Margaret Ruiz, Gina Turner Ruiz and Gina Margaret Turner Ruiz when Digby phoned. He said, 'Where the fuck are you?'

'I told you,' I said. 'I've done the early shift every day for two weeks, I've done the late shift too for several days. I'm taking the day off. I told you yesterday.' I hadn't, but intention counts for something. 'You fat capitalist toad,' I finished, 'you are in breach of fair employment regulations. So shove that down your greedy throat and choke on it.'

'You're fired!' he shouted.

'Too late, I already quit,' I shouted back. I cut the call. Sometimes the only way I can score a day off is when Digby cans me.

I mused about the job I'd started. My client thought he recognised his step-sister's voice on a fraud recording designed to frighten someone so much about the threat of losing their money that they risked losing much, much more. It was due to accelerating greed. When I'd turned on my laptop that morning I'd had to delete two offers of cut price Viagra; a different kind of offer from Yolanda, who thought I was cute and promised she would do all the dirty things other women refused to do; an attempt by an insurance company who wanted to frighten me into buying cover against nuclear war and the end of the world due to the climate emergency – whichever came first; and an investment expert who wanted to double my savings in less than a month. I'd missed calls from a double glazing salesman, someone who would tarmac my drive, and a man who promised to analyse my water supply because of threats to contaminate it with an extremely dangerous organophosphate compound.

The so-called forces of law and order are nearly toothless against the greedy, grinding jaws of online capitalism. Firstly, the perps are always at least one step ahead, and secondly, it's usually international – some of it even being foreign-government sponsored and designed to destabilise. So, sorry folks, you'll just have to sharpen up your native wits and suspect everyone you don't know of trying to steal from you.

But back to work. In the UK there was no record of a death or another marriage registered under any of Gina's names. Which of course doesn't rule out any number of alternatives including my favourite, a quickie in Vegas.

My contact in Cardiff told me that a car had been registered to Gina Margaret Turner four years ago. This was the name on her driving licence – so she hadn't gone through the rigmarole of changing that. He gave me an address. Now I had a splinter of hope that I would be able to pick up traces in this country. Anywhere else I would be useless: a transcontinental operative I most certainly ain't.

Gina, as far as I could see, had no presence on Facebook, Twitter, TikTok, Instagram or any other of the antisocial platforms I know about. Nor did she have a website I could find. This, for an actor, was a bad sign. Her three drama school friends were represented: one was getting small parts especially in historical TV dramas like

Downton Abby; another had small parts in police and medical series; the third gave up acting quite quickly, joined a band and died a few years later of drug abuse. Life's tough in the arts.

All of this took dreary time, backache and caffeine.

I stripped my bed, bundled up the sheets and most of my overflowing laundry basket and took them to the Clean Machine Launderette on the high street. I am not allowed to use Eleanor and Olive's washing machine or dryer. 'We've had misuse problems with tenants before.' It was the only explanation I was given.

Fortunately I like the damp warmth of a launderette. I find the clunk and hum of the machines peaceful and the smell of soap powder doesn't make me sneeze. I could work there and send business-like messages requesting interviews to Gina's living friends and relations. No one had to know I was catching up on two weeks worth of laundry at the same time. And who's to know that my hair, soaked by a sharp rain shower, has dried lop-sided, and I'm wearing torn trackies and a sloppy sweater with a large hole at one elbow.

So, wouldn't you know it, that's when I met my next client. He walked like a man with a bad back. I supposed he was in his seventies except that he had rather trendy facial hair, a twinkle in his sad eyes and a beanie, probably knitted for him by someone with a sense of humour.

He said, 'I've seen you at that sandwich place in the Common. Someone told me you used to be a police officer.'

I waited. He looked kindly and, in spite of the badly knitted headgear, nearly sane. But as every woman worth her salt knows you need more proof than just appearances.

'What am I interrupting?' he asked, politely ignoring my revolving filthies. I hoped the soap suds camouflaged the worst of it.

He went on, 'I've heard you sometimes use your expertise to solve the kinds of problem people are reluctant to make official.'

'That's me,' I said, stuffing my phone in a pocket and holding out my hand. 'Hannah Abram.'

'Carl Barber,' he said. We shook.

'There's a coffee shop a couple of doors down, next to the tattoo parlour,' he said. 'Can I buy you a coffee?'

'Tempting,' I said. 'But a month ago someone pinched my nearly new duvet cover out of the dryer. These days I don't leave my laundry unguarded even to buy a paper.'

'Understandable,' he said. 'But there's always take-away.'

'Are you a client or a pick-up artist?' I asked. 'Either way you might be disappointed. But if you want to consult me professionally it'll cost you a flat white and a *pain au chocolat.*'

'You're on,' he said and disappeared out into another sharp shower.

I shouldn't let an old guy with a bad back get cold and wet and perhaps catch his death of Covid while buying me coffee and a pastry. But he offered. Who am I to turn down what might be the only offer I'll have all day? I am, after all, technically unemployed. And as such I've lost my 'office'. One day Digby won't re-hire me. Maybe he's already grooming Dulcie to take over my position as underpaid drudge, but with extra duties my skin crawls to imagine.

Carl Barber came back wet but with two large coffees and a pleasantly greasy paper bag. I warmed to him.

His problem was simple but wearying. It was caused by someone he called The Rubbish Vigilante. I thought he was joking, but he wasn't. He lived in the basement of a four storey house in a small street nearby. Every Wednesday night someone tipped the rubbish left out for collection next morning over the railing and down the area steps outside his bedroom window. It wasn't any old rubbish: it was rubbish that had been left out too long, unsorted or not bagged properly. This included kitchen waste which was like a three-course dinner to gulls and pigeons, especially urban foxes. And rats.

The poor old geezer didn't like having rats feeding and breeding so close to his bedroom. And who could blame him?

'It isn't just me,' he said. 'He or she does target other houses sometimes. But I receive by far the most attention. I'm beginning to take it personally. And it's always the night before the recyclers and bin men come. So every Thursday I have to get up early, clean the steps and the area, re-bag all the garbage and hope the bin men will take it away.'

While telling his story the old guy seemed to age before my eyes. I said, 'You've no idea who's doing this?'

He shook his head. 'I've stayed up as late as I can, and got up as early as possible but I've never caught anyone.'

'The council?' I asked. 'The cops?'

He shook his head.

'Just to be clear,' I said, 'what exactly do you want me to do?'

'Find out who The Rubbish Vigilante is. I want to talk to him or her.'

'Hmm,' I said. 'You know, this kind of action looks obsessive and not exactly sane to me. Don't you have cameras on your street?'

'There's one at the Common end where the most expensive houses are. But it's just for show – it hasn't worked for years.'

'What about neighbourhood watch?'

'It's not a very neighbourly neighbourhood,' he said sadly. 'Are you saying you don't want the job?'

'No. But I might have to stake your house out for one or two nights, which will cost money. Also, someone who's mentally unhinged might not be a person you'd want to tackle alone.'

Suddenly my phone purred. 'Excuse me,' I said to Carl. I had a text from Gina's brother, Gordon. It read, 'Since Gina did not have the decency to come to my father's funeral last year she can rot in hell as far as I'm concerned.'

Not a helpful reply to my oh-so-polite enquiry. I sighed and turned back to Carl who seemed mesmerised by my washing which was just finishing its spin cycle.

'Give me a minute to think,' I said.

So he nicked my newspaper and settled quietly in a corner.

I transferred my disreputable washing to the dryer and thought about replying to Gordon. Several smart and cutting replies crossed my mind but I settled for 'I'm so disappointed you feel that way. Do please stay in touch.' I added a kiss and then deleted it. Some people just don't get sarcasm.

While my laundry tumbled like dead babies I considered Mr Barber who seemed to have nodded off. Asleep he looked nearer eighty. What was he doing living in a basement being harassed by someone who would probably turn out to be a neighbour? He should be living in a pretty village, dozing in a stripy deck chair, his straw hat tilted to shade his eyes, while chubby grandkids played around his feet.

Then, because I'm self-centred and everything revolves around me, I pictured my ideal flat. There was, of course a utility room. In it my good looking partner was folding fresh, colour-separated laundry and calling, 'Dinner's in the oven.' Absolutely, categorically *not* the same good looking bloke who'd used me as a dirty joke to make his workmates laugh, which in turn led to my trying to drown a superior officer. I lost everything and ended up with Digby, Eleanor and Olive, and not a lot of hope about starting from scratch in a depressed economy.

When I was a lot younger I saw life as having an inevitable upward trajectory. I didn't take into account the equally inevitable banana skins, pot-holes in the road, and sexist baboons. I told the sexist baboon that if he wanted his diamond engagement ring back it was at the bottom of the canal where the Sergeant ought to be. He laughed and said it was cubic zirconia, second hand and so cheap he was surprised it hadn't floated. Am I bitter? You bet I'm bitter.

Carl Barber woke up in time to help me fold the sheets. I even remembered to thank him.

After I'd stowed the laundry in my car we took a short walk to Cottham Road, where he lived in a row of Edwardian buildings. He told me the houses had been built for a growing population of middle management families at the beginning of the twentieth century. There'd been a semi-fashionable renaissance in the sixties and seventies when North London prices had rocketed out of reach of the arty class. Since then most of the houses, except the posh ones with a good view of the Common, had been split into flats. His was about halfway down between the Common and the tattier High Street end where there were more doorbells per front door, student bicycles chained to the railings and, yes, some rubbish bags that had been attacked by gulls, their rotting contents littering the pavement.

Carl showed me the gate in the railings. It was chained and secured by a stout padlock which he unlocked and led me down an iron staircase to his front door. His bedroom windows were double glazed and shuttered. The front door was protected by three bolt locks.

He said, 'I had a break-in a couple of years ago. They took my computer, my TV, my piano and all my clean towels. I've been more security conscious since then. But coming in, especially with shopping bags, is wearisome.'

'Your *piano?*'

'Korg keyboard and synth,' he said.

'Towels?' I countered, on safer ground.

'That puzzled me too,' he said sadly.

I pictured him, with his aching back, on a rainy morning in the cramped basement area in front of his door, cleaning other people's garbage off the ground and the iron stairs. I felt sad too, and then annoyed at him for making me sad.

I said, 'Okay, you look more respectable than I do at the moment, so we'll go back to the High Street. There's an estate agent's office almost opposite the end of your road. Go in and ask if there's any property for sale.'

'Oh?' Then he brightened. 'You think this might be someone trying to smarten the street in order to drive up property prices.'

'I don't think anything yet.'

'But it's a start.' He smiled. 'I feel less victimised already. I hate feeling victimised.'

'Me too,' I said and we trotted off towards the High Street.

He gave me a fifty pound note as a retainer even though he'd done most of the work.

7

Dulcie texted at about two-thirty when the lunchtime panic usually calmed. 'You've got to come back,' she wrote. 'I can't cope. Digby's in a total rage.'

So quit, I thought. But I didn't reply. Let Digby vent his existential anger on someone else for a change. I had two clients. Count 'em. *Two.*

My phone rang while I was turning the mattress ready to put clean sheets on the bed. It was Fiona Knight, the actor who specialised in TV costume dramas. She said, 'I wonder why Myles didn't ring me personally. I'd love to see him again. Gina's half-brother. Such a clever little boy.'

Neither accuracy nor memory seemed to be Fiona Knight's strength, but I said, 'He's quite worried about her, so if you have any recent information he'd be very grateful.'

'Well, let me see, sorry, I've been so busy lately. Do you watch Bridgerton or Downton Abbey? Because those two shows are taking up a lot of my time, even though these days I always seem to play someone's mother. Ha-ha. It's the fate of any performer who's even a couple of years over eighteen. Still, I mustn't grumble when so many fine talents are out of work nowadays. Oh right, Gina. Yes, I got her on a cattle call for a movie about Queen Victoria. I'd already been cast, you see, but I thought it might be fun if Gina and I could work together again. But no one was interested, and I can't say I was surprised – she was so tired and thin. No, I don't mean slim. She was scrawny. I was shocked. It's so embarrassing when an old friend can't even get cast as an extra. Don't you think? Oh she was full of stories about Havana and New York, but if you ask me, marrying that greedy bugger from the Royal Ballet and following him to Cuba was the worst career move a young actress could've made. You have such a short time, as a woman, to get noticed, and put yourself out there. You've got to work your butt off while you're young or no one will remember your name later. But Gina had all these leftie principals, about immigrant rights and fair play for gays of colour, as if they didn't already hog the dance and musical scenes. Sorry I shouldn't have said that. I don't want to be cancelled, ha-ha. But Gina genuinely thought everything would be different in Cuba. I don't know what happened but they didn't seem to want her there either...'

Fiona seemed to be enjoying Gina's downfall a little too much so I almost shouted, 'Do you have an address or number for her now?'

'Let me see. I'm waiting for a call from my agent on the other line but I can spare a couple more minutes.'

Ten minutes later she gave me the same address my contact at the Licensing Centre had given me, a mobile phone number, and far more about the life and stellar career of Fiona Knight than I'd ever remember.

I rang the number and was sent straight to voice mail. The message was spoken by a pleasant, middle-English voice. I'm not good at voices so I couldn't tell if it was the same as the scam one Myles had recorded. I didn't leave a message but I rang Myles and gave him the number. He said he'd ring me back.

I finished making the bed. Myles did not ring me back.

I looked up the Driving Licence address and found it to be in Potters Bar. That's in Hertfordshire and doesn't count as London, even though it's at the furthermost tip of the Northern Line. I'm a South Londoner – even the words Northern Line strike fear into my heart.

I went to the supermarket and restocked my single shelf in the fridge. I had to buy almond milk rather than cow's milk and rennet-free cheese. But it was okay to murder any vegetable I chose so long as it was organic. This is why I eat Digby's crap leftovers so often.

Myles still hadn't rung. I sighed and rang him. I was told by a posh male voice, not his, that he was unavailable.

Dulcie left another message, sounding even more desperate. 'Couldn't you just sort of mumble "I'm sorry" very quickly to him?' I didn't answer or ring back.

It was almost time for Eleanor and Olive to come home from work so I put my coat on and left the house. I have absolutely nothing against veganism or any sexual preference as long as it doesn't hurt anyone else, but I really hate the missionary zeal with which they lecture me about *my* choices. I absolutely loathe being dependant on their grudging approval for my bed and small attic room.

I climbed into my battered old Honda and set my GPS for the wasteland, the tundra, that I expected to find in Potters Bar. If it weren't for Tom the Poison Bomb I'd still have a small flat of my own and a job I could sometimes be proud of. It was his idea that I sell my lease and move in with him. It was my idiot idea that we pool our resources, to refurbish and refurnish his dilapidated but larger accommodation. Me, Hannah Abram, living with a guy. I was next door to being married. Unheard of. No one had ever asked me before. I wasn't blonde; I was neither stacked nor willowy; I didn't flirt; I didn't have a rich daddy but I did have a big gob. What's not to fancy?

Women are supposed to know what men want and act accordingly. But if there's one thing the spate of obscene emails has taught me, it's that whoever's sending them think men want something pornographic and often painful. I don't want to know in detail, but it's a country mile away from snuggling up on a sofa with wine and crisps to watch the football.

I seem to have spent a lifetime dealing with the rubble left by men, and the heart-broken, disappointed, bruised women they leave in their wake. You'd think I'd know better, wouldn't you? Well, I didn't. I guess it was just my turn. Later, when I talked to his ex-wife and some of his so-called mates I realised that almost everyone, except me, knew about his gambling and his habit of conning stupid women out of their savings.

Am I broken-hearted? I asked myself, as the traffic finally allowed me to crawl across Battersea Bridge. I don't know. I'm still too pissed off with him *and* myself to feel anything but anger.

North of the Thames feels like another country to me. It's smarter and shabbier, cleaner and dirtier, richer and poorer, more and less diverse than my patch. You crawl through urban village after urban village, five miles taking over an hour to drive. All your fuel is used up idling at roadworks, jams and traffic lights, but you can't find any petrol stations. A cloud of anxiety and ill temper seems to hang in the air. There are just too many vehicles and way, *way* too many people. And all the while my GPS barked orders at me in a posh accent. Which made it difficult to plan what I would do after I 'reached my destination'. No wonder I arrived at Flat 2, 57 Waterford Road, feeling resentful and alienated.

Before leaving home I'd Googled the address. I couldn't find it, but discovered that Potters Bar was used for the location of a movie called Bloodbath at the House of Death. An endearing claim to fame, I thought. Less endearing was the location of Gina's last recorded address, which was above a boarded up café called Tasty Treats in a failing commercial road which looked like every other damn row of unsuccessful businesses, anywhere in the UK. There were two floors above the café, and two bells on the wall next to the side door. I pressed both buttons – a long impatient sort of ring.

'What?' yelped a male voice.

'You flat one or two?' I growled.

'Two.'

'Okay. Parcel for Miss Gina Turner.'

'Who?'

40

'*Gina Turner*,' I bellowed, sounding like every pissed off delivery guy I'd ever heard.

'No one called that here,' he snapped back, sounding like every pissed off guy who'd just got out of the shower to answer a buzzer.

'How long you been there? Any forwarding address?'

'No. No. And fuck off.'

I fucked off back to my car.

After driving in a slow circle round the block I parked in another spot where I could watch the door. I cut the engine, sat back and waited, wishing I'd brought a tasty treat of my own to pass the time with.

There was no reason to wait, except that I'd driven for what felt like half my waking life to exchange about thirty words with an ill-tempered bloke. I'd discovered zilch except that said guy had nothing to say to me.

Myles's phone was still going straight to voicemail. Maybe he'd already found Gina and was indulging in twenty years-worth of missed yak. Maybe he'd want his dosh back.

I texted him: I'm outside Gina's last recorded address. She's not here. Instructions?

There was no reply, but after half an hour the shabby door opened and a young guy with wet hair and skinny jeans came out, turned right and walked off. He was wearing shiny white ear buds so I didn't bother to close the car door quietly. I let him walk about fifteen paces away before crossing the road and pressing both buzzers again. There was no answer. I peered through the letter box and saw a narrow hall strewn with unwanted paper.

Skinny Jeans was still in sight so I ambled after him. He turned a corner and I got there just in time to see him enter a kebab shop called Tenerife Kebabs. He was at the counter as I walked past.

I gave him a few minutes before coming back to study the menu on the window. I could have anything as long as it was a kebab or a burger. There was acne on Skinny Jeans' neck. He looked as if he was

41

trying to chat up the woman behind the counter. She was filling a sick yellow styrene box with kebab, chips and salad. He made her remove the green stuff.

He came out brushing past invisible me and looking disgruntled. I went in, just in time to hear the woman mutter, 'And don't come back,' as the door shut.

''Scuse me?' I said as she stared at me with blank eyes.

'Not you,' she said. 'Him. He's in here near on every night and he always has the same effing order, and he always says he wants salad and then makes me take it out. And he won't take no for an answer.' 'Creep,' she added judiciously.

'Creep,' I echoed, just to be friendly. I ordered a chicken burger plus salad and took it away to eat in the car. It wasn't as bad as it looked.

There was a light on in the top flat window. But I know a dead end when I bump into one. I finished my burger, switched the GPS to Home, turned the car round and left.

8

When I got home I found Olive and Eleanor watching something called Discovering Witches on their telly. I tried to get upstairs without being heard but Olive turned and said, 'Your tub of yoghurt is leaking. Please would you clean it up.'

And Eleanor added, 'If you're going out again tonight, would you *please* have a little consideration about the front door when you come home. Some of us have to work in the morning.'

They turned back to the screen without waiting for a reply. So I didn't give them one although several came to mind, all containing the words sanctimonious and bitches. It really hacked me off – me, a feminist in good standing, reduced to insulting my landladies.

It took me ninety seconds to wipe a couple of spots of yoghurt off my shelf in the fridge. Then, instead of going to bed for an early night, I went out again and drove to Cottham Road.

I spent over an hour of double parking before a suitable space opened up where I could see Carl's house without a street lamp shining in my eyes. I put on a black surgical mask, tilted my seat back and started asking my phone questions, like who owned the property at 57 Waterford Road, Potters bloody Bar.

I made several mistakes on a site I know well and before the name Emir Yilmaz popped up my vision was blurry. It occurred to me that my eyes were tired and I closed them for a minute.

*

I was hanging from a branch of a giant oak tree. A huge woodpecker was hammering away inside my head. Being as small as a mouse was

43

a risky business when birds had grown so big, I thought. I must've missed the nuclear war.

I opened my eyes and checked the time. I'd been asleep for nearly ten minutes and someone was knocking on my window. The hand wore a ring with a big yellow stone.

'Stop it,' I yelled.

'Get out of the car and face me,' an enraged voice yelled back. I couldn't see her face. She went on, 'Stop sneaking around in the dark. I know what you're up to.'

Well, sneaking around in the dark is often my damned job. But all the same I lost my temper. I shoved my door open so suddenly the effing be-ringed woodpecker had to jump backwards to avoid injury. I hate being woken up abruptly when I've only just fallen asleep.

She was about five foot six inches tall, probably in her fifties, wearing a padded jacket that perfectly matched her hair, which was fawn and helmet-like.

She was wearing a mask too, so I got in her face. 'What's your game?' I hissed.

'What's *my* game?' she hissed back. 'I'm not the slag who's waiting for me to clear out so she can steal my boyfriend.'

That nearly floored me. I gulped, but rallied enough to say, 'I'd be an idiot to go after anyone fool enough to fancy you.'

We stared at each other. She had a fixed, obsessive gaze. She said, 'You *would* say that, wouldn't you? But I've suspected him for months. He's a lying, cheating monster. But he's clever. I've never had proof till now.'

'What proof?'

'What's your name?'

'Mind your own business.'

'See?' she crowed triumphantly. 'If you were innocent you'd tell me who you are and what you're doing skulking out here.'

'And if you were halfway sane you'd apologise and sod off.' I switched on my phone torch and shone it in her face.

She looked so ordinary: a middle-aged woman trying to look younger. She did not seem bat-shit crazy. The sane thing for me to do would be to get back in my car and drive away. Ah! Perhaps she was creating a scene so that she could nick my parking space.

I looked at all the neighbouring windows, wondering if anyone was watching or listening. All I saw was blank glass, curtains and not many lights still on. Even so, I reckoned she'd ruined my pitch for the night.

I started to turn away, but to my surprise she hauled off and swung at me. I caught her wrist before she connected.

Slap me? What had I done? Well, I've done plenty, but not to her.

I folded her little finger down towards her palm and applied pressure – a technique I hadn't used since secondary school when Amanda Gribble said something anti-Semitic.

The woman screeched just like Amanda had.

I said, 'How fucking dare you? Who are you and what's your problem?'

The woman burst into tears. So I let her go.

She said, 'I'm Deena. He's mine, but he's always looking for someone younger. They all do. They're all pigs. We've been together for ages but he still won't introduce me to his family and he won't give up on his ex-wife. They go to weddings and family parties together when he should be taking me.'

'That sucks,' I said. 'But it has fuck-all to do with me.'

'I found poems on his computer when he was in the shower. He wasn't writing about me. He never shows me what he writes.'

'Well, nobody writes me poems either,' I said.

'But here you are. You're probably twenty years younger than I am and you're hanging around outside his house.' She turned and pointed.

To my dismay I saw that she was pointing at Carl Barber's house. It was definitely time for me to go home.

Of course the woman was barmy-bananas. But if she made a habit of haunting Care Barber's house, maybe she'd seen who was harassing him. Or was *she* responsible? I'd have to talk to Carl. I would not, however, interview her.

9

Had I not, with great foresight, switched my phone off before falling into bed, I would've been woken at six when the increasingly desperate texts and calls from Dulcie began. As it was I slept sweetly through till after nine when I had the house to myself. The sun was shining, the birdies were whistling and yesterday's cock-ups were behind me.

I went out to a high street café for breakfast. While I was waiting I plugged in my headphones and logged the calls that were worth logging. One of these had come in at 7:10 am and was from Myles. He gave me a landline number to ring and said his iPhone was 'tied up'. This was a sudden insight as to why I'd constantly been sent to voicemail. I pictured him obsessively punching and re-punching the number I'd given him for Gina. He must've got caught in a loop, listening to her voice and ringing, ringing, ringing; leaving message after message. I hoped he'd managed to stop for some sleep. But I doubted it if he was asking me to use his landline.

I wondered whether I should ring his godmother or if I should treat him as an adult who had learned to solve his own problems. I'd never had dealings with an OCD person before.

My coffee, orange juice and pastry arrived which postponed rational decision-making. I do miss the Met. When I was a cop they told me what to do and where to go. So of course I argued and thought orders were stupid, but at least I had a solid scaffold on which to hang my day.

One of my 'missed calls' was from Digby himself. 'Okay,' he said. 'I forgive you. You can come back for the lunch shift, and we'll say no more about it.'

Wouldn't we, though? He could stick his head in the microwave with the baked spuds before I caved in. At very least he could do his fair share of the work instead of relying on me to do every shift and all the cooking and serving while he schlepped off with his latest nooky provider. Poor Dulcie was untrained and inexperienced, and the only reason he'd given her a job was because she was too effing hopeless to realise what the deal was.

I made up my mind to leave my server a big tip. Working in hospitality is not a soft gig.

While I was licking the last of the Danish off my fingers a call came in from Carl Barber.

'Good morning,' he began. That's what I like about the granddad generation: they learned manners in their youth. Of course manners waste a lot of time, but it's way better to be greeted with, 'Good morning', than, 'Okay, I forgive you.'

'I hope I'm not interrupting something important,' he went on.

'You're a client,' I assured him. '*You* are something important.'

'This call is probably unnecessary, but I wanted to remind you that tonight is when my street puts its rubbish out – the night of the vigilante.'

'I hadn't forgotten,' I said. 'But I was going to ring *you* this morning to ask if you know someone called Deena.'

'As a matter of fact, I do. May I ask why?'

This was where the safest course of action would be to say, 'I'm asking the questions.' That is what a cop would say, but cops don't have clients they have to be polite to.

I paused and then, when he didn't fill the gap, I said, 'I spent a few minutes last night checking out what was normal activity in Cottham Road late at night. She approached me.'

'Oh,' he said. The next pause was his. He went on, 'That was very diligent of you. Thanks.'

'Just part of my normal service,' I said, although I'd only gone out again to avoid another unpleasant exchange with Eleanor and Olive.

'Well,' he said reluctantly, 'I should ask if Deena was rude to you.'
I hesitated.

He went on, 'Because I think somehow she got the wrong impression about where our... er... friendship was going.' He cleared his throat. 'So I'll have to have a little word with her. She won't disturb you again.'

Oh, I thought, as we finished the call, so you can be in the granddad generation, have lovely manners, and *still* want sex without an ongoing relationship while kidding a woman otherwise. I shouldn't have been surprised, but the thought was depressing.

When I was about thirteen, at school, a slim paperback was passed hand to hand among my sniggering classmates. The title on the cover was Sex For The Over Sixties. All the pages were blank. We thought that was hilarious.

Sometimes what pisses me off most is my own lack of resilience. And my longing for a future when there's no more insecurity about sex, love, money, my appearance or my place in the would. I'm bummed out because my life, career, finances, and self-respect had been smashed like skittles in a bowling alley. All because I fell for the flattery of one bad-bastard bloke.

Thinking about Carl Barber and Deena didn't make me feel more confident about my future in these precarious times so I rang Myles's landline instead.

He picked up on the seventh ring and said, *'What?'* in a clipped impatient tone.

'Hannah,' I said. 'You told me you'd ring me back.'

'Why?'

'I'm working for you,' I said, annoyed. 'I gave you a number for Gina. You were going to tell me if the voice on the answer message matches the fraud call you played for me. What I do next depends on your answer.'

'Oh,' he said. 'Look, I'm on the other phone. I'm waiting for call.'

I was right about him. I said, 'It's not going to happen. If she hasn't done it already Gina will not listen to your massages and she won't ring you back.'

'She will in the end. I have to keep calling.'

'She won't.'

'You don't know that.'

'Yes, I do,' I said, although I didn't. 'She's your friend. She *knows* you. If she was still connected to that number she'd have picked up immediately. She wouldn't leave you hanging.'

He didn't answer immediately and I heard him blowing his nose repeatedly. Then he said, 'Are you still outside her house in Potters Bar?' He sounded exhausted.

'No. She doesn't live there anymore.

'So what will you do now?'

'I'm waiting for old lists of tenants off past electoral rolls. The landlord seems to have done a bunk off to Turkey. But the present tenant has to pay rent to someone. I'm chasing it down. What I really need to know from you is about the voice. Is it Gina?'

'Yes,' he said without hesitation.

'And does it match the fraud call?'

'Well,' he said.

I waited.

'Yes. I was sure a couple of hours ago. Now I think maybe the fraud call is too generic. Maybe it's too actor-ish. She sounds as though she's learned the lines. And sometimes she sounds as if she's reading them. And then I wonder if it doesn't sound like her because there's someone in the room threatening her. She has a gun to her head and she's sending me a message by subtly not sounding like herself. Or maybe it's someone else pretending to be her. She had friends who are actors and quite capable of such cruelty. Or…'

'Stop,' I said. 'Listen to yourself – you're overcooking. Keep going like this and you'll combust. Why don't you get some sleep and I'll call you when I hare some news. If I find Gina she can tell you herself.'

'But I know she's in danger.'

'No you don't,' I almost screeched. I was quite worried about him. But I was more worried for me, because my client sounded like a maniac and he was dragging me down into his personal snake pit. 'Call Sophia,' I instructed.

'*Who?*'

'Sophia Smithson,' I almost yelled, 'your godmother.' I cut the call and ordered another coffee. Just to make myself feel better I asked for another pastry too. After talking to Myles I needed the ballast.

My client was demented. I could almost see his phone melting, spewing steam and melted silicon down the front of his immaculate shirt. I shouldn't be taking his money. But I had taken his money. I'd even done some work for him, and jotted down my mileage in my little spiral notebook. I wasn't going to give his lovely money back, so I'd better do a bit more work for him.

First I tried to find Emir Yilmaz on social media. This was, it seemed, a bit like looking up John Smith. I gave up. Then I Googled Tasty Treats because although it looked as though it had been out of business for years people rarely delete their information. The internet is littered with dead people and defunct businesses.

So I spent the next two hours chasing every damn business of that name I could find all around the web. They say you can find anything and everything there, but only if you already know where to look. I have access to a lot of public information most of it legally sourced, some of it not. Even so, after hours sifting through scores of hits, Emir Yilmaz and Tasty Treats remained elusive. It would be a longer process of elimination than I'd predicted. So tired, hungry and cross-eyed I bought a roast beef and horseradish sandwich, and scrolled through missed messages and calls.

As usual junk outweighed every thing else. Natasha had taken, especially for me, thirteen photos of her beautiful lady parts and would allow me an exclusive peek for a token sum. I consigned her offer to the bin. Of course there was no real Natasha, any more them there was a Flavius Murillo who guaranteed to make me rich if only I'd give him my bank details so that he could release to me money from stock I didn't know I owned. And on it went: the never-ending gimme, gimme, gimme game.

I deleted three more missed calls from Dulcie but played one from Digby. He said, 'If you come in today I'll have your severance pay ready for you. Also a new client's been asking about you. Shall I arrange a meeting?' Oh the devious, clever son of a blister!

The call had come in at twelve-thirty. I looked at my watch. It was now just past one – the epicentre of the lunch panic. Just how stupid did he think I was?

I was about to consign the call to the bin with all the rest of the trash when I noticed a text that had only just arrived. It was an emoji: a pair of brown hands folded palm to palm as if in prayer.

'BZee,' I said out loud. That emoji was BZee's way of saying he wanted a meeting. The place we always met was just outside the Sandwich Shack, and I would, nine times out of ten, bring him something to eat. Don't get me wrong – I'm not his effing social worker. It's not my responsibility to make sure he's fed, washed and warm. But I have been a cop and I was trained to stick my shnoz in where it isn't wanted – in the public interest, of course. BZee and his dodgy ways do provide me with some work. I pay him but as, technically, he's a child, the least I can do is give him a sandwich,

I cursed Digby and the unwise parents who hadn't strangled him at birth. Then I returned his call.

'Oh, Hannah,' he said, as if I was some very distant acquaintance he'd almost forgotten. 'How nice of you to call.'

'Oh Digby,' I replied. 'You called me. Is your Alzheimer's playing up again?'

'Are you ever polite to *anyone*?'

'I'm polite to *everyone*, except you,' I lied. 'You're *special*.'

Opening courtesies over, he told me to come in for my pay packet.

'What about this so-called job you've got for me?'

'I'll tell you when you get your lazy fat arse over here. Better hurry or I'll change my mind.' He cut the call, leaving me with a mouthful of unshared insults about the appearance of *his* arse. He's bloody addicted to the last word. It's a very annoying habit.

On my way over to the Shack I bought a huge white baguette filled with ham, cheese and brown sauce, just the way BZee likes it: I also bought him a can of high octane Coke which is his tipple of choice. I would not, absolutely not, fill Digby's pockets by buying the overpriced shit he sells.

When I got to the Shack I found a very long queue at the takeout window, Dulcie in tears and not even a hideous smell where Digby should have been.

'He said to tell you he had urgent business,' Dulcie sobbed. She'd cut her finger and was trying to staunch the blood with a dirty dishrag. I sent her off to the loo with the first aid box and instructions to wash the wound with lots of soap and running water before covering it.

'Thank God you're back,' said an elderly gent, one of the Common People, a walking club that met every Wednesday for a brisk pre-lunch trot around the Common. 'That new girl's useless. She hasn't even cleared the outside tables.'

I told him, in a loud voice, that I wasn't back, I was only helping poor Dulcie out of the kindness of my hard heart, and that Digby'd canned me. I basked in the murmured support from the Shack regulars even though I was sure not much of it was sincere.

In the end I persuaded the Common People to clear the outside tables themselves in return for free coffee while I dished out sandwiches, mac and cheese and fried egg rolls. Nobody was difficult. In fact everyone seemed to enjoy pitching in. I whirled around like a Dervish, keeping the microwave humming and the coffeemaker bubbling, saying, 'You'll miss me when I'm gone,' to all the customers.

BZee, seeing that Digby wasn't on the premises, sidled in. I gave him his Coke and baguette and settled him in a corner. When I next had time to check on him the food was gone and there was barely a crumb on his plate. He was asleep with his head on one bent elbow.

Dulcie returned after way too long a comfort break. Her finger was badly bandaged and her eyes were swollen and red. Instead of yelling at her I handed her a clean pair of surgical gloves and set her to washing up and filling the steriliser.

See how sweet natured I am! When I'm trying to prove a point. My point is that Digby needs me very badly indeed, so if he wanted me back he should give me a hefty raise, fewer hours and more consideration. Pity he wasn't around to notice.

By two-thirty the flood of customers had shrunk to almost nothing and the area behind the counter was as clean as it ever is – it *looks* good but it wouldn't pass a Health and Safety inspection. I told Dulcie to mop the floor, stole a large slice of apple pie and an oversize scoop of chocolate ice-cream and woke BZee out of his deep sleep.

While he demolished the pudding I went back into Digby's office to look for my pay packet. Shock, horror! It wasn't there. So, giving myself a raise, I found his badly hidden petty cash box at the bottom of the dirty laundry sack and awarded myself two hours pay. I didn't bother to leave him a note to tell him what I'd done. I didn't have to. He'd know.

Dulcie went outside for a cigarette. It looked as if, in the last twenty-four hours, she'd taken up smoking. I wonder why. I heard her coughing her lungs up while I was talking to BZee.

His problem was pretty simple. All he needed was an adult who wouldn't rip him off or sick the social workers on him: yesterday his friend Petra had borrowed her mum's bike without permission. 'She too lazy to fix her own chain an' there was this party at Chubby's cos his people went to Egypt. Okay? So the bike got nicked, yeah?'

'Yeah,' I replied, trying not to drum my fingers on the table top.

'Yeah, then Petra's mum so craze she unsafe. Right? So Petra, she know I gotta name. So she tells her mum I'll find the bike today.'

'And?' I said, impatient. I didn't want Digby showing up and giving BZee and me grief.

'See, Petra and me got on her laptop and, check it out, the bike advertised on Facebook and eBay. Big guy at same party. Left school last year. Pumps crack in the yard. Got backup.'

'Oh,' I said. 'And you think...?'

'Yeah. Cos you 'n' me, okay, do good with the K9s, right? So we could do good with bikes. This guy selling shit-loada bikes. Him gotta name for doltish...'

'What do you want me to do?'

'Be nice English lady want to buy that pretty gold bike him showing on eBay.'

'Why me?'

'Him stupidy-stupidy. But he white.'

'Oh,' I said, 'I get it.' But I was pretty sure I didn't, exactly. And looking at the expression on his face I could see that BZee was one hundred percent *convinced* that I didn't.

He turned his head away, almost politely and said, 'Got cheesecake?'

I went to the chiller cabinet, cut him a double slice, and the moment passed.

He showed me the picture of the bike on his phone. I copied the details into my phone. Then I dialled the number. It was answered almost immediately. Stupidy was out and about. I could hear the whoosh of passing traffic.

'Yeah?' he said.

'Am I speaking to Kevin?' I asked hesitantly. 'The gentleman who's selling a gold-coloured bicycle?'

BZee grinned. He seemed to think 'gentleman' was a nice touch.

Stupidy did too. He put on a posh accent and said, 'I am himself.'

We dickered around the questions of condition, age and price. I sounded fussy and hesitant; he sounded increasingly impatient. In the end he said, 'Look, lady, d'you want it or doncha?'

'Oh I do, I do,' I stammered nervously. 'But… '

'No buts,' he said. 'Bring the cash and take the bike. It's simple as that.'

'Now?' I asked, getting up and nodding to BZee who got up too.

'Now or lose it,' Stupidy ordered, showing his true colours; although what the true colour of a bully is I can't imagine.

'You,' I said to BZee as we crossed the common. 'You keep me in sight but don't let Stupidy see you. He'd recognise you wouldn't he? You were at that party too, weren't you? And you go or went to the same school. Right?'

He didn't answer. He was hopping around like a dog with ADD on too short a lead. Anxiety and mistrust radiated off him like the smell of sweat. 'What you gone do?' he asked in the end.

'Wait and see,' I said, because I didn't exactly know myself.

We went to the double row of lockups and garages that runs between St Marks and St Andrews Roads. It's known as Saints Alley. Stupidy Kevin was waiting about halfway down outside a blue painted roll-up door.

I sent BZee round to the other end where there was more cover from wheelie bins. He would keep his phone handy and the connection between us open. He was not on any account to show himself. That was one part of my instruction I was sure he'd respect. Stupidy was big and beefy. He looked as though he'd copied his dude-fashion statement from YouTube.

I walked hesitantly towards him, my bag clutched protectively in front of me like an intimidated older woman.

'Mister Kevin?' I asked, shy and tremulous.

'Mrs... ?' He had clearly forgotten my false name already.

'You have a gold coloured bicycle in good condition for sale?'

'Told ya,' he said. 'Liquidated stock. Kosher.'

'May I see it please?' My manners were so good I was impressing myself.

For an answer he rolled up the garage door. I got a quick glimpse of about half a dozen bikes, before he pulled the gold one from where it leaned against the wheel arch of a Kia Picanto. He pushed it into the daylight. It was a very flashy article indeed.

'Ooh,' I said admiringly. 'My niece will just love this. Do you mind if I take a closer look?'

'No buy, no ride,' he intoned, clamping his large pink paw over the saddle.

'I wouldn't dream of it,' I said, although pedalling away at top speed into the sunset had been an option.

So I tested the breaks, lights and all the shiny reflectors. Then I knelt and took a pencil torch from my pocket. I ran the light over the place where the gears and crank met.

'Oh dear,' I said, standing up and putting the torch away.

'What?' Stupidy said.

'The serial number of this bike.' My tone changed from faltering to official. 'My infrared light reveals to me that this bicycle has been registered on the stolen vehicle list. Which means that you, Kevin Vaughn, are in possession of a stolen item, and are therefore guilty of attempting to sell same to a serving police officer!'

He looked so furious I was afraid he might hit me. Instead he threw the bike at me and took off down the alley like a rabbit. I sat on the tarmac with the bike on top of me laughing my head off.

'BZee,' I said into my phone, 'did you catch all that?'

'I told you,' he said, 'him stupidy-stupid. Got Petra here.'

'Good. Send her along. There are six other bikes. What do you want to do?'

'Liberate,' he said, and hung up.

Petra was very pretty, well dressed and well spoken. She was also well brought up enough to thank me and pretend to admire my tactics. I told her that the stolen bikes should not on any account be sold. She said she'd put the descriptions and serial numbers up on her Facebook page. If anyone wanted to donate a reward she'd give it to BZee.

Then he and a posse of ragamuffins, all younger than him, descended on us and began to gut the garage. I retreated. I should've sent an anonymous call to the cops. But I didn't. They didn't care about stolen bikes. The world was full of crimes too small to grab their attention, or too big for them to cope with, so it was their own silly fault if the woman who stepped up and did their job for them didn't bother to let them know. Maybe I should advertise: Hannah Abram, Jobbing PI – no case too small or dirty.

I walked back to the Shack. Digby still hadn't shown his ugly mug and Dulcie seemed to be managing fine. She said, 'Can't you make it up with Digby? I'm not cut out for all this stress. I'm too slow for fast food.'

'Quit,' I advised. 'You can do better than the Shack. And definitely better than Pig Digby.'

She shook her head. 'No qualifications.' She was too young to be so utterly lacking in hope or self belief. Someone had done a very complete job on her if she couldn't see anything better in her future than Digby.

'Dulcie,' I said, 'you're kind, hardworking and young. There's work in the caring professions, for instance, where you can go in at entry level without qualifications. That's just an example. There are jobs where you'd be appreciated for what you *can*. It's a real shame to see you beat yourself up for what you find difficult. There's nothing wrong with *you*. But there's definitely something wrong with this job.'

Dulcie started to cry. 'Oh bloodyell,' I said. I put an arm around her shoulders, gave her a quick squeeze and buggered off as fast as I could. Maybe I was good at small stuff, but bolstering Dulcie's self respect was way beyond me. I wouldn't last five minutes in the caring professions.

10

As the sun went down I was circling around Carl Barber's house looking for a parking space. I had a thermos of strong black coffee, a packet of four cheese and pickle sandwiches, two packets of chocolate biscuits and a Shewee, which I was hoping never to use, on the seat beside me. Not for the first time I wished I had a van. Finally a space opened up a couple of doors down and I slid my grubby, anonymous Toyota in.

Neighbours came and went; lights went on and off; people started to put their rubbish out for collection next morning. Carl's neat array of black bags and sorted recycling went out at ten. He looked up and down the road but didn't spot me.

Later the residents of the other three flats above his dumped untidy heaps of unsorted, badly bagged garbage in front of the railings. The two houses on either side of his were equally thoughtless. Perfect temptation for a rubbish vigilante, I thought.

I waited. I listened to the radio on my phone. And waited. I recharged my phone. And I waited. Midnight came and went. The sandwiches disappeared one by one, and then the biscuits. And still I waited. Cottham Road settled down and, I presumed, went to sleep. I very nearly did too.

Then, an erratically driven Jaguar wove its way down to the posh end of the street. Two seemingly rat-arsed young guys got out and stumbled, giggling, to a house nine doors away from the one I was watching. After blundering around with dropped keys and too small locks they disappeared inside. Lights went on, off and on again upstairs.

That's it, I thought, the night's action is finished. I had to make up my mind whether or not to wait for the early risers. I was thinking about it when movement caught my attention. Someone was coming out of the door the smashed guys had gone into.

A man in an overcoat pulled on over his pyjamas appeared. It seemed he was being towed by a young, muscular Dalmatian.

I made myself very small and motionless as he went past. I could hear him saying, 'Fucking get on with it you horrible dog.' But the dog was acting as if this was a treat, sniffing lampposts, railings and, yes rubbish, which he attacked whenever he smelled un-bagged food. The man made no attempt to stop him as he raised his leg on the piles of rubbish bags. He was a middle aged man with an office worker's stoop. His hair was sticking up on one side and clearly he was not as muscular as his dog.

Several yards further on the dog pooped on the pavement and the owner didn't pick up the mess. As I watched, the dog tore a black bag open and pounced on a takeaway pizza box. He started to guzzle the contents.

The man snatched the box away, picked up the vandalised bag and chucked it over the railings.

'Gotcha!' I muttered aloud. I pointed my camera at man and dog and started the video function as they turned back towards home. The man didn't pay attention to every pile of garbage his dog had investigated, but when he got to Carl's house he paused and picked up every single bag and box, including the small meticulously tidy pile of Carl's, and deliberately dropped the lot over the railings onto the iron steps and front door step. I filmed this and kept the camera going till he disappeared through his own front door.

I got out of the car and took a picture of the front of the house that clearly showed the number. It was a single occupancy house close to the posh end of the road, and although there was quite a lot of rubbish it all looked as though it had been generated by one household.

I was tempted to throw the vigilante's rubbish over his own railings but stopped myself. Carl had only hired me to find out who the vigilante was, not to take revenge or tip the perp off that he was busted. I could have phoned Carl and maybe helped him clear up the mess outside his door, but by then it was after three and I was too pleased with myself to get my hands dirty. I'd scored with bikes and rubbish. Success – small to be sure, but success is success, so don't knock it.

11

Digby phoned me at seven-thirty, eight, eight-thirty and nine. I ignored him the way he'd ignored me yesterday. Less than five hours sleep often makes me cranky. And Digby *always* makes me cranky. Double cranky is dangerous. I turned my phone off and went back to sleep until nearly noon when someone started banging on the front door.

I pulled a sweater on over my PJs and stuck my head out of the window. There was Digby, abusing the doorknocker.

'Shut the fuck up,' I shouted. 'And piss off. I've nothing to say to you.'

'I'll stay here knocking till you let me in,' he shouted back. 'I'll sing The Red Flag at the top of my voice till all the neighbours complain to your landladies and they chuck your sorry arse out on the street.'

He began, 'The people's flag is deepest red... '

I hate to admit it, but Digby can hold a tune and he has a pleasant tenor voice. But it's very, very loud. He's trained in musical theatre techniques – one of which is extreme projection. Also he's in a Kinks tribute band, and someone told me that one time when his mic blew halfway through Waterloo Sunset he carried on without it. Everyone could hear every damn word, and the lead guitarist had to tell him to dial down the volume.

'Beneath its folds we'll live and die,' he hollered, probably smashing glass all around South London.

My only weapon was a tooth mug. I filled it with cold water which I poured on Digby's head.

He just laughed at me. 'Are you so bourgeois now you can't take a little left wing ditty? Let me in or I'll start the second verse.'

Most irritating was the fact that the street where I lodged *was* the kind of place where tidy liberal vegetarians lived. Olive and Eleanor were not the only right-on, self-satisfied householders here. Everyone pretended to be left wing but never voted for Socialist councillors or MPs. They joined radical groups on FaceBook but never went to meetings. They might have *claimed* to be more offended by Rule Britannia than The Red Flag, but such are the wondrous ambiguities of gentrification that the residents here cared more about property prices than politics.

'I'm not letting you in,' I shouted down to him. 'But I'll meet you at the Sun in Splendour on the corner in twenty minutes.' I slammed the window shut and went away to wash and dress. For once, in my long power struggle with Digby, I was holding most of the cards. And to prove it, when I got to the pub ten minutes late, not only was he waiting patiently but he'd bought me fish and chips and half a pint of best bitter. Believe me, even given Digby's company, I've had far worse breakfasts.

We sat at a small corner table. He waited till I'd doused my food with salt and vinegar and taken a swallow from my drink. I was staring at him.

'What?' he asked, suspicion leaking out of every pore.

But actually I was remembering why I hadn't killed him in forty different ways during the year I'd worked for him. Yes, he was a sexist arse, a terrible employer and a sarcastic, heartless, mean, penny-pinching son of a baboon. But nobody's perfect. If you asked him he'd say I was as nasty-ass as he was. And he'd be right. Life-lessons have taught me how.

But when push comes to shove the penny-pinching son of a baboon does sometimes do the right thing. And he *had* employed me when I was jobless and living out of my car. For which favour he exploits the shit out of me. And that's what I now had the opportunity to re-negotiate.

I took a huge forkful of hot cod in crisp batter and followed it with one of salty, deep fried potato. There's nothing better, unless you eat the same thing by the seaside.

'Damn if that doesn't look good,' Digby said. 'I should've got some for myself.'

'Do it,' I said. 'Cos you ain't getting any of mine.'

Ten minutes later, anyone seeing us sitting together, tucking into fragrant food, would have taken us for friends. The illusion lasted only as long as our gobs were too full of fish to talk. Then he said, 'Okay, greedy-guts, what'll it take?'

I could've pretended I didn't know what he was talking about, but I was tired of playing time-wasting games so I said, 'I want to be promoted to manager and be paid accordingly. I want use of the office whenever I need it. I want flexible hours. I want a contract that stipulates I only take the early shift seven times a month, similarly the late shift. If you deviate from that I get paid time and a half. I want a proper assistant – not just some poor bitch who lets you shag her. You can abuse women on your own time. I will *not* suffer from your alley-catting.'

I took a breath, and just had time to notice that his complexion had turned from sallow to purple before he yelled, 'What the fuck you talking about?'

'Dulcie,' I yelled back. 'She doesn't even know how to make a plain ham sarny, she's scared of the coffee maker, she hyperventilates when there's more than one table in use. If she's a proper employee, effing train her, and do it double quick, cos she's a waste of space as she is. If she's your girlfriend treat her better. If she's just another shag, well, shame on you.' I was amazed at how angry I was about Dulcie. I took another breath.

He leaped to his feet. Digby standing is, if anything, shorter than Digby seated with his legs dangling. Even so, Digby in a rage is quite an impressive sight.

'Listen, bitch,' he began at the top of his voice.

My phone rang.

I didn't want to listen to Digby so I answered it, grabbed my bag and marched outside. I couldn't fail to notice that the men in the pub were sniggering at the row, but a couple of the women gave me a thumbs up.

'Hannah?' Carl Barber said.

'*Yes?*' I walked away from the pub to a recessed doorway in a quieter part of the street.

'Are you alright?'

'*Why?*' I said, and then realised I'd snapped at him. I was speeding. I took a deep breath and let it out slowly. 'Actually, Mr Barber, I was just about to phone you but was interrupted by an idiot.'

'Do you have time to speak now?' he asked, with his beguiling good manners. 'I could ring back later.'

'No, no. I didn't want to call you last night because it was very late when I got home, and this morning sort of got away from me.' No lie: I'd slept through it, but that's not the sort of thing an efficient private investigator tells a client.

'I was wondering if you saw anything. The rubbish vigilante visited the street again last night.'

'Yes, I know. I've got something to show you. Will you be at home in about an hour?'

'Yes. I'll expect you then?' He sounded as if he was accustomed to being let down – a malady we all suffer from these days.

I needed to decompress from my high pressure breakfast with Digby, so I walked across to Carl's side of the Common and then dropped into Tania's Tea Room for a small pot of English Breakfast tea. I sat in a comfortable armchair surrounded by china figurines, crocheted doilies and linen napkins. Tania's interior decoration is claustrophobic and very English. But Tania is from Bulgaria. She makes a killer pot of tea strong enough to wipe my mind clean of Digby's mess and let me focus on my iPad.

I began with one of my favourite tasks, which is to delete unwanted messages from my inbox. Then I noticed that one of my lines of enquiry about Tasty Treats in Potters Bar had paid off: the building that housed the defunct café and the flat which Myles's Gina used as her address was being administered by a company called North Potter Holdings. NP Holdings apparently managed several properties in the area including a burger and kebab bar called Tenerife Kebabs. It seemed weeks ago, but only a couple of nights back I'd followed a guy in skinny jeans, who was apparently living in Gina's old flat, to that place.

I rang Myles's number and was sent straight to voice mail. I told him I had a lead and cut the call without telling him what it was. If he still had Gina's old number on perpetual redial I wouldn't be hearing from him anytime soon.

I paid for my tea and went out into watery sunshine and a brisk breeze. At Cottham Road I found Carl's gate unchained. His iron steps and the area in front of his door had been swept clean.

He answered my knock and showed me down a dark passage to a bright living room. This was untidy – there was paper and recording equipment cluttering every inch of space.

Carl offered me tea or coffee. I refused. He then removed a guitar, a tiny Korg keyboard and about six hundred books and papers to reveal a small sofa. I sat down. He opened a canvas director's chair and sat opposite me.

'You were outside last night?' he said. 'Watching?'

I nodded and took my phone out. I started last night's video of the man with the badly trained Dalmatian dog and handed it to Carl.

I watched him watching it. He was poker-faced. If he recognised the vigilante not even the flicker of an eyelid gave him away.

He asked if he could download the video onto his own device. While he was doing this I asked, 'Do you know him? He's a neighbour – well, nine doors away. But it seemed personal. It looked as if he was giving your rubbish special attention.'

Carl finished what he was doing and handed my phone back.

I waited. He smiled at me and said, 'Are you sure you won't have a hot drink?' I shook my head and he went on, 'You've done very well in a surprisingly short time.' He tapped his pad. 'This is everything I need to know. I'm impressed. Thank you so much.'

He gave me another fifty pound note and before I knew it I was wafting back to my flat on a cloud graceful gratitude. I was halfway there before it occurred to me that the information I'd given Carl had meant a whole lot more to him than he'd told me. I'd been seduced by fifty quid and a handful of compliments. It was such a sharp contrast to my skirmish with Digby that I hadn't noticed that I'd been politely but efficiently evicted.

*

I sat on a bench facing the Common and accessed Companies House where I discovered that North Potter Holdings (Maintenance) had an office in Watford. Which, after a quick search on Google Maps, I learned is a town adjacent to Potters Bar. There was a phone number which I copied into my mobile and rang. After a couple of minutes a woman said, 'You have reached Head Office of NP Holdings. Due to a heavy volume of enquiries none of our operatives are available at present. You are, at this moment in time,' pause, 'number sixty-four in the queue.' I hung up.

I looked at my phone. The voice belonged to a nice, well-bred Englishwoman. I wished I was better at voices.

The right thing to do now would be to forward the number to Myles for his verdict. What would he do, given his obsessive reaction to my last request for voice recognition? Might he simply explode?

I'd just about decided that this would be *his* problem, when someone sat down heavily on the bench beside me, reached out and tried to grab my phone. I smacked the hand away, turned and saw that the would-be snatcher was Deena.

'You are phoning Carl,' she said as if she was in possession of an undeniable fact.

'Are you crazy?' I countered.

'Don't lie to me,' she said, eyes narrow. 'I saw you come out of his flat. I expect it was an all-nighter. That's how he begins. He gets your hopes up and then dashes them. He's only pretending to be interested in you to torture me.'

'You really *are* dipsy-doodle,' I said, getting up. 'Now bugger off.'

'I followed you here. I'll follow you to your home and your place of work. I won't give up until you sign an affidavit in front of a Justice of the Peace undertaking never to have congress with Carl Barber ever again.'

I stared at this perfectly ordinary middle-aged woman. She was neatly turned out in a fitted jacket, a smart straight skirt and sensible shoes. Her conservative pink lipstick was carefully applied – so apparently she could colour inside the lines. She didn't look like a lunatic.

I knew it was useless, but I had to try. I said, 'Deena, I have absolutely no idea why you're saying all this. My business with Mr Barber does not, and has never, in the *two days* since I met him, included "congress". And, in case you haven't noticed, he's way, *way* too old for me.'

'You would say that, wouldn't you?' She made another grab for my phone. I pushed her away, but she went on, 'I know all about women like you and father figures, even sugar-daddies.'

'*Sugar-daddies?* What century are you living in?'

'Gold digging tramps then, groupies. You're like flies on turds.'

I got up, turned my back and walked away. I was going to Google Carl Barber when I got a chance. Maybe he wasn't the sweet old geezer he presented .

I walked quickly, but so did she. If I wasn't careful she really would follow me home and I was not at all keen on a maniac knowing my address.

I led her all around the body of water known as The Drain in the middle of the Common. It's too big to be a pond and too small to be a lake. A few years ago a gay guy was drowned in it a by a bunch of National Fronters who couldn't find a person of colour to murder.

I was tempted to drown Deena because I couldn't shake her off. Unfortunately my car was parked outside my house. Had it been anywhere else I'd have got in it and driven to Watford. It was a ridiculous problem, and one of the things I resented was that it made me look silly.

I've spent all my working life trying to undermine the male world view that if you scratch any woman, under her veneer of competence, you'll find a silly incompetent female. That was why Toxic Tom's photos of me in the shower which he circulated among my colleagues and superiors did so much damage to me and my prospects. Those fucking photos are still out there. Even if T. Tom takes them down, I'll be dead long before *they* die. Just what a woman wants to be remembered for.

And here I am being stalked by a lunatic accusing me of being a gold-digging tramp with an oldie three times my age.

I walked all the way to Clapham, and then, figuring that a woman in jeans and trainers could run faster than one in a straight skirt, I sprinted to the station.

'Welcome to the heart of Battersea', said the sign over the concourse. Before the sickness crushed the life out of high streets, the concourse used to look more like a shopping mall than a station. It's sadder and wiser now – like a lot of the shoppers and travellers.

I raced through to the barriers and, slapping down my travel card, I lost myself in the maze of stairs and platforms that is Clapham Junction.

I got on a train to Wimbledon but disembarked before I got there. Then I sat on an out of the way bench for twenty minutes Googling Carl Barber.

He had once fronted a long forgotten band called Gravity Lite. Almost famous for a number he wrote called I Wanna Be Seventeen Like You, the band once opened for Tom Jones on a West Country tour. The song itself became famous again when it was banned by the BBC in the nineties for, apparently, encouraging paedophilia. But the band had imploded twenty years previously. Now Carl was better known as a song writer, especially for two disco songs sung by Princess Bootyful, which went stratospheric in the late seventies and are still played regularly at birthday parties, hen parties, weddings and bat Mitzvahs.

That explained a lot, including Deena's accusation of groupydom.

I yawned and rang NP Holdings number again. I was still sixty-fourth in the queue – which wasn't possible if it was a genuine number and a kosher queue. I forwarded the number to Myles with a note explaining that all I wanted to know was whether or not he recognised Gina's voice.

Then I took down my ponytail, combed my hair with my fingers, removed my jacket and caught the next train back to Clapham Junction.

While I was on the train a call came in from Digby. I let it go to voicemail. I didn't want to talk to him but I did want to know what he had to say. The message surprised me: 'Look, Hannah,' he said, 'we got off on the wrong foot. Please, please come in and talk to me. I've been giving your proposals serious consideration.'

'Oh *really?*' I said out loud. 'I don't *think* so.' But I was pleased to hear that he sounded desperate.

Every now and then I think I ought to try to be a better person – take a course in niceness or something. But every time I do I remember that my love of humanity has never made me a penny, and that humanity's neglect of me has constantly landed me in the shit-house.

As if to prove my point, as I exited the station, I saw the back view of a woman in a fitted jacket and a straight skirt turning and just beginning to walk away looking disconsolate. Demented Deena hadn't believed my protestations of innocence. Nor had she believed that I'd gone somewhere on a train. See what I mean? If I'd simply dotted her one and pushed her into The Drain I wouldn't have wasted an hour by being nice enough *not* to. I *am* innocent and I *have* been somewhere on a train. But my honesty has made no difference – the bloody woman waited over an hour and is only now giving up. I swore – I can recognise a long-term problem when I see one.

I watched her walk away. I was thinking, Maybe I should give her a taste of her own poison and follow *her*. I could find out where she lived and harass her. But I didn't, even though I wondered how much she'd make me pay for my niceness.

12

I arrived at the Shack just as Digby was locking up. Had I come any earlier he would have probably found a way to make me help Dulcie mop the floor. Now he unlocked and said, 'Wait in the car,' to her. She looked exhausted and pink-eyed.

As we went through to the office I couldn't help noticing, to my great satisfaction, how grubby and untidy the Shack looked after only two days away.

'Okay,' he said, as he sat behind his desk 'You win. I'll give you a raise.'

I'd had more cash work than I could cope with so I could afford to wait him out.

He named a figure. I laughed and turned towards the door.

'And you can call yourself the manager if you want to,' he added hastily.

I reached for the door handle, still laughing.

'Wait!' he almost yelled. 'I'm offering to raise your take-home pay by a third and you can be a proper manager. I'll even have a badge made for you.'

'You can stick your badge,' I said evenly. 'What you don't seem to understand is that the hospitably sector is on its way down the honey-bucket. No one can get good staff anymore. And that's the fault of people like you, Digby, for paying wages no one can live on and working your staff – me – to death. I could walk out of here and get a job, say, at Tania's Tea Room for twice what you're offering me.'

'Is that bitch poaching my staff already?' Digby roared. 'And I suppose she's offering you the use of her office so you can moonlight with your other "clients"?' He made 'clients' sound dirty, but I kept my temper.

'That's another thing,' I said in the reasonable tone I knew made him crazy, 'when I first came to work for you, use of the office was a condition of employment. Nowadays you've made it a privilege you can dole out or withdraw according to your whim. That's not good enough. I have another job. You've always known that.'

'You wouldn't last sixty seconds at Tania's,' he grumbled. 'She expects polite service with a fricking smile.'

There was a tap on the door. '*What?*' howled Digby.

'Can I have the car key?' Dulcie said, looking terrified. 'It's started to rain.' She was already drenched.

Digby threw the key at her. She fumbled the catch and had to crawl on the floor.

'Now get out,' he ordered. 'Can't you see I'm busy?'

She backed away leaving wet footprints behind her. She might've been wearing a sign proclaiming 'Victim' on her chest.

'Okay,' he said turning back to me 'You get your raise, you're elevated to management, and you can use the office whenever so long as it isn't at the lunch scrum.'

'I want that in writing,' I said.

He glared. 'You write it,' and pushed his lap top towards me.

I opened a document and called it Letter of Agreement Between Hannah Abram and Digby Walsh. Then I made a list of his undertakings while he leaned back in the revolving chair that was far too big for him. He looked like a malevolent child, swinging from side to side, distracting me and threatening a tantrum.

I ignored him and turned my list into plain English that no one could weasel out of – hourly rates, overtime, my duties, his obligations. As a cop I'd been trained to write statements that would stand up in court. It was a skill I put to good use.

Finally I turned the screen toward, him and let him read what I'd written.

'I'll think about it,' he said.

'Okay,' I said equably. 'Then I'll think about coming back.'

While he'd been scanning the document, I'd had a peek at the Shack diary. I'd reminded myself that the day after tomorrow there was an event. It was called The Big Sleep Out. Every year, the Friends of the Common and a bunch of local charities jointly staged an event in support of the homeless. Well-meaning middleclass residents, school kids and recreational users of the Common turned up at sundown with sleeping bags, tents and bed rolls to pledge solidarity with the street people they ignored for the rest of the year. There was music, wine and kegs, so people had a good time as well as bolstering their charitable cred.

Digby made quite a wedge of dosh out of the event because the Shack stayed open all night and the breakfast trade was extraordinary. Last year I broke all records for how many breakfast rolls I could dish up in an hour.

Digby needed me urgently. I had him over a barrel, under a barrel and in a barrel.

'Alright, alright,' he said furiously. 'I'll sign.'

I had to stop myself doing the 'I scored' dance. Instead I turned my back and sorted out the printer cable.

'I'll do that,' Digby said. 'We'll have a beer to seal the deal. Or drown my sorrows.' He handed me the key to the secret cooler he kept behind the counter. It was where he hid his private stash of Tiger beer. It had to be well hidden because Digby did not have a liquor licence and wasn't allowed to keep alcohol on the premises. For The Big Sleep Out it was the organisers who acquired a temporary licence and provided the alcohol.

When I got back to the office with two opened bottles, the printer was chuntering like a car with a bad battery. Digby made three copies of the agreement: one for himself, one for me and one for the files. I watched him sign, digging his pen in aggressively to show his displeasure. I signed all three copies too with a lighter touch and a much lighter heart.

It was only after I'd gulped down half my drink that I noticed his malicious smirk and did what I should have done before signing. I checked the Agreement and saw that, while my back was turned, he'd added another clause. It read: 'It is the job of the Manager to train any new staff the owner deems suitable, for which duty there will be no extra pay.'

I choked on my beer. He burst out laughing. 'Gotcha!' he crowed, happily.

*

It was one of those transition days. The rain and brisk wind made me think that winter was stalking me like a creature that would bite as soon as it came close enough. I don't like winter. It lasts too long.

I walked back to my loveless digs thinking about digs and Digby. Because, up to a point, I probably needed him as much as he needed me. Given my wiped-out financial status in the middle of an economic melt-down, my ability to pay the rent on the aforementioned loveless digs depended on unlovable Digby.

I'd had four cash-paying clients in the last few days and that gave me the confidence to roll what could have been suicidal dice with Digby. Okay. But, let's be realistic, there hadn't been even a sniff of a job in the fortnight before that. Four clients do not make me a financially secure self-employed person. I needed an office with my own name on the door, and that, at the moment, was an unrealistic fantasy.

I arrived home just as another squall of rain stopped as suddenly as it started. There were lights on in the house. Eleanor and Olive would be hogging the kitchen and having one of their endless discussions about the nutritional value of a liquid diet based on pulverised… what? … grass?

I put my door key back in my pocket and went to sit in my car. I scanned the street, aware that Deena might be on the prowl. What *was* the deal between her and old Mr Barber? If she became a real nuisance I'd have to ask him. And to be honest, I didn't really want to know. It was something he said he 'wasn't proud of', so was my reluctance to find out an example of my own sexism and age-ism?

I opened my bag and released the iPad. First I looked again at the Companies House entry for NP Holdings and noticed that in a list of unpronounceable names I recognised one Emir Yilmaz. He was one of the NP Holdings company directors. I had already tried a search for him on Social Networks and discovered that it was such a common name that it'd take me weeks to find him. All I knew was that he'd been Gina Turner's landlord and that he'd left the UK. The name seemed to be most popular in places like Turkey and Armenia.

This triggered my xenophobia about the sort of foreign based internet scams that Gina might or might not be fronting. I was an ex cop; xenophobia and racism were diseases cops are horribly vulnerable to. When they feel threatened they tend to fall back on prejudice. It's something I'm sadder and wiser about since I left the Met. But every now and then it pops up like a festering sore from an ill-fitting shoe. In case you haven't noticed, I'm not perfect.

I ran through missed calls, texts and emails. There was nothing from Myles.

13

Friday was spent back at the Shack cleaning up after my own absence, making lists and preparing for the big Saturday night event. People started gathering at the designated campsite not far from us by mid-afternoon. The wimps put up tents, the hardy ones brought sleeping bags, and the macho ones just came with blankets.

The Big Sleep Out welcome packs included one token per person entitling those who'd paid to one free breakfast roll and one cup of coffee in the morning. No token, no free breakfast; Digby would be policing that. Anything else had to be paid for. A lot of the campers brought picnics, but by midnight, when the munchies set in, I would do a roaring trade. So, early that morning, I made a huge vat of vegetarian chili and an equally huge pot of mac-cheese.

The rest of my time was spent trying to teach Dulcie the mysteries of the coffee machine and tea urn. I failed, but Digby brought in a college kid called Fred who had successfully worked at the Shack one summer holiday and whose mother owed Digby a favour. Things went more smoothly after that. Dulcie became the server and did quite well at it.

Digby himself brought in car-loads of the supplies we'd need to get us through the night. He also organised black sack rubbish collection. And I have to admit that when there was no time to be snarky we worked well together.

Of course the dog walkers were out in force. A handful of the dogs were ones I'd 'rescued', including Moira Lancer's Gus who came running, tail wagging, to have his ears pulled, and as I liked him better than I liked Mrs Lancer, I pulled his ears and made a fuss of him. She said, 'When you have a minute, Hannah, there are some people I'd like to introduce you to.'

'Okay,' I said. 'Who?'

'You know the allotments on the other side of The Drain?'

I did. There were fourteen carefully tended allotments worked and maintained by a group calling themselves Common or Gardeners.

'They've got a problem,' Mrs L continued. 'I told them about you.'

'Okay,' I said. 'I'll be here all night. Tell them to come over when things are a little less frantic. I'm glad to see Gus looking so well.'

'All you need is love,' she said, misty-eyed. And then stiffening, she snapped Gus's lead onto his collar and stalked away.

That reminded me; I swilled out the three large stainless steel dog bowls and filled them with fresh water. A manager has to think of everything. BZee appeared at about six-thirty, lurking at the edge of the crowd, looking famished. I waited till Digby had his back turned and then sent Dulcie over to him with a heaped plate of mac-cheese.

'He missed you,' she said when she came back. 'He got quite cross when I told him you'd quit.'

'Tough,' I said. 'Listen, Dulcie, if you don't stand up for yourself you won't be able to stand up for anyone else.'

'Oh?' she said and turned away, disbelief written all over her face.

At about seven-thirty an acoustic band got up on the little stage and began with a Beatles medley.

Digby, Dulcie, Fred and I worked non-stop handing out tea, coffee, outrageously overpriced bottled water and paper-platefuls of food. The organisers' wine and keg stand was kept equally busy.

There were a couple of dog fights, and a couple of fights about dogs. Some children cried. Older children whined about missing their TVs. Even older children missed everything because their heads were buried in their phones and tablets. On the whole though the mood was mellow.

There was a Portaloo break between acts. The next one was Digby's Kinks tribute band, the Just Kidding Kinks. For this, Digby wore a leather biker jacket on his top half and a frilly pink skirt plus sparkly platform soled shoes on his bottom half. This explained why the band always opened with Lola. I have absolutely no idea why he does this except that he's the sort of awkward bugger who is always trying to piss off absolutely everyone. So it probably annoys him that a lot of people who don't know him are charmed and amused by the very short person with the very big voice. The band followed Lola with Dedicated Follower of Fashion and Dulcie sidled up to me and whispered, 'He was singing this the first time I ever saw him.' Dulcie, star-struck by Digby – I couldn't think of a single thing to say to this, but when she crept closer to the stage I let her go. Fred and I could manage on our own for awhile.

There were probably about five-hundred people monging around. Maybe two-thirds of them had paid and the rest were being guilted into feeding the donation buckets the charity workers were holding out to them. I was amazed by how many people I knew after working for a year at the Shack. I was also amazed at how many people I didn't know. One of these was a middle aged anorak of a guy with poor posture and a badly behaved Dalmatian. He complained that the dog bowls were dirty. Fred served him at the takeout hatch while I sluiced and refilled the bowls. The man didn't thank either of us.

'That's a good-looking dog,' I tried experimentally.

'You like him, you can keep him,' he said morosely. 'He's a Covid dog. It wasn't my idea. It was my wife's.'

'Even so,' I began.

'Then she buggered off, and guess who was left with the bloody dog and the even bloodier kids?'

'What's his name?' I couldn't think of single sympathetic utterance for the guy.

'Is that all you've got to say to a suicidal man? What's his name?' The guy turned away, juggling with his too hot cardboard cup of coffee and the Dalmatian's lead.

'What was all that about?' Fred asked.

'He doesn't like his dog or his kids.'

Fred shrugged and turned to his next customer.

Okay, I thought, but he lives at the expensive end of a pretty nice street and his sons get pissed and drive a Jaguar. And he is harassing a neighbour. Why?

Then the Just Kidding Kinks finished their set with a reprise of Lola and the stage was taken by one of the charity organisers who wanted to tell us what each and every one of us could do to solve the problem of homelessness. It was therefore no surprise when Fred and I were suddenly swamped.

Digby pranced in on a performance high, dragging Dulcie by the hand towards his office.

'*Oy!*' I yelled. 'We need a little help here.'

But he pretended not to hear me and disappeared with poor Dulcie, slamming the door behind him.

'*Really?*' Fred said, awed.

''Fraid so,' I said. And those were the last words we exchanged until the next band went onstage and we could sit down and take a breather.

That was when Moira Lancer chose to introduce three members of the Common or Gardeners allotment society.

They were Yurek and Magdalena Luczak and Candice deRousseau. They were neatly dressed and very polite.

'There's a problem at the allotments,' Mrs Lancer explained. 'I was telling Magdalena that sometimes you're successful with the small crimes the police don't bother with. And I have warned her that you are expensive.'

'Well, I'm so glad you decided to pay the kidnappers as well as my exorbitant fee.' I narrowed my eyes at her. 'The aim was to get

Gus back in one piece, wasn't it – whatever the cost, weren't those your instructions? My fee was the least of it.' I was tired and my back ached. I wasn't going to accept any of her snide criticism; especially when Gus had his head on my knee and I was pulling his ears.

'If you say so,' she snapped back. 'Well, I've done my civic duty. Come, Gus, beddy-byes.' And away she marched, head high, convinced of her righteousness.

'Okay,' I said to the trio who had witnessed the exchange and remained expressionless. 'I'm expensive. Mrs Lancer said so. It must be true.'

Yurek Luczak cleared his throat. 'Back home,' he began, 'my wife was school teacher. Here she is cleaner for Mrs Lancer, so we know, as you say, she pinches pennies. We discus fee after problem.'

'Good. What's happening?'

Candice deRousseau said, 'We represent the Common or Gardeners committee: fourteen gardeners – more when you count partners and children. We had a meeting and we all agreed we need help. I'm telling you this so that you will understand that together we can afford to hire you.'

'It is harvest,' Yurek said. 'We work all year. Now is time to pick bean, dig potato, collect fruits.'

'Now,' said Magdalena, 'our harvest stolen. We come to our place and find destruction, crop gone.'

'It's heartbreaking,' Candice said. 'There was *some* pilfering last year. But this year it's so much worse. I know we're all more and more dependant on what we grow. And we know other people are feeling the pinch too. But we worked so hard only to become prey for vultures.'

'Yes, vultures,' Magdalena said.

'You help?' asked Yurek.

'I can try,' I said and started asking questions and taking notes. I was too tired to have any bright ideas but I could lay the ground for having them tomorrow.

It was nearly midnight by the time the gardeners left. Most of the small kids had been put down to sleep or taken home. The last band left the stage and bunches of big kids smelling of weed, urgently needing burgers and fries, descended like packs of laughing hyenas on the takeout window.

Digby came out of his office looking refreshed, ostentatiously adjusting his trousers. He was followed by a miserable Dulcie. An interesting contrast, I thought, between the stud strut and the walk of shame.

I sent Fred off to get acquainted with his sleeping bag for a couple of hours and pointed Dulcie at a dangerous pile of pans, plates and implements to wash or put in the steriliser. Digby took over the hot and cold drinks. I kept my position at the griddle and the deep fat fryer.

Trade was unrelenting until about one-forty-five when, just as I was passing a plate of food through the hatch, a woman said in a piercing upper class accent, 'I wouldn't eat anything that dirty whore cooks.'

It was Deena. Of course it was Deena.

The kids started to laugh and stuff food in their mouths, which annoyed her even more.

She said, 'You'll all get syphilis.' Which made my customers laugh even harder.

As I was too tired to be as tactful as I usually am I said, 'Everyone knows insanity's contagious. She'll give you all monkey pox if she breathes on you.'

'I'll sue you for defamation of character,' Deena shrieked.

'I'll counter-sue you,' I shrieked back. 'You defamed first. Now eff off, you're making an arse of yourself.'

'I know you, you man-crazy little tart.'

The queue at the takeout hatch was gathering around her as if she was part of the entertainment.

Digby, noticing that she was interfering with lucrative business, put down his stack of paper cups and rushed out to deal with the problem. He shoved himself between her and the hatch, and said, 'That's enough. I don't know what your beef is, lady, but move it away from here, or I'll call the cops on you for creating a disturbance and interfering with lawful trade.'

There was a disapproving murmur from the crowd which was mainly young and didn't want police intervention.

'She's been stalking me,' I said, 'and harassing me. She's wearing barmy-boots and if she wasn't so scary I'd be sorry for her.'

'Shut up, Hannah,' Digby said over his shoulder.

Deena looked down on him, an expression of contempt on her ordinary middle-aged face. 'You,' she screeched, 'you're the perverted little dwarf in the pink skirt.'

At this, the crowd, who hadn't raised any objection when she slagged *me* off, rolled in to defend poor innocent little Digby. And a big guy who I recognised as part of an amateur rugby team that trained on the Common hustled her away. What could've been a catfight was averted, and my stoned, hungry customers didn't know whether or not to be disappointed. I served the first few with some extra fries till Digby noticed and stopped me.

Yeah, how do you spell Deena? T-r-o-u-b-l-e. That's how.

Finally, at about three in the morning I tore off my surgical gloves and mask. Most crucially, I kicked off my shoes and tried to massage my sore feet. I had a wash in the ladies loo and pushed two chairs together in a dark corner of the Shack and closed my eyes. I left Digby and Fred to cash up, feed stragglers and prepare the kitchen for breakfast. I'd been on my feet for twenty hours straight. We'd hauled in moolah hand over fist, and I could almost hear Digby purring as I dropped off the edge of the world.

I remember thinking, while trying to ignore my swollen feet, that when I was sixteen I could stay up for nearly forty-eight hours at an illegal Dance party, floating on a cushion of Drum'n'Bass and, yeah, a tiny dose of ecstasy. I thought then that I could go on dancing forever if only I didn't have to drag myself to school on Monday morning. It's a whole other experience in a kitchen, believe me. When it's your job to serve fast food non-stop to the people who are having fun your feet start calling you rude names after only a couple of hours.

I was dreaming I was crippled and in a very uncomfortable wheelchair that was being pushed to the edge of a cliff when Digby shook me awake.

'I was dreaming,' I mumbled. 'I think it was about fear of aging.'

'Then you won't mind waking up.' He grinned cruelly. 'There's someone here who wants to talk to you.'

'No!'

'Yes, lazy-arse.'

'Fuck off. What time is it?' I sat up, aching all over.

'Four-fifty. I told you I'd got you a new client.'

Had he? Oh yeah – but I'd thought he'd said that just to scam me back into working at the Shack.

'Wake up,' he said kicking one of my chairs. 'He's here and he wants to meet you. So get up, wash up and drag a comb through that crap excuse for hair.'

I would've kicked him back if I'd had the energy. I washed face, hands and armpits, then retired to the office to put on the clean shirt I'd left hanging on a hook behind the door. Digby was right about my hair – it made wet string look good, and worse, it smelled of beef fat. There was nothing to be done about that except to twist it up and hide it under my Doctor Dre baseball cap.

There was a man waiting at a corner table. Digby brought over two proper china mugs of coffee. The man got up and Digby introduced me to Mark Ferguson. He had iron grey hair, a thin handsome face, good teeth and dark straight brows over warm brown eyes. He smiled, making me wish I was better looking, better dressed, cleverer and, most importantly, more fragrant.

He held out his hand, saying, 'So you're the detective.' Even his hand, dry and cared for, made me feel clumsy.

Digby said, 'Well, she used to be. Now she's my griddle girl. But she's still got useful contacts.' He just couldn't resist cutting me down even while he was selling me. I glared at him.

Mark Ferguson ignored him, and said, 'I've heard very good things about you.'

My first thought was, Where did dog-face Digby meet a charmer like this?

I sat down and took a mouthful of hot coffee. I said, 'Well, I can't return the compliment: I haven't heard anything at all about you. How do you know Digby?'

'Our paths occasionally cross at local enterprise get-togethers – where events like this are planned.' He waved a hand towards the camping ground outside the Shack. 'The Lions underwrote this particular venture. But I'm pleased to see that the organisation has worked perfectly.'

He smiled in a complimentary way at Digby who smirked and said, 'I'll get back to work. Our clientele will be waking up any minute now.'

This was directed at me, but Mark said, 'I was in the area this early to check on how everyone was getting on and to offer assistance if need be. But I can see that apart from touching base with Hannah here, my journey was wasted.'

'Always a pleasure,' Digby said. 'We're grateful for the thought.' This was such blatant brown-nosing that I almost laughed out loud. Digby noticed and gave me his evilest baby-killer look. But he turned away and went back to the counter where he could take comfort from his overflowing cash register.

Mark fixed his warm brown gaze on me and said, 'I can see you're exhausted and this was the wrong time to introduce myself.'

'You're saving me from the deep fat fryer,' I said. 'What's the problem?'

'This will be one hundred percent confidential – even from Digby?'

'Especially from Digby.' I made the cross-my-heart sign and grinned, wishing I'd managed to clean my teeth before meeting Mr Practically Perfect.

'My domestic problems are already a matter for gossip in the local business community but no one knows the true facts. I don't want them to.'

'I'm water-tight,' I said.

'This is painful.' He coughed and looked embarrassed. 'Then, in a nutshell, and for your ears only, I'm looking for my soon to-be ex-wife. She ran away with a younger man. I've been told that he abandoned her and that she's returned to South London. She has not been in touch with me, or asked for my help. It's past the point where we can repair our marriage, but I do still care. I'm worried about her. I believe – well, I've been *led* to believe that she lost everything. I could help. I don't want three years of marriage to end in such a colossal failure, or even a tragedy.'

He looked down at his hands and I couldn't help noticing that he was still wearing a wedding ring.

'Tragedy?' I asked.

'I don't mean to sound dramatic. It's just that she's a lot younger than I am, so even now it's all over, I feel I should have protected her better. I know how easily she can be crushed and humiliated.'

I tried to think about anything except how much I'd have appreciated the thoughtfulness of someone like Mark after I'd been crushed and humiliated. 'So,' I said, pulling myself together enough to pretend to be practical. 'So you think she's come back to this area? Has she got friends or family round here?'

'She's from Malta,' he said. 'We met there. So, no, she's very much on her own.'

'Might she have gone there?'

'Almost certainly not. You see, if she's lost everything she'll be too broke to travel. Further, her family is Catholic and a failed marriage, for whatever reason, will shame her. No, I think she'll be holed up somewhere, hiding, feeling guilty.'

'Have you checked out Catholic churches in the area?'

'It's a possibility, but I doubt it. Catholic upbringing seems to breed guilt and shame in the bone.'

'Look,' I said reluctantly. 'I'm just one woman who already has a pretty, er, demanding employer. There are a couple of other firms in the area who have a much larger personnel list.'

'I know. But I already know their CEOs and, I repeat, I'm not keen on talking to men who I meet socially.' For the first time he showed a touch of impatience. 'One of your strengths is that you know and are known by people who, through no fault of their own, have been rejected by society. And you're a woman. A woman looking for a woman isn't at all threatening.'

I raised my eyebrows.

He caught my expression and said, 'I only mean that she's very shy. And if she's already feeling guilty – well, I don't want to distress her any more than she is already.'

I wanted to ask, 'What're you afraid of?' But just then Digby yelled at me.

Mark got to his feet and said, 'Have you a card?'

Of course I hadn't and was forced to write my email and phone numbers on a napkin. At least the napkin was clean.

'I'll be in touch,' he said, tall in his smart-casual weekend clothes, holding out his hand.

I had one of my stumble-bum moments, getting to my feet so clumsily that I barged into the table, knocking over the coffee mugs.

14

A cook who doesn't live entirely in the present gets burned. I have several scars to prove it. It's surprising I didn't collect more that morning: I'd been cooking without a proper break since seven-thirty the previous morning and, as well, I'd been given two new cases to get stuck into. It hadn't occurred to me to turn either one of them down although I'd barely had two hours kip. Now there were *two* missing women and a load of stolen vegetables to track down. It's either feast or famine in the PI game. Because of this it was hard to keep my mind on cooking.

The truth is that I'm not a cook. All I do is make sarnies and throw together platefuls of whatever can be sizzled on the griddle. So I can do an edible chili or mac'n'cheese, but those aren't what I'm interested in.

Okay, let's admit it, slinging crispy bacon and a fried egg into a bun isn't the way to meet men like Mark Ferguson. But thinking like that *is* the way to add another blister to the inside of my wrist.

'Fukkit!' I yelped.

'Whatsa matter?' Digby snarled. I looked at him. I could see he was dying to say something like, 'If you can't stand the heat get out of the kitchen', but couldn't risk me taking him literally. Which, by seven o'clock, I was more than ready to do.

People were taking down their tents and rolling up their bedding. Most of the children had already been dragged away by sleep-deprived parents. Only the very hardy and the very stoned remained. Demand slowed. Fred and Dulcie were sent out with black plastic sacks to begin the clear-up.

One of the organisers stopped by to begin counting the redeemed breakfast tokens. Digby kept a close eye on her in case she shorted him by even one meal. She was red-eyed and drooping with fatigue, but very pleased. 'Hardly any trouble at all,' she was saying. 'Nothing major went wrong.'

So of course that was when someone started screaming.

Fred and Dulcie were just tying off and depositing their first load of bulging garbage bags. Fred was laughing at something she'd said. It hit me suddenly that she'd do so much better if she paired up with him instead of Digby. It was an irrelevant thought, born of exhaustion, that hardly lasted two seconds. It was over by the time Digby and I reached the door.

A young woman in jeans and an enormous man's sweater was standing by a blue two-person bender tent. A small crowd was gathering behind her. She was looking down, her hands up to her face – the cliché gesture of horror you see in every damn horror movie ever made. A woman screams. A woman always screams. Why do film makers think all women always scream when they see a dead body? They just stand there and scream. It's the model – women think that's what they're supposed to do and it's very annoying.

Of course I wasn't actually expecting a dead body. Maybe someone had trashed her tent or used it as a latrine. I was thinking this as I strode the fifty or so yards that brought me to the screaming woman.

Of course I was wrong. There *was* a body. And it looked pretty dead to me.

I wanted to scream too – not because the body clearly *was* dead, but because it was Deena, and if you still want to know how to spell Deena it's still T-r-o-u-b-l-e.

There she was in her polite straight skirt, padded jacket and sensible shoes. She was lying prone but her head was at an excruciating angle. There was mud on the heels of her shoes, and one of the shoes had partially come off. Mud was smeared on the heel of her American tan stockings as well. Also, because her jacket was rucked up under her armpits it seemed probable that she'd been dragged, face up, into the tent and then flipped over.

This took all of two seconds to notice and then someone tried to push me out of the way to take a photo.

I went straight into cop mode. I turned to face the curious crowd and said, 'Stand back, everyone. Stand back. This is now a scene of crime.' I turned on the teenage girl who was trying to take pictures and said, 'Use your phone to dial 999.'

'I can't,' she said. 'My mum will find out I didn't spend the night at the church.'

The screaming woman stopped screaming, took her phone out of her pocket and handed it to me. So I called 999 and reported a very iffy looking death. Then I co-opted a handful of the less stoned, more responsible looking people, including a couple of the event organisers, to keep the crowd away from what a ghoulish youngster kept referring to as 'The Death Tent'. Dulcie, who had followed me, ran back to report to Digby and fetch my phone.

The screaming woman was the owner of the tent. She was Irena Durham, a member of the *a cappella* group who'd gone on stage after the Just Kidding Kinks. She was very cagey about why she and the cousin she was sharing with hadn't spent the night in her tent. Not my business. The cops could sort that out. All I wanted was her name and address, and the names and addresses of everyone nearby. When Dulcie rocked up with my phone I took pictures of everything and everyone I could see.

Once they realised that the cops would turn the scene into an official enquiry, many members of the rubber-necking rabble snuck away. Again, not my problem. All I wanted to do was the knee-jerk cop thing – preserve the crime scene. No one would thank me. They'd just wonder why I hadn't done it better.

My other and opposite knee-jerk reaction was to creep away unnoticed as soon as I saw that the body was Deena. How many people here had heard her call me a syphilitic whore? It had been rather too public a row to pretend it hadn't happened, or that I'd never clapped eyes on the damn woman before.

My total lack of sympathy was not entirely down to sleep deprivation. Quite a few people who know me will tell you that I'm not a very cuddly person. The list includes several police people including a poisonous ex boyfriend and a soaking wet Sergeant. Both of them know I'm famous for carrying a grudge. And both of them might be among the first team of investigating officers. T-r-o-u-b-l-e.

Irena Durham was talking to me: 'I'm a wreck. So when can I get my things? I'm supposed to be home by nine. I'm shaking – look at my hands.' She held out her hands for my inspection. They were fluttery.

I said, 'Just wait till the police get here. They'll tell you what to do. Who does the other sleeping bag belong to? There were two of you, weren't there?'

'So couldn't I just, you know, go home now? You've got my name and address.'

'Yeah,' said a belligerent guy with what looked like a painful hangover. 'Who made you the boss of everything?'

'No one,' I said. 'Do what you like. But haven't you ever watched TV? It's way more bother to leave the scene of a crime than to stay. Unless, of course you're guilty of something…' I let that hang.

'What're you saying?' Irena snapped. 'I haven't done anything.'

'Didn't say you had. Just saying it'll save time and trouble if the police don't have to come knocking on your door.'

A woman in a long hippy skirt and a man's sweater pushed through. She looked at Irena and me standing in front of the tent flap and said, 'I need my toothbrush.'

I wanted to laugh, but Irena said, 'Lara! Something dreadful's happened.' She stood aside briefly to let her look into the tent. Lara rocked back on her heels and said, 'Who's that? What's she doing in our tent?'

'Do neither of you recognise her?' I asked.

Both women shook their heads so emphatically that their hair flew.

Then two uniformed police women showed up and began the official procedure. They were both young and if they knew me at all it was as a Shack employee. They let me go back to work only stipulating that I should 'keep myself available'.

I trotted back to the Shack where I was met a barrage of questions from Digby, Fred and a bunch of customers. Everyone was buzzing with excitement and curiosity. Sudden death has that effect. The only one immune from the drama was Dulcie who, as usual, seemed to shrink into invisibility.

Without actually lying, I just said that no one, not even the owners of the tent, admitted to recognising the dead woman.

Then I was too busy filling breakfast buns to talk to anyone except to warn Digby that the cops would turn up in force. This didn't upset him in the least. Cops are almost always hungry and thirsty. Also, he, like most people drawn to performance, loves a bit of drama.

But between blisters I worried about what I'd say to the bizzies when they showed up. I'd seen Deena three times. Once in Cottham Road, very late at night when there had been, as far as I knew, no witnesses; once at Clapham Junction where there had been plenty of potential witnesses; once here at the Shack where she'd caused a memorable scene. At that time I'd told everyone within earshot that she was stalking me. When will I ever learn to keep my fool mouth shut? Not in this lifetime, I answered myself sadly.

I worried too about which bizzies would turn up.

On the whole, I decided it would be best simply to relate all the facts. But then I gave myself some more blisters worrying about dragging Carl Barber into a messy investigation by naming him as the gent Deena was obsessing about.

Then I realised I should warn Digby because he'd been part of the fracas at the serving hatch. He'd shouted at Deena too.

So, during a quietish moment I said, 'I didn't get more than a quick look at a woman lying face down, but I'm pretty sure she's the one who was so angry earlier on. You know, the one who called you a pervert.'

'You mean the one who called you a dirty tart? Good thing we've both got such reliable alibis, eh?' He had to be as exhausted as I was but he started laughing uncontrollably. I didn't feel like it, but that didn't stop me doubling over in a fit of the giggles. How inappropriate could we be?

'What's the joke?' Fred asked. We ignored him, and went back to work.

The busy-body detectives showed up with the rain and turned Digby's office into a make-shift interview room. They were led by DI Chloe Mwezi. I didn't know her at all, but her assistant, DC Evans greeted me with an unpromising leer. My guts lurched – he'd seen Poison Tom's photos.

By that time the campsite was almost empty except for the Death Tent and a few supposed witnesses the uniformed cops had corralled.

Digby closed the Shack. But we couldn't go home yet. We were all dead on our feet and our feet were dying horrible deaths too. But we had to clean up. We had to make coffee for the cops. We had to serve them with leftover pastries and breakfast buns. Digby tried to make them pay double, but he was lucky he got them to pay at all.

Finally he managed to kick them out by claiming they were violating our human rights and that sleep deprivation was an internationally recognised form of torture.

My interview started like this: Johnny Evans, 'We hear you had a very public fight with the victim only minutes before her death.'

Me, 'I don't know when she died and nor do you yet.'

JE, 'Just answer the question.'

Me, 'Just *ask* the question.'

JE, 'Did you or did you not have a fight with the victim at about 10:45 pm last night?'

Me, 'It wasn't a physical fight, it was a brief slanging match.'

'Did she or did she not call you a whore?'

'She did.'

'Why?'

'I expect that was what she was thinking.'

'Oh for fuck's sake,' Evans snarled. 'Stop taking the piss.'

'I'm not,' I said. 'A couple of days ago she accosted me in the street and accused me of shagging her boyfriend. I did not even know her name. And before you make the mistake of asking, I am not shagging *anyone*. Get it? *Any* one. I was tired. I'd been working for fifteen hours straight. I wasn't at my most tactful.'

'I was told you had a temper,' he said.

I blanked him and turned to Mwezi, saying, 'Before the uniforms fetched up I took a bunch of pictures of the crime scene and the people close by. Do you want to download them?'

She held out her hand. I found the pictures in my album and gave the phone to her. She turned away from Evans who was trying to muscle in and exchanged a nano-second's glance with me. She was interesting. I wondered how hard it was for a woman with a tag like Mwezi to make detective. It had been virtually impossible for a woman with a tag like Abram. But then, I have a temper. And she's probably way, *way* better at tact and diplomacy.

15

I crawled up to my attic bedroom almost on all fours. I showered, washed my hair and went to bed with my head wrapped in a towel. I did not turn on my phone to check emails, texts or messages.

I crashed so completely that I don't suppose a meteor strike would've disturbed me.

*

The Shack would be closed till Tuesday so I did not have to wake up till nearly eleven on Monday morning.

I was achy and starving hungry so I dragged my wayward hair into a ponytail, scrambled into clean jeans and a long-sleeved t-shirt. The long sleeves were supposed to hide the evidence of careless cookery. I couldn't bear to cram my poor feet into trainers so I wore flip-flops instead. I would've gone barefoot but I am *so* not a hippy.

Then I went out for brunch. Let someone else cook for me, serve me and clean up afterwards. But I would definitely tip well. Most of us who work in hospitality know that life without tips is life on the breadline.

The rain had started sometime in the night but at midday there was sun and a steamy heaviness in the air. A British autumn is no longer crisp, cool and smelling of bonfires. Instead, like every other season, it will display three quite different climates in one week.

I left the house and walked away from the Common. I didn't want to meet anyone I knew. I'd had it up to my eyebrows with the small world around the Shack – the gossip and speculation about a death, about who had slept in whose tent, and mostly, about why a dead woman had called me a dirty little tart. Or whatever she had called me. Even I couldn't remember now. It was just one damn incident in a day and a night of unrelenting incidents, insults and blisters. If I could've walked to the seaside and paddled at the edge of the ocean with a packet of fish and chips in my hand and nothing in front of me but blue sky and ruffled water I would have.

Instead I went to Yak and Yeti to eat many small dishes of differently spiced and textured food with a satisfying mound of fragrant saffron rice. Nothing could be further from burgers and fries than Tibetan food. It was so tasty that I didn't even switch my phone on till every dish was empty and my plate licked clean. Not *quite* licked – I've got a few table manners left after life with the cops, followed by the even lower standards of the Shack. After two cups of hot tea I felt strong enough to engage with the outside world and discovered that the outside world had been knocking on my door for more than twenty-four hours. The most insistent was Myles Emerson who had sent me a total of seventeen texts, eleven missed calls and six emails. He'd ignored me for days so I ignored him. Actually, I realised I'd forgotten what I'd learned about NP Holdings and the significance of it. I'd have to consult my notes. Maybe I wasn't in as good shape as I thought I was.

His godmother, Sophia Smithson, had left two emails, one of which was in red and marked Urgent. I sighed and read it. It said, 'Dear Miss Abram, I believe I instructed you not to do anything to increase the obsessional anxiety from which my godson suffers. You have chosen to disregard my instruction. Unless you can remedy the situation promptly I will be forced to set in motion remedial actions of my own which will most probably result in his hospitalisation. Yours sincerely, Sophia Smithson.

Someone calling herself Martha E Brown from Wyoming told me she had only eight weeks to live and because she didn't trust her dead husband's family to do their Christian duty and give her $8.7 million to the charities she'd designated, she'd chosen me to take charge of the money, and out of the Christian love and honesty she knew was in my heart she was sure I would help her. It was a religious twist to the old Nigerian Prince scam. Delete, delete, delete.

Yurek Luczak texted to remind me that I was to visit their allotment that afternoon.

Chloe Mwezi wanted to see me at the cop shop in Clapham. She did not want to send someone out to bring me in. She sounded tired. I would have to deal with her quickly. But first I wanted to ring Carl Barber.

I hadn't mentioned his name when questioned about Dead Deena but only because no one had thought to ask me where I was when Deena accosted me and why I was there. Nor had anyone asked me if I knew who was the cheat I was supposedly screwing around with. Carl had been a client, but that case was closed. I probably didn't owe him confidentiality anymore – especially in the face of a police investigation. But I liked the old guy with the wonderful manners – not enough to screw around with of course – and I felt I should give him a heads up before I talked to Mwezi.

I rang him and he picked up sounding cautious.

'Have you heard about Deena?' I asked, jumping in with both feet.

'Sort of,' he said.

'Have the cops been in touch?'

'No. Why?'

'Because,' I said, 'last night, at an event at the Common, she accused me very publicly of… '

'Oh lord,' he said sounding depressed. 'Did she name me?'

'No. And nor did I. But she made it very clear I'd stolen her, er, man-friend. She described me in pretty insulting terms. And I was tired enough to retaliate. The police want to interview me this afternoon. And if they dig even a little bit they'll find out about the connection to you. So I'll be obliged to come clean. Maybe they already worked out a connection between you and her.' I paused, waiting for him to respond.

After a bit he said. 'Well, thank you for telling me. Of course I'd rather not be involved, but I'm sure that horse has already bolted. And I can also see that any lie or evasion from you will only serve to complicate matters. So keep it simple: tell them what you know.'

'I don't actually know much.' I waited again. This time he let me hang. So I said, 'How implicated might you be? Where were you last night?'

'I don't think I can be implicated at all. But thank you so much for your concern. Maybe you could ring me after your interview? To let me know if I have inadvertently caused you any trouble. If it's possible to keep the rubbish vigilante out of this it would simplify things. But if you can't, you can't. I understand that.'

'Okay,' I said. 'I'll try. But it's best not to dick around with information they can get from other sources.'

'I think you and I are the only ones who know why I employed you. I paid in cash so there's no money trail. We could just be two people who got chatting in the launderette and went for a cup of tea afterwards. No one saw you visiting me.'

'Deena did,' I pointed out. 'She could've told someone.'

'Yes,' he said sighing audibly. 'I made a really serious mistake when I got involved with her. I'm not the best judge of character where intimacy's involved.'

'I hear you, brother,' I said. And when we cut the call we were both laughing sadly.

Five minutes later, when I got through to Chloe Mwezi, I said, 'Look, I can come in tomorrow if you want me to sign a statement. But would it be possible to start on the phone? I don't want to schlep all the way over to Clapham. I was on my feet yesterday for over twenty-four hours straight and today they're killing me. Besides, I need to visit my dad. He's sick and I won't get another day off this year if my boss has anything to do with it. You've met Digby, haven't you?'

'Oh yes,' she said in her soft, strangely stressed accent. 'Okay, let's start on the phone and see where it takes us.'

It took me out of Yeti and Yak and across the Common in the direction of the allotments while she asked her questions and I gave her straight answers. That particular problem was already sorted for me because someone had told her that the dead woman, Deena Barrymore, was obsessed with Carl Barber. I told her that I'd done a small job for him and that he would most probably tell her what it was. But that if I blurted his business to her at her first time of asking it would damage my reputation for confidentiality. She did not tell me if she'd already questioned Carl. In fact she didn't tell me squat, except that there were plenty of people who could vouch for my whereabouts at all times between the how's-your-father with Deena at the Shack and when she was found in the Death Tent. I, in turn, vouched for Digby, Dulcie and Fred.

I said I'd see her after three the next afternoon.

Just before ringing off she said, 'One or two of my colleagues told me to give you a hard time, to see if I could make you lose your temper. Who do you think they are setting up?'

I said, 'Have you heard the phrase "killing two birds with one stone"?'

'What d'you take me for?' she snapped back. 'You think I'm just off the plane from Africa?'

We were both laughing grimly when we cut the call. She'd probably told me more about herself than she wanted me to know. Plus she definitely told me more about *myself* than *I* wanted to know.

I walked slowly across the Common and BZee caught up with me before I was halfway there.

He said, '*Man,* you look wreck.'

'Thanks,' I said. 'What you see is what you get.'

'I see wreck.' He sounded horribly cheerful. 'You know that dead ol' lady? She say mean stuff 'bout you, know it?'

'I know it.'

'You not the only one she mouf-out.'

'Who else?' I didn't even look at him. He spooks easy.

'Coupla big guys and they girls. She call the guys "pimp". An', like, they raking up girl-garbage – hos like you.'

'*Oy!*' I couldn't stop myself.

'Like what she *say* to you.' BZee grinned, unfazed. 'Feds give you grief?' he went on, looking all around, clocking everyone nearby for threat or opportunity.

'Not yet,' I said. 'But I have to go in tomorrow – make a statement.' I didn't even bother to ask *him* about the cops: bizzies come, BZee go. Nothing in between.

'What's her name?' he asked suddenly. 'Lady with sweet face, stupidy-stupid choose of man?'

'Dulcie.'

'Dulcie, yeah,' he said. 'Same foster home when I very little. She nice to me then, nice to me now. Where you at now?'

'I'm going to the Common or Gardener's allotments.'

'They robbed.' He nodded.

'You know anything about that?'

'Eugh! Veg-tables!' He said this with such revulsion that I laughed.

'They hippies.'

'They nice people trying to feed their families,' I countered. 'And they're *paying* me to help them.'

He let that thought settle for a few seconds. Then he said, 'Saw a van. It parked at end of St Martin's Walk. Late, late, coupla night back.'

St Martin's Walk was a footpath that led from the main road to the north side of the Common. It was the closest access to the allotments.

I said, 'You want to come with me?'

He made the universal money gesture.

I said, 'You help them, I help you.'

He nodded, and we walked on in silence.

Yurek Luczak and Candice deRousseau met us at the gate to a couple of acres of plundered allotments. There were fourteen small sheds, grassy walkways separating the plots and a single water tap. While Candice was introducing me to some of the other gardeners BZee hung back and began to examine the gate and the fence.

Everyone raised their eyebrows at the skinny kid in scruffy gangster clothes. It made me notice how middle-class and white we all were.

I said, 'I asked BZee along because he's a kid who keeps his eyes open. He saw something a couple of nights ago that might be helpful. He's an extremely good ally to have.'

Candice said, 'Wow, you *have* moved quickly.'

Yurek said, 'Magda making tea. The boy like?'

'BZee,' I called. 'You want a cup of tea?'

BZee shrugged without looking at me.

'And *cake*,' Yurek added loudly. 'Welcome.'

BZee trailed us over to Yurek's plot where Magdalena, waiting outside her shed, presided over an enormous metal teapot. We were introduced to a few other gardeners including a man with a snake tattooed on his shaved head.

Behind her trestle table the shed was immaculate, the tools clean and shiny, the hose coiled and hung up to drain – all in sorry contrast to the wreck of the garden. Magda had laid out mugs, plates and forks. In the middle sat a perfect homemade lemon drizzle cake.

Of course BZee would've preferred chocolate but he managed to force down two thick slices of lemon drizzle without complaint. He sat on a canvas chair next to Magdalena, and I saw what I'd missed the night I'd met her: she, like Dulcie, had a very sweet face.

When everyone, BZee, me, Candice, the Luczaks and a few other gardeners whose names I'd already forgotten, had finished, an oldish geezer who looked like everyone's image of a retired colonel wiped his white moustache with a spotted handkerchief and said, 'Well, young man… ?'

For two seconds BZee stared at him in disbelief. Clearly he had flight on his mind. Then he turned to Magdalena and said, 'Sometime some women, like, on benefits, come when no one around and take beans, marrow, strawberry.'

I could see the Colonel winding up to ask for names, addresses and National Insurance numbers. I raised a finger to stop him and Candice put a hand on his sleeve.

I looked at the end of the Luczak's patch and noted that about two thirds of the ground had been roughly dug. From the leavings I could see that at least twenty leeks and a lot of potatoes and carrots had been dug up. Further away I could see the same damage repeated over and over. Corn stalks had been stripped, some of the fruit trees had broken branches. It was a sad sight.

'These women,' BZee said, excluding everyone except Magdalena, 'they don't do this.' He waved his hand in the general direction of the damage. 'Council high-rise,' he explained as if he was talking to children. 'No spades, see.'

He seemed to be making perfect sense to every one except perhaps the Colonel.

BZee went on. 'One sleep before last night.' He looked at Magdalena.

'Yes,' she said, counting on her fingers, 'not Sunday or Saturday but Friday?'

BZee nodded. 'Late, late, was a white van out on High Street, next to St Martin Walk.'

I knew the Colonel was aching to ask about the make, model and registration number because I too had gone into cop-mode and was having to restrain myself.

BZee continued, 'Ain't seen no high-rise ladies drive no Mercedes Vito, 1.6 litre diesel power van. *New,*' he added with a showman's flourish.

I wanted to applaud. The Colonel's jaw dropped.

Then we walked the perimeter because the gate, chain and padlock had been untouched, leading a couple of the gardeners to suspect an inside job.

It was interesting: at first sight it didn't look as if there had been a forced entry. This was puzzling but, almost by accident, I saw a very small shift in alignment in the chain link, rabbit-proof fence that protected the allotments. On close inspection I could see that the part of the fence closest to St Martins Walk had been carefully cut and then, astonishingly, almost invisibly mended with fishing line. This was not thievery as I knew it.

'Good lord!' Candice said, putting on reading glasses, which she needed because the mend was so well camouflaged.

'Who on earth would do a thing like that?' the Colonel bellowed.

The guy with the snake tattoo joined in: 'That's not normal. What's normal is a quick entry and a quicker exit. Thieves don't sit around for hours repairing the damage, do they?'

'Has anyone noticed someone who shouldn't be there hanging around that part of the fence?' I asked.

Nobody had. I looked at the ground. There'd been heavy rain since the break-in. I didn't expect to see any traces of a barrow or a trolley and I wasn't disappointed. We walked slowly out of the common by way of St Martins Walk. There were signs of bicycles being ridden and prams and pushchairs being wheeled, but not the sort of handcart that'd be needed to shift the number of vegetables that had been stolen.

'My two dozen cabbages,' mourned the Colonel.

'Nearly all my potatoes and purple sprouting broccoli,' countered Snakeman. 'And most of my apples.'

We stood on the pavement of the street at the end of the Walk.

'They parked illegally,' the Colonel said in a disapproving tone, pointing to the double yellow lines.

Snakeman looked as if he was going to criticise his priorities, but Candice jumped in. 'BZee,' she said, 'was there any writing on the van?'

'Dark.' BZee turned away.

The Colonel already had a finger up, pointing to the street light, but this time *I* butted in: 'Or a picture?' I asked.

'Big sofa,' BZee said, looking bored. 'Purple.'

'Anyone recognise a big purple sofa as a logo?' I asked.

'Rings a bell,' Snakeman said. Then he shrugged.

Everyone else shook their heads uncertainly.

'Well, let's all keep our eyes open,' Candice said. 'You too, BZee, if you have time.' She pulled him aside. I saw her open a purse and hand him something. Whatever it was vanished into a pocket, and suddenly he looked a lot less bored. I grinned sourly at him. And he made big innocent eyes back.

He bunked off soon after that.

'Who is he?' demanded the Colonel. 'What's his proper name? Doesn't he go to school? Where does he live?'

'If I asked him questions like that I'd never see him again,' I said.

'That's not a responsible attitude.'

I couldn't disagree.

'Anyway,' he thundered, 'a kid like that can't be trusted.'

Yurek, who'd been very quiet up to now said, 'A kid like that does what he has to do. Survive. Not be taken away.'

'There are safeguards in place,' the Colonel said. 'You're foreign, you wouldn't understand.'

'You English,' Yurek replied. '*You* not understand.'

Candice took the Colonel's arm and they began to walk away together. He liked her, I could see that. She had surprised me – there were hidden levels of tact and understanding. Maybe *I* had hidden prejudices against women with good haircuts, Barbour raincoats and green welly boots.

Snakeman, watching them walk away together, said, 'He asked her to marry him a few days ago.'

'She refuse,' Yurek said, watching too. 'She tell Magda; Magda tell me.'

'So that's why he's been in such a foul mood,' said a thin woman with red hair.

It was like visiting a miniature village where everyone knew everyone – a real sense of community that disappeared from my life when I got dumped out of the Met.

16

I walked back across the Common giving the Shack a lot of space. If Digby was still cleaning up and he spotted me he'd find some loathsome task for me to perform in spite of my promised day off.

I found a dry place to sit under a chestnut tree and switched on my phone again. I hadn't yet had time to read through my Tasty Treats and NP Holdings notes so, instead of phoning Myles, I called his godmother. Her message had struck me as borderline threatening. She picked up on the second ring.

'What on earth do you think you're doing?' she said, launching an attack almost before she'd drawn breath. 'Myles is going out of his mind. He's convinced the two messages you recorded for him were left by his step sister, Gina Turner. He can't work or do any of the tasks that stabilise his day. I told you to be careful but apparently you've chosen to ignore my warning and his safety.'

'Ms Smithson,' I cut in. 'I've been trying to carry out his instructions. The job itself is predicated on whether or not he has correctly identified the first message he heard as Gina's. Apparently, according to you, he's done that. I'll have to take your word for it. I haven't been able to talk to him. I texted him, asking him to get in touch to discuss my findings and to ask for further instructions. He hasn't replied.'

'That's because he has both his mobile phones and his landline on permanent re-dial to the numbers you provided. This is your fault – you should have consulted me before giving him any information that could start him on a downward spiral.'

I cut in again, 'And now you're threatening to have him sectioned. Okay. But he's the one who paid me. Not you. So if you want me to stop my enquiries, get *him* to speak to me in person or send me a signed quit notice.'

'Don't you care?' she almost shouted.

That stopped me. She'd started the call so aggressively that what I actually cared about was winning the argument with her. The moral of that story is, Never shout at a cop or an ex-cop. But I'm in civilian life where, however pissed off I feel, showing myself to be helpful, cuddly and caring, and being liked, is an aid to growing my business; winning arguments isn't.

I took a deep breath and said, 'I only met Myles once. He struck me then as reasonable. He might have a few weird quirks, but he and his behaviour made sense. I liked him. I had no idea that he was so very fragile.'

'Well he is.' She sounded like a dog that won't give up her bone.

'You must see that, as his employee, I can't give up on your say-so alone. What I can do is text him again and tell him I can't proceed without his expressed instructions. That should give you time to influence what those instructions might be.' My problem was that he had sent numerous unanswered calls and texts while I was doing my twenty-four hour griddle stint for the homeless, and I hadn't yet had the space or energy to deal with them.

But Sophia didn't know that and she sounded a little mollified. 'Well, alright. I suppose I can accept your offer – weak though it may be. I know he's a difficult man. But I did promise his mother I'd look after him.'

'I understand,' I said, oozing sympathy I didn't feel. Self-employment has upped my hypocrisy quotient no end.

Fortunately for me Ms Smithson seemed to accept my assurance. While I was speaking to her two more calls came in. One was from Nattie, my brother, who sent a voice text. For the first time in weeks I heard his voice, and my lie to Mwezi about my sick father came back to bite my bum.

Nattie said, 'Hannah, where are you? I went to your place of work and your screwy little boss said it was your day off. You need to come with me – Dad had a fall. He's broken his pelvis. He's in St George's. No one's visited Mum in a week. Kirsty's having a crisis at work and it's all fallen on me. You've got to step up.'

My gut clenched. But I clicked onto another missed call and heard a warm unhurried voice say, 'Hannah, it was so good to meet you last night.'

My gut unclenched and Mark Ferguson went on, 'We need to have a proper talk. Perhaps we can meet over a drink this evening. Shall we say Lord Melville's Wine Bar in Dover Street at seven?' It wasn't really a question, and my mind immediately went into a spin about what I could possibly wear to such a posh venue.

Mark continued, 'I gather there was a big drama in the early hours. That's not the first murder on the Common in recent years, is it? If I remember correctly, one of them was committed by a serving police officer in the Metropolitan Police Force. So you can see, can't you, why I worry about the safety of my ex-wife.'

He wasn't wrong. Gardeners, dog walkers, bird watchers, tennis players and other recreational people may be benign, but they aren't the only ones to use the open spaces the Common provides. And cops, freakily, do have agendas other than serving and protecting. Don't *I* know it?

I stood up, suddenly overwhelmed by the number of commitments on my shoulders. Just a few days ago I'd been sitting in my car, bored out of my gourd, watching a husband-stealing woman's bedroom window. The only other item on my list was the return of a kidnapped dog. Now I didn't know what to do first. And to my shame the most important item was wishing I had a sister or a girlfriend who would lend me an outfit I could wear to Lord Thingammy's Wine Bar – someone the same size as me, who would know without being told that I needed something classy but approachable; someone who would also lend me matching shoes.

Dismissing my unworthy panic I texted a three-word confirmation to Mr Ferguson and rang my brother.

17

Ten minutes later we were in my brother's car on our way to St Georges Hospital, Tooting, and I was leafing frantically through my notes.

All of Myles' texts and emails contained the same message: where was I, what had I found out, where was Gina Turner, what was I doing to rescue her from a lethal gang of foreign fraudsters?

Because it would be quicker to talk to him than to send a long email I called each of his numbers in turn. All of them were tied up. I hate typing in a moving car but there was nothing else to do. I wrote: 'So far, my contacts at Vehicle Licensing have given me an address in Potters Bar. She no longer lives there. The property was owned by Emir Yilmaz. It was bought by a Company called North Potter Holdings. The café downstairs is out of business. But a kebab shop round the corner is being run by the same company and one of the officers of that company is Emir Yilmaz. My contact at Companies House tells me that he is now registered as an Off-shore director. This is confirmed by another contact who says Yilmaz is now resident in Turkey.

'I can continue researching NP Holdings but I'm not sure how close that will take us to an actress who might or might not be Gina Turner, who might or might not have made the recording that sparked your initial interest, especially as this is, seemingly, turning into the kind of international operation I told you I couldn't pursue.'

I should have rewritten the last massive sentence, but by the time I'd finished it Nattie was parking his car as close as he could to the hospital. So I ended tamely with, 'I await your instructions.'

Natty didn't look at me as he said, really sarcastically, 'Sorry to interrupt such important business. I've had to take a day off work too, you know.'

'You work for a big company,' I said. 'You take a day off you still get paid. I don't. I'm on a zero hours contract with Digby, and otherwise I'm self-employed. I can't afford to turn anything down.' I was already regretting my email to Myles. I wished I could take it back.

'Well, whose fault is that?' said my overindulged brother. The one who was the only son and therefore the only child my parents wanted. The one they could afford to keep at school and send to college while I had no choice but to find work. The one who thought Poison Tom was a prize I didn't deserve, all because he played football in the Met's first team. The one who had all his meals cooked for him, all his clothes laundered, et cetera, et cetera, by the domestic goddess he was married to. The one who lived in the three bedroom house bought for him by, jointly, his parents and her parents. Shall I go on and display, shamefully, that there's no resentment or envy so sharp as between siblings?

Nattie strode towards the hospital entrance with me trailing mutinously behind. The woman at the front Enquiry desk sent us on a long and winding road to the Accident and Emergency Enquiry desk. The guardian of that particular gate to hell made us sit in an overcrowded waiting area. I took one look and put on my mask. Nattie, reluctantly, did the same.

'Will this never end?' he asked.

'No,' I said flatly, in no mood to placate him. And in fact, that day I was right, because when, after a fifty minute wait while there was no news at all, an administrator showed up and told us bluntly that we couldn't see our father. He had, she said, tested positive for Omicron BA4. 'He'll be in isolation,' she said. 'If you want to make a fuss, make it to someone else. BA4 and 5 are spiking this week and we're inundated. Has Mr Abram got his phone with him? Yes? Then

I suggest you stay in touch that way.' And away she went looking sicker and more tired than anyone waiting for treatment.

'This is outrageous,' said my brother who occupies an important managerial position in his important place of work.

'Where do you suppose he picked the virus up?' I asked. 'When did you last see him?' I was glad I hadn't been to see either my father or my mother in the last month. I run enough risks in the hospitality trade. I couldn't afford to get sick.

We got up and left the hospital by the nearest exit.

Nattie said, 'Actually I haven't seen either of them for a couple of weeks. Nor has Kirsty. She's been having staffing problems at her company.'

'So we're pretty safe from that source of infection?'

Nattie whipped out his phone and called Mother's care home while I leaned against a red brick wall and thought about a hospital that started life at Hyde Park Corner in Central London and ended up jammed between two cemeteries in South London. My mother's care home is round the corner from a cemetery too.

Then I remembered how close I was living to a churchyard full of ancient graves. There are thousands of churches in London and all of them used to have graveyards of their own. There are plague pits and bomb sites still hiding the dead. London was an ancient city that has been built and rebuilt for millennia over the bodies of the dead. Lovely thought. I wondered where Deena's body lay.

Which led me to search through scores of missed calls and unanswered texts and emails in case Carl Barber had got in touch. Yes. He'd called twenty minutes ago while my phone was switched off. He'd left no message. I wouldn't call him back, I thought. I didn't want to be involved in Deena's killing. It was a police matter, I was glad to say. I was not living in a movie where a PI solves a case that baffles the cops. I was scratching a living from their leavings: bikes, dogs and rubbish, the small miseries of ordinary life, which fell through the cracks. I'd taken such a pounding in the last year that

I'd lost my appetite for big dramas. Thinking small was big enough for me at the moment.

Nattie came over. He was staring at his phone as if it was an unexploded bomb.

'You won't believe this,' he said. 'Ma's got Covid too. They want to send her home to isolate till she's better.'

'Whose home?' I asked, anxiety rising in my throat like a fart in a bath. 'Bluebells *is* her home. That's what Dad's been paying for.'

'That bloody snooty supervisor says they can't get the staff.' Nattie raked his finger's through his curly black hair, making him look a lot less like the well-groomed young executive who'd picked me up in a nearly new SUV a couple of hours ago.

'I think they thought Dad would look after her. I told the damn woman he had Covid too and a broken pelvis. And even if he hadn't, he'd sold his house to pay for her care and, when not in hospital, he was living in a one-bedroom flat that wasn't at all suitable.'

I knew what was coming next and rushed in first: 'Don't even think it: I'm lodging in a tiny attic room at the top of two flights of stairs. I have landladies who barely tolerate me on my own. And if that wasn't enough Mother hates me. Last time I went there she said, "I want my son." And if I remember right you were, at the time, really pleased to hear it.'

'Well, I can't take any more time off work. Nor can Kirsty.'

'Nor can I,' I said emphatically. 'But you do have enough room for her plus enough money for twenty-four-hour home care.'

'I knew you'd throw that at me,' he whined. 'It's not my fault you got yourself fired from the one decent job you ever landed. And it's not my fault Ma prefers me to you. You never bothered to learn how to handle her.'

'And it's not my fault I had to leave school at sixteen to work for Argos to help pay for your university place and digs. You got the education, the course in business studies, the good white collar job and the three bedroom house. Now fricking earn it.'

'You're turning your back on your own mother! I never heard of anything so selfish.'

'Don't you shout at me about selfish,' I shrieked. I turned on my heel and marched away to the nearest bus stop. He could stick his SUV up his jaxxy for all I cared. There's nothing so bitter as the quarrel that started in the nursery.

18

Myles Emerson's text came in while I was on the bus back to the Common. It read: Phone me in exactly five minutes.

Eat worms, I thought, because I was still in a red hot snit with my brother.

But, even while thinking evil thoughts, I was looking through the smeary window at a charity shop. And there, in the rather meagre display, I saw the perfect garment. I leaped to my feet, rang the bell and got off the bus at the next stop.

My mood changed from feverish resentment to optimism at a single stroke. I am a terrible shopper, so the sight of a solved wardrobe problem at a price I could probably afford put almost everything else out of my tiny little brain. But not quite. While trotting back to the Women's Aid charity shop with unreasonable hope in my heart I went to my contact list and touched Myles' number.

'*What?*' he barked, picking up immediately.

'Hannah!' I barked back.

'You're waiting for my instructions,' he said more evenly. 'My instructions are that you should tell me what your next step would be and carry on.'

'Okay,' I said. 'But first I need to know that you're not going bozeyquat and wrecking your life by obsessively ringing numbers that I've told you are obsolete. I told you that the number I gave you for a mobile phone of Gina's and the number for NP Holdings are dead ends. But I can't get in touch with you because you won't believe me. How can I work for you if you won't take my calls? Or you won't believe me or take my advice?'

'You've been talking to my godmother,' he said, clearly annoyed.

'She's been talking to me.' I was annoyed too. 'And as you probably already know she's blaming me for tipping you off your skateboard. Sorry to be blunt.' I wasn't, but I needed him to know I was serious. 'Listen, Mr Emerson,' I went on, 'there's one more step I can reasonably take, and that is to go back to Potters Bar to ask questions of another business administered by NP Holdings. But if you want the company and Emir Yilmaz investigated you should employ someone with contacts in Turkey. I can give them any information I have. But as I told you, I'm too local and small-time for that kind of job.'

He was silent for so long that I started again. 'Mr Emerson, what... '

He interrupted me. 'I could send you to Turkey....'

I interrupted *him*. 'No you couldn't. I'd be useless there. Plus I don't want to go. I have commitments here.'

'For heaven's sake!' he said. '*I'm* the one who's allowed to panic. Not you.'

'Then don't threaten me with abroad and airports and foreign languages. Potters Bar is bad enough.'

'Alright, alright. Finish what you started. What are you thinking?'

'I don't want any more grief from your godmother, so if I tell you, will you promise not to go into a wind tunnel?'

'I've swallowed a lot of pills today so take advantage of the medication. Go ahead.'

'Well,' I began doubtfully. 'You've probably thought of this already, but none of Gina's friends have heard from her for years. Yet the mobile number I gave you is still connected. Someone is paying the charges. Who? If it's her, she'd surely answer or monitor calls. If it isn't, who and why?'

'Oh,' he said. 'Actually I haven't let myself think ahead like that. I've been, as you put it, in a wind tunnel just listening to her voice. And, by the way, I haven't definitively identified the voice on NP

Holding's number as hers. But nor have I definitively ruled it out. I'm sorry. It's driving me mad. But supposing she is paying her phone charges, might it not be that she's in danger and keeping the phone as a back up?'

'Or it could be someone who wants anyone interested to think she's alive.'

'You mean someone killed her and doesn't want an investigation?'

I could hear an edge of panic in his voice. I said, 'You always knew there was a possibility that she might have died. Especially in the last few years, with the virus and society in meltdown – anyone can find themselves in the red zone. It doesn't have to be suspicious. I mean I've got five people on my contact list who died unexpectedly and I can't bear to delete their names. It could be that someone, not unlike *you*, might be paying to keep her voice close to him. Or her.'

While I was talking I was looking through an unwashed window at an emerald green tunic with a scarlet, yellow, grass green and pearl grey embroidered panel down the front. It managed to look both dressy and bohemian. It was coupled with darker green slim slacks. If they fit, I thought, they'll make me look taller and less sturdy.

Myles was saying something that ended with, 'But I can't help fearing the worst.'

'I know you can't,' I said distractedly.

'So you'll go to Potters Bar now and follow up your enquiry?'

'Okay. But you've got to be available to report to.'

'I'll try,' he said.

I cut the call and pushed into the Women's Aid shop. It was only when I was in the cramped cubicle trying on the clothes that I registered that I'd agreed to go to Potters Bar '*now*'. But even that failed to dim my pleasure at seeing myself in the mirror as someone who didn't look like the scrag-end of mutton. I could walk into Lord Thingammy's Wine Bar without inspiring pity. The whole outfit, plus a pair of wedge-heel sandals for extra height, came to less than fifty pounds. I was ecstatic even though I'd broken my own rule about never buying second-hand shoes.

There was even enough time to go home to shower and do something about my face and hair. I had to try, because I knew only too well what an unappetising picture I'd presented to Mark Ferguson after countless hours working at a hot griddle and a deep-fat fryer. This time I'd be fragrant, clean and presentable. What could possibly go wrong?

*

I walked into Lord Melville's Wine Bar five minutes late. Mark Ferguson was later. I found a seat at the bar and ordered a spritzer. It was crowded and very hot. The weather that afternoon had done a lightning switch from early autumn to sticky high summer. It's amazing to be in England unable to rely on rain to cool things down. Sitting at a bar alone, trying not to sweat, while waiting for a man was not a favourite pastime so I was quite glad when my phone rang.

It was from a cop I used to know, Sid Nailer, who I'd tried to ring while hanging around outside Gina's last recorded address in Potters Bar. He said, 'Hello Hannah Hot Hips. I was told you were looking for me.'

Hot Hips was one of the nicer things my so-called friends in the Met called me after Toxic Tom posted those malicious photos.

I got up and took my drink and the phone to the door in case I had to shout at him in an uncouth unladylike way.

'Hi, Sid,' I said cautiously. 'I spoke to Mary Whatsername from your department, and she was really snotty with me. So I thought maybe I'd become an untouchable.' I wished I hadn't used the word untouchable but when Sid answered there was none of the dreaded leer in his voice.

He said, 'Take no notice of her. The truth is that I've left the Force. I've gone private and started my own business.'

'Blimey,' I said surprised. 'I thought you were a lifer.'

'So did I,' he said. 'But you know, read any news-feed, they'll tell you the Met's under-funded, unsupported and the pension's not worth the paper it's written on. I've got marketable skills so I'm marketing them – a nice little earner – my own company. It's called Device Detectors. I suppose the bread and butter business is with people who've lost their own phones but I do more interesting stuff too.'

This changed everything. I'd been prepared to grovel for a favour but now I didn't need to. Even though he couldn't see me I straightened my back and stuck my chin out.

'I have a client who needs to trace a phone belonging to his stepsister,' I said with dignity.

It was his turn to be surprised. 'You have client?' he said. 'You've gone private too? I did not know that. Your ex said you were waitressing.'

'I'm managing a café while building up my client base. You aren't the only one with marketable skills, you know. And,' I went on with even more dignity, 'persons who continue to think my ex knows anything about me at all are deluding themselves.'

'I hear you,' he said. 'So you have a paying client who can afford my services?'

'You'll have to send me a list of fees,' I said. 'But yes, I have a client who can and will certainly pay the bills. In fact I'm meeting another one now.' Up the street from the wine bar I saw Mark Ferguson climb out of the sporty little Aston Martin he'd just parked.

'Yes,' I continued proudly. 'If he can afford to drive an Aston Martin in today's financial climate, this one won't be short of a bob or two either.'

'Well, well, well,' Sid said. 'Maybe we can put a spot of business in each other's direction.'

'Indeed we may,' I said loftily, as the tall nearly handsome man came closer. 'All right. This has been most interesting. I'll wait for the details.' I rang off.

Mark Ferguson walked past without recognising me. Obviously I'd done too good a job cleaning myself up.

'Mr Ferguson?' I said to his broad-shouldered back.

He swung round. 'My, my,' he said. 'You *do* scrub up well.'

'Oh, the sacrifices I'm prepared to make on behalf of the homeless,' I said, mock pious. 'Blood, sweat, blisters and *really* bad hair.'

'Now you're making my hefty donation look insufficient.' He opened the door for me and we went into the loud chatter, perfume and canned music of an overcrowded bar.

'What are you drinking?' he shouted. 'If you can push your way through the throng, there's a garden outside the back door.'

I pushed and found a cluster of tables in a rather untidy garden of browning grass, overgrown laurels, burnt buddleia and tangled roses that needed dead-heading. I was lucky and bagged a table from a departing trio of suits. A hot, tired server removed their glasses, plates and overflowing ashtray. She swiped a damp cloth over the surface and gave me a challenging look. I grinned at her as she turned away. She'd managed to survive nearly two weeks employment at the Shack a few months ago and probably thought Lord Melville was a step up from Loud Digby. She didn't recognise me.

Ten minutes later Mark appeared with a bottle of something red and two glasses. He sat down saying, 'I've taken the liberty of ordering a tray of tapas. They do a proper menu as well, but with the crowd in tonight we'd be waiting for hours.'

That was fine by me. But he didn't wait for me to reply, moving on quickly to, 'Give me your phone. I want to send you pictures of Paulina.'

I handed him my phone. While he was sending the pictures I watched his strong, well-shaped hands with their clean, buffed nails and thought, He wants my phone number. He now *has* my phone number. It was idiotic, but I realised I hadn't felt this girlish since a handsome, athletic, football-playing colleague came up to me after a burglary and ABH we'd both attended saying, 'Hey Hannah, the pubs are still open. Fancy coming for a drink?' He'd smiled at me with a wicked, complicit twinkle in his blue, blue eyes, and I'd said, with studied cool, 'Sounds like a good idea.'

Mark Ferguson had warm brown eyes and a kind mouth. His greying hair and smile lines told me he was probably in his late forties, too mature and sophisticated to play cruel games.

While I was studying the pictures he'd sent he poured the wine and said, 'I know you'll think she was far too young for me. But when we met in Malta the parents she'd nursed through their terminal cancer had recently died. The father left everything, including the house she'd lived in while nursing him, to her brother – who sold it immediately. He allowed her to live in his own house but only as an unpaid nanny to his three children. His wife treated her like the maid. Paulie had given up her college place to look after her parents and now she couldn't even begin where she'd left off. She had no money and nowhere else to live. I was very sorry for her.'

I sipped my wine, listening and scrolling through pictures of Paulina. Because the long dark dress she was wearing was too big for her, she looked immature and pathetic. There was nothing glamorous or seductive about her at all – unless you counted the expression of helpless devotion she aimed at the camera.

She was so unlike the kind of wife I would've expected him to have that my first impression could be summed up by 'a nonentity in need.' Bitchy, I chided myself. But *he* was … what? I don't know. Good looking didn't cover it. Nor did distinguished or smooth. What was it? He looked at me as if he saw me? Yes. Maybe that was it. Plus all of the above. Had I Googled him? Well, yeah, I had. Was I impressed? You bet I was.

I looked up then and saw him watching me as I gazed at images of his lost ex-wife. Our eyes met and he half smiled. I felt suddenly warmed. But the next time I looked up he was eyeing a young woman who seemed to be dressed entirely in thin black straps and, for no good reason, I felt a shiver of insecurity.

I cleared my throat and his attention instantly switched back to me. He rolled his eyes at the strappy garment and said, 'Is that really a frock?'

I laughed at his use of the word frock, and said, 'It's the next best thing to skin. *Meeow!*'

He laughed too. He said, 'So what do you need to know from me?'

As I'd just been talking to Sid Nailer, I started with, 'Did your wife have a mobile phone?'

'Certainly,' he said. 'But either it's switched off or she's got rid of it – maybe sold it for cash. Why?'

'One of my contacts used to be a digital forensic technician in the Metropolitan Police. He's recently set up in the private sector. A phone, and possibly its user, can usually be traced.'

'Now you're talking,' he said enthusiastically. He jotted Paulina's phone number and the phone's make and model down on a blank page of my notebook.

'If it looks possible and we decide to use his services,' I said, with a judicious note of warning in my voice, 'I'll send the bill to you. I don't know what he charges these days.'

'Not a *pro bono* relationship then?' he asked with a roguish twinkle.

'Have you noticed *anything* that's *pro bono* in the private sector lately?' I asked sounding more aloof than I'd intended.

He gave me his wry smile and refilled my glass. The wine tasted fine and mellow. I changed the subject and asked about the circumstances of Paulina's leaving.

They'd been living in his cottage in rural Somerset, he told me. It was supposed to be his weekend retreat, he said, but after his marriage to Paulina and her pregnancy he felt country life would be more peaceful and healthy for her and the baby. Previously they'd been living in his riverside flat in Battersea. He spent four days each week in London and three in the country with Paulina. All was fine until her miscarriage. This was a tragedy for both of them, but unfortunately his business was going through some crucial upheavals so he was only able to take a week off work. He blamed himself for missing the danger signs.

There was a photo of Paulina in the dappled shade of a fruit tree. She was looking away from the camera, expressionless and alone.

I said, 'A miscarriage can be really devastating.'

'Yes,' he said. 'I talked to a doctor friend – too late, I'm afraid. He said that the surge and dip of hormones can affect a woman's mental stability quite severely. I wish I'd known that. But Paulina was always so quiet that I didn't realise she was more than normally sad. If I'd known, I would've hired a nurse, or taken her back to Battersea with me.'

'You said she ran away with someone?'

'Yes.' He looked suddenly grim. 'There was a young man employed by the management committee of my building. His name is Kyle Yardley and he was a sort of concierge-stroke-maintenance man. He'd, for instance, organise the cleaning of windows, or if a plumbing problem developed he'd sort it out. This was for the building, you understand, paid for by all the owners. But he was available too for small jobs for individual owners or their tenants. I think the first time he met my wife it was because of a blocked drain in my flat.'

'They got friendly?'

'Of course not.' He sounded annoyed. Then, hearing himself, he went on, 'Well, actually, of course they *must* have. But the husband's always the last to know. It turned out a couple of the neighbours on my floor had seen them together on my balcony, but no one thought to inform me.'

'So he went to Somerset, or she came to London?'

'Neither.' Mark Ferguson got a bit tangled in all the details, but the gist was that his bank informed him that his and Paulina's joint account had been emptied, he couldn't contact her by phone, his flat was broken into, some cash was taken and his floor safe tampered with. Kyle disappeared. And a few days later he was told that a woman of Paulina's description had changed three hundred pounds Sterling to Euros at a Bureau de Change at Heathrow Airport. A couple of hours later she'd changed the Euros back to Sterling using the same Bureau.

'At quite a loss, as you might expect,' he added ruefully. 'There wasn't much more than that in the joint account as it was. It was only set up for household expenses.'

'She had no money of her own?' I asked.

'I gave her everything she wanted,' he said, sad and bewildered. 'She only had to ask.'

He must've seen a less than complimentary expression on my face because he raised his eyebrows and said, 'What're you thinking?'

Not a question you want to answer honestly when sitting in front of a paying client. I stifled the obvious retort at birth and said instead, 'Where was Paulina's passport kept?'

'You're quicker than I was,' he said, again with the rueful smile. 'In the floor safe, of course. Your conclusion?'

'Off the top of my head and untested,' I warned, 'she wanted to leave the country and realised that since the UK is no longer in the Euro zone, she'd need Euros and her passport. Either she or Kyle tried to find it but failed, so she had to swap back to Sterling. If true, this doesn't sound like a well planned scheme.'

'It wouldn't be,' Mark said, raising his hand to his eyes as if the fading light was too bright. 'Paulina's not a schemer or a gold digger. And Kyle, while being an adequate handyman, isn't exactly a mental giant.'

'You say some cash was stolen?'

'I keep cash in a locked drawer in my desk – only about a thousand in case of emergencies.'

Only a thousand in cash? I nearly laughed.

'That's why I'm convinced it was Kyle who forced my desk drawer,' he went on, without noticing. 'Paulie would never, *ever* steal.'

But *someone* told Kyle about the emergency stash and where to find it. I didn't voice the thought – Mark's faith in his ex-wife's honesty was too touching to puncture. Yet. But I was suspicious.

I said, 'Did she have a credit card?'

'Yes, on the joint account. But it hasn't been used.'

'Have you closed the account?'

'Yes, immediately.'

So he didn't trust her *that* much. 'If she, or he, tries to use the card, will you be informed?'

'I believe so.' He was still hoping she might return to him having had a breakdown and needing his support.

The food came. At the same time, the woman dressed in black straps left the garden with her perspiring escort. She floated past, wearing more perfume than clothes. Mark raised an eyebrow at me, and said, 'I'm feeling old. You wouldn't go out in public like that, would you?'

'Not in a million years,' I said truthfully.

He'd noticed what I was wearing! I helped myself from several small dishes to keep from blushing, and said, coolly, 'Well, it seems that you've done all you can. What exactly is it you want from me?'

The food smelled delicious. I was hungry, but I didn't want to start stuffing my face in front of someone who looked as fastidious as he did. I waited until he'd served himself and taken a few bites before digging in.

After the respectful silence the tapas deserved, Mark said, 'As I told you when we me met on Saturday night – or was it Sunday morning – I'm concerned with privacy. Gossip about a failed marriage is bad for my kind of business. However someone, a resident in my block, told me he'd seen Paulina on the Common. He's a jogger, you see, goes out most mornings.'

'I'd like to speak to this guy,' I said.

Mark gave me his crinkly smile. 'Certainly. He's in New York at present, but I'll give him your number as soon as he returns.'

'Was Paulina alone when he saw her?'

'Apparently she was with a woman of colour who had children. My friend said she looked ill.'

'You said the guy she left with – Kyle Yardley – deserted her. How do you know that?'

'He was easier to trace as the management committee had his address and employment records. And unbelievably, the little weasel put in for back pay only ten days ago. Can you believe the nerve and stupidity of him?'

Having just confronted a moron who advertised stolen bicycles on Facebook, I could.

Mark continued, 'Naturally I went to his last address myself. He had been lodging with his sister's family in Kennington and he'd left owing a lot of back rent. The sister was so angry with him she told me everything she knew. He said that a rich woman from the building he worked at fancied him.'

Mark's face now went stony with hurt. It was a scary expression.

'Yes,' he said. 'The bastard told his sister that he had a fling with her and she was so impressed that she gave him a lot of money. Apparently he left her at the airport. He *said* she was going to Rio for cosmetic surgery. Can you believe it? *Can* you?' Even his voice had clenched teeth. 'And she wanted him to go with her but he couldn't "walk out on his responsibilities in the UK". Even the sister didn't believe him. And, let me assure you, Paulina was far too sensible to contemplate surgery – she didn't even wear lipstick.'

He emptied his glass and refilled it with a trembling hand. As there was nothing but the bleeding obvious to say, the best way to deal with a clearly shaken man was to keep schtum.

After a few beats he said, 'I thought I'd achieved a rather more Zen-like calm. Apparently I haven't. I apologise.'

I raised my hands in a don't-worry-about-it gesture.

'You're a good listener,' he said, and I tried to remember what a good listener looked like.

We ate a few more mouthfuls of the tapas and then he pushed his plate away. This was a pity as I was far from finished but didn't want to be seen as greedy.

'The sister doesn't know where Kyle went but thinks it must be somewhere in the UK – he doesn't like foreigners. It will be close to a casino. The idiot's obsessed with blackjack. She says he'll come back when he's broke and then she'll contact me.'

Eventually I said, 'So there's no point my trying to find him.'

'Unless revenge is my game.' He snorted. 'Which it isn't. Although, clearly, I'm rather more tempted than I hoped.' The smiley eyes returned. 'No, the marriage is over. Paulina voted with her feet. What I want from you is to ask around casually and subtly. Find out if she's alright, and what I can do to help.'

I was about to speak when my phone rang. I looked at the screen, saw it was Carl Barber and switched to silent.

'Boyfriend?' Mark asked, staring at my phone.

'If I told you who was ringing me, what would that say about my discretion?'

I switched the phone off altogether and stowed it in my bag. This seemed to reassure him.

He asked how I intended to begin, and I said, 'Carefully.' Given his wish for discretion I needed to think about Paulina's options before rushing around showing everyone her photos. I was more likely to find her if no one knew I was looking.

I presented this thought to him as a sort of philosophical concept. He gave me a strange look but nodded his approval. I felt warmed.

19

It was fully dark by the time I parted from Mark outside the wine bar. He offered me a lift home but I said I preferred to walk. Walking, I told him, was an aid to thinking. Actually, doubt was beginning to creep up on me in the stealthy way it always does when I've bent over backwards to court compliments. I remember smiling too much, tilting my head, not interrupting even when impatient, pretending to think when I'm not thinking and using poncy words like 'philosophical concept.'

'Aargh!' I said out loud, startling an urban gull that was about to attack some smelly rubbish sacks. The gull flapped away, screaming unearthly insults at me like a ghost in the half dark of a city night. 'Knackers to you too,' I screeched back, and marched off, digging in my bag for the phone I'd hidden from a nearly handsome nearly attentive man.

Carl Barber had rung twice but only left one message. 'Call me back,' he said, huskily. I wondered if he'd been crying. And if so, had he been crying for Deena?

The thought of Deena and tomorrow's interview with Chloe Mwezi made me call him back immediately. I started apologising for ringing so late, but he cut me off saying, 'Hannah, I have to warn you. I've tested positive for one of the Omicron Bs. You should test as soon as possible.'

Yes, I should. But what good would it do when I'd been cooking for hundreds of people non-stop during the Big Sleep Out? If I was positive there was no way I could warn all my contacts. And I'd have to tell Digby. Oh shit – I wouldn't be able to work for a week, and, and, and…

This was the second reason to be furious with Carl Barber. In fact I couldn't for the life of me remember why I liked him. Then, of course, I remembered that he was a paying client. He'd paid me upfront for a couple of nights' work and expressed satisfaction and admiration for the result.

Now he said, 'If you're symptomless I don't think there's too much danger for you because we haven't met for a few days.'

'What are your symptoms?'

'Sore throat, fatigue, can't taste or smell food, fever. None of it too bad yet.'

'Well, fingers crossed,' I said, remembering with relief how delicious the tapas was and how revolting the garbage sacks smelled. 'When did you start feeling bad?'

'This evening.'

'What about the police interview?'

'Oh,' he said. 'I suppose I should ring the police station.'

'Probably,' I said. 'But just so's we're on the same message when I see DI Mwezi tomorrow, did you tell her about your previous relationship with Deena? Because plenty of people heard her call me a gold-digging tramp and she's going to want to know why.'

There was a typical Carl Barber silence. Then he said, 'I told her we'd been to the movies a couple of times and that Deena started to act like she was my wife – coming round at all hours, even when I was working, calling several times a day. And, you know, sort of stalking me, and of course, harassing women she'd seen me talk to.'

'And?' I prompted, thinking, you might've warned me.

'And? Well, of course I told her to leave me alone. She didn't take any notice. So I told her to bugger off and blocked her calls and left the chain and padlock on the gate twenty-four-seven.'

'And that's why she attacked me outside your house? You took her to the movies a couple of times?'

Again with the silence.

'Is that what you told the detectives? What did they say?'

'Erm, well, Inspector Mwezi sounded a bit sarcastic and asked if I'd taken *you* to the movies a couple of times. I said of course not.'

'You'd better have,' I said. 'So did you tell them about the rubbish vigilante?'

'Well, yes. Mostly.'

I waited. He coughed pathetically.

'Mostly?' I said, stony hearted. 'I need to know what you want me to hold back, if anything. But I'm telling you now, I'm not going to lie for you – that's the shortest route to the lock-up I know.'

'Okay, okay. I told her I'd asked you to find the vigilante. I said you'd done a satisfactory job. I said it was someone I already knew, and that it was nothing at all to do with their present inquiry, and I wasn't going to name names. I said I'd told you that the work was confidential. She said you had no privilege but she'd try to respect my wishes.'

'But you didn't tell me who he was. All I gave you were the pictures.'

'So delete them. After all, the enquiry's over.'

'I can probably do that with a clear conscience,' I said, thinking it over. 'It's got nothing to do with a murder anyway.'

'That's what I told Mwezi.'

'Did you tell them that Deena's first approach to me was outside your house?'

'No.' Another pause. Then he added, 'If you can keep that quiet I'd be grateful. This is already too personal.' His voice was getting more and more husky.

I said, 'You should be in bed with a hot drink.'

'That's exactly where I am,' he said.

I took a chance. 'How do you feel about Deena being gone?'

'All I feel at the moment is sick and worried in case this goddamn thing goes to my chest. But that's cos I'm nearly eighty and at the moment *my* possible death is more important than hers. She always said I was an "emotionally withholding" sort of guy.'

'Fair enough,' I said, wondering if I'd mistaken his beautiful manners for kindness. I'm often wrong about people. He was certainly withholding the truth about his relationship with Deena. I wasn't wrong about that. But there he was, very old and sick. That wasn't my business either. I wasn't even going to look after my demented mother or my father with his broken hip.

Never mind, I thought as I trudged the rest of the way home through the heavy airless streets – if I tested positive for Covid no one could make me look after anyone but myself.

I remembered how, when I first went to work for him, Digby never closed the Shack. He kept open through all the health scares, simply nailing a sign to the door claiming 'All staff tested negative.' Of course no one took the nail out and read the back of the sign which continued, '… for brains.' Now *there* was a fluffy caring individual I could use as a role model.

I came home to a dark house. Not knowing if the Tedious Two were out or asleep I crept upstairs. I hung up my pretty new clothes and took a shower. Then I used my last lat-flow test. While I waited I deleted the pictures of the vigilante. While I was at it I deleted the pictures of unfaithful Mr Reynolds I'd already forwarded to Mrs Reynolds. And then I cleaned the rest of unwanted unasked for pictures from my gallery. I got stuck on a two-shot of Tom and me dancing. Unusually, I did not look like a rabid dog and Tom was looking at me, not through me. My finger hovered over Delete Now. And then, of its own willpower, moved on without tapping.

The timer beeped. I scrutinised the test kit. It told me I was uninfected.

I was on the early shift in the morning so I set the alarm, lay down and let the remains of Mark Ferguson's good red wine do its work.

20

Amazingly, the Shack was relatively clean when I opened up in the morning. I felt as if I'd been away for a week, but there was trodden down grass and bare patches in front of where the stage had been. A couple of abandoned sleeping bags littered the ground. Police tape still fluttered round the site of the Death Tent. But all the drama seemed a lifetime ago.

I turned on the lights and, starting with the coffee maker, all the equipment. I was wondering why no one ever took police tape away – except maybe kids. It was single-use plastic and environmentally unfriendly, I thought primly, as I drank my first fix of caffeine.

I emptied the dishwasher and steriliser and assembled the tools I'd need for the breakfast rush. I took eggs, bacon, ham, tomatoes, burger patties, milk, cheese, and pancake mixture from the fridge. I broke open a new package of buns and a new loaf of bread. I filled the hot water urn, fired up the griddle and made sure the toaster was plugged in. Then I took the outdoor tables and chairs from the storeroom and set them up in the area outside the takeout window. As always, someone had put the tables away dirty. I cleaned them, and while I was doing that my first customers arrived. It was six-thirty and already the sun was hot. It had been a weird, unstable summer, and autumn was promising more of the same.

Amazingly, everyone was pleased to see me. And equally amazing, no one annoyed me by expecting service with a smile or happy chat. To complete my astonishment the pastry delivery was on time so no one could complain when there were no fresh croissants or Danishes.

Dulcie fetched up at nine on the dot, wearing her usual kicked kitten expression. There was a customer lull so I set her to whipping up tuna mayo for the sandwich rush. I took my coffee and toasted cheese outside to sit in the sun before the drink got too cold and the sun too hot. While I was there the drinks machine guy arrived to refill the vending machine. He saw me and my coffee and said, 'Some people have all the luck.'

Even this failed to annoy me and I said, 'If you promise not to sit with me or talk to me you can have one too.'

He accepted saying, 'That's what I like about you, Hannah, you're such a people pleaser.'

'Take it or leave it,' I replied, and went back to failing at Saturday's crossword. He sat as far away from me as he could, and Dulcie, who'd overheard the backchat, brought him a steaming mug without me telling her to.

Digby arrived at ten-thirty and went straight to the office without picking a fight on the way.

Riding my luck, while Dulcie was making the first sandwiches, I opened my iPad and looked up local furniture shops. A lot of them had gone out of business recently but I found one whose logo was a dark crimson sofa. It wasn't purple, but it was worth a try. I wondered if any of the Common or Garden people had already done that so I wrote a note and tucked it in the back pocket of my jeans.

When, an hour later, I noticed BZee lurking on the outer perimeter of Digby's domain, I carried a beef sandwich and a coke out to him and asked him to take the note to Magda. He wolfed the sandwich, glugged down the drink and took off across the Common towards the allotments. He seemed happy with the assignment and I hoped he'd continue to bond with the Luczaks. The more people who fed him the better. He wasn't going to put on much weight courtesy of the Shack while Digby was on site.

My eight-hour shift ended, and Digby didn't complain when I washed my hands and changed my shirt on the dot of two-thirty.

I quit the Shack, turned left and walked off towards the Incident Room the cops had set up half way between Clapham Junction and the Common. I'd hardly gone a hundred yards when I heard my name called. It was Candice and the Colonel. They were holding hands. I didn't stop walking but I slowed down to let them catch up. 'Ms Abram,' the Colonel started, huffing and wiping sweat from his neck with a mustard coloured handkerchief. 'Can we talk?'

'If it's on the hoof,' I said. 'I have an interview with the police about what happened at the Big Sleep Out. They hate to be kept waiting.'

'So do I,' he said. 'But where were they when I reported a burglary from the allotments? They didn't even ring me back. Turn up and investigate? Oh no! A few cabbages are a waste of their precious time.'

'I know, I know.' Candice squeezed his hand. 'That's why we asked Hannah for help.' She turned to me. 'Thanks for your note. Magda and I went to the address you gave us and we found, round the back, two vans exactly like the one BZee described. What should we do now?'

'Nothing,' I said. I hadn't stopped walking. 'All we know is that a van owned by the Cosy Couch Company was parked close to your land at an appropriate time. I need to establish a connection between the company or one of their employees and the theft before we can act.'

'And how do you expect to do that?' the Colonel asked. 'Why don't we just go there and confront them?'

'Confront who?' I said. 'What I'll do first is to find out a bit about the company and who runs it. Then I'll put the names through a search engine and see what comes up. I'll inform you immediately to see if anything rings a bell with you. In the meantime, are you in touch with any other gardening groups in the area? Because if you are, we may get more information that way. And maybe you could pool resources and ideas about how to protect yourselves.'

'That's not such a bad idea,' the Colonel said grudgingly. Clearly he was action man: as long as he had a job to do he'd be easier to manage.

'When do you think you'll have some information for us?' Candice asked.

'Possibly by tonight,' I said at random, and picked up my pace. I needed some quiet time to think through what I didn't want to say to Chloe Mwezi.

'Ring me,' Candice said, catching up and pressing a business card into my hand. We said goodbye and I hurried on.

Of course it wasn't the cops who were kept waiting – it was me. I sat on a plastic stacking chair in a grey painted corridor while busy cops rushed to and fro. Some of them knew me; some greeted me; some stared; some ignored me. I feared the worst. And, naturally, the worst happened.

I was trying to keep busy – no – I was trying to *appear* busy by logging on to the Companies House site to research the Cosy Couch Company when the dreaded familiar voice said, 'Well, hi there, Hannah, long time no see.'

'Not long enough,' I said to Toxic Tom, who would be dead by a humiliating misadventure if wishes were telekinetic orders and a cartoon anvil fell on him squashing him to the shape of a beer mat.

There he was, dark blond hair endearingly rumpled, blue-blue eyes twinkling merrily, white teeth gleaming between smiling lips – the man of my nightmares.

'Looking good,' he said insincerely. 'I hear you're mixed up in this murder enquiry.'

'Nope,' I said, closing my iPad. 'I'm here to return my library books.'

'But I heard you were working hardly fifty yards from the action.'

'Nope,' I said. 'I was at my sister's watching Love Island.'

'You don't have a sister,' he said. To my great joy, he was beginning to look annoyed. 'You only have a brother.'

'Nope,' I said. 'He transed. Catch up, Tom. Call yourself a detective?'

'And you can call yourself a waitress,' he said meanly.

'Nope,' I said. 'I can call myself equerry to Prince Harry, as far as a nosey, pervy bastard like you is concerned. Now get out of my space, you're polluting the atmosphere.'

He was standing much too close to me and I thought he might hit me. Perhaps I wished he would. Then I could break his snotty nose and mash his ding-dong so bad he'd be in a truss for a month. Which is what I should've done eighteen months ago.

Chloe Mwezi saved his ding-dong and my dignity by appearing in a doorway further down the corridor. She must've noticed his balled fist and angry red neck, plus the fact that I'd climbed halfway to my feet in readiness. She began to hurry towards us, calling, 'Ms Abram, I am sorry to have kept you waiting.'

Toxic Tom stepped away immediately. 'Watch your back,' he whispered. 'You aren't on the force anymore. I can still screw you up rotten.'

'Don't you threaten me,' I said, loud enough for Mwezi to hear. 'Haven't you done enough damage?'

Tom gave her an I-don't-know-what-she's-talking-about shrug and sauntered away with the macho jock's swagger I used to admire.

Mwezi said, 'Follow me.' And then, over her shoulder, 'You have a history. Yes?'

'Oh yes,' I said. And we both shut up about it. She'd heard. She wouldn't comment because he was still on the job and I wasn't. She was keeping to the code. As I knew she would. The most vulnerable stick to the rules; the makers of the rules are the ones who bend or break them.

She was meticulous. She covered the hours between when Deena insulted me at the Shack's takeout window to when I'd gone over to the Death Tent in response to the scream. She wanted to know who I could vouch for and who I couldn't. To my relief she didn't waste time playing games, pretending I was a suspect. She behaved as if I was being as helpful as I possibly could. In fact the pictures I'd taken of the scene before the police arrived had been printed, enlarged and stuck to the wall behind her desk. She asked me to identify everyone I could and wrote down everything I said.

Only when she'd completed that part of my statement did she go back to my quarrel with Deena.

She asked me how I knew Carl Barber and I told her that I'd done a small job for him. She told me straight up what he'd told her about it and I confirmed his statement.

I told her, as apparently he already had, that I'd passed the video and photographs I'd taken of the vigilante to him, and that he had not told me the name of the person I'd seen.

'You have them now?' she asked.

'Sorry, no. I always delete anything pertaining to a case from my phone. It's hard to keep a client's secrets in the electronic age. Password protection isn't enough. Also,' I went on, 'I like the guy, but he isn't a friend. He didn't confide in me. Far from it – he seems to be a very private bloke.'

'So you do not know why Deena Barrymore attacked you?'

'Actually,' I said, 'this is the first time anyone's mentioned her full name.'

Chloe Mwezi waited.

I went on, 'I think she must've seen me outside Mr Barber's flat and followed me. He told me, eventually, that she was stalking him. She tried to snatch my phone and shouted abuse at me.'

'What did you do?'

'I think I asked her what she was on about, but it was clear that there wouldn't be a rational conversation. So I took evasive action because I didn't want her to know where I lived.' I was factual and straightforward in my answers, but all the time I was aware that, while telling the truth, I was not telling the whole truth. I hurried on to the scene Deena made at the Shack and described everything I could remember about who had been there at the time, Digby's intervention and the rugby player who had hustled her away.

'So,' Mwezi concluded, 'she accused you of having sexual relations with her lover, and of alienating his affections, and of having designs upon his wealth?'

'Wow!' I said, 'I wish she'd put it so politely. She was screaming slurs about me that I didn't want strangers to hear. But yeah, that was the meaning of a far ruder message.'

Mwezi smiled tiredly. 'The English language, which seems so poetic, has many more vivid insults and curses than words of respect.'

'I can't disagree,' I said. 'But however it was expressed, the allegation simply wasn't true. No way. No how.'

She considered me coolly before saying, 'I will get your statement ready for your signature. Thank you for your time.'

'Before I go,' I said, 'I've got a question.'

She stared at me with that neutral cop look that reminded me that, even though I'd been on the job myself, I mustn't take advantage.

'Am I the only one?' I asked. 'Should I take Deena Barrymore's abuse personally? Were there others?'

She considered. Then she said, 'There were others. Including Mr Barber's ex wife.'

'Thanks,' I said. 'That helps.'

We shook hands and that was very nearly that except that when I left I found Toxic Tom lurking outside with one of his mates. I tried to ignore them, but they blocked the pavement.

In a carrying voice, Tom jeered, 'They're saying Hannah Abram is so desperate for a shag she's pulling half blind pensioners.'

'Well,' I said, just as loudly, 'even a half blind pensioner would be a better shag than you, Tom Tiny Tool.'

I pushed past the two twats and made off as fast as I could, sure that Mwezi wouldn't have approved. Sometimes the worst aspects of the English language are the only weapons I can lay my hands on.

21

On my weary, tedious drive up North I thought about the walk back from the incident room to my lodging house. It had been carefree, without glancing suspiciously around, looking for a hovering madwoman. The fact that my happy-go-lucky walk came at the expense of Deena's life did not spoil the thought that, in spite of clashing with Tom, so far it hadn't been a bad day. Sometimes I'm that superficial.

But good things float away like birthday balloons on the breeze when you drive to Potters Bar. I tried to use the unbearable stop-start-go-stop journey productively. For instance I found from the Companies Registry that the Cosy Couch Company was a one-off local business, not a franchise. I made a note of its officers – a married couple and two others. Then I received Sid Nailer's eye-watering price list and forwarded it to Mark and Myles. This is not the legal way to drive through traffic. But whoever made the legislation has clearly never tried to drive up the Edgware Road in a hurry. I noticed drivers doing crossword puzzles or Sudoko. I saw a taxi driver with a paperback. The stifling heat meant that there were a lot of open windows so I caught blasts of loud music, the radio and audio books that kept drivers' frustration damped down.

There was a heart-stopping message on WhatsApp supposedly from my mother saying that she needed my help urgently. An electronic glitch at her bank meant that she couldn't access her account to pay her gas and electricity bills. Please would I help her out of a jam by sending five hundred and sixty-six pounds immediately as the power company was threatening to cut her off. A fearful two seconds passed before I remembered that my mother no longer paid any bills and it had been a couple of years since she'd written a coherent text. Another gimme scam. I deleted the message.

Wouldn't it be ironic if Myles' longing for contact with a stepsister who'd been kind to him many years ago led to the uncovering of a serious international scam?

I called Sid and gave him the number of Gina's phone – the one that Myles was still endlessly calling – and asked him to track it down. Myles hadn't yet approved the expense, but I was sure he would. At the next stop for road works I texted him to report what I'd done. He didn't answer.

My brother rang. I let it go to voicemail. I'd already had a scam-induced panic about my mother. I didn't want another so soon after it.

By the time I arrived in Potters Bar it was well after six o'clock. On the drive I'd failed to come up with a clever strategy so instead I took two twenties and one ten pound note out of the stash Myles had given me and walked into the greasy, sticky burger bar called Tenerife Kebabs. If anyone other than the discontented woman I'd seen four nights ago had looked up from the counter I would've bought a packet of fries and left. But the tired blonde, who was leaning on her elbows looking at the pictures in Hello magazine, was familiar.

She straightened when I came in, and this time I noticed how tight her apron stretched around her belly. She looked about five months pregnant. And because she was obviously suffering through a late shift I thought that this might be my lucky night. Taking advantage of pregnant women is not the sort of thing I'm proud of. But what the fuck – she clearly needed money, and I clearly needed information.

I'm sure there must be more elegant ways of opening such a conversation, but I just raised a hand fanning fifty quid in the air in front of her and said, 'Hiya. Could you use a little extra bunce?'

'I could use a lot of extra bunce,' she said, staring past the money and into my eyes. Almost as an afterthought she added, 'What's your game?'

I put the money down on the counter and held out my hand. 'I'm Hannah,' I said.

'Orla,' she said cautiously. We shook. Her hand was as limp and tired as her hair.

'I'm working for a guy who's looking for his sister,' I said economically. 'Her last address was in Waterford Road above the Tasty Treats café.'

'Just round the corner,' Orla said. 'I used to work there before it went bust. How long ago are you talking about?'

'Her car was registered to that address about four years ago,' I said, unreasonably hopeful.

'Are you going to eat anything?' Orla asked.

'Maybe soon,' I said.

'Cos I'm not supposed to gossip to customers.'

I looked around. It was a cramped space. The counter was built on a small platform so Orla seemed a lot taller than she was. I could not see any cameras.

'How will your boss know?' I asked.

'He'll be here soon to collect the lunch-time takings. He comes early evening and closing time. We don't hardly keep no cash in the till.'

I nodded. Digby's policy with cash was similar.

'They'd of gone over to card-only yonks ago except it cut profits in half. Not everyone hungry got a bank card.' She didn't touch the money in front of her, but she counted it with her eyes. 'If I knew your friend's sister, would it be worth more than fifty?'

'Depends.'

'Look,' she said. 'I got three kids at school. Fifty quid don't even buy the oldest boy's shoes. Know what I mean? Now this little bugger's on the way. Didn't plan it. I'm over forty and if I'd known in time I'd of stopped it. You get me?'

I nodded again.

'My other half's on disability – his back, y'know. I'm it, as far as earnings go. Working for the Erdigans ain't no picnic, I can tell you. I can't hardly pay my bills as it is so I can't afford to lose this job. Even if they don't take no notice of health and safety, there's a Christmas bonus if I can hold out that long. If this little bugger don't decide to pop early.' She ran a less than tender hand over her bulge.

I had a quick think about how Myles would react if I failed to pay someone who was hinting she knew Gina. I said, 'Pick up the cash. It's yours whatever you tell me. If you give me something I can work with I'll double it.'

Quick as a weasel, the cash disappeared under the waistband of her stretch pants.

'Okay,' she said. 'Now you buy yourself a burger and pay for it. If the old bastard comes in I'll make it for you and you can go out and sit in your car. Alright?'

'Yes,' I said. I asked for a chicken burger and paid in cash. But just to make sure I said, 'Who do you think I'm asking about?'

'Well, I dunno, do I?' she said, tiredly. 'But there was a Gina living above T.T. She was a toff down on her luck. Getting warm, am I?'

'Smokin',' I said. I fished one of Myles' photos out of my bag and showed it to her.

'That's her. Now put it away.' She grabbed a breaded chicken fillet out of the chiller and shoved it and a split bun on the griddle.

I didn't turn round when the street door opened. I just stared at the food on the grill.

An elderly man, smelling of cigarettes, pushed past me and lifted a flap in the counter. He didn't look at me or greet Orla. He just went through the plastic strips that acted as a door to the back and disappeared leaving the flap up.

Orla said, 'That'll be six pounds seventy-five.'

I put cash on the counter. The elderly geezer came back with a canvas money bag. He was stout and had a ragged moustache and a mono-brow. A bulbous nose was squashed in between.

Orla put my money in the till. She flipped the chicken piece and put the split bun out ready to receive it. It was a practiced move, almost graceful. I could've done the same bloody thing myself just as quickly.

'You want salad on that?' she said without looking up.

'Yes, please,' I said.

The old geezer squeezed past me unnecessarily close, making me jump. Then he was gone.

'Dirty old git,' Orla said, and went on making my sandwich. She'd almost finished when the door opened again. I tensed, but it turned out to be the spotty guy in skinny jeans I'd followed days before.

Orla sighed as she slapped my food into a yellow styrene box and handed it to me.

'Thanks,' I said, and walked out.

My car was parked across the road. I sat in it and ate the crap food I'd paid for. I made a note of my expenses so far, and watched the ritual exchange between Orla and the spotty guy through the window. I was hot and sweaty. The heat was suffocating enough to feel more like Florida than Potters Bar. I wondered what it could be like to do that job in such a cramped shop when five months pregnant. As far as I could see the poor cow had it a lot worse than me.

The skinny guy wanted to hang around but Orla got rid of him. I watched him shamble his lonely way home to Waterford Road. I checked the sparse traffic and then went back to Tenerife Kebabs. Orla opened the street door and sat on a plastic stool wedging the door open with her body. It was debatable which was more airless, inside or out. She stretched shapely legs with slightly swollen ankles and sighed. 'Fuck him,' she said of the spotty guy. 'I know he's just a saddo, but I *so* ain't got the energy.'

I sat on the doorstep next to her. We both wasted a moment staring at the street. Then she said, 'If someone comes you'll have to buy a portion of fries.'

'Or a cold drink,' I said.

'I got Fanta,' she said. But neither of us moved an inch.

'So,' I began, 'you knew Gina. I was beginning to think she didn't exist. Nobody's seen or heard from her for years.'

'Well, me neither. But see, I was working at Tasty Treats when she showed up. TT went bust a year later and she just sort of disappeared.'

'That still makes you the last person I can find who saw her.'

'What d'you want to know?'

'Where she is now,' I said hopefully. 'But failing that, anything you can remember.'

'A couple-a weeks after I started work here I asked Mr Mo how she was, cos, y'know, he was the one who moved her in. And he said she was sick and gone to hospital. I asked where. Cos, y'know, I might of gone to see her if I could find the time, and he said she'd gone back to Canada where her mum lived.'

'Canada?' I interrupted. 'I don't think so. Also her mum died years before that.'

'I thought he was telling porkies,' Orla said without surprise. People lied to her all the time, I thought – something else we had in common.

'But she *was* sick. She had that thing that makes you shake and fall over sometimes. Mr Mo said she used to work for him but now she was a charity case. Hah! Don't make me laugh – he wouldn't know charity if it smacked him on the snoot.'

'Was that Mr Mo who collected the cash?' I asked.

'Him? No. That's Papa Erdigan. Mo's one of his sons. Or maybe a nephew. Gina said she and Mo used to live together. He took her to Turkey, y'know, where he come from. But he wouldn't marry her cos of religion or something. There's always a reason, right?'

'Right,' I said.

'Still,' she went on, 'it was sad. I went up to that flat once. I had one of those emergencies. Endometriosis, y'know, and she helped me out. It was horrible up there. She tried to make it nice, but there was damp and mould and none of them windows fitted. Charity, my arse! But she told me she and Mo had a baby over there. She said if it'd been a boy and lived she might of got the ring. But it was a girl and it died. It's true, isn't it, you always mourn a dead baby, even one you didn't want?'

Orla didn't wait for a reply, which was just as well; babies are *so* not my area of expertise.

'One way or another we didn't see much of each other. But I liked her even though she was a toff. She said she were an actress, but she didn't look like one.'

'She was a trained actor,' I said.

'Oh. I'm glad *she* weren't telling porkies.'

Just then a small herd of teenaged girls gaggled their way across the road. Orla made to get up but failed until I gave her a hand. She went back behind the counter and threw four burgers and a couple of kebab sticks on the griddle. The girls, it seemed, were regulars.

Reluctantly I sat in my car. Shadows were stretching and the car was now in the shade. Even so in only took a few minutes for my bum to stick to the seat.

After the girls left a mother with two preteen kids arrived. Then a couple of middle-aged women with just-home-from-work written all over them. So it was about twenty minutes before Orla came to the door carrying two bottles of poison yellow Fanta. I paid her for both of them. It went without saying that the Erdigans would be as generous with freebies as Digby. Even so, working on the Common seemed to be a whole heap better than what Orla had to put up with.

When she was settled on her stool in the doorway and sipping on he cold drink I said, 'Did anyone come to visit Gina that you know of?'

'Her brother, she told me, but he only stayed half an hour and made her cry. I expect she asked him for help. He looked like a tight arse from what I saw. Which wasn't much. There was a posh old biddy who stayed for hours, but if anything she was sicker than Gina. She had to call a taxi to take her home. The old dear couldn't seem to remember where she lived. Alzheimer's, Gina said. She said she hardly had any friends left – she'd lived abroad too long. I was sorry for her. She was so nicely spoken and sort of kind. She wasn't hard like me. Believed everyone. A bit of a dope, to tell the truth.'

I took this in and let it sit uneasily with what I'd been told about the Turner family. In particular I remembered Gordon Turner's curt dismissal of my request for help in finding Gina. He could've saved me some work if he'd told me about Tasty Treats, but she hadn't gone to his father's funeral. She was the sister who didn't toe the Turner line. She led a messy life and deserved all the bad cards she'd been dealt.

This, of course, is what my father and brother thought of me. It seemed to be my evening for identifying with other women. I shook the thought away and asked, 'Anyone else?'

'You gotta remember I was only on from nine in the morning till three so I could take the kids to school and pick 'em up after. So I don't know who she saw or talked to or phoned. We weren't friends. Just friendly.'

Orla closed her eyes and tipped the last of the Fanta down her throat. She went on, 'There was the social worker, of course. Except she said he wasn't one. See, I thought maybe she'd complained to the soshe about living conditions. That was before she told me the Erdigans owned the property and it wasn't nothing to do with social housing. She wouldn't complain to Mo, would she, or she might of lost what little she had.

'She could get around a bit, see, but she couldn't work. One time when I was really strapped, cos the girl helping me just didn't show up, and she started clearing tables for me. But she was so slow and shaking so much I had to stop her. If she'd of dropped a pile of plates it'd come out of my wages. Soon after that, she couldn't hardly walk without a stick cos she said she'd taken a coupla tumbles. It took her forever to come down them stairs from her flat.

'About then Tasty Treats went bust. I was lucky cos the Erdigans took me on here. If you call that luck. Well *I* did at the time. But I didn't know till the last minute what would happen to me, so I wasn't thinking about Gina. Then, like I told you, Mo said she went to Canada.'

'This guy who wasn't a social worker?' I prompted. I wanted to get as much information as possible before the next cluster of customers turned up to distract her.

'I don't know, do I?' she said, telling me as clearly as a woman can without opening her mouth, that she was tired and her back ached.

'When do you get off work?' I asked.

She sighed and shrugged. 'When that mucky shit-face says I can go. My other half's feeding the kids tonight, so I'm covered. He's a useless streak of gob-shite mostly, but he does know how to open a tin of spaghetti hoops and work a toaster.'

Remind me never to have kids, I thought.

I really did not want to wait much longer. And I certainly didn't want to come back to Potters Bar. Emergency measures were required. I got up and went over to the car. I unlocked the glove compartment and extracted a hundred pounds in twenties from Myles's stash. I gave Orla another forty quid and let her glimpse the rest before I stuck it in my pocket.

'What can I tell you?' She rotated her spine to ease the pain. 'I dunno if I even saw him twice. He was there to help her, I'm sure of that. She spilt her tea and he came to me for a cloth. He mopped the front of her shirt and the table. She just sat there and I could see she wanted to cry. He said something like, "I'll see what I can do," which is what social workers always say before they do sweet fuck all.' She stopped talking for a minute, closing her eyes and trying to massage her own shoulders. Then she looked at me straight in the eyes and said, 'His name was Rafael. Yes that's it. She said, "He's my angel." And she told me he was going to help her cos he knew all about her condition. There! I remembered something good, din't I?'

'I hope so,' I said, because the last piece of information had given me a few ideas, and if any of them panned out I could bypass the Erdigans and NP Holdings.

I thanked Orla and paid her. I didn't want to see her again but if I needed to I knew where to find her. I'd paid her far too much but I was hoping I could justify the expense. It wasn't only that I recognised Orla as another member of the Fast Food Family, it was because she'd given me hope when previously I'd been going through the motions of tracking down an out-of-work actress through an internationally held company. That wasn't something I was qualified to do on my own. But I could, without much trouble, list the symptoms of shaking, slowness and falling over on my iPad while stuck in a traffic jam, and think about what to do next.

22

It was dark by the time I got back to my home patch south of the river. All I wanted to do was have a cool shower and to stretch out on my bed to ease the tension from my neck and shoulders. That's what driving North does to me. It's physically painful.

But one thing I'd stressed about on the drive was that I had four jobs on the go all at the same time: find Gina, find Paulina, track down a veggie pincher and, of course, short order-cooking. I'd got somewhere with Gina this evening, thank you Orla; I hadn't even started on Paulina, sorry gorgeous Mark – I promise I'll start tomorrow afternoon; last, I'd neglected the Common or Garden gardeners.

With this in mind, and dutifully putting duty before cleanliness, I drove to the street where the Cosy Couch Company had its premises. It had a double shop front, and there was a driveway between it and the next shop that led round the back to an asphalted yard. There, two vans were parked with their rear doors facing a loading bay. All as reported by Candice. I noted down the registration numbers of the vans – force of habit I suppose, or more likely, habit of the Force. I know that in law everyone is presumed innocent. But when you've been a cop the ingrown knee-jerk presumption is that it's safer to presume everyone is guilty. Of something.

Round the front again I saw that the shop next door to Cosy Couches dealt with computer repairs. 'We repair ALL electronic devices', read the notice on the door. I wrote down the phone number and email address. That was for my own private insecurity about all my electronic devices. The window was protected by steel shutters.

On the other side was a cut price shoe outlet. This was a useful street to know about, I thought.

I drove slowly round the block. Nothing caught my eye until three doors down from a Balti House I saw a green and gold shop front called Father and Mother Earth. A handwritten chalk board in the window claimed, 'Everything natural, vegan and ethically sourced'. I didn't exactly jump up and down shouting *'Bingo'*, but I did think, Hmm, interesting.

Then I drove home. It really had been a good day.

23

One good day did not predict another.

I unlocked the Shack's door and was greeted by a flood.

Someone had left a tap dripping over a blocked drain in the main sink. It was not anything as simple as a rag left over the plug-hole. And if I'm honest I'd noticed since before the Big Sleep Out that the sink had been draining slowly. In fact I'd warned Dulcie not to empty the grease trap into it.

One of my least favourite things in the universe is cleaning out a u-bend. But *you* try to get an emergency plumber out of bed at five-thirty on a Wednesday morning. Believe me, it's not even worth trying if you want to be open for business at six.

First I turned the tap off properly. Then I used the industrial plunger we keep in the cupboard next to the customer loo. I dislodged the blockage enough for the sink water to dribble away. Then I took off my clean jeans and, clad in just t-shirt, knickers and socks set about mopping up as much of the floor water as possible. Lastly, in the same sophisticated, alluring attire, I fetched a bucket and a plumbers grip and attacked the fittings that attached the loathed u-bend to the rest of the pipes.

Good mornin', Hannah, hope you slept well. Cos today's starting like a total bastard!

To make matters even peachier, I found, when I turned on the fan, and opened doors and windows to dry the effing Shack out, I'd collected an audience of startled early risers wanting coffee and pastry. They showed their appreciation for the floor-show by shuffling their feet and looking embarrassed.

I said, 'Morning all. If you can't wait ten minutes, go elsewhere.' Head held high, with as much swagger as I could muster, I marched away to wash and dress. I was proud of myself for not telling everyone to fuck off.

Actually my customers were much nicer to me than I was to them. Mostly, their comments were sympathetic, except for one old geezer who said, as he paid with a ten pound note, 'Keep the change. I suggest, if you're going to make a habit of working in your underwear, that you run down to Marks and Spencer pronto to buy a new pair of knickers.' I kept the change and resolved to spit in his tea at the first possible opportunity. It was only a very small hole, which he'd only be able to see by staring very hard at my arse.

By the time Digby and Dulcie rolled in fifteen minutes late I was in a lousy mood. I greeted them by launching into my complaints. 'You're late,' I snarled, 'and someone poured grease down the sink, blocked the drain and caused a flood by leaving a tap running. The emergency plumber cost two hundred quid which I paid out of my own pocket cos I couldn't find the key to the petty cash box. I've spent every free sodding moment since then mopping up and drying the floor. So pay up right now. I've had it with you two.'

'Where's the invoice?' Digby asked wisely.

'Didn't give me one.' I glared furiously at him. 'He wanted cash up front and just as he was finishing he got another call so he buggered off. I want cash up front too.'

'I'll give you fifty now,' Digby said, 'and the rest when I see the invoice.' He knew I was ripping him off. And I knew he knew. But he'd had an effective plumbing job and clean-up for diddly squat and I wasn't penny-pinching about fifteen minutes overtime. So he probably thought it was worth it.

'A ton,' I countered, furious because my back ached.

'Seventy-five.' His face was scrunched up like a wrung out dishcloth.

'Done.' I know when Digby is about to do his famous imitation of a hand grenade. Another time I might have welcomed being fired yet again. But twice in one week is a bit much, even for me. Besides, I'd paid Orla too much without okaying it with Myles first.

Digby was growling like a hungry guard dog. But I stood my ground. Eventually he forked over the money. I snatched a chicken salad sandwich from the counter and left without paying for it. Dulcie looked terrified.

I would've sat somewhere quiet in the shade to calm down and eat my lunch but BZee materialised from behind a beech tree. He looked hungrier than I felt so I gave the food to him.

Luckily for both of us he's good at reading faces, because the only thing he said before tucking in was, 'You fight with little-man-big-noise again?' Another time I might've laughed. Not today. I ignored him and pulled my iPad out of my back pack.

I quickly stabbed in the links I would've looked at during my morning shift if my morning shift hadn't been such underpants.

Suddenly I was more cheerful. In just fifteen minutes I'd found connective tissue in two cases, and that made me feel like a detective. To be realistic, it was my iPad that was the detective. But that was a secret I meant to guard from my clients for ever.

First, though, I emailed Myles, saying, 'Ring me please. I have news.' Then I turned to BZee. 'Fancy a walk over to the allotments?' His permanently anxious expression cleared and he gave me a cheerful grin. On our way around The Drain I rang Candice and asked if anyone could meet me in ten minutes. She said she was already working on her patch, but she'd collect as many of the gardeners as she could.

'Magda coming?' BZee asked.

'I hope so,' I said. 'And I hope she brings cake.'

She did – a tin full of blueberry and raspberry muffins with a white chocolate topknot on each one. BZee was clearly smitten with her; or her baking. I'm too insensitive to tell the difference.

She'd made a huge pot of strong tea and as she handed me a mug and a muffin I felt a bit smitten myself. I love and hate motherly women equally. I don't understand it, and I don't want to ask myself why.

Magda effortlessly served about ten people including Yurek, the Colonel, Snakeman and Candice. When everyone was comfortable the Colonel handed me an envelope, saying, 'I was reminded that we hadn't paid you anything for your time so far. Here's a hundred and twenty pounds. We all agreed to hire you so we had a whip-round. Those of us who can afford to chipped in at least ten pounds. Now we'd like to hear your news. If *any*.' He couldn't help himself.

But I accepted the money. And taking my cue from the Colonel's officious, sceptical speech I straightened in my folding chair and adopted a cop-talk tone of voice.

'As I expect you realise,' I began, 'I have a few contacts not available to the general public. So while investigating the owner of the van BZee noticed I discovered that the Cosy Couch Company is registered to four people including a married couple. Of course I noted their names and addresses for further investigation. Then last night, while familiarising myself with the neighbourhood of the Couch Company I noticed a vegan whole food shop called Father and Mother Earth. This might have proved to be irrelevant, however when I ran the name and address of this business past my contacts I discovered that a company calling itself Father and Mother Earth is registered to the same married couple who are co-owners of the Couch Company – Lily and Kyron Daffid.'

'Lily Daffid?' Candice said, looking around at the group, horrified. 'But Lily's one of us.' She took a breath and went on, 'I don't mean she's got an allotment here, but she…'

'Same thoughts,' Magda said, shocked.

'Sometimes when we had a glut, she'd buy our surplus,' Snakeman said.

'She'd *never*,' Yurek said.

'Not *ever*,' Magda said, almost at the same time.

'Not so fast,' the Colonel put in. 'Just because she approved one-hundred percent of our methods and philosophy does *not* mean that she is totally honest.'

'We're living in hard times,' said a woman I hadn't seen before. She wore her hair in snow white plaits but was otherwise dressed all in black. 'Shopkeepers are crashing right, left and centre. The supply chain is disintegrating. Has anyone, other than me, tried to source seeds for next year yet?'

BZee helped himself sneakily to his fourth muffin. I sat silently, watching the group coming to grips with the unwelcome information I'd given them. They seemed to be discussing the collapse of society or capitalism. I couldn't work out if that was going to be a good or a bad thing.

But time was passing and I wanted to start on Mark Ferguson's enquiry. I said, 'Look, I have to go now. But when you've decided how you want me to proceed, let me know. However, if you want my advice, it would be for one or two of you to go *quietly* to the shop, just to have a nose around and a *friendly* chat. Don't immediately accuse anyone of anything. Just look for whatever signs and hints that'd mean something to you lot but not much to me.' I couldn't imagine how anyone could tell one apple or spud from another. But maybe they could.

I got up, and BZee after a short internal struggle about whether to stay with the muffins or follow the money opted for leaving with me. I knew what he was thinking so, when we were out of sight of the allotments I took four five-pound notes out of the Colonel's envelope and gave them to him. He took them but held them in his hand rather than squirreling them out of sight immediately. He transferred his gaze to me.

'What?' I said.

'You keep lots, give I little,' he said accusingly.

'Ms deRousseau already paid you. The rest of the work was all mine. I got expenses.'

'School start,' he replied promptly. 'I need books.'

We stared at each other. Then he burst out laughing and I joined him. 'Come on,' I said, 'I'll buy you lunch. You choose where.'

While we walked towards the part of town where his mother lived I showed him one of the pictures of Paulina and asked if he'd seen her.

He shrugged and wrinkled his brow. 'Maybe.' He pointed vaguely in the direction of Streatham. 'With baby-mothers, got no man. What it worth?'

But just then we'd arrived at the van which called itself Carrib Cookhouse, and he ran up to the hatch. A guy with all his dreads crammed into a Rasta hat, said, 'What you want? What you got?'

BZee waved me forward with a lordly flick of his wrist, and then fell into serious discussion with the cook. The result smelled wonderful and looked awful. I'd hardly ever seen BZee look happier. I paid up and walked away unnoticed wondering how well the huge bowlful would sit with the chicken salad sarny and half a dozen muffins he'd already gobbled.

24

I wandered, rather aimlessly, in the Streatham direction. I realised that Magda's muffin did not fill the gap left by BZee eating my lunch. Leaving the Common, I started looking for a sandwich shop but settled instead for an all-day breakfast place where I ordered two lox and cream cheese bagels. There were tables outside on the pavement so I sat at one of them in the mottled shade of a lime tree.

While I ate I scrolled through emails. Tatiana still wanted me to pay for the privilege of looking at her not-so-private parts. And 'A Friend' wanted me to send him a shed-load of bitcoins for not exposing my online gonzo porn consumption. Maybe 'Friend' and Tatiana were in cahoots: she set 'em up, he knocked 'em down. He was the more dangerous as he appeared to have partial information about one of my passwords. I sighed. I'd have to change them all again. I knew it made sense, but it was such a time-consuming pain in the petunia. So many electronic processes that are supposed to be more secure, save me time and save paper, cost me security, time and paper.

Find Paulina Ferguson I told myself sternly. Then I got up and bought another flat white. I was thinking about Mark's contact who reported seeing her walking on the Common beside a woman with a pram. Now BZee said he might've seen her with a baby mother. So I asked myself if there was a home for unsupported, destitute mothers in the area. Did those still exist? I didn't know. That thought led me to think about the Women's Aid shop where I'd bought Monday night's finery.

When I walked out of Toxic Tom's flat after the ugliest fight I'd ever had with anyone, I literally had nowhere to go. So I spent the rest of the night trying to sleep on the back seat of my car. In the morning I called in sick and waited till Tom had strutted off to work without a care in the world. Then I let myself in, had a shower and collected all the clothes and toiletries I could cram into a couple of bin bags. I couldn't take my furniture, of course, or whatever we'd bought jointly.

I rang my brother to ask if I could stay with him till I got sorted, but he told me that his wife's sister and their child were staying. Later I found out that this was a lie. When tackled, he excused himself by saying he was hoping that I'd patch things up with Tom if he made it difficult for me to leave him. Obviously he liked Tom better than he liked me. I've never forgiven him.

I rang a couple of friends and sofa-surfed until I found something better. Then, the Met fired me, the sickness engulfed the city, and I became homeless again. There are times in a lot of women's lives when there's no choice but homelessness.

You can ring your local council and ask for help. The council's obliged to house you provided you meet certain criteria. If you're very lucky you might be put into temporary accommodation, like a hostel. But if, like Paulina, you aren't British and you can't lay your hands on even your Maltese passport – what then? Charities?

It was the obvious thought because, as far as I'd been told, Paulina had no friends in the area. The only friend she appeared to have made for herself was the git she'd run away with.

I swiped through the photos Mark provided. There was no contact list. His wife ran away with a thief. End of story.

For the umpteenth time I wondered what sort of loser would swap Mark for a predatory handyman. Maybe it was insanity caused by hormonal imbalance.

Mark told me she'd be too ashamed to turn to religion, but just for the hell of it, I Googled Greek Orthodox Churches in South London and discovered that there was a Cathedral in Camberwell. It wasn't in the area he'd asked me to search. But it was worth a shot, and there was a phone number. I was about to dial when the phone rang. It was Myles. I'd forgotten I'd asked him to call me – or rather, I hadn't expected him to call me back.

'I hope you got good news for me.' He sounded bone-tired. 'My godmother is threatening to have me hospitalised.'

'I'm sorry to hear that,' I said, cautiously. 'Is there any way I can tell you my news that won't drive you dipsy-doodle?'

A harsh bark of miserable laughter exploded in my ear. I hurried on. 'I mean, have you got meds you can take, or… '

'Stop digging,' he said. 'You're about as tactless as anyone I've ever met.'

'And *you're* going to ruin any chance of me making the contact you want with Gina unless you can effing control yourself,' I snarled. '*Tactless* – my sainted arse! Listen to yourself, why don't you?' I was almost hoping he'd cut me off so I wouldn't have to deal with him. But he owed me a hundred and fifty quid so I gritted my teeth and ploughed on, 'If this new lead goes tits-up because you've gone bozeyquat again and jammed up more switchboards it's on you, mate, not me.'

'I've paid for the information,' he yelled.

'You paid for my time and expertise,' I yelled back. 'But *I* paid for this new information out of my own pocket. It's called "expenses" which you agreed to in writing.' There was a sudden silence that went on for so long I thought my phone had frozen.

Then he said, 'I'm going to take a pill and talk to my doctor. I'll call you back in half an hour.'

He sounded so small and reasonable that I almost apologised, but managed to restrain myself. He cut the call abruptly, and I thought about what he might be like if he didn't have money. He'd probably be a rough sleeper. This thought led me to think about the homeless charities that clubbed together to organise the Big Sleep Out. An obvious place to start Mark's inquiry, I told myself, wondering why I hadn't thought of it before.

I was walking through the door of the Pilgrim House charity shop before I realised that I had not rung St Mary's Greek Orthodox Cathedral. Myles had that effect on me.

In Pilgrim House I bought a nearly new sky-blue, long-sleeved t-shirt for five pounds as a token of my good will. The woman who took my money was, I guessed, about sixty, kind-faced and looking as though she was wearing her own merchandise. I thought I'd seen her rattling a donation tin at the Big Sleep Out, so we talked about that. She said it was a lucrative event for Pilgrim House. It helped fund their Outreach program. Apparently volunteers went out at night with supermarket trolleys full of sandwiches, donated clothes and blankets. She loved her job, she said; people were so grateful – not only those who received, but those who gave were happy to have the opportunity to give.

I couldn't help thinking we inhabited pretty different worlds. But I asked her if Pilgrim House sponsored a shelter for the homeless. No, she said. They didn't have the funds or the premises. I asked her who did, and specifically if anyone ran a shelter locally especially for women.

'I really do wish our church did,' she said. 'Around here, nine out of every ten murders or serious assaults are perpetrated on women. Look at that poor woman who had her neck broken at The Big Sleep Out I'm told that the police are questioning her husband. Apparently the marriage was in trouble.' She looked at me as if I was an expert. 'Why,' she went on, 'is it so often the men who should love and protect them who do the most harm to women?'

I shook my head. At first sight she looked like the average late middle-aged, middle-class, middle-English woman who had to fill empty hours with charitable works. But she spoke like someone with a history that she'd never tell me.

'So,' I said, 'if I was looking for a Greek friend who seems to have disappeared?'

'You could try Women's Aid,' she said doubtfully. 'They have two or three houses around here for abused women.'

'Oh, she isn't abused,' I said. 'Her husband's a really nice guy. But she made a very bad mistake with someone else.'

'Well,' said the kind woman whose name I couldn't be bothered to ask for, 'I hope you find her and she's alright. But I should warn you, charities that help women are very cautious about enquiries from outsiders.'

That made sense, I thought, as I was walking away stuffing my new t-shirt into my bag. Except that Mark Ferguson was not an abuser, and Kyle Yardley was somewhere close to a casino in hiding himself. Or was he?

My only experience of homelessness was one night in my car. But what if I'd had no car, no friends or no bank account? Toxic Tom's treatment of me didn't really count as abuse the way it was officially defined, but it had, over several months, cost me everything. Surely the cyber-bullying that followed Tom's 'sharing' of the pictures he took of me should count as abuse? If I had circulated pictures of him soaping his crotch in the shower nothing in any way resembling the onslaught I'd suffered would've happened to him.

I've said it before, but I'll say it again, the very same thing that makes a man a stud makes a woman a slag.

I walked away from Pilgrim House – just another charity shop in a row that had three such shops amongst several – like a photographer's studio and a hair dresser – that had gone bust and were boarded up. There was the Heart Foundation and Save the Children, both of which had nothing to do with the homeless. But further on, at the end of the street, I saw a sign for St Martin's Helping Hand which, I remembered, had helped with organising The Big Sleep Out. This time I didn't buy anything but asked the elderly woman behind the counter if there was a hostel or shelter for women supported by St Martin's Church.

At my question the woman became fluttery and nervous. She didn't ask why I wanted to know but launched into a prepared speech which began, 'I'm so sorry, but I am expressly forbidden to divulge any information about this subject. I suggest you address your questions to head office.' She waved vaguely in the direction of St Martin's Church.

When I left she was blotting sweat from her powdery upper lip.

Outside, I found my notebook and wrote, 'St Martin's has a hostel for women', on the page headed Paulina. I walked on looking for somewhere suitable to sit and search the charity online.

It occurred to me that forty-five minutes had passed since I spoke to Myles and he had not called me back. It was more comfortable to think about that than to remember what I knew about the behaviour of abusive men, and why charities concerned with the safety of women might want to keep their activities secret. I'd been involved as a police officer in trying to persuade a woman to bring changes against a violent husband. The operation had ended in disaster for the woman who had been forced to give up her children and left her so traumatised that she fled to Wales. The campaign to get her kids back was still being conducted from there.

We'd failed to protect and serve a frightened, injured woman. And I, still a rookie, had taken my cues from the more senior men around me: I'd shrugged, blamed the Crown Prosecution Service and got on with the next case.

25

I sat in The Lamb and Flag pub with half a pint of draught lager and a packet of salted peanuts and opened my trusty iPad.

St Martin's Helping Hand Foundation did indeed possess property they used for the benefit of the homeless. But the patient saintly-voiced man I talked to resisted all my charisma and reasonable arguments. He refused point blank to give me any information about locations and whether or not any space was dedicated to women. In turn I resisted the urge to call him a tosser.

I could find out for myself by searching records and Land Registration. Which would cost me long, boring hours. But even if I found a bunch of useful addresses I would face the same problem – the carers' code of confidentiality.

I tried to think about alternatives, but it had already been a very long day. I was tired. The drink relaxed me to the point where I almost found the golf tournament on the pub's TV entertaining. Traffic-polluted air wafted from an open window and the sound of heavy vehicles sang the Londoner's lullaby.

I'd almost nodded off when a brilliant thought occurred to me. I was *not* going to find Paulina by the usual methods. Therefore I would let Paulina find me. How's *that* for a clever piece of lateral thinking?

I bought another half pint and a packet of salt and vinegar crisps for extra energy. Then I turned the iPad on again and began to write.

That was when Sophia Smithson, Myles's godmother, rang me. The bossy old-lady voice said, 'Hannah Abram?'

'Yes,' I said, when by rights I should've hung up.

'My godson has been prescribed a stronger sedative,' she began. 'He's been directed by his doctor to sleep for as long as he can. But of course he cannot get your last conversation with him out of his mind. He has therefore delegated his authority to me. I will hear your news and make decisions on his behalf.'

Oh, you will, will you, I thought. I crunched a salt and vinegar crisp before saying, 'Certainly, Ms Smithson. As soon as I receive Mr Emerson's instructions to that effect I will do as you both wish.'

'I thought you'd say that.' The old bat almost crowed. 'For your information, I'm in his bedroom right now. And we are on speakerphone.'

'Really?' I said with a sinking heart. 'Hi Myles, how're you doing?'

'Not well,' he replied groggily. 'So please, Hannah, will you speak to my godmother? I don't want you to lose time and impetus because of me. Try to get along with Sophia. And you, Sophia, please, please try too.'

'Of course,' she said, with a lot more certainty than I felt.

There was a pause. Then she said, 'Alright. Now I'm in the drawing room with two doors closed between me and the bedroom. I know he'll try to fight the sedative if there's even half a chance he can listen to our conversation. So, what have you discovered?'

'Okay,' I said, trying hastily to put my thoughts in order and find the right places in my notebook and iPad. 'First, Ms Smithson, I'm quite happy to talk to you because now I won't have to double-think what I'm going to say. You're much better qualified to judge what will or won't upset Myles.'

'I'm glad you agree, at last,' she said, so snottily I almost blew a raspberry into the phone.

As patiently as I could I went on, 'I tracked Gina Turner's last known address through her car registration. The property in Potters Bar is owned by a company called NP Holdings which is owned and, apparently, run by company officers from Azerbaijan and Turkey. There is only one phone number given and, as you already know, the message on voicemail was, according to Myles, most probably recorded by Gina. Her own phone is also permanently on voicemail. I told Myles that I was not equipped to pursue enquiries into an overseas-held company, but the fact that Gina's phone, even though she isn't answering it, is *live* means that someone is paying the bills. Which, if Myles is lucky, may mean that she's alive, and there's a possibility that I can find her. He urged me to go ahead.'

'Stop right there,' Sophia ordered. She must've thought that unless her own voice was heard this was not a conversation. 'You know you're offering my godson a pig in a poke, don't you?'

I bit my tongue. 'There's a chance of *finding* a pig in the damn pokes' I said, trying to sound as snotty as she did. 'And if you'll just let me tell you what I've discovered you can make up your own mind and advise Myles accordingly.'

'Continue,' she said loftily.

'Well, Gina was living in really substandard accommodation above a closed-up café called Tasty Treats in a pretty run-down neighbourhood. But I found out that NP Holdings also owns a kebab shop not far off. I went there yesterday... '

'You've actually been to Potters Bar?' She sounded startled.

'More than once,' I said. 'What do you think, Ms Smithson, that I just sit on my elegant arse and make phone calls?'

'It had crossed my mind,' she said. 'This *is* the electronic age, in case you hadn't noticed.'

I should get an effing medal for not telling her to sod off and then hanging up. Instead, because Myles still owed me a hundred and fifty quid plus petrol and burger money, I said, 'Know what? We'll get on a lot better and *faster* if you use your ears rather than your mouth.'

As an awed silence followed this evidence of my wisdom and good manners, I went on rather less than accurately, 'After making exhaustive enquiries *on the ground* I interviewed a woman who used to work at Tasty Treats and who knew Gina. I had to pay for the information, by the way. Quite a lot.'

Sophia Smithson remained silent so I went on, 'Here's the hard part: Gina had an affair with a Turkish guy called Mo Erdigan. She got pregnant but lost the baby. Mo dumped her but let her stay in the flat above the café. She was already ill by then. From my informant's description it was a progressive neurological condition. My informant also described visitors, one of whom I believe was Myles' mother, already ill herself. Another was, I believe, Gina's brother Gordon, who was unhelpful. He "only stayed half an hour" and "made her cry". Well, it sounds like the man I tried to speak to, anyway.'

'Agreed,' barked Sophia.

'Okay,' I said, surprised. 'The third visitor was a man my informant thought was a social worker. Gina denied this but said he knew all about her condition and was going to help her. By now, she could only walk with a stick. She could barely manage the stairs to her flat; she'd had several falls and had a permanent tremor. So I thought... '

'Parkinsons,' Sophia supplied. 'Or something similar.'

'Yes,' I said sullenly. I hate it when someone steals my punch-line. 'And further,' I added quickly, 'I thought the man who wasn't a social worker might be from a local branch of, for instance, the Parkinson's Society. It's a charity... '

'I know what it is,' Sophia said. 'So you thought you'd just ring up and ask if they had a case file on a woman called Gina Turner. Is that what you thought?'

'No, as a matter of fact it wasn't.' She was bugging the snot out of me. 'I'm sure they have exactly the same security in place to protect vulnerable clients as most charities do. But I did think they might be more accommodating to someone who could prove that he or she was a relative. Who, if push came to shove, might even employ a lawyer to front the enquiry.'

'That is not an unintelligent conjecture,' Sophia said. 'I'll take over from here.'

'Fine,' I said, relieved but offended. 'There are two outstanding matters for you to settle first. I have initiated a search for Gina's phone which you'll have to pay for even if you decide to cancel. And Myles will need to pay my expenses.'

'Send me an itemised invoice and your bank details,' she said. 'As to the phone – what have you done, what guarantee is there for success, and how much will it cost?'

'I don't give my bank details to strangers,' I said flatly. 'Myles respected my request for cash only.'

'I will not collude with tax evasion,' the old bag said, sanctimony oozing from every damn word.

'Then we have a problem,' I snarled. I should've started with the money. I was furious with myself. I'd given away a very big bargaining chip. Of course I hadn't thought I'd need one. But that's why not thinking ahead when dealing with a spiteful person is always a bummer.

There was a silence which I had to break. I said, 'I am not your plumber or your dressmaker. Myles employed me because I have contacts and informants on the *street*. Are you following me? They don't have bank accounts or bank cards. This is not a question of undeclared income. It's a question of me buying information from very poor, sometimes homeless people. I need cash to do that.

'I go where you can't go and I talk to people you don't want to talk to. If you walked where I've been with your poncey attitudes and sanctimonious sermons you'd be as much use as a jelly door-knocker. Myles knows that. Talk to him. And if you still want to protect him from me, do it quick, before *I* contact him with *my* effing invoice. Till then, I'll stay active on the case and you can go and microwave your own head.'

This was not my most endearing speech ever. I compounded it by using my thumb forcibly on the off switch. Well, the bloody woman got up my hooter. Send her my bank details? I'd send her a flaming dog turd first.

I went to the bar and ordered a celebratory rum and orange. The barman said, 'Sounded like you were in a fight. Who won?' He was a fair-haired good looking student type so I grinned and said, 'Me.'

He grinned too and slipped an extra tot of rum in my drink. But when I went back to my seat and calmed down, I had to wonder how much damage I'd done.

Losing my temper feels wonderful at the time but it really doesn't work for me in the long run. I thought about how my Sergeant looked covered in dirty water and duckweed, with a face on him like a humiliated gorilla as he tried to crawl out of the canal. I could remember the elation and release – as if I'd conquered not only the dirty old prick but also the force of gravity. I almost felt I could fly away. But I paid for that pleasure. Oh yes.

So I felt almost, but not quite, apologetic when fifteen minutes later, Sophia rang me back. Fortunately she was a woman who liked to get in first. She said, 'I suppose, as always, I'm forced to be the bigger person. Alright then, I accept that, in your trade, you need a large cash float. Send me proper invoices and I'll make sure you will be recompensed in coin of the realm.'

'Okay,' I said, and then shut my mouth even though I wanted to tell her that enquiry work was not a trade – it was a profession. Shutting my gob is often the right thing to do and every now and then I do it.

She went on, 'Please do *not* contact Myles directly.'

She said, 'please'! I win!

'I understand that you and I have had something of a culture clash. But if we can agree to co-operate I believe we'll do a lot better than each of us on her own. So I propose that I should use my contacts in the charitable world to work with the people concerned with chronic neurological conditions. You in the meantime would be much better employed tracking down Gina's phone. That is a technical matter I'm not qualified to pursue. I will undertake to inform you of my findings and I expect you will reciprocate.'

'Alright,' I said. 'I'll send you an invoice. But you do understand, don't you, that my informants have to remain anonymous?'

'Very well,' she said. And after exchanging contact information we cut the call.

I have to admit that I was relieved. I'd already, that day, come up against the protective fence surrounding charities. I was trying to get around all that with local charities in order to find Paulina, so I didn't want to take on national organisations as well.

It occurred to me then that my life was creeping out of control. I had too much to do and not enough sleep. When was the last time I'd cooked a healthy meal for myself – with green things in it? I couldn't remember. And yet, when you're self employed, you can't afford to say no to anyone even if it means turning your back on fruit and vegetables.

I finished my drink and crisps. The letter I'd begun on my iPad stayed unfinished and I was in no mood to think in words. Instead I walked slowly back towards the Common, avoiding the Sandwich Shack even though I knew that by now it would have the closed sign on the door. I would eat a healthy meal, I thought, and get an early night.

With this in mind I trudged slowly towards Father and Mother Earth.

26

There seems to be a law which states that whenever I try to do the right thing complications follow.

When I pushed through the glass door into the shop I was greeted by a dull, potting-shed smell. It was caused, I quickly decided, by the fact that nothing was packaged. Dried beans and lentils for instance came in burlap sacks. Scoops hung nearby. You were supposed to bring your own bags. Vegetables weren't wrapped. Potatoes still clung to the earth they grew in. Carrots came in all shapes and sizes – except the perfect cones you find in supermarkets. Lettuces and cabbages had holes in the leaves, proving beyond doubt that they'd grown up without benefit of pesticides.

I don't normally shop like that. I rush into a place where brilliant lighting reflects shiny off plastic. I can buy spuds without getting my hands dirty. I don't have to weigh my own dried goods, or soak them for forty-eight hours. I don't have to slice my own bread. In I go; out I come with a bag full of stuff ready to cook or eat. Easy-peasy. Buying food in Father and Mother Earth would mean that shopping, cooking and eating would take five times as long. I am way too busy to be a vegan. Or is the word I'm looking for 'lazy'?

I was standing in front of the box of potatoes wondering if soil analysis would help the Common or Gardeners when I heard voices from behind a tall stand of brown rice, brown pasta and other brown dry goods. To my horror I realised the angry voices belonged to Eleanor and Olive. My landladies, it seemed, were arguing about whether or not biological men were justified in identifying themselves as lesbians. This made a change from overhearing their arguments about what to put in the blender for their green drink.

But I didn't want to be caught. I wasn't prepared to face a charge of eavesdropping so I quickly scraped a clump of earth off one of the dirty spuds and folded it into a tissue. Just as quickly I picked up a small cauliflower and went to the checkout.

Of *course* Eleanor and Olive would shop at Father and Mother Earth. I should've known there might be a danger of running into them.

Still, if they were lingering to enjoy a fight, I might have time to rush home and boil up the cauliflower. I'd smother it with non-vegan, non-kosher grated cheddar, stick it under the grill till it was covered in melted cheese and rush up to my room to eat in secret.

This is exactly what I did. I even had time to clean up after myself. But there was no doubt about it: I would have to find a change of digs. Somewhere I didn't feel guilty about what I ate, what I wore, and what my gender politics were. Feeling guilty is not what cops are trained for.

I know I'm a loudmouth, so don't laugh when I say that there are times when I feel overwhelmed, insecure and alone.

I was thinking about charity shops – high streets dominated by them, strung out like lifebuoys on a rope keeping the torpedoed local economies afloat. I needed some other woman's cast-offs so that I could look okay at an up-market wine bar. See, I *think* I'm doing alright: I can make next mouth's rent and I still have a bunch of cash in my pocket, but even so I can feel poverty and scarcity swimming like sharks in a pool just waiting to use their razor teeth to tear chunks out of me. I'd hate to be an *old* woman these days.

Speaking of whom, where was I before the Old Bag Supreme phoned? Answer: in a pub writing an extremely important letter.

I dragged the tablet out of my bag and set to work again. It was tricky. I had to persuade a total stranger to trust me. And how hard is that at present when I'd just received an email telling me that my Supermovie.stream account had been frozen? All I had to do to restore service was to send my bank details to Larry at Custamer

Relations in Hong Kong. It took me a couple of beats to remember that I didn't have a Supermovie.stream account, and that you spell customer with an O not an A. Do *I* trust everyone who offers to help me? Or, in fact, *anyone?* So I wracked my brain for words of sympathy, empathy and comfort.

I'd just started the first draft when the phone rang, saving me from a brutal editing job.

Carl said, 'Can you come over?' He sounded shaky.

'What's up?'

'There are people outside. I think I need a witness.'

'I'll be there,' I said. 'Ten minutes tops.' I'll do anything to get out of writing letters – even after dark when I've promised myself an early night. And even with a mask on and anti-Covid wipes in both hands. I hadn't forgotten his positive test.

*

There were three men outside Carl's house. I switched my headlights up to high-beam and drove slowly towards them – two big guys and one smaller.

One of the big ones turned and looked into the light, raising his hand to shield his eyes. He said something and they all turned to look. I kept the Honda moving relentlessly straight at them.

All three turned and hurried away, jogging up the posh end of the street that finished at the Common. They paused for some argey-bargey before skirting the bollards that protected the Common from dirty old Hondas like mine.

It wasn't that I recognised any of them. But as Carl had previously been harassed by someone who lived at this end of Cottham Road I had my suspicions. I switched back to low beam, made a U-turn and drove away. At the T-junction at the end of the road I turned left, parked illegally and hurried back on foot to Carl's house. I was just in time to see the three guys emerge cautiously from the Common. They were looking for a vehicle, not a pedestrian so they didn't see me duck down between two parked cars. I wished I'd had time to whip out my phone and video which house they went into, but I saw it clearly. It was the same house the vigilante and his Dalmatian had entered. It was also the same house entered by the two drunk lads who owned a Jaguar.

Busted, I thought. But if Carl wanted evidence an eye-witness would have to do.

I went to the railings and shone my torch down the iron stairs to the area in front of his door. The ground was covered with builders rubble and broken glass. The brick that broke his bedroom window seemed to have bounced off the interior shutters. Otherwise his bedroom would've been showered with glass. This looked a lot more serious then a few bags of rubbish. It was the kind of vandalism that could injure an old guy.

I took out my phone and called him.

'Who is it?' he asked, a tremor in his voice.

'Hannah. Can you open your door and chuck up the padlock key? Take care, there's broken glass.'

'Have they gone?' he asked. And a few minutes later he appeared at his basement door. He'd thoughtfully put his whole ring of keys into a sock which he threw to me.

He looked a lot older than when I'd last seen him and he seemed to have shrunk.

'What the hell, Carl?' I said as I picked my way down the stairs. I followed him into the passage to his chaotic living room.

'Did you see them?' he asked. He lifted a bottle of single malt and poured himself a stiff one that was clearly not his first. He waved the bottle in my direction.

I shook my head. 'Yeah, I saw them.' I cleared newspapers, unopened letters, and sheet music from a chair and sat.

He slumped down opposite me. There was a music stand between us and he pushed it aside with one foot. It fell over but he didn't seem to care. He was wearing thick, lumpy, hand-knitted socks. He caught me looking at his feet and said, 'Deena knitted these for me. I didn't ask her to; I didn't want her to. It was like she wanted to own my feet. I don't know why I'm... ' He bent, tore the socks off and threw them at the sofa. Being socks, they didn't travel very far. They lay there, like an accusation, amongst all the other detritus on his floor.

I wanted to say, 'Okay, Carl, what the fuck's going on? Spill.' But for once I restrained myself. Maybe explaining the socks would be what broke down his bullet-proof reticence and good manners. Or maybe it'd be the single malt.

As if he was ejecting the last air in his body, he sighed. 'They're saying I killed Deena.'

Silence.

In the end I broke it. 'Why?'

'Why do you *think?*' He sounded almost irritated.

'It's *your* story. Don't make *me* tell it.' I was irritated too.

He stared at me. Then he took a small notebook from an inside pocket and scribbled in it with the blunt stub of a pencil.

'*What?*' I said through clenched teeth.

'Could be a line for a song.' He sounded distracted. '"It's your story, you gotta tell it",' The words came out in a rhythm.

He was really beginning to piss me off. I stood up. 'Sod it,' I said. 'I didn't schlep over here to play Yoko to your John. You called me.' And I started for the door.

'Please,' he said brokenly. 'Please stay. I'm sorry. This is all my fault. I made it happen.'

'What?' I turned to face him. 'Are you saying you killed... ?'

But he didn't let me finish. In fact he hardly let me start.

'There was a small charity event I was playing at. She came over and said how much she loved my work, how the damned disco songs had been the soundtrack to her life. She said she loved music and creative people.'

He stopped. I said, 'So?'

'I was depressed. I'd been introduced as a "one hit wonder". She came on like a fan. Sometimes it only takes something as worthless as a woman coming on to me, putting out, whatever you want to call it. I wasn't even attracted to her. Before she approached me I hadn't even noticed her.'

Another silence. He drank some more and sat back as if he'd explained everything.

'So?' I said again. When he didn't answer, I said, 'So, out of nowhere, with no input or encouragement whatsoever from you, she suddenly started knitting you socks and attacking anyone she thought was stealing you away from her?'

'I told you it was all my fault. She said she was forty, and of course I'm nearly eighty. I was flattered. I don't have to like someone to have sex with them. It was the same for her – if I hadn't been playing at a charity gig she wouldn't even have *noticed* me. It wasn't love at first sight or any of the imbecility you young people believe in. She wanted to score a musician for her own damn reasons, so don't look at me like that. Anyway, she lied – she was over fifty. And she gave me a dose of thrush. *And* no one told me she was a nut job.'

I'm not sure why I was so dismayed. Was it because he was doing what I did when I jumped into bed with Toxic Tom after a few drinks, without getting to know him, or seeing if I actually liked him? He was glamorous, and I was flattered.

Without any sympathy or thought I said, 'Don't you blokes ever look before you leap? Or think before you fuck? Don't you learn *anything* when you grow old?'

'Apparently not. *You* try getting to my age still needing someone, *anyone,* to want you. You try getting old without making hundreds of wrong decisions. Just try it, and then listen to some twenty-something year-old give you a lecture about looking before you leap.'

'But Deena's dead,' I almost yelled. 'And three of your neighbours, one of whom was already harassing you, are accusing you of killing her. That's a bit more than a "wrong decision".'

'God – you sound like that cop.' He looked defeated. 'You know she even hauled my ex-wife in to ask her if I was the "protective type", because someone told her Deena was attacking her too. Have you any idea what that means? My ex-wife is the mother of my daughter and she's the only woman I've ever felt truly safe with. I want her back. I want to spend what little time I've got left with her. Not an attractive prospect when Deena was stalking her, and Deena's husband was harassing me.'

He stared at me as if I'd understand. While I was thinking, Blimey, what a complicated old geezer you are! Mwezi must've thought you had a motive for murder. Then I latched on to what was really important in his little speech.

'Carl,' I said, awed by the stupidity of the Y chromosome, 'please don't tell me you were humping the wife of a guy who only lives a few doors away. Don't tell me that the rubbish vigilante is Mr Barrymore?'

'Not the brightest button in the box, am I?' he asked so humbly I almost leaned forward and patted his hand.

On second thoughts, though, I found myself really irritated. 'And please don't tell me you knew who the Rubbish Vigilante was all along.'

'No, no,' he said quickly. 'I didn't know. I thought it was possible, but actually I was afraid it might be Deena herself. Also there's my daughter's husband who thinks I'm a waste of space and wants me to sell the flat and sign my music rights over to him. Plus the grandson of the drummer on the recording of the bloody disco songs thinks I gypped his granddad out of his fucking royalties. You know, Hannah, success is as much a curse as a blessing.'

This time I said it out loud: 'You really are a complicated old geezer, aren't you?'

'Life doesn't get simpler or easier the older you get,' he said tiredly. It was a reproof, but said gently.

'Yours surely doesn't,' I replied. 'Those big lads outside, are they the vigilante's sons – Deena's sons?'

'All one happy family,' he said bitterly. 'Deena and Robert Barrymore and their delightful two lumps of sons, Schwartz and Egger.'

'Joke?'

'I think it's more like Phil and Bill. They play rugby and hang around Boss Bods Gym. Not exactly Brains of Britain. Deena said they were a big disappointment to her.'

'Well, they're big alright.' I was actually picturing the large rugby player who hustled Deena away from the Shack on the night of the Big Sleep Out. I'd half recognised him as a member of a team that trained on the Common. Not a regular – I didn't know his name. Nor could I connect him with Swartz and Egger aka Phil and Bill Barrymore. But maybe Mwezi could. I said, 'Did you tell Chloe Mwezi that Robert Barrymore was the Rubbish Vigilante?'

'The policewoman? She was only interested in my, my, oh hell, I can't even call it a relationship. In the end she was only interested in where I was when Deena died and who could vouch for me. I didn't tell her why I employed you except that it was a personal matter.' He poured himself another shot of single malt. This time, too tired to think straight, I accepted one myself even though it meant removing my mask. Well, alcohol's a good steriliser, isn't it?

'Didn't you think that Robert…' I began.

'Might've killed Deena?' Carl jumped in, energised by alcohol. 'Well, no. He was taking his anger out on me in a mean and sneaky way, and I was only afraid that he'd find newer and nastier ways of doing that. I was maybe a bit scared he'd be violent to *me*, but only if I met him face to face. According to Deena he wanted her back.'

'She wasn't scared of him?'

'Well, no. Well, sometimes at the beginning, when we were secret, she dramatised the need for secrecy. But then, almost before it'd begun, she told him. That was a shock.'

'So why didn't you end it then? How long does it take to knit a pair of socks?'

He laughed suddenly. 'The duration of an affair measured in hand-knitted socks – a novel concept. It lasted three pairs of socks, a beanie and a jumper that doesn't fit. You may not believe me but I was scared of her. Well, you've seen how weird she was. I didn't want to antagonise her. I just wanted her to go away.'

He re-filled both our glasses. I was feeling super-relaxed and light-headed.

He said, 'Thank you for not asking if I killed her. Truth: I was afraid she'd kill me. And, again, I don't think Robert did either. He was too sneak and weakly – I mean weak and sneaky.' This was the first clue I'd had that the single malt had gone to his head.

Then, hesitating, he asked, 'I don't suppose I could persuade you to stay, could I? I'd feel safer with someone else in the house. I'll pay, of course.'

Although I wondered how much an old guy would pay me to spend the night with him I drove home. I was lonely, but not pissed enough to be tempted. Also off-putting was the fact that he was a secretive weasel. And I couldn't help noticing that he'd neatly ducked telling me how long his non-relationship with Deena had lasted. And how he was downloading all fault onto the victim of murder. Humorous and charming, yes; truthful, no. But I still liked him. What the fuck was wrong with me?

I was definitely over the limit so I drove carefully and took an uncharacteristically long time over parallel parking. It was a hot, humid night and very late. I would have to get up early again in the morning. I was feather-quiet about letting myself in and creeping up to the attic, where I found, taped to my door, a note which read, 'You put the outer leaves and stalk of a cauliflower in with general waste instead of in the compostable receptacle. Please rectify.'

Please kiss my arse, I thought as I tumbled into bed without rectifying.

27

I was not greeted by a flood when I opened the Shack the next morning, but I did find BZee asleep under one of the outside tables Dulcie had failed to put away yesterday afternoon. At least it had been a hot night, and nobody had pinched the table.

He followed me inside and watched while I filled the kettle, filled and turned on the hot water urn, turned on the grill. While it heated up I shoved four slices of bread in the toaster and fetched eggs, sausages and bacon out of the fridge. I made strong tea for both of us and spooned five sugars into his mug. I buttered three pieces of toast for him and one for me. I hadn't had any breakfast either.

He sat at his usual table in the darkest corner and gobbled his toast while I put sausages, eggs and bacon onto the griddle. When they were ready I made a bacon buttie for myself and shovelled the rest on a plate for him. He went to sleep as soon as his plate was cleared. We hadn't exchanged a single word so I didn't get the chance to ask him about his split lip or the swelling that closed his left eye.

He wouldn't have told me anyway and I was too tired to do more than go through the motions. I suppose I would've felt better about myself if I'd done more than dump a plateful of fatty food in front of him, and get on with my joyless job. But I didn't.

I trudged through the first couple of hours of my day on auto-pilot, and for a miracle nothing went wrong till Digby came in an hour early and saw BZee asleep in the corner. Fortunately I'd removed his plate and mug and any sign of free food. But, enraged, Digby said, 'What the fuck's he doing here?'

I was busy shoving two Americanos, one macchiato, three lattes and one flat white through the service hatch. The sun was already hot and the Walkers were sweating. They'd have been better off with cold drinks, but habit is a cruel master. Besides, not many people like to dip their croissants in orangeade.

I turned in time to see Digby kick BZee's chair, dumping him onto the floor.

'This is your doing,' Digby said. 'Get him outa here.'

What helped was the Walkers peering into the Shack and murmuring like disapproving bumblebees.

I said, 'You're mistreating the guy who prevented your café from being burgled last night. Now everyone will think you're an ungrateful racist erk as well as all the other things they think already. You owe BZee a night watchman's wage.' I said the last sentence loud enough for everyone in the queue and at the outside tables to hear.

'What the buggering hell you talking about?' Digby was too fuming to be careful.

I said clearly and at top volume, 'Either you or the other member of your overworked staff failed to put all your outside furniture away. BZee kept it safe all night.'

'You're the sodding manager,' he yelled. 'It's your responsibility.'

'Even managers don't do sixteen hour shifts.' I turned the volume up to eleven. 'You're the *owner*. But if you want me to make *all* the decisions, even the ones that should be yours, get out the petty cashbox and pay BZee fifty quid. He's earned it – look at him!'

'He's been in a fight, is all.'

'Protecting the property you're too bone idle to look after yourself.' I was only interested in scoring points. Truth and reality could go hang themselves from a lamppost.

But Digby was in an even fouler mood than usual. So, to forestall the inevitable firing I started to take my apron off.

Bless their sweat-wicking cotton socks, the Walkers went into panic mode. They banged on the counter, on the window and the door.

'Don't you go *anywhere!*' one of the octogenarians screeched at me.

'If you let her leave again we'll picket this place and organise a boycott,' shouted another.

A trio of dog-walkers, including Mrs Lancer and Gus, joined the throng. She said, 'Hannah's an asset to the community.' Which I thought was going a bit too far.

So did Digby. But having taken the threat of a revolt seriously he decided to roar with laughter instead of lashing out.

'Okay, okay, sorry,' he said not sounding sorry at all. 'I had a bad night and must have put on my grumpy boots this morning.' Nobody believed him, but I had to smile.

'Pay the kid,' insisted one of the Walkers who, I think, used to be a union organiser. 'Fifty pounds, isn't it?'

I nodded. I still had my apron in my hand but I didn't have to lift a finger to defend BZee or myself.

'Twenty-five,' Digby countered.

'Forty.'

'Thirty-five.'

I cocked an eyebrow at BZee and he gave me a micro nod. I started to put my apron back on.

'Done,' said the union organiser. His friends patted him on the back. But as we knew Digby quite well we all waited until he'd counted the thirty-five pounds into BZee's hand.

BZee left before anyone could change their minds. I could've done my winner's strut, but was wise enough not to. Nor did I ask where Dulcie was. I was pretty sure Digby'd find some way to blame me for her absence.

Eight-thirty, nine, and nine-thirty came and went without Dulcie showing up. At ten-thirty Digby took over drinks and pastries while

I started prepping the lunches. Rush hour began, and I have to say I didn't miss Dulcie much. In fact there were fewer spills to clean up. But Digby still hadn't said a word about her.

We both worked quickly and hard. But as one-thirty approached, when my eight-hour shift was supposed to end, I began to get anxious. I had a busy afternoon ahead: I needed to finish and print the letter I'd started yesterday, talk to Sid Nailer about Gina's and Paulina's phones, I had to contact the Common or Gardeners about possible soil analysis, maybe ring Chloe Mwezi about what I'd found out last night, ring St George's to find out how my father was, and ring my brother to find out how my mother was. I was sure there was something else but I couldn't think properly while making egg salad sarnies, keeping track of pizza slices in the microwave, and juggling chicken nuggets and burgers on the griddle.

At one-twenty-five, Digby said out of the side of his mouth, 'Gimme one extra hour at time and a half and you can have the office to yourself all afternoon.' He was too busy even to look at me.

'Done,' I said slapping a burger and onions in a bun. I didn't look at him either.

I don't know why that day was so crammed. Outside, the temperature shot up into the high nineties; inside, it was like cooking in a sauna. But apparently it wasn't too hot to eat hot food. I don't understand our clientele at all.

So I worked flat out for another hour. Dulcie didn't appear, Digby didn't explain and I was too damn sweaty to care.

28

Sid Nailer said, 'There is no trace of a phone registered to Paulina Ferguson at the number you gave me; or any other number under that name that I can trace. Either it's been destroyed or the SIM card has been removed and it's been sold on. It could be anywhere in the world.'

'It was a long shot,' I said. But I was disappointed. 'Please invoice that search separately from the next one.'

'Sent,' he said without a pause, and my inbox pinged. Instant invoicing. Doncha just love technology?

'Thanks,' I said. 'Next?'

'Gina Turner, okay. Still live, as you know. I've located it. It's a little odd because it hasn't moved anywhere for years as far as I can see. But of course it's paid for.'

'Give me the location,' I said. And immediately he sent me a post code.

'Thanks,' I said again. 'Do you know who's paying the bill?'

'No,' he said. 'It's a VocalPhone account paid by direct debit from the South Midland Building Society. I won't be able to get around South Midland's security but there's someone I know at VocalPhone. I could have a stab at that if your principal's willing to fork out. And, of course, only after they've paid the first bill. Sorry, but a guy setting up in this kinda business gotta be careful.'

'I hear you,' I said. 'Send it over and I'll forward it stat.'

'I like your style,' he said. 'Any chance of meeting up for a drink sometime?'

It was only after we'd broken the connection and I'd forwarded the two invoices to Mark and Sophia that I remembered I'd gone to his wedding eighteen months ago. But he hadn't asked for a date, had he? Or had he? I'd been cooking for over eight hours, I was a walking armpit, and so unaccustomed to feeling fanciable that I really didn't know.

It would be a mistake, I thought, to tell Myles I'd found Gina's phone, so I would only tell Sophia about it if she started accusing me of not working hard enough for my money. The post code Sid supplied was in a street in Watford, a dormitory town not far from Potters Bar, also at the wrong end of the freaking Edgewave Road.

I turned Digby's desk fan up as far as it would go and got on with writing a letter to Paulina Ferguson.

Dear Paulina, I wrote, and then stopped. Dear Paulina …what? Who am I kidding? Dear Paulina, give me the information I need so that I can look clever, capable and willing to take pains for the comfort of a charming, intelligent, handsome man.

Dear Paulina, you may be half barmy with grief for a lost child, but why on earth would you walk out on a guy like Mark? And steal from him?

Dear Paulina, you don't deserve a man like Mark, so come out of hiding and let me prove that *I do*?

'Woh!' I said out loud. 'Stop right there!'

I got up, went through to the café and poured myself a cup of coffee. Digby, astonishingly, was cleaning out the grease trap. I said, 'Whatever you do, don't pour that down the sink.' He didn't even look up, but grumbled a sentence that contained the words, 'Grandmother, suck, and eggs,' along with a few revolting expletives.

'Where's Dulcie?' I asked before I could stop myself.

'I don't fucking know, do I?' he snarled. 'If I knew that, she'd be down here on her hands and knees cleaning out this fucking trap instead of me!'

Good for you, Dulcie, I thought as I went back to the office. You *have* got a brain in your head, in spite of evidence to the contrary.

There was something about this brief exchange that made me ring St George's Hospital instead of continuing my letter to Paulina.

After a recorded message that told me I was eighty-seventh in the queue to speak to the Almoner, I hung up and rang my brother instead. He was not in the office, nor was he answering his private phone. Chloe Mwezi was not in her office either. I could leave a message. I asked her to ring me when she got a chance. No one wanted to talk to me.

I looked back at my iPad. 'Dear Paulina,' I'd written. If I changed that to Dear Dulcie, what would I write? Go girl? Dump Digby, you're doing the right thing?

Paulina was doing the wrong thing. But did she know that? Obviously not. She would be confused. Ashamed of her actions. Afraid, unnecessarily, of the consequences. Okay. So?

I wrote, 'Dear Paulina, My name is Hannah Abram. I work at the Sandwich Shack on the Common. Maybe you've seen it. Maybe you've seen me.

'I hope you are well and being looked after by people who will protect you – people you trust.

'I'm writing this letter, not so that I'll find you, but because I hope you can find a safe way to contact me. I don't need to know where you are.

'All your husband has asked me to do is to assure him that you are safe and well. And to let you know that he will help in any way you want. I believe he is sincere.

'I'd be grateful if you would put my mind at rest and get a message to me. My email address and phone number are below.

'I sincerely wish you well. Hannah Abram.'

I reread this for mistakes and, although it made me feel squirmy, I printed off half a dozen copies. Then I addressed several of Digby's envelopes to Paulina Ferguson, care of all the charities in walking distances of the Common that supported refuges or hostels.

Of course the Royal Mail was at sixes and sevens. Deliveries were random and uncertain because the postal workers were on intermittent strike. I would therefore save on stamps and deliver my letters by hand. More time spent tramping the streets. Would I have used the car before fuel prices became absurd? Yes, probably. But now I even resented the necessity of driving out to Potters Bar. Twice in ten days!

I was stacking my letters into a neat pile when my brother rang back.

'Nattie,' I said with a sinking heart. 'How's it hanging?'

'Good of you to enquire,' he said with brutal formality. 'Your father is still in isolation and your mother is in Cousin Esther's spare room. Kirsty and I are at Heathrow Airport on our way to The Balearics. We have both been forced to take a medical break due to stress-related symptoms.'

I couldn't believe my ears, so I hung up. Cousin Esther was over sixty and suffered from emphysema. But she had a spare bedroom which was all the qualification needed to be a twenty-four hour carer of my Covid-sick mother who has early-onset dementia.

I didn't want to think about any of it. I had a job to do; several jobs in fact, no time and no spare room. I was exonerated from thinking.

I put the letters in my computer bag, used the washroom basin, then I changed my shirt.

In the café Digby was buttering a teacake just out of the toaster, and swearing about his singed fingers. As I made for the door I said, 'Just to remind you, Digby, I'm not on the early shift tomorrow. I won't be here till eight-thirty.'

'Stop!' he shouted, shoving the teacake and a bottle of fizzy water through the hatch at a startled woman. 'You're the manager. You're supposed to manage a staffing shortage.'

'But,' I said sweetly, 'you haven't told me about a "staffing shortage". Okay, Dulcie didn't come in today. But you haven't told me whether she's got Covid, a toothache or a dying grandmother. You know, but you haven't told me. So manage it yourself.' And with this I slammed out of the shack and made for the street as fast as I could. Not that it mattered – Digby was on his own and he'd never leave the cash register unguarded. It was, anyway, too hot to run. I slowed to a walk. The heat settled like a wet sack over my head.

I'd delivered three of my letters before BZee found me. His face was even more swollen than it had been this morning. We diverted from my postal trek into a Café Nero. Everyone inside looked ill and exhausted in spite of the air conditioning, but I was the only one accompanied by an abused boy. He stacked three sandwiches on my tray along with a large slice of chocolate cake and a can of something fizzy. The only thing I could face was iced coffee.

'Want to talk about it?' I offered when we were sitting at a not very clean table.

'Nah,' he said. 'Fam'ly.' He didn't meet my eyes but began to stuff his mouth with so much food that talking was impossible.

As usual I began to worry about what my responsibility was. He was technically a child, but he was living independently, making his own decisions and his own money. He was clearly in need of care and attention, but he wasn't in a gang, he didn't take drugs, and he kept in as close touch with his mum as she or her 'friends' would allow. He didn't, as far as I knew, hurt anyone. But sometimes people hurt him. When that happened he didn't complain. He wasn't exactly a petty criminal but he sailed pretty close to that rocky shore. And he hated, with a passion, schools, teachers, social workers, cops and preachers. He was bright, quick, funny and helpful. What was I supposed to do about him?

Almost anyone I knew would tell me to let the experts or the courts decide what was good for him. But for no very rational reason I preferred to think that the best expert on what was good for BZee was BZee himself.

After he'd bought, with his own money this time, a gigantic bowlful of pistachio ice-cream with sprinkles and eaten it all I told him I was touring charity shops. He thought I was stupidy. But we left Café Nero together and walked slowly to my next destination which happened to be Women's Aid.

Old women are wonderful. I had the right envelope in my hand. All I had to do was to hand it to the woman with a severe grey bob and a yellow and lime green cotton frock. But she took a look at BZee and steered him towards the men and boys' clothing section.

He surprised me too. I was sure he'd tell her to get stuffed, that if a garment didn't sport a sexy label he wouldn't wear it. But he didn't. He picked a plain scarlet shirt and a pair of black Levis that had nearly all the starch laundered out of it. Wordlessly she pointed him at the curtained off corner where he could change. Astonishingly, he went where she pointed.

She came back to the counter where I was waiting and whispered, 'I'm sorry, but we don't accept donations of underwear.'

'We'll manage,' I answered weakly, not knowing if BZee's underwear policy actually included underwear.

'You aren't his social worker, are you?' she said, eyeing my own appearance shrewdly.

'Just a sort of friend and neighbour,' I admitted. 'The official system – how shall I put it – has some holes in it.'

'How shall I put it,' she responded sourly. 'I think "sucks big time" just about covers it.'

I grinned at her. She was my kind of cynic.

I put my letter to Paulina Ferguson on the counter, and said, 'I understand that you will never tell me if this woman is being cared for in one of your refuges. Women's safety first – I really get that. But if she is, please would you give her this letter? I'm distributing six letters. They're addressed to every charity I know in the area that supports a hostel or a refuge. It isn't just Women's Aid. So if she does get in touch with me it won't compromise your security.' I showed her the remaining two envelopes.

'I'm just a volunteer,' she said, shoving a pair of half-glasses onto her nose and examining the envelopes. 'I don't know where the refuges are, let alone who is staying there.'

Just then, BZee came out of his corner wearing the red shirt and black jeans.

'The devil's colours,' the volunteer murmured. 'Young man, you'll need a belt if you want to keep your backside covered.' She pointed him to a rack of belts. 'Okay,' she said while he was trying on belts. 'I'll pass your letter on to head office and let someone responsible decide what to do. I hope there's nothing criminal or private in there because I'm pretty sure someone will open it.'

'I should hope so,' I said righteously.

BZee came back wearing a sort of cowboy belt with an elaborate brass buckle that was, like everything else, too big for him.

The old woman sighed and brought out an ancient hole-punch from a shelf under the counter. She handed it to me and I punched a hole where BZee told me to.

The old woman charged me thirty pounds and five pence for everything. The five pence were for the used plastic bag BZee needed to carry his old clothes in.

'Need shoes,' the ungrateful little toad said, by way of thanks.

'Not here,' the volunteer said, waving us goodbye as we set off for the next venue.

'You think Petra like?' BZee fingered the cuff of his new previously-owned shirt. 'Red her favourite colour.'

'It's very red,' I said. 'You seeing Petra?'

'Sometimes,' he said, not looking at me.

'What about her mother?'

He shrugged. 'I bad influence.'

'You can make that work for you,' I said, remembering the lure of the Bad Boy when I was just pre-teens, and suffocating in respectability.

'Sometimes,' he admitted. 'Sometimes not much.'

'But you got her bike back.'

'No one told Mama 'bout her bike gone,' he said. 'That the point.'

'Petra knows.'

'Yeah,' he said, smiling at last.

Our next stop was the St Swithins charity shop where BZee once again earned me points by trying on and yearning for a pair of nearly new Nike running shoes in racing green with orange go-faster stripes.

I argued for the plain white Reebok tennis shoes which looked more practical and weren't so expensive. I gave in when BZee complained loudly that I had 'old lady' taste. The elderly gent behind the counter couldn't help laughing but promised to see that my Paulina letter went to 'someone in charge.'

That left Women and Children First. But I was grumbling that the economy was so awful I couldn't even afford charity shop prices which disgusted BZee to the point where he peeled away and ran off without saying goodbye. That, I thought, should teach me not to buy him running shoes.

As I trudged on alone the sky began to darken. It wasn't a slow build-up of cloud-cover – more like a black curtain being drawn across the sky. There was a sudden flash of white light and a simultaneous crack of thunder so loud that everyone out on the street stopped in their tracks and then ran for cover even before the rain fell on us like a burst dam. I was already drenched to the bone before I could find a doorway that wasn't sheltering ten people. The road turned instantly from melting tarmac to a river that blocked all the drains. But the temperature remained unbearable. Traffic slowed to a stop and drivers turned on their headlights.

The raindrops were as big as grapes. It was how I imagined a tropical rainstorm would look and feel. I was thrilled and also pissed off. The envelope in my hand fell apart, almost melting in the warm water. Without the letter there was no point in going on or even standing in a doorway waiting for the deluge to stop, or for Noah's ark to show up.

Suddenly I felt as if I was on holiday. I wanted to take off my shoes and paddle in the running water. I left my doorway and took the quickest route to the Common.

29

The Common was a mess. Branches had broken off from the weight of water. My precious little dream of walking barefoot on the grass was shattered by the sight of parched brown turf and worn away patches turning into to muddy pools where dead worms were floating. We seemed to have gone through three seasons in a week.

I wanted to see if The Drain had flooded but on the way I was distracted by thoughts of the allotments so I sloshed in that direction.

I stood at the gate. Any green growth overlooked by the thieves had been flattened by the rain. The place seemed deserted. I was about to turn away, depressed, when someone called my name and I saw the Colonel waving to me from the door of his shed. I went over. He seemed almost elated. Thievery angered him, but natural disaster was energising. 'The plums were almost ready to pick anyway,' he said instead of greeting me. 'There'll be plenty on the ground that'll only take a day or two to ripen. And look, the rain's slackening off.' He was wearing thick hairy socks, his boots were upside down in front of a smelly oil stove and his raincoat was hanging, dripping, over a tripod of two hoes and a broom. He seemed to be enjoying himself. 'Reminds me of monsoons in Sri Lanka.' He rubbed his hands together. 'You look like a drowned rat. But good of you to call round to see if we're surviving.' He sounded as if he was going to offer a fellow expat a gin and tonic and a bowl of cheese straws to go with the 'sun-downer'.

'How're you all doing?' I asked as if that was what I'd come for.

'We're gardeners.' He bellowed with laughter. 'We expect the worst and hope for the best. Scratch the skin off any one of us and you'll find an optimist underneath.'

'How true,' I murmured, because I'd just caught sight of a rather large flask lying on the work bench beside a bunch of flower pots.

My phone buzzed. It was Candice who said, 'I saw you arrive. Is Rupert sozzled yet?'

So the Colonel was a Rupert. 'Not entirely,' I said. 'How are you?'

'I'm at Yurek and Magda's. Come over?'

'Okay.' I cut the call and turned to the Colonel, saying, 'I'm going over to Magda's shed.'

'Well,' he said, 'I'm not putting on wet boots just for a slice of cake. Stay and have a proper drink.'

Sharing a flask of un-named booze with a Rupert was not on my wish-list so I went out into the rain again and puddle-jumped my way to Magda's larger, warmer potting shed.

She greeted me with a mug of hot strong tea and a thick slice of Victoria sponge.

'How's Rupert?' Candice asked anxiously. 'He's a teddy bear normally, but I, er, don't like him much when he's drunk.'

I said, 'He's certainly drinking, but I really don't know how drunk he is.'

'One follows other,' Magda said, sympathetically topping up Candice's mug with hot tea. 'Nothing you can do to stop night follow day.'

I warmed my hands on the mug. And then remembered to check in my computer bag. It was made from heavy-duty canvas, but nothing could have saved the contents from the storm. I opened it. Magda gave me a dry cloth to wipe down my iPad but my notebooks were soggy and a lot of the notes were illegible.

'Effin'ell!' I exclaimed. I'd just found at the bottom of the bag a sopping wet tissue with liquid mud attached. 'I need proper evidence bags,' I said out loud. Actually sandwich bags or freezer bags would've done just as well, but I hadn't thought, now that I was no longer a cop but not yet a kosher PI, that I'd be collecting evidence.

'What?' said Candice.

Yes, what was I? I thought, suddenly gloomy. Just a short order cook masquerading as a glorified problem-solver.

I scooped up the tissue and mud into a cupped hand and held it out. 'I went to Father and Mother Earth yesterday, and collected some of the dirt clinging to the spuds. I thought soil analysis might connect it with the soil in whatsis-name's patch. Y'know, the guy who lost most of his potatoes – the one with the snake tattoo.'

'Harvey,' said Candice. 'What a good idea.'

'We went to Lily Daffid's shop,' Magda said, swinging her index finger from Candice to herself. 'We spoke. Yes.'

'Yes.' Candice nodded. 'Just Magda and I. The guys seemed to have made up their minds already. We didn't want a confrontation. We wanted to talk to Lily alone – without her husband. She told us she was having a real problem with supplies of fresh vegetables.'

'They collect from wide area,' Magda said, sweeping her arm in a circle. 'But petrol cost through roof. Also no drivers.'

'Also no migrant workers to pick fruit and dig veg.'

'But couldn't they use their own vans?' I asked.

'They don't have vans of their own,' Candice said. 'But she admitted that at a pinch they borrowed vans from the furniture shop, Cosy Couch Company – the van your friend BZee saw. But that was a problem because the vans had to be cleaned immaculately for transporting new furniture. Fresh produce and soft furnishings don't mix.'

'So we tell her our gardens ransacked,' Magda said, looking unhappy. 'And then she cry. Big tears.'

'She said she had nothing to do with it.' Candice took up the story. 'She told us that when she opened up the shop – it was the morning after our allotments had been raided – I checked the date, and it matched. She said she walked in and the bins and display baskets were full. Magic. It was like Veggie Santa had visited, she said.'

'She didn't ask questions?' I said, suspicious.

'She very careful with husband,' Magda said, even more unhappy. 'He has big, big temper.'

'Apparently Kyron had been out late that night delivering a double bed somewhere in Berkshire and didn't come back till four in the morning.'

'Delivering a double bed after midnight?' I said sceptically.

'I know,' Candice said. 'Lily knows too. But she was working in the shop all day, and when Kyron got up at lunchtime he went straight out to Cosy Couches, and when he came home he was in a foul mood.'

'Big temper,' Magda reminded me. 'But…' she held up one finger. 'She find his *boots*. Boots clean in afternoon, dirty, dirty, dirty next morning.' She spread her hands, appealing to me to join the two of them in an obvious deduction.

Oh the reasoning powers of ordinary, observant women! 'Okay,' I said. 'I'm with you. There *are* conclusions to be drawn. But no proof. How far do you want to pursue this?'

'You mean the police? Lawyers? Civil action? That'll be very expensive. But I'm afraid that's the direction the chaps might want to take.'

'Or everybody get bad, bad temper and fight, and bleed, and maybe die.' Magda clasped her hands under her chin as if she knew what happened when bad-tempered chaps fought each other.

Candice nodded, and in spite of my knee-jerk reaction that a clear crime required an unequivocal response from the law, I nodded too. The law had been given its chance but kicked it into touch: not important enough.

'But,' I said, holding up a warning hand. 'You'd all better control yourselves and the blokes. If this comes to violence, the police *will* get involved and they won't care who did what to who.'

'So what would you advise? We're having an allotment owners' meeting at The Red Lion this evening. Can you come?"

'I can't,' I said. 'But here's my thinking... useful?'

'Go on,' said Candice.

I held up the handful of mud and the disintegrating tissue. 'This is contaminated and useless. But Lily and Kyron don't have to know that. Why not say you can prove that they're selling, whatsisname, Harvey's spuds?'

'Tell lies?' Magda was shocked.

'Yes,' I said, 'but only if you have to. Only if Kyron wants to play rough, deny everything et cetera. Also you can say or imply that a witness can identify the van. I'm just saying that you have a couple of strategies that might prevent a legal action that none of you, Lily and Kyron included, can afford. Also I can give you a list of tariffs associated with vandalism, causing an affray, GBH and ABH that might deter the more militant-minded in your group from taking the law into their own hands.'

'Thank you,' Candice said. 'That'd be great. Anything else?'

'Well, that depends what you want. The thing is, Father and Mother Earth must be broke or they wouldn't be stealing. But you could, for instance, get the Daffids to give all of you a ten percent discount if you shop there. Or you could get them to arrange and help pay for security lights or better fencing here. Negotiate. It's so much cheaper and quicker to settle things yourself – if, that is, you can do it sensibly and don't start a vegan turf war.'

Magda was staring at me, but I noticed that Candice was recording me on her phone. I was quite proud – not many people had taken me so seriously in the past couple of years. I went on, 'See, if the bloody economy stays on the downward slope, we should all assume crash positions. Co-operation is way cheaper and safer than war.'

I could see Magda nodding vigorously, and thought, Blimey, I'm a woman of influence. Who'da thought it? Better quit while I'm ahead.

So, feeling inspirational, I took my leave and slipped and slithered through the mud towards home and dry clothes.

30

The Drain had flooded to almost twice its size. Now that the rain had slowed to a persistent drizzle it was shrinking slowly, leaving at the edges a lot of dead and dying fish, some of them still flopping desperately. A flock of screaming urban gulls was feasting and fighting over the banquet. There was a stench of death and decay.

I'd never heard of this happening before and I hurried away, disturbed and disgusted.

The Common was deserted. I'd never experienced that in daylight either. Another time I might have enjoyed it, but now, cold, drenched and uncomfortable in mind as well as body, all I wanted was to hurry home to the familiarity of a hot shower and a warm dry towel. I trudged on in squelching shoes thinking that anyone who didn't believe in a climate emergency must be blind, deaf or optimistic to the point of imbecility.

The lights were out at the Sandwich Shack. That was no surprise: heavy rain, no punters, no cash in the till – therefore no need to spend money on energy bills and of course, no Digby.

Except for a lonely compact Mercedes, the car park was empty too. It looked like one big pool of standing water though. There's always a danger of this happening, especially now when the council has cut back on clearing fallen leaves from gutters and storm drains.

So I was surprised, as I splashed past, to hear the car door slam and someone call my name.

I turned just in time to see a wine bottle flying towards me. It was attached to the hand of an angry man.

Too late I flung an arm up to save my head. But I only felt the first blow. Then I was reeling sideways, trying to control jelly legs and the angry man was coming at me with a now broken bottle.

*

I was lying face down in three inches of water, enough to drown in if I didn't turn my head. *Then* I felt the pain.

Someone said, 'I can't believe it – he was going to drive straight over her.'

'He would have if you hadn't started yelling and waving your arms. That was so brave.'

'You did too.'

'Only after you did. I was thinking, "What if he's the Death Tent killer?" I was thinking more about protecting myself. I mean us.'

I raised my head a couple of inches and choking was agony.

'Shit – they said not to move her.'

'She's got to breathe.'

'It's a *head* injury.'

'Yeah but… '

'I can't breathe,' I mumbled through blood and blubber.

'Fuck it.' It was a women's voice. 'I'll support her head and neck. You try to turn her a bit. Pass me her bag.'

Merciful blank for uncounted seconds. Then there was something rough and unyielding under my head and neck. Not a pillow.

'Thanks,' I whispered, taking some painful gulps of cold air.

*

In an ambulance, neck in neck-brace, arm in arm-brace, counting fingers, remembering prime ministers.

Time passes. I think, Hey, I don't have to drive to Watford.

*

Having my skull x-rayed, I realise I'm in the local clinic, not at St Georges. At St Georges they have all the latest scanning kit. And, after a new surge in infection rates, they have a crisis, oh, and my father, on their hands. Obviously I'm in no danger of dying or they'd have me too.

In the clinic they could spare a nurse to pick broken glass out of my face and hair. I was lucky.

*

The doc is putting stitches in my scalp, my left cheek and the side of my nose. I reek of wine.

'A nice Chianti,' she quips as she adds more piercings to my already punctured skin. 'I'm very good at this,' she adds more sympathetically. 'I got my training in Afghanistan. You won't have much scarring.'

'Thanks,' I lisp. The back teeth on that side of my mouth feel loose. A lot of the blood turns out to have come from a self-inflicted wound – I'd bitten through my tongue.

She tells me that my thick skull has not been fractured. Nor has my arm. Both areas are swollen, bruised and cut. I have a sprained wrist. My jeans are torn and my knees are grazed. Someone cleaned the grazes but I can't remember when. No one cleaned my clothes. They dried on me from the heat of my body.

Casually, she asks if I have anyone at home to look after me or bring me clean clothes. I think blurrily of Eleanor and Olive and say 'no'. She says they're keeping me in overnight for observation.

This means being woken every hour to have bright lights shone in my eyes. At five in the morning I remember to text Digby to tell him where I am and why I won't be doing the early shift.

A seven-forty, he texts back demanding to see a doctor's note.

I send him a selfie instead.

'Sexy!' he replies. But I hear no more about doctor's notes.

They brought me a cup of tea and a cheese sandwich for breakfast. I was too queasy to eat more than half of it.

At around ten a different doctor came to re-look at the x-rays and check the wounds, stitches and dressings. He pronounced me fit for release, but added, 'There are two policemen here who want to talk to you. We need the bed so you'll have to go to the waiting room.'

In the waiting room I found Toxic Tom and his mate Stoat Staunton flirting with the receptionist.

'Frankenstein's monster,' crowed Tom.

'All you need is the bolt through the neck,' added Stoat – always a follower, never a leader.

'That's not very sympathetic,' the receptionist said. But she was smiling.

A very old, overweight lady, who was knitting something tiny in electric green, snorted loudly. I was too weary to stand so I flopped down on one of the clinic's grey plastic chairs.

'Somewhere more private?' Stoat asked the receptionist.

'I'm stopping here,' I slurred. I really, *really* didn't want to go somewhere private with Tom. I wanted as many witnesses as possible.

'So, which of your admirers did that to you?' Tom began.

'Or don't you recognise them with their clothes on?' Stoat is so *very* original.

Even the receptionist looked quite shocked at this.

The old woman with the knitting harrumphed loudly, and, bless her heart, said, 'You two should be ashamed. Haven't you read the Common Echo this morning? She was attacked by the Death Tent Killer.'

'Is that what she said?' Tom looked stupefied. 'I never read the local rag.'

'Then you bleedin' should,' the old knitter wheezed. 'It might make you better informed, and less insulting to hurt women.'

Tom turned his back on her. 'So,' he said to me, 'did you recognise the person who attacked you?'

'I can't remember what happened,' I said. 'Concussion.' I tapped my head. I was thinking, I'm not telling you doodly-squat, you arsehole. You want someone to make your job easier? Go to the zoo – I'd rather help the Death Tent Killer. Another time I might've said some of those things out loud but presently I was almost too tired to think them.

'Not very co-operative,' Tom said. 'C'mon, you must've seen something.'

'Tom,' I said, almost too weary to move my swollen tongue. 'I can't even remember being in the car park, let alone what happened there.'

'Hah!' Stoat cried. 'So you *do* remember being in the car park.'

I looked at Tom. Being Stoat's mate had never caused him to be a *loyal* mate. He'd often told me Stupid Stoat stories when we were together. And, shoot me now, I used to laugh at them.

'Whenever I asked what happened, someone told me I'd been attacked in the car park,' I said, 'by a man with a bottle.'

'She would say that,' Stoat said to Tom.

'Waste of good wine,' Tom said. 'And she's a waste of good time.' He made a show of stowing his notebook in his pocket and climbing to his feet.

'Aren't you even going to give her a lift home?' the old knitter said.

But Tom just walked away without another word, followed by his lack-witted lackey.

'If no one's coming to collect you I'll call an Uber,' the receptionist offered.

'Thanks,' I said, and allowed myself five minutes to drift off – relaxation – a result of Tom and Tom's little helper going away.

But I was not at my best when I staggered out into the cold morning air to find two teenaged girls with porcupine hair and kicker boots waiting for me. There was also a reporter and a photographer. The girls closed in on either side of me as if they were propping me up – which wasn't far from the truth – and the photographer snapped off some pictures.

'Meet Sass and Mindy,' said the reporter. 'They saved your life. Can you remember anything about your terrifying time in the car park?'

'I'm sorry,' I said. 'I can't remember a thing.' Having said that to the police I'd have to stick to it.

'We were walking past the entrance,' said Sass or Mindy. 'And we saw you on the ground.'

'And we saw this guy,' said Mindy or Sass. 'He was getting into his car and it looked like he was going to drive straight over you.'

'So Sass rushed forward, waving her arms and screaming,' said Mindy.

'And so he reversed and then drove round you and out of the car park like a bat out of hell,' finished Sass.

The reporter looked at me expectantly.

'Well, I'm very grateful,' I said. 'I don't know how to thank you properly.'

The reporter said, 'We know you work at the Sandwich Shack. Maybe you could treat the girls to a free meal?'

'Of course,' I said, with a sinking heart. 'I'd love to – as soon as I'm back at work.' I hate feeling grateful and obliged to return favours. But my sore face, aching head and bruises insisted that I did owe Sass and Mindy quite a lot. I tried to smile and felt my split lip open up again.

'She's bleeding,' the reporter said excitedly. 'Get another shot.'

'Oy,' yelled the Uber driver. 'I can't sit on a double yellow line all day.'

'We'll take you home,' Mindy decided. 'We'll see you settled.'

'No,' I said.

'Yes,' Sass said. 'You should be in bed.'

Before I could collect my scattered brains Mindy, Sass and I were crammed in the back of a pine-scented Uber and barrelling along to Eleanor and Olive's house. I didn't realise till we got there that the reporter had followed us.

I was shivering. I'd left the house in a heat-wave, got soaked in a tropical storm. The storm had brought down tons of leaves and branches. The trees, till then looking dark with late summer foliage, were now almost bare. The season had changed abruptly while I was unconscious. And I had slept in my damp summer clothes. A lot had altered for the worse since yesterday morning, and right now I couldn't cope with any of it.

Of course neither Sass nor Mindy had any money so I paid the driver with cash I still had in the back pocket of my crumpled jeans. I should look in my computer bag for my wallet, I thought. But Sass was saying, 'Have you got a can of chicken noodle soup, Hannah? That's what my mum gives me when I'm sick. Soup and toast always does the trick.'

My nan made chicken dumpling soup. We used to laugh at her for presenting it as a cure-all. But I wasn't laughing now.

I gestured at the front door and said, 'I rent a room at the top of this house. The owners are vegan. Chicken noodle soup sounds wonderful but if I allowed chicken into their kitchen I'd be evicted.'

'You're kidding,' Sass said.

'I'm not,' I said. 'But you're right – this is insane. I've got to find somewhere else to live. Right now all I want to do is have a hot shower and sleep for a month.'

'That's so unfair,' my teenage protectors said in unison. They were very sweet, with their aggressive hair and tough-girl boots.

I said, through split lips and swollen tongue, 'Don't worry. You've done enough and I thank you. I'm grownup and responsible for my own decisions. Some of which are crap.'

'What're you talking about?' asked the reporter who had been ear-wigging shamelessly. 'What did you do to deserve getting glassed in a car park?'

'I don't know,' I said. 'I wish I did. But I can't remember.'

'If you do, will you tell us?' Sass watched me scrabble in my bag for my keys. I gave her my phone and she entered her number on my contact list while I opened my door.

She didn't want her adventure to end like this, but I couldn't bear for it to end any other way. When I closed the door on three disappointed faces it was like leaving hungry puppies out in the cold.

See, if the cops sent out to interview what seemed to be a victim of random violence hadn't been Toxic Tom and Stoat Staunton, and if those two cops hadn't begun by insulting me, it might've been a whole other story. But, having lied to two sexist, racist, possibly bent cops with whom I had a totally diseased history, I couldn't tell the truth to an effing reporter asking the same questions, could I?

I dragged my heavy carcass upstairs one step at a time, feeling that it was my whole life. I was living one step at a time. There was no plan, no structure. All I seemed able to think about was making the rent one day at a time, forgetting that my success at this pathetic ambition could make other people very angry.

I threw my torn, crumpled, bloody clothes onto the floor and stepped into the shower. I wanted to wash my hair but was afraid of the stitches in my scalp. All the cuts and grazes burned and prickled, but after ten minutes I was as clean as I could be. Then the hot water ran out.

I didn't check my phone or iPad for messages. I turned everything off and crawled into bed.

31

I woke at midnight, almost too stiff to move and with a raging thirst. After drinking several tooth-mugsful of cold water I crept down to the kitchen. On my shelf in the fridge were one elderly pot of yoghurt and some milk. I ate the yoghurt. Then I put cornflakes and grapenuts into a bowl and poured the milk over them. I took the bowl back up to bed with me and waited for the contents to soften. Chicken dumpling soup was just a distant fantasy as I sucked the cereal slush off the teaspoon which was the only thing I could fit into my damaged gob.

I'd slept for almost twelve hours straight, so I turned out the light and tried for another twelve.

*

I almost made it. It was after eleven when I finally woke up.

Someone was knocking on the front door. I ignored it and turned on my phone instead. It started ringing immediately.

'What?' I snarled. My mouth felt as stiff and achy as the rest of me.

'It's me, Candice,' said the horribly cheerful voice. 'I'm at your front door. Let me in.'

I went down in my PJs and opened the door. There she was, oh so respectable in her Barbour raincoat, holding up a plastic container. 'Chicken noodle soup. Magda and I made some because the Common Echo Online said you didn't have any. Can I come in?'

'Okay,' I said. I could feel tears building up behind my eyes so I turned my back and led the way to the kitchen.

'I know you said this is a vegan house and you'd be evicted for bringing meat into it, but surely, under the circumstances… ?'

I was starving, so I said I'd risk it.

Candice borrowed one of Eleanor and Olive's pristine pans and heated up some of the delicious smelling concoction. I would definitely go to hell for this, I thought. But it was worth it.

'Having guests and eating at the kitchen table are against the rules too,' I remarked to Candice who was sitting across from me while I ate. 'It was the best I could do at the time, but I really must find somewhere better.'

'After the Echo piece, you might have some offers.' She took her phone out of her bag, found the article and began to read out loud while I sucked soup off a spoon. 'The headline is "Local Angel of Mercy Attacked in Car Park".'

'*Excuse me?*' I protested.

'Don't blame me,' she said grinning broadly. 'I didn't write it. Anyway, it calls you "A good deed in a naughty world", and it says you feed hungry children, find lost dogs and return stolen bicycles. You kept the café open single-handed during the worst of the pandemic when there was nowhere else to go. You work tirelessly for homeless charities. And you refused to co-operate when the café owner wanted to make it a card-only business.'

'*Whoa!*' I said. 'I only did that to annoy Digby. Where's my well-earned reputation for bad temper, foul language and bolshieness?'

'Air-brushed out. Your character is spotless. The trouble is that those two girls must've told the reporter that they thought your attacker was the Death Tent Killer, and she's bucking for a job with one of the sensationalist papers. I tried to look her up, but I think she's just done an online course in online journalism. She seems to have dramatised and misrepresented just about everything.'

'Who are the kids?' I asked. I was trying to eat as much soup as possible. I couldn't even imagine the consequences of polluting the vegan fridge with the remainder.

'Good, aren't they?' Candice said with a smile. She consulted her phone again. 'They're both fourteen years old and go to St Michael's Comprehensive. They call themselves New Punks and Rebels, but they did a mini course in First Aid last term. Actually I think you were very lucky they were passing – they were positive you were going to be run over.' She considered me shrewdly for a moment. 'You don't seem surprised. Hannah – you *do* know who the man is.'

'No, I've absolutely no idea who the Death Tent Killer is,' I said, giving her my direct I'm-honest gaze.

She laughed. 'I'm sure that's literally true,' she said. 'But you *do* know who attacked you, don't you?'

I put my spoon down. Kind Candice had stopped being my favourite person.

'And don't you narrow your eyes at me,' she went on mildly. 'I used to be a deputy head teacher at an all-girls' school, and I have an advanced degree in the body language of female liars using literal truths in a dishonest way.'

My speciality, I thought ruefully. We stared at each other. I wasn't at my best so I broke first. I said, 'Okay, but if you tell anyone – anyone at all – I'll drench your whole plot with weed killer and salt. You won't be able to grow anything for years.'

She nodded. 'Probably for decades. Not very trusting, are you?'

'You be me,' I replied. 'I've been a mug too many times.'

'It's better to trust than not to trust.'

'Not in *my* life.'

'All right,' she said. 'There's a story I know nothing about, and it's your decision to tell or not to tell.'

'That's right,' I said. But just then I didn't know if we were talking about my whole-life experience of treachery and betrayal, or simply the bloke in the car park.

I said, 'I lied to the police. The man in the car park is the cheating husband of a woman I did a job for a few days ago. I gave her the information she wanted and he must've found out the informant was me. He was insanely angry, so maybe she's claiming all the community property.'

Candice nodded. 'And you couldn't tell the police without breaching confidence? But surely the violent attack on you trumps your protection of your client's privileged information?'

I was stunned. The idea that I owed Mrs Reynolds or her lying, cheating husband privacy had never crossed my mind. People seemed, at the moment, to be falling over themselves to assign to me better motives than I had. It was ludicrous but useful, so I said, 'People need to be able to trust me.'

'But that should work both ways, shouldn't it? The woman you were working for shouldn't have told her husband about you.'

I hadn't thought about that either. I said, 'The information needn't have come from her. Also, Candice, I get most of my jobs from word-of-mouth recommendations.'

'And, I suppose, most of your beatings too,' she said dryly. 'Speaking of which, your advice was very effective at our meeting last night. And at the meeting we had with Lily and Kyron Daffid this morning. I'm mentioning this because Kyron wanted to bluster his way out of all the accusations and kept saying, "Who told you that? It's all lies." He's very bombastic. Yurek practically had to sit on the Colonel's head to stop him retaliating. I don't think anyone mentioned your name, but I can't swear to it. So watch your back.'

'Did the women manage to keep a lid on things?'

'Just about.' She smiled again. 'And we were partially successful. As you speculated Father and Mother Earth is hanging on by a thread. They're thinking of closing down completely and declaring bankruptcy – which actually would be in nobody's interest. So we settled for a five percent discount and they're definitely going to help with the fencing.' She sighed. 'Magda and I were wondering if we couldn't put on some sort of benefit for them. You know, like a vegan picnic.'

'Bloodyell,' I said. 'Isn't that taking forgiveness a bit far?'

'Sort of a "Truth and reconciliation" day,' she said. 'Do you think the Shack might want to be involved?'

I laughed, which hurt my face quite badly. 'What, *Digby?* Going all Nelson Mandela? And *vegan?* I think it's one hundred percent against his religion.'

'Now *there's* a challenge,' she said thoughtfully. She took the pan and my empty bowl and washed them thoroughly. She packed up the left-overs, promising faithfully to give them to BZee. Then she left having ordered me back to bed – an order I was only too happy to obey.

I slept without moving for another three hours, so it was mid afternoon before I woke with enough energy to look at texts, emails and phone messages.

These began with the usual collection from Myles, Sophia and others wanting to know why the hell I hadn't been in touch. Then the tone changed. I suppose it was when the Echo's creative interpretation of my 'accident' in the car park began to get around.

To Myles and Sophia I wrote,' Thanks for your concern. I would have driven to Watford yesterday, but I'm afraid I'll have to delay the trip for a couple of days.'

Mark Ferguson got a rather fuller apology and, inspired by Candice, I added, 'This is one of the hazards of being in a confidential business when someone wants information I have to protect.' There was no harm, I thought, in making myself out to be rather more heroic than I actually was.

I found the links to the Common Echo's articles about me and forwarded them to my brother and his wife: some nice reading matter to entertain them while they were sunning themselves on the beach. The links included the picture of me leaving the clinic all bloody and bruised, proof that I couldn't do anything helpful about our parents. There it was, in colour, in the Echo. So it must be true.

Of course there was a lot of spam, and because of that I almost overlooked an email from someone I didn't know. I was about to delete it when I noticed that the name Paulina was on the subject line.

It read, 'Paulina would not have replied to your note had she not seen the articles about you in the Common Echo. She expressed great sympathy for you as a victim of male abuse, and is prepared to trust you. Reply to this email to begin negotiations about a meeting. From the pains you took to get in touch with her, we think you are aware of the danger she's in and the need for extreme caution. Please tell no one about this.' It was signed Les Goodall.

Score!

I'd thought something out, made a plan, executed it. And scored.

On second reading though I wondered about what danger she could be in. I looked back at my notes. The most obvious danger was Kyle Yardley, the maintenance man, who she'd run off with. He'd tampered with Mark's safe, stolen a grand from Mark's desk and disappeared to somewhere close to a casino, leaving Paulina in the lurch at Heathrow Airport. I'd bet the grand was long gone. Had he been stalking Paulina? Could he still be seeing her as a cash cow? Might he have tried to blackmail her? Maybe he hadn't heard her marriage to a rich man was over. Come to think of it maybe *Paulina* didn't know that Mark wasn't trying to breathe life into a dead marriage either.

I went downstairs to make a mug of tea before replying to Les Goodall. While the kettle boiled I decided that I couldn't go far wrong by paying attention to Paulina's obvious, if mistaken, desire for secrecy.

Somehow, I fitted my split lip to the rim of the mug and drank. Then I wrote, 'Dear Les Goodall, Thank you for replying on Paulina's behalf. Please would you ask her if she would be more comfortable meeting me online than in person. I can offer Skype or WhatsApp. Very best wishes, Hannah.'

The phone rang just as I finished. It was Sid Nailer. He said, 'Sorry to hear about your trouble.'

I said, 'Thanks. It looks worse than it is.'

'I should hope so,' he said. 'You looked like one of the undead.'

I laughed. It hurt.

Sid went on. 'So who do I knock down and kick for you? Are you still concussed or has your memory come back?'

My scalp prickled. I said, 'I think I'm okay now – I've had a lot of sleep.'

'So what does the Death Tent Killer look like?' He made it sound like a joke.

I didn't laugh. 'Actually Sid, I meant I'm not concussed anymore, but I still can't remember what happened in the car park. I can't even remember *being* in the car park. All I know about it is what I've read in the Echo.'

'Really?' He sounded sceptical.

'Did Tom tell you to ring me?' There! I'd said it.

'Fuck, no!' he said. Just a micro second too late. He laughed, 'Paranoia, Hannah – not your most attractive trait.'

'Aha, the P word!' I said. 'You *have* been talking to Tom. One of his favourite insults when I was trying to get the truth out of him: "all Jews are paranoid".'

'I'm not Police any more,' he said. To an outsider this might sound like a random reply, but it wasn't.

I said, 'Nor am I. But I still know the "mates rules". And I still know they don't apply to women.'

He was silent, but he didn't ring off. So I jogged his memory. 'I'm a client now. Shouldn't different rules apply to clients? Cos if they don't, you've had your first and last jobs off of me.' I knew Sophia had paid him promptly for the information about Gina's phone because she'd told me so in her last voicemail.

'Hannah,' Sid said eventually. 'You're putting me in an awkward position.'

'You rang me – remember? Who told you to do that? Our "position" was quite clear till then.'

'So what can I tell Tom?'

'You can tell him to lick custard off his own balls,' I said. 'Or you and his other *mates* can do it for him. Your choice.' I cut the connection. My hands were sweating.

He called me back immediately. 'Listen, Hannah, I'm so sorry. I really don't want to get caught in the middle here.'

'There's no *middle* to be caught in. It isn't like a quarrel. Tom's choosing to harass me long after he shot our relationship down. I'm not harassing *him*. I'm out of it, long gone. Where's the "middle" in that, Sid?' I was shaking with anger. Tom still thought there was an advantage to be had from hurting me.

'What's his game now?' I blurted out.

'Oh crap.' Sid sounded tired and... could he possibly be *embarrassed*? 'I think he's got it in for Mwezi. I think he's really pissed that someone like her got promoted over him. I think he's trying to use you to get a leg up with the Tent Killer enquiry.'

It was my turn to be silent for a few beats. Of course! Of *course* Chloe Mwezi would be everything Tom despised about so-called 'inclusive policing'.

In the end I said, 'Sid, you've got to walk away from old, tired, poisonous cop culture. It can only harm you if you want to make a success of your new business. The world is a way bigger place than just a bunch of white men scratching each other's backsides and feeling superior. You're within a fraction of an inch of losing another paying client.'

I was afraid he'd be hacked off with me for saying this. But he only sighed and said, 'I was a cop for a long time, Hannah.'

'I know,' I said. 'A long time of pretty effective mind control – brain washing, in fact. I'm not immune either, and I'm not a white male.'

There was another pause. Then he said, 'My missus said something similar just the other day.' Another pause, longer this time.

Suddenly tired and bored, I said, 'Your missus might be right.'

'That's what *she* says.'

'So? What's up, Sid? You got something else to say?'

'Listen Hannah,' he said in a rush. 'I swear it wasn't anything to do with me. And you didn't hear it from me. Okay? But there's pictures of you and Mwezi. I mean pictures of you *with* Mwezi. *With*. Know what I mean? It's all deep-faked, with girl-on-girl porn obviously. And Hannah, I don't know who posted it. I'll *never* know that. Gottit?'

'Where?' I was shocked.

'YouTube.' Sid sounded miserable. 'FaceBook. Instagram – you name it.'

'*Son of a syphilitic snake!*' I didn't know where to begin. 'How long's it been up?'

'Since the Echo started the Saint Hannah stuff.'

'Take it down, Sid,' I said. 'You're supposed to be Mr Techspert.'

'*Don't you shout at me!*' he shouted. 'I told you. I didn't do it!'

My head was ready to explode. I took a deep breath and said, 'Isn't deep-faking illegal, Sid? It fucking should be, if it isn't. You can take it down without being caught, can't you? Or report it? How would you feel if someone did this to your wife? It's worse than harassment. What's it going to do to Chloe Mwezi's career? Look what those shower pics did to me! Remember that, Sid? Did you think that was fair, Sid? Or was it so funny you didn't even consider whether it was fair on not? Is that it, Sid? It's okay to wreck a woman's life if you get a laugh out of it?'

'Calm down, Hannah. Please.' He sounded upset. But I was too distressed to believe him.

He went on, 'I'll do everything I know how to take the effing lot down anonymously. And I'll report it. Maybe the Sex Crimes bods are already on it. But you gotta swear you won't nark on me, y'know, to whoever you think did it.'

I was exhausted when I put the phone down. All I wanted to do was to cover my head with a blanket and never show my face again. Instead I phoned Chloe Mwezi. She didn't answer so I left a message.

Sorting through the rest of my messages, texts and emails seemed too much like work I wasn't up to.

I was about to bury my head under the pillow when someone tapped on my door. It could only be one of my landladies. Arguing with them about using unauthorised saucepans was something else I couldn't face. I would have pretended to be asleep but Olive opened the door uninvited and came in. She was carrying a small tray which she handed me before sitting down on my one and only chair. On the tray were a mug of green tea and a plateful of mashed potatoes. I only just managed to stop myself from bursting into tears.

She said, 'I know you think our beliefs are ridiculous, Hannah, and that what we're trying to achieve is rigid and restrictive to you, but we care about the future of the planet, about biodiversity and sustainable farming methods. We're really trying to find a more rational way of living. And I'm really sorry it doesn't include chicken noodle soup when you need it. But I hope you'll accept some mash made with organic, locally grown potatoes, vegan butter and kosher salt.'

'That's so kind,' I stammered. 'I don't think your beliefs are ridiculous, honestly. The chicken noodle soup was someone else's idea. It was kindly meant, but tactless.'

Olive continued, 'And now we know that lodging in our house doesn't suit you. Even so, we hope you'll take time to heal properly before you start looking for somewhere else to live.'

Clearly Eleanor and Olive read the Echo. I should've kept that in mind when mouthing off in front of a reporter. Now I was being passive-aggressively evicted for my own good.

'I'm sorry you feel so unappreciated,' I said. 'This is a clean, well-organised house and I've always felt safe here.' I touched my stitched up face with trembling fingers. Two could play the guilt game, I thought.

I put a forkful of the mash into my mouth. It was smooth and not at all bad. It didn't need chewing and my teeth were grateful.

I went on, 'This is so generous of you. I apologise for bringing the results of male violence to your house. I can't remember what happened, but I must've made the man who did this very angry.'

'Don't you *ever* blame yourself for male violence,' Olive said forcefully. 'Women are *never* to blame for that.'

After she'd gone, and before going back to bed I thought two things: one was schizo – real woman, me, agreed with Olive, but cop-woman, me, thought that she was making a knee-jerk political statement that I didn't agree with at all. The other, muzzier, thought was that maybe I'd just eaten the last of Snakeman's organic, locally grown potatoes. Stolen goods. Was I an accessory?

32

Next morning the phone woke me at seven o'clock. It was Chloe Mwezi so I answered. She said, 'Did you look at the postings? Was that why you called me yesterday?' Her soft musical voice sounded stiffer, even a bit rattled.

In my experience it's not a good idea to talk to police while lying down. I sat up. 'I didn't look. I was told. Is it very bad?'

'Bad, yes. But also badly done – obvious fake.'

'Obvious is good,' I said. I was thinking about Tom who always bought the latest hardware, apps and gismos but was too impatient to learn how to use them properly. He seemed to think that the skill should be included in the package the device came in.

'Do you know who's responsible?' I asked.

'I thought you might know,' she said.

'There's an obvious suspect, but no proof. Which leads me to ask if it was you who sent the obvious suspect and his partner, Staunton, to the clinic to question me.'

'I did not.' She sounded almost grim. 'I did not at that time know how badly you had been hurt. I was making such an enquiry when I learned that two officers had already used their own initiative. Both have been reprimanded.' She paused, then went on, 'You have a history with this "obvious suspect" of course. So I wondered if he was punishing me for censuring him, *and* punishing you for lying about what happened in the car park.'

'Yes,' I said. 'I wondered the same thing myself. But when I was questioned it was very soon after the incident and I was really confused. Concussion – I'm sure the attending medics will confirm that. But the two officers treated me as if I was being wilfully obstructive.'

'And since then?'

'I've slept like a marathon runner after a race. I can now tell you that I *do* know who attacked me. It was another angry man connected with a surveillance job I did for a local woman. And I don't want to press charges. There's an issue of confidentiality.'

'I'm sorry, but you are a private citizen.' Mwezi quite suddenly stopped being a co-victim of male sexual abuse. 'You cannot claim privilege. If you refuse to answer official questions I will be obliged to charge you with obstruction. This, of course, is an *unofficial* chat. I do not have to write down or otherwise record what you say. So I will not be obliged to act on information received. I am using my own phone. I am not in the station.'

I thought about this for a moment or two. Then, deciding to trust her, I said, 'The man who attacked me is Ryan Reynolds.' I gave her his address, assuming Mrs R had not already chucked him out on his arse. 'But,' I added, 'I am *not* making an official complaint. My reputation has taken a few too many knocks lately.'

'So has mine.' She coughed. I could almost hear her sliding back into her professional self. 'Then how did the rumours about Deena Barrymore's killer occur?'

'I suppose it was fourteen-year-old girls plus an ambitious journalist who put a large dose of hogwash and excitement together to make a drama. But, Sergeant Mwezi, do you have a minute for a question?'

'Go on.'

'Remember, in my statement, when I told you about the big guy I'd pegged as a rugby player who trained on the Common? The one who came and hustled Deena away when she was making a nuisance of herself at the Shack?'

'I remember.'

'Well, I was told later that both Deena's sons play with that team. And then the two young women who owned the tent Deena was found in showed up in men's sweaters about a hundred sizes too big. It's probably nothing – two girls vacating their own tent to hook up with two guys after a homeless charity event. No big deal. But I wondered if any of the dots joined up.'

'Dots?' Mwezi asked stiffly.

'Connections,' I said, wishing I'd never started. Mwezi obviously didn't like not knowing stuff – what cop does? 'I mean, rugby players, sons, big guys, big sweaters, at least one guy who knew the girls' tent would probably be empty all night?'

There were a few seconds of loaded silence. Then she said, 'I must insist that you do not share this speculation with anyone, especially journalists.' She sounded even more buttoned up.

'Of *course* not,' I was offended. Just a couple of minutes ago we were both victims of male sexual abuse. Now she was an officer of the law while I was just a know-nothing nobody who couldn't be trusted.

'Very well.' Mwezi rang off.

'Very well, my big bum,' I hissed into the empty air and crept downstairs to make a mug of hot, strong tea.

I needed it. My next call was from Digby.

'Status?' he demanded.

'Good morning, Digby,' I slurred, sounding as injured as I possibly could. 'How are you? I hope you slept well.'

'Don't bullshit me. I'll need a doctor's note if you want any more days off work.'

'Okay,' I said equably. 'But I'll need another day off to arrange that. You know – the NHS is in crisis. It took me hours to even talk to a receptionist, let alone a doctor. I tried first thing this morning and the automated message told me I was fifty-seventh in the queue.' The lie slipped so easily off my tongue I was almost shocked. But not quite. I could hear Digby growling. Yes, *growling*.

Eventually he said, 'Okay, Hannah, you win. I have to go to the wholesaler, and Dulcie still can't cope with the lunch rush by herself. Can you come in at around eleven and stay till it's over?'

I let my silence mature like a fine old cheese.

'*Please,*' he said furiously. 'And I'll say no more about a sick note.'

'Big of you,' I said sweetly, knowing it would annoy the crap out of a little person.

It did. He ditched the call. I am *so* not a nice woman.

Next, I looked at emails and found, to my relief, a reply from Les Goodall saying that all Paulina wanted was for me to arrange the return of her passport and birth certificate from her ex husband. But there were unspecified difficulties. I couldn't see what the problems were, but quickly sent a note saying I hoped very soon to make a suggestion acceptable to both parties. Then I wrote to Mark Ferguson saying that I had made contact with Paulina and that she seemed to be well and wanted her documents.

I glanced in the mirror on my way to the shower and then stared, shocked, at my stitched-up, rainbow face, the shaved patch above my left ear and my half-closed left eye. It had never been a pretty face in the conventional sense but now there were no two ways about it – I was ugly and I didn't want Mark Ferguson to see me that way.

I'd been beaten. I'd had a bottle broken against my head. Glassed. South London Kisses. Worst was the defenceless, unsafe, humiliated look in my one and a half eyes. Come to think of it I had the same expression I'd seen in women like Paulina and Dulcie's eyes. No, I certainly didn't want to meet Mark Ferguson looking like that.

What I needed was a bracing fight with Digby. I wanted to trade insults with someone I hated. I wanted to win.

I showered thinking about Digby. He was a rotten boss and a bit of a crook. He exploited the weak and he was my enemy. No doubt about that. But did I actually hate him? I knew where I was with him. He didn't pretend to like me or fancy me. When he tried to deceive me it was always for short-term gain to do with time and money, and sooner or later, I was always on to him. He never disappointed me because I always expected the worst. He couldn't hurt me because I didn't love him. It was, in many ways, as open and honest a relationship as any I'd ever had.

I was in my bathrobe when Eleanor knocked and came into my room. In all the time I'd lived under their roof until now, neither Eleanor nor Olive had ever come in. While I was there, I mean. I knew they came in and inspected while I was out because every now and then they'd leave me stuffy little warning notes about cleaning hair out of the trap in the shower or washing the window. Now it was twice in two days.

Eleanor handed me a bowl of her very own home-made muesli. It looked like horse feed floating in oat milk. Who knew you could milk an oat?

I hid my fear for my sore mouth and thanked her. I didn't believe my landladies were acting out of genuine sympathy or kindness. I thought they were trying to prove to me and readers of the Echo that they were sweet, fluffy women. But what do I know? I'm a suspicious, mean-minded ex cop. And I suppose, in my present state of decrepitude, I don't need kindness to be genuine. All the same I want my enemies to show themselves in their true colours. I don't want the women who're aiming to evict me to bring me food and pretend they care. I'd rather be attacked in a car park.

No I wouldn't. I was over-thinking and confusing myself.

Just then Mark Ferguson rang. He said, 'Very well done, Hannah, good work.'

I straightened my aching shoulders and glowed with the warmth of his voice.

'I can't tell you how relieved I am that you've made contact and that she's safe and well. Where is she? When can I see her?'

'Slow down,' I said quickly. 'We haven't got to that yet.'

'What do you mean?' He sounded as if I'd offered him a gift and then snatched it away.

'Wait,' I said. 'I told you that it looked as if we'd have more chance of success if she came to me rather than me aggressively pursuing her. I thought it was most likely that she'd be living in some sort of women's shelter. If that was true I'd have to work very cautiously indeed. Shelters are notoriously secretive about and protective of their residents. So I don't know where she is. All I've done is to make her and a carer, Les, feel safe enough to contact me.'

'Les?' Mark said flatly. 'Who's he?'

'I don't know. And I shan't ask yet.'

'I mustn't make assumptions and get ahead of myself,' he said sounding contrite. 'And of course I don't want to scare anyone off. But if she wants her passport et cetera there'll have to be safeguards, won't there?'

'Yes,' I said, although I hadn't yet thought it through. 'They're official documents that shouldn't get into the wrong hands. Does she have a Maltese passport?'

'Yes,' he said. 'And Malta's in the European Union, so it's quite a valuable document. The safest thing I can think of would be if I could put it directly into her hands.'

'I agree,' I said. 'But there may be difficulties because of the shelter's protocol. Let me think about it and I'll get back to you.'

In fact, I couldn't think at all. My head was banging and conversation was hard because my tongue was too big and my lip was stitched. I was wasting a lot of energy trying to sound strong and competent. I managed to finish the call without giving the game away but then I took two pain killers and lay down.

33

I wore a Chicago Cubs baseball cap to hide the head wound and to shade my eyes. All the same Digby said, 'Try not to frighten the customers.'

Dulcie said, 'You should be home in bed.'

Digby said, 'She would be if you could manage on your own.'

I said, 'I would be if you weren't so effing mean about sick pay.'

He said, 'You aren't as sick as you're ugly.'

I said, 'If ugly was a race, you'd win by a country mile.' I was feeling better already.

To Dulcie's obvious relief he left with a sour grin. She said, 'He's been horrible. I think he was really worried about you.'

'No he wasn't,' I said.

'No, he wasn't,' she agreed, blushing. 'And he had to give me a raise or I wouldn't have come back.'

'Well, look at *you!*' I said. 'Well done. What happened?'

'My nan was really sick,' she said, handing me a clean apron. 'But he wouldn't give me any time off and he still expected me to go round to his place between six and seven every night. Know what I mean?'

'Please don't tell me,' I said. 'What then?'

'My nan died.' Tears welled up in her eyes. 'So I didn't have to stay home and care for her after all. And my step-dad said I'd have to go back to work cos he wasn't going to let me live in his flat rent-free. But I remembered what you said, so I went round to the Angela House assisted living place and asked about a job.'

I tied the apron on and took latex gloves from the box under the counter.

237

I decided to make another batch of mac-cheese on the grounds that I'd probably be able to eat it myself if I over-cooked it.

While I was assembling the ingredients Dulcie served a few coffees and pastries.

'You were right, Hannah,' she said, when she finished. 'They really do need me there. But I have to have some training before I can start, and they can't do that till next week. But I filled out all the forms.'

She served another pair of customers and then, almost mumbling, said, 'I gave your name as a reference. Do you mind?'

'Course not,' I said. 'You go for it, hear?'

'You aren't going to tell Digby, are you?' she asked.

'Absolutely not,' I said, and then I got busy cooking and slapping sarnies together while she made coffees and cleaned tables.

After a while I stopped keeping an eye on her. Something was changing: she spoke to customers while looking them in the eye, and she didn't wait for me to give her orders before doing what needed to be done. The customers, however, took up a lot of time, commenting on my appearance and asking what happened and repeating silly questions about what the Death Tent Killer looked like.

Some of the regulars gave me a round of applause for having cooked mac and cheese while wounded. And the Common or Garden people sent a three-woman delegation with a tin of banana bread.

In fact I attracted quite a crowd. I would've been touched if I'd been a nicer person who was less busy and less self-conscious about her messed up face. Also the headache had marched back in army boots.

But I was pleased to see BZee who sidled in as the lunch rush began to subside. We hid him in a corner and fed him two burgers, a mountain of fries and a hefty wedge of coffee cake. In return he demonstrated his sense of humour by calling me 'Zombie Lady' at every opportunity. That'll teach me to waste my short supply of human kindness on him.

At two o'clock, I sat down at an indoor table, leaned forward and cradled my thumping head on the crook of my arm. I closed my eyes. I was vaguely remembering sitting in my car in the dark, watching a bedroom window. Behind the curtains, Ryan Reynolds was having a way better time than me. He didn't know I was there. He didn't know he was being followed. He didn't know my name, or how to find me. I didn't exist. I simply had to sit there, camera ready, and wait. The task was not to go to sleep. The task was... and then Dulcie shook my shoulder.

'Sorry, sorry,' she said.

I croaked, 'He didn't know my name or where to wait for me. Until his fucking wife told him.'

'What?' she said. 'Hannah, there's someone waiting to see you.'

'Who?'

'I dunno. An old lady. Very posh.'

'Give her a hot drink. On the house. I need to pull myself together.'

I staggered to the loo to wash my hands. I was still in my greasy apron. According to my phone I'd been asleep for twenty minutes. According to the mirror above the basin I was, as BZee said, a Zombie Lady. There was nothing to be done about it except remove the apron and straighten my baseball cap.

The posh old lady was, of course, Sophia Smithson. She was tall, thin and dressed in navy blue linen. She leant on a black cane. In other words she looked exactly like she sounded on the phone.

'You shouldn't be working,' she said, without even a greeting.

Already she was telling me what to do. All I could think of to say was, 'Come through to the office.' Then to Dulcie, 'Would you bring me a black coffee and plenty of sugar.'

'Coming up,' Dulcie said cheerfully. 'And a hot chocolate for the lady.'

'Thanks,' I said.

I sat in Digby's enormous office chair behind the desk. Sophia took the hard chair opposite, and sat yard-stick straight with her gnarly fingers folded over the handle of her cane.

She said, 'Myles insisted that I come. In my opinion he should have waited a couple of days. Sometimes even *I* cannot dissuade him from a foolish course of action.'

I was searching for the bottle of paracetamol Digby keeps in his desk drawer. I could only nod. My head didn't approve.

'What can I do for you?' My voice sounded muffled by too much tongue.

'Myles wants a situation report. He wants to know if you are fit to drive to Watford. And before you think he's heartless – yes he *is* a mono-maniac – he can't help it. But he was concerned that you might have been attacked by an imaginary Azerbaijani hit man, even though the online news stream he was reading had an equally ridiculous theory. It's part of his condition to place himself at the centre of whatever situation is current, and he thought he might be responsible for your injuries, and that by sending you back to Hertfordshire he was putting you in more danger. Having said all that, yes, he does want you to go back there.'

I would've laughed except my mouth hurt. Dulcie came in with two mugs and saved me from an immediate reply.

When she'd gone, I said, 'Funnily enough I was on my way to pick up my car for the drive north when the attack happened. I'd had to wait out the storm so I was later than I would've liked. It had nothing to do with Gina or the people she was involved with. And the Echo Online is full of sh… completely inaccurate.'

'So you do know who assaulted you?'

Everyone wanted to know that. I said, 'Yes, so do the police. Don't worry, Myles is in no danger from his association with me.'

'I wasn't… ' she began, and then gave her weird little bark that was supposed to be a laugh. 'Yes, of course I was worried. And of course he was too.'

'So,' I said, 'to be clear – neither you or Myles have anything to fear. But I won't be driving to Watford today. Tomorrow possibly. I wouldn't mind a progress report from you though.'

'Very well.' She took a typed sheet from her handbag and slid it across the desk. 'As you will see, the Neurological Society is active in Watford – which is where your contact located Gina's phone. They have on their books a counsellor by the name of Rafael Freshford. He also works for a mental health facility in Langley Road, Watford. I've included a phone number. But you were correct about the security with which these people surround themselves. I'll leave that to you.'

Rafael the 'angel' slotted into place, a missing piece not missing anymore. I couldn't understand why I felt almost tearful. I buried my face in the coffee mug and then read what was written on the sheet of paper. When I could, I said, 'Thank you, Ms Smithson. You've been an enormous help.'

She looked surprised. 'Well, without the information you supplied I wouldn't have known where to begin.'

Blimey, I thought, after she stalked out like the Lady of the effing Manor, you can find allies in the oddest damn places.

The temperature dropped again as I scurried home, checking out parked cars and recessed doorways, constantly looking over my shoulder for would-be assassins. I hated my own wussiness, but I couldn't stop.

The wind came in gusts from the west, bearing rain. After the suffocating heat followed by the tropical storm this felt like normal autumn weather. I used to complain about normal but these days it feels like a blessing.

My phone pinged four times, but I didn't answer. All I wanted was to lie still in a dark room and maybe eat the overcooked mac and cheese I'd put aside for myself.

I was done for the day but the day wasn't done with me. The first saved message was from my Aunt Esther who said, 'Hannah dear, please come and sit with your mother on Monday while I go to the dentist. It's an emergency appointment and I really can't miss it.'

The second was from Carl Barber. He said, 'Sergeant Mwezi wants to interview me again today at five. Please would you come with me?'

Thirdly, Mwezi herself said, 'I need to review your testimony regarding the Barrymore brothers and the Durham cousins on the night and morning of the Big Sleep Out.'

Mark Ferguson said, 'I'd like to talk about safeguards we need to put in place when returning Paulina's documents.'

Everyone had urgent, justified claims on me. I didn't even take my shoes off when I fell onto my bed and closed my eyes.

When I woke up nearly two hours later it was because one of my wobbly back teeth was hurting. This was why the first call I made was to my aunt Esther. I asked her when her dentist's appointment was. Nine-thirty, she told me. Could I get to her house by nine o'clock to be on the safe side?

'Hannah, dear,' she went on, 'I know you're most frightfully busy. I wouldn't ask except your mother has Covid and in any case can't be left alone. But I've had an abscess for nearly a month and I can't cope. So *please* come.'

I told her I'd tested negative for the virus, so she said I'd have to wear a mask and that there was hand sanitizer in every room. 'I'm trying not to get infected myself,' she said without much hope. 'If I do, the dentist will refuse to treat me.'

She then warmed my heart by criticising my brother for abandoning his mother for selfish, frivolous reasons. She used, for her, quite strong language and she even quoted the Talmud. I'm small-minded enough to enjoy hearing my righteous brother who can do no wrong being slagged off.

I rang Digby to say that I needed to take another sick day. He said my job was hanging by a thread. I didn't believe him. Threats are expected – they seem to be a cherished facet of our relationship.

I left a message for Chloe Mwezi saying I'd be at home all afternoon if she wanted to come and see me or call, but that I was in bed.

I did *not* say that to Mark Ferguson. I sent a voicemail in my most competent tones to say that I'd try to arrange a secure exchange as soon as possible.

I looked at my watch and saw that it was nearly five o'clock – too late to help Carl Barber with his police interview. I texted him: So sorry, I wish you'd given me more notice but I really can't come now.

I don't know why I'm so reluctant to admit to men, except for Digby, that I'm not well enough to do what they're asking me to do. Sorry Digby, you irredeemable egotist, I do not walk this earth solely to do your bidding.

But against all my instincts for survival I decided I'd have to go to sit with my mother at Aunt Esther's. Maybe it was just to prove I was a better person than my brother. But I promised myself it would be a one-time-only offer.

34

Fortunately, nothing much happened on Sunday – everyone, it seemed was taking a day off. But on Monday morning, without any hope in my heart, I went to Aunt Esther's small house in Lambeth.

My mother was sitting in a wheelchair. She was dressed in a quilted housecoat and fluffy slippers.

Aunt Esther was wearing a grey suit that exactly matched her hair. Worryingly her skin was grey too. Having toothache and a batty sister-in-law in her front room can do that to a woman.

The TV was showing re-runs of Murder She Wrote and my mother was staring vacantly at it. She'd put on a lot of weight since the last time I saw her.

'Look, Ruthy,' Aunt Esther said in a bright tone of voice that was also close to bawling. 'Look who's come to see you!'

When there was no response, she added, 'It's Hannah.' Long pause, then, 'Your *daughter*. Isn't that nice?'

At last my mother looked at me. 'You're ugly,' she said clearly so that there'd be no mistake. Another pause. Then, 'I don't like you. Go away.'

'Oh *Ruthy*,' Aunt Esther said, so sadly that I felt she was the one who needed comfort.

'It's okay, Aunty.' I gave her a perfunctory hug. 'She's felt like that for as long as I can remember. She won't change now.'

'Maybe it's because you're wearing a mask,' she said hopefully. 'And you're so cut and bruised. I do wish you'd told me, dear; I'd have tried to make other arrangements.'

'Aren't we a pair?' I pointed to her swollen jaw. 'Go and get your tooth fixed. We'll be alright here.'

She was gone for over two hours and when she came back she was haggard and her mouth was bleeding. 'The butcher pulled the tooth out,' she lisped through numb lips. 'I'm sorry, I'll have to lie down.'

So I sat with my mother in front of the endless stream of classic stories from Cabot Cove, wishing my problems were easy enough to solve in forty-five minutes with a cheery smile.

Instead of suffering from PI envy I caught up with my electronic messages.

Once, my mother said, 'Where's my tea?'

When I brought it to her she drank three-quarters of it and then threw the mug at me.

'Bitch,' she said, while I was mopping up the mess and standing between her and the television.

I made a cheese and cucumber sandwich for her lunch, and was relieved when she didn't spit it at me. Then Aunt Esther came down looking a lot better and I heated up a can of soup for her.

'Thanks so much, dear,' she said.

'Hideous cow,' my mother added. 'Where's my son?'

And that just about summed up my family relationships.

Maybe it was because there seemed to be too many women with slowly crumbling brains in my life, that, instead of going home to lick my wounds like a sensible PI, I turned my car north and drove slowly towards Watford. Someone had hired me to find Gina Turner, a despised and rejected daughter like me. The fact that someone wanted to find her seemed, just then, very moving. If I found Gina maybe, in the future, I too would be found.

Magical thinking isn't clear thinking. I have to admit I wasn't at my best. But the day had been so bruising that I didn't feel even a drive up the Edgware Road could make it worse.

The trip was not entirely speculative. I'd rung the number Sophia provided and made an appointment with Rafael Freshford who conveniently had a late afternoon cancellation. I'd used my poshest, most persuasive accent when talking to the local Society secretary and mentioned a lot of the Society directors' names that Sophia had used as her informants about Mr Freshford's credentials as a well-qualified counsellor.

I didn't know anything about his qualifications although I saw several framed certificates on the wall behind his desk. What I found was a tired middle-aged man with a high hairless forehead and absolutely no vanity about clothes or disguising a small paunch. His right arm was in a garish blue hospital sling and his cord jacket, slung across his shoulders, looked decades old. His shirt collar was rumpled, half up and half down.

I wasn't exactly a pretty picture either, but he hardly blinked at my wretched face.

What broke the ice was when we both remarked simultaneously, '*You've* been in the wars,' and then burst out laughing.

He said, 'I'd offer you tea or coffee, but… '

'Do *you* want one?' I asked.

'To tell you the truth,' he admitted, 'I'm gagging for a cup of tea.' He showed me the little kitchenette at the end of a corridor, and I made mugs of builders' tea for both of us. While I was boiling the water he explained that, late for an appointment and running full tilt, he'd tripped on an uneven paving stone. He'd hit the ground so hard that he'd broken his arm next to the shoulder where, he was told, it was impossible to put a cast. It was up to him to keep his own arm supported and immobile. He was dependant on pain killers to get him through the day.

'So why the fuck did you agree to see me after five o'clock instead of going home?'

'So why the fuck have you spent nearly two hours driving here instead of going home?'

'I asked first.'

'Well, my excuse is that the colleague who had promised to drive me home forgot and made a date. I can't drive a stick shift one-handed.'

'And I have a car,' I said.

'That was a bonus.' He smiled. 'Also I have a personal interest in Gina Turner, and I wanted to see who was looking for her.'

'Why?'

'Too long a story,' he said. 'But I met her when I was transferring from social work to psychotherapy. I had an interim job assessing needs for the Neurological Society. Gina was my first assignment. I can't tell you more than that.'

'My confidentiality rules probably aren't as strict as yours. But they exist.'

'Okay. So what do you want to know? And why did your employer not come him or her self?'

'Well, he's a complicated guy. He doesn't get out much. He's sort of obsessive-compulsive. He knows he's a pain in the tuchus, but he can't help himself. Has Gina described anyone like that in her past?'

'You see,' he said slowly, 'I really do need to know who might, and who might not harm Gina.'

'I do see,' I said. 'It all depends if she can talk to a guy who feels very grateful for her past kindness but who has absolutely no impulse control whatsoever.'

He sipped from his mug and nodded approval. We went back to his office. Instead of sitting behind his desk he took an armchair and I sat on a saggy seated sofa that smelled comfortably of dog.

'Why now?' he asked.

I'd decided, while driving, how much I'd tell him. Now, my instinct about him told me he was someone I could trust. My record concerning trustworthy blokes, on the other hand, told me otherwise.

I said, 'My client received one of those bogus phone calls about fraudulent activity on his debit card.' I waited.

He said, 'I expect we've all had a few of those lately.'

'Yep.' I took a drink of hot tea. 'This has nothing to do with the fraud itself. But my client thought he recognised the pleasant middle-class voice of the woman fronting the fraud. As I hinted at the beginning, once this guy gets an idea in his head he's a slave to it.'

'Which makes normal life impossible for him and very difficult for everyone around him.'

'Yeah,' I said with feeling. 'This is probably more understandable to you than to me. Which is why I've told you about it. You protect your clients; I protect mine – even the impossible ones.'

We stared at each other. He shifted uncomfortably in his chair and sighed. 'My pills. I left them on the desk. Would you…?'

I got up. There were two blister packs and a carafe of water on the desk. I was just going to hand them to him. Then I remembered Candice and Magda's chicken noodle soup, as well as Eleanor and Olive's mash.

I said, 'How many?'

'Two of the white ones, one of the blues, please.'

I cracked open the blisters, imagining how clumsy I'd be if I could only use one hand. I poured some water into a plastic cup. I left pills and water on a small table beside his good hand. Now he was going to think I was a caring, considerate sort – which shows how wrong even a guy with certificates can be.

He said, 'In that little kitchen, in a cupboard under the worktop to the left of the sink, is a packet of custard creams.'

He needed a couple of minutes to think, I decided as I walked back along the corridor. I took my time.

Out of respect for my back tooth I softened my biscuits in the hot tea before eating them. He was a cruncher, and a thinker. I watched him thinking. It was a peaceful activity. I rummaged in my bag and took a couple of painkillers myself.

Think as long as you want, I said to myself. I was not looking forward to the long drive home.

'Your injuries,' he began at last. 'Can you tell me what happened?'

'Okay,' I said, because I thought I knew why he was asking. 'I busted a cheating husband – gave his wife conclusive proof. He blamed me. I guess she told him where to find me.' It was my turn to look thoughtful. He was probably better at it than me, so I said, 'It had nothing to do with finding Gina. It seems, though, that she was in contact with some rough people. If you want an impenetrable barrier between them and Gina I'd really understand. All I can say is I don't think my enquiries have alerted anyone.'

'All the same,' he said, 'it seems remarkable that, beginning with nothing more than a recorded voice on the phone, your "enquiries" have brought you to *my* door.'

'I can tell you where the weak link is. But if no one but me has bothered with it after all this time I think she's fairly safe. My client himself was afraid she was being exploited.'

'What do *you* think?'

'Dunno. But what little I know about financial fraud or slum landlords make me suspect that she was desperate and someone exploited the situation. Then she got sick with some degenerative neurological condition, so he, or they, dumped her. I think you're worried that if anyone from, let's say, NP Holdings found out I was investigating them, someone, somewhere might think she has inconvenient information.'

'How likely is that?'

I could lie to him, I thought. But suddenly I was too tired to make up a story. I said, 'All the connections I made between financial fraud and a shady property company came from a place any member of the public can access: Companies House. It seems clever to my client, and maybe you, but it isn't. It's free information – like the Electoral Roll. All you have to do is use a search engine.

'I knew Gina was still alive because her phone is alive. She may not be using it, but someone is still paying the bill. Phones can be located.' I was so tired, I leaned back in the sofa and waited.

When Rafael said nothing I went on wearily, 'I got to you by interviewing someone who remembered your name. That was a lucky result of legwork. I'm not very clever, even my friends will tell you that. Again, anyone could take the same route.

'So, yes, Gina could still be in danger. Okay? But I'm assuming she's pretty sick with something incurable, and that you are sheltering her.' I closed my eyes. All I wanted to do was drift away and wake up nine hours later in my own bed. I forced my swollen eyelids open and saw that he too was stretched out in his armchair, eyes closed.

I said, 'Have you heard one bleeding word I've said? You better, cos I'm not fucking repeating myself.'

'I heard *every* bleeding word you said.' But he didn't open his eyes.

We sat in silence for over five minutes. Maybe he was collecting wise thoughts. But I certainly wasn't. I'm the sort of woman who doesn't know what she thinks till she hears it coming out of her mouth. These days I keep remembering the advice my old supervisor repeatedly gave me when I was a probationer, 'Just shut your gob and give your ears a chance,' and I realise I'm still an effing work in progress.

Eventually he said, 'Hannah, I think you're on the level, but I can't tell you much without clearing it with Gina. Okay? So here's the deal: I'll tell you what I can and then you'll drive me home.'

'Deal,' I said. 'But can I say that recently I've discovered that when searching for someone, instead of running them to ground, it's much better if I give them the choice of coming to me first.'

'That kind of reverses the process, doesn't it?'

'It means that I, to begin with, give you more information than you give me. As I have already. So I guess I think you're on the level too.'

He smiled at me then, and I smiled back. It was like shaking hands except that we were both too tired for such an energetic activity.

35

I woke the next morning at eight, hungry enough to eat a whole monster pizza. I'd gone to bed early without a decent supper although I'd scrambled six eggs for Rafael and me as a last favour after driving him home. I liked him and I hoped he'd had as peaceful a night as I had.

Missed texts, calls and emails remained missed till I was sitting comfortably at Tania's Tea room, eating kedgeree and drinking English Breakfast tea. The wobbly, painful back tooth seemed to have healed itself during the night.

I was on the mend – a fact I would not yet share with Digby. His deluge of missed calls had started at five-thirty while my phone was turned off and I was still in the land of nod.

Myles too hadn't been able to restrain himself, sending five texts and seven calls asking for progress. I would've ignored these except that he was panicking because, 'The last time I called Gina's number, at eleven forty-three last night, an automated voice told me the number was unavailable. What does this mean?'

I was tempted to tell him that he had broken Gina's phone by going on ringing and ringing instead of stopping when I told him to. Instead I silently thanked Rafael for taking one of my suggestions seriously. Then I rang Sophia Smithson.

'I went to see Gina's counsellor yesterday. Thanks for the information that made him so easy to find.'

'You're welcome,' she said in that insulting tone of surprise she used whenever I showed the slightest hint of good manners.

'Rafael Freshford was the right person to talk to. He's Gina's case supervisor. This is the situation: Gina is confined to a wheelchair.

She's being cared for by professionals in an assisted living facility in Hertfordshire. Don't ask me where, because I didn't ask, and wasn't told. She can still talk but her speech isn't easy to understand. She is as comfortable and contented as sponsorship from the Society can make her. She's definitely one of the lucky ones.'

'I'm so glad,' Sophia said. 'And my godson will be too.'

'There's an extra layer of protection around her,' I said. 'You see, Myles was right – that *was* her voice on the fraudulent recorded message, and on NP Holding's number too.'

'I'm astonished,' she said. 'I thought he was having one of his obsessive fits.'

'Being a pain in the bum doesn't make him wrong *all* the time.' I was happy for once to be the self-righteous half of the conversation.

'I should remember that more often,' Sophia said, icily.

'But, you have a point: Myles could make things difficult for Gina. His persistent calls, for instance, are the reason why her phone contract has been cancelled. Not because she's heard any of them, but because if I can trace her through her phone, so could anyone who thought she could do them harm. Just looking for her could've kicked over the anthill that went unnoticed for years.'

Sophia jumped in, offended, 'Are you insinuating that my grandson's wish to make contact with someone who was kind to him has put her in danger?'

'Well, yes,' I said. 'He got an idea into his poor old head and couldn't let it go. I don't know, and nor do you, what he'd do if I told him where to find her. His intentions might be great, but his self-control is absolute crap.'

'Mind your language, young lady,' she said automatically. 'Myles is a very intelligent man. He's open to reason.'

'Intelligence has sod-all – 'scuse me – *nothing* to do with it. Reason doesn't stand a chance against obsession.'

'You know nothing at all about my godson,' she barked.

'Correct,' I said, but she'd rung off in a huff before I could get the word out.

'Not very helpful,' I muttered to myself. I wondered if ringing her back would be a sign of weakness but before I could make a decision Tania herself came over and offered me a free pot of tea. She'd seen the pictures in the Echo Online and wanted to commiserate.

Then she told me that she thought a delivery man was stealing from her. Could I help? She didn't want to make it a police matter. I asked if it was urgent, and she said it wasn't – she could wait till I was fully recovered. We shook hands and I started on my fresh pot of tea.

I picked up Digby's next call. It was the same as yesterday's – he needed me to help with the lunch rush.

Then Les Goodall texted me asking for a WhatsApp video call in five minutes.

'Give me fifteen,' I replied. 'I'm in a public place.'

This was one of the problems of not having an office or even a flat of my own. I could never rely on privacy – which is a bummer when you're trying to build yourself up as a *Private* Investigator. I could, if I ran, get to the Sandwich Shack in ten minutes, but Digby would be there and he'd say that if I was well enough to conduct business I could do a proper day's work.

In the end I asked Tania if she had a small room where I could be alone for an urgent call. Surprisingly, she showed me upstairs to her own flat. On the way she said, 'You know Magdalena Luczak?' This went a long way to explaining why she might trust me.

'Magda bakes some of cakes I serve here,' she went on. 'Magda is excellent baker.'

'And a very kind woman,' I replied, thinking of BZee.

'Too kind ever to be rich.' Tania sniffed and opened the door to a neat, over-crowded sitting room. 'No one disturb you now. No one hear secrets except Illya.'

Illya was a very large ginger cat who raised his head and yawned when he heard his name and then went back to sleep.

'I think I can trust him to keep his mouth shut,' I said.

'Not in kitchen,' she said, without a trace of humour. She went out, shutting the door behind her.

I cleared a space on a table in front of small window, set up my iPad and drew an upright chair towards it. I took the Ferguson folder out of my bag and quickly scanned the contents.

Les Goodall called a few minutes earlier than I would've liked. A round pink face topped with short sandy hair filled the screen. I said, 'Les Goodall? Thanks for getting in touch.'

Instead of replying she held up a passport in front of the camera. I squinted at it and saw that the face belonged, unambiguously, to a Lesley Anne Goodall.

'Thank you,' I said, hiding my surprise. 'I don't have my passport with me. Will a driving licence do?'

'Probably not,' she replied. 'Judging by all the bruises and swelling you won't look anything like your photograph. But hold it up anyway.'

I fumbled my licence out of my wallet.

'Okay,' she said. 'You have Hannah Abram's licence even if you don't have her face.'

'Sorry about that.'

'I bet you are.' Les grinned cheerfully at me. 'Want to meet Paulina?'

I was so surprised that I could only drop my wallet and croak, 'Yep,' as I bent to pick it up.

When I straightened I saw that Les had pushed the camera away from herself and showed me that she was sitting beside a small, dark woman with long black hair.

'Paulina?' I said stupidly.

'I have no passport,' she said softly, 'no certificate of my birth. I am, in this country, a woman without identity. My husband owns all the proofs.'

'He wants to give them back to you,' I said.

'Does he really?' Les asked, one eyebrow shooting up. 'What did he say?'

I looked at Paulina. 'He said of course you should have your documents.'

'But?' she said quietly.

'Well, of course, he was concerned about how to get such valuable papers to you. He wants to be sure you have security in place, that the passport doesn't get into the wrong hands.'

I was looking for clues. Les and Paulina sat side by side, just head and shoulders in shot, with their backs to a blank sky blue wall. Les was wearing a green and red plaid shirt; Paulina was in a grey long-sleeve T with a pink strip around the neck. She looked a lot less bedraggled than she had in the photos Mark gave me – although next to Les she looked like an underfed child. Les's face was so round that her features seemed tiny and squashed between her cheeks. There were no clues about their location.

I went on, 'I told him I'd try to arrange a drop that would satisfy your need for security and his at the same time.'

'Has he asked for an address?' Les said.

'No.'

'He will,' Les said.

'Look,' I said to Paulina, 'I don't know what you're afraid of, but I told Mark in no uncertain terms that if you were in a women's shelter no one would give him – or me – the address. He understood that.'

'Did he?' Les said, one eyebrow up again. 'Did he really?'

I looked from one to the other, perplexed.

Eventually Les said, 'Did he tell you that he reported Paulina here as a missing person?'

'No,' I said, remembering Mark's embarrassment at the thought of any of his business associates gossiping about his affairs. 'Why?'

'He *couldn't* tell the police. And he won't want any official to examine her documents.'

'Why?' I said again. They were both looking at me as if I was the dumbest bunny in class.

Les nudged Paulina who said, 'My birthday was two weeks ago. Only now am I sixteen years old.'

Les said, 'And now that she has passed the age of consent in this country he can begin a very sneaky search for her. What exactly did Mr Ferguson tell you?'

I could feel myself turning into a slack-jawed bumpkin. I stammered, 'I don't understand.' There'd been absolutely nothing about Mark that could possibly have rung warning bells. Had there? I was trying so hard to think that my brain went on a spin cycle and all my thoughts stuck in a damp, shapeless clump somewhere behind my eyes.

'Did he tell you we met in Greece?' Paulina asked.

'Malta,' I said through numb lips.

'I cannot prove without my passport, but I am from Estonia.'

'Why would he lie about that?'

'Because,' Les said, 'he'd already arranged a different passport for her *before* he met her. And he thought he'd have a better chance of her documents not being examined when she entered the UK if that's what was presented at immigration at a crowded airport. Where in any case a lot of people were wearing masks.'

'Did he say we married?' Paulina said.

'Yes.'

She shook her head. 'No. There is a pretend marriage paper from Greece. But no one ever asked.'

'It's Covid,' Les said. 'Before Covid he went to Thailand or the Philippines. Normally he wouldn't have brought a "bride" home. Covid clipped his wings.'

'B-b-but… these are all *crimes*,' I said. 'These are crimes – sex crimes, false documents, trafficking … I don't know where to begin.'

'And so,' Les said, 'you thought you were simply carrying out a search for a confused young woman who needed her husband's help and forgiveness.'

'Well, yes.' *I* was the confused woman who needed help. I hadn't caught up. Mark Ferguson, the guy I longed to impress, the guy I'd *dressed* to impress. The guy who somehow seemed, at the wine bar, to be more of a date than a client? Who did I believe? Who did I want to believe? Where was the proof on either side? Watching two women on a video screen suddenly seemed like watching a movie on TV. Pure fiction.

'You like him,' Paulina stated gently. 'I understand. I liked him too. I thought I was lucky.'

'It's okay,' Les said to Paulina. 'Don't blame yourself. How were you to know? We'll keep working on it.'

'Who are you?' I asked Lesley Anne Goodall.

'I guess you have a right to ask. I am a certified councillor and advisor to the women who end up at my employer's shelter.'

Two qualified shrinks in two days, I thought. How lucky can an ex-copper get? At this rate I was going to need one. I gave myself a mental shake and tried to take my brain in hand.

I said, 'Okay. But if what you say is true, why are you talking to me? Aren't you taking a huge risk? And why are you *not* talking to the cops?'

'Mark Ferguson knows the Chief Constable,' Paulina said. 'Also immigrant status is not clear and I have no papers. I need someone to take my passport from this man.'

When Mark told me about Kyle Yardley trying to break into his safe and then stealing money from his desk drawer all I'd really heard was that Paulina had sent her boyfriend to steal from her husband. I had not concentrated on the fact that she was waiting forlornly at the airport for the guy she thought would bring her the means of escape from the UK.

Les cut in, 'We decided to give you the benefit of cautious trust because you understood shelter policy.'

'And I Googled you,' Paulina said. 'And I saw that you too suffered from male domination.'

'And male brutality.' Les pointed at my unlovely mush. 'And then there was the faked pornography of you with an ethnic minority police officer. Also, from your name, you are probably Jewish. We thought you might be more predisposed then most white middle-class women to take Paulina's story seriously. And therefore less likely to recommend the straight, white solution.'

'But,' I said sadly, 'I'm ex-police. When I hear of a crime I think about the law.'

'Even so, you must be aware that, with crimes against women, especially against women like Paulina who fall between the cracks of society, police are more likely to compound the crime than to right the wrong. You do know that, don't you?'

'Yes,' I admitted even more sadly, thinking of the times I'd failed. Worse, thinking of the times when my own colleagues punished *me* for offences *they* committed against me. Even now.

'Listen,' I said, feeling a sort of despair. 'I have been told two contradictory stories. My bigotry makes me think the rich, yeah, white male is telling the truth; my experience makes me believe you two.'

Gina Turner, I thought, and Paulina Ferguson, two women who, for very different reasons, needed to be protected from the men who'd paid me to find them. I longed for the simplicity of kidnapped dogs and stolen bicycles; I wanted the safety of flipping burgers and fighting with Digby.

When you're a cop your actions are decided for you by the book of rules, the law. Without that, you have to make up your own mind about right and wrong, fair and unfair, just and unjust, who to believe and who to doubt. I'm a single, not very bright, woman. How can I do that all on my own?

Les Goodall said, 'Will you at least let Paula, here, tell her own story?'

36

Paulina said, 'I didn't know anything about it but my father advertised me for sale a year before I had my fifteenth birthday.'

'The age of consent is fifteen where she comes from,' Les put in. 'This man, her father, wanted to stay within the law of his country.'

'He is a poor man who suffers from a withered leg, who drinks much and does not work,' Paulina said. 'But he ordered me, from when I was small, to learn English from English people online. As he told me just before I left home with Mr Ferguson, it increased my market value. English speakers are the rich people, he once said. I thought he meant that *I* would be rich. He did not.'

Assisted by Les, she told me that as long as she could remember she'd been hungry. She now thought that stunting her growth and delaying menses was part of a long-term strategy. But at the time it seemed normal for men to eat first and more than women.

She was taken by a brother from the forest where she'd lived all her life to Tallinn where she was handed over to someone she thought was a priest. The priest spoke English but was, like her, a native of Estonia. He tested her conversational English and seemed to be upset because hers was better than his.

He told her she was to marry an Englishman. It was a normal arranged marriage. But, she protested, arranged marriages were *not* normal in Estonia. He told her, as her father had several times, that girls should pay their families back for their upkeep, clothing and education. That if this ungrateful child refused she could live, homeless, on the streets of the city and experience what would happen to her if she refused this great opportunity for herself and her family.

She met Mark Ferguson in the lobby of The Tallinn Hilton. She was overawed, overwhelmed and totally unprepared. He was older than her father, but handsome. He had beautiful manners and smelled clean. He treated her with great courtesy. She said again that she thought herself lucky.

The priest gave him an envelope and Ferguson gave the priest a heavy travel bag and a small key. The priest departed, and before she knew what was happening she was in a cab on her way to the airport. She left Estonia on her own passport, but arrived in Malta with quite different papers. None of this was ever explained to her.

She wanted her original passport back. She didn't think she could get anything straight with UK authorities without it.

She started to cry when she told me that her real name was Emma Paulina Tamm.

Did I believe her? What a question!

'Yes,' I said, thinking yes, no, yes, maybe. And, this is such a wasp's nest. How the hell can I talk to Mark again without telling him some of what I'd been told, giving him a chance of rebuttal?

As if psychic, Les asked, 'What will you tell Ferguson next time you speak to him?'

'I don't know,' I said. 'I really don't. But I expect he'll want proof that the person I've been talking to is indeed Paulina. So can I suggest that you let me take a screen shot, without Les in the picture? And as you already show nothing of your location in the background that should satisfy both him and you.'

While they conferred in whispers I thought, The only clue *I* have is Lesley Anne Goodall's passport. Quickly I keyed the name into my phone and found a friendly website which offered psycho-therapy and counselling to anyone searching for mental wellbeing, serenity training or advice. There was a picture of her with a big mongrel dog. They were both smiling. An email and a phone number were at the bottom of the page.

If I believed Emma Paulina's story Les's identity had to be hidden too. If it wasn't, she'd be very easy to trace, as would any shelter that employed her.

Les looked up and said, 'A screenshot's acceptable.'

She ducked out of sight and I took one. Paulina stared, expressionless, into the camera.

When Les came back into frame I said, 'At the moment, Les, *you* are the weak link. So far Mark only knows you as Les. But you and your clients would be very easy to trace if I told him any more.'

'Will you tell him any more?' She seemed suddenly appalled and aggressive.

'No,' I said. 'Actually, the fact that you showed me your passport makes me more likely to believe you both. Anyway, I haven't heard the whole story yet. There are a lot of questions begging to be asked.'

I would've gone on but without warning Illya, Tania's big ginger cat, leaped onto the table and walked in front of the camera. Les gave a shout of laughter which startled Illya who reacted by sitting on the keypad and cutting the video link.

'Outstanding,' I said to him as I tipped him onto the floor. 'Really freaking outstanding,' I repeated as I failed to reconnect.

Les phoned me. 'The link crashed and I can't get it up again. Is that your cat?'

'It is not.' I said through gritted teeth. 'I was out when you texted. I'm in someone else's flat.'

'Could you be overheard?'

'No,' I said. 'Confidentiality's the name of the game.' But I suddenly realised that I wasn't working for Les and Paulina: they weren't my clients. Mark Ferguson was. I'd accepted the job and he'd paid me real money – in cash.

'This is an ethical dilemma.' I said it out loud without meaning to.

'No it isn't,' Les said. 'What's right is right; what's wrong is wrong. You said yourself a crime or crimes were committed against Paulina.'

'Yes. If she's telling the truth, but… '

'Don't you believe her?'

'Yes, I do. *But*… but my belief doesn't make a thing true.' My recent past was scattered with lies I'd believed. People call me cynical but I don't think I'm half cynical enough.

I went on, 'But I promise that for now at least I'll behave as if what I've heard is the truth. Okay?'

'Okay,' Les said grudgingly. 'What will you do?'

'I'll keep it simple. I'll send Ferguson the screenshot to verify. I'll tell him that Paulina hardly said a word but that she looked healthy. And I'll wait to see what he proposes.'

'You know he'll insist on a meeting.'

'Probably. And I'll tell him that's unlikely. I'll be helpful and unsuspicious. If I'm not he'll just find someone else to employ. The reason he's searching in this area is because someone recognised her walking on the Common.'

'Who?'

'He said it was an acquaintance who lives in the same block of flats.'

'Hang on,' Les said. She must've muted because I didn't even hear whispering.

When she came back she said, 'Paulina doesn't know who that could be. He kept her locked in, out of sight. You don't think he's got someone else on the hunt too?'

'I'd never thought of that,' I said.

'Maybe it's a man who wasn't getting anywhere. Maybe he thought a woman looking for a woman would be less threatening.'

'No one would get anywhere by following me,' I said. 'I don't know where you and Paulina are. There's no information to give away. And, please notice, I'm not asking.'

'Yet,' Les said grimly. 'Okay, we'll leave it there for now. I'll get in touch tomorrow to see what that bloody man's had to say.'

'Fine,' I said, offended by her tone. 'But please would you try to remember that I have other work. I need more notice, and the late afternoon is a safer time.'

'Noted,' she said, and cut the call.

'Bollocks to you too,' I said, only half addressing myself to Illya who was winding his fat, furry body around my ankles as I stowed the phone and iPad in my bag. I tried to arrange Tania's doodads where they'd been before I'd made a space for myself. Arranging doodads doesn't feature in my skill-set. Tania would not be pleased.

Downstairs I thanked her profusely for allowing me internet access. She reminded me that she had a job for me when I was free. I told her she was top of my list.

I was fifteen minutes late for the Sandwich Shack, and Digby was fuming. Situation normal: no ethical dilemmas there.

37

It was a tough, annoying shift, but at least I managed to recharge my electronic devices at Digby's expense, under Digby's desk. A small victory, but given the sniping I received without complaint, I'll take it.

'Can't you wear some make-up to hide the worst of the bruising?' he demanded. And, 'Why don't you wear a surgical mask all the time? You're putting my clients off their food.' And, 'There's too much filling in the sandwiches. I'm not made of money, you know.' And, 'When do you think you'll be "well enough" to open up? You're heaping unwarranted pressure on me.'

'On me, actually,' Dulcie said. '*I* opened up the last two mornings. And I don't mind a bit. You take your time, Hannah. You've been through something horrible.'

'Thanks, Dulcie,' I said, trying to sound fragile and fatigued. I didn't have to try very hard. All I wanted to do was go home, shower, and put my feet up. But just as I was removing my greasy apron Carl Barber shuffled in.

He said, 'Can we have a private word, Hannah?'

'That's the last sodding straw,' Digby snarled furiously. 'You walk in here, into *my* place of *business*, demanding time from a member of *my* staff, and you don't even have the courtesy to order so much as a cup of coffee to pay the rent.'

Carl, and everyone within earshot, stared at him in astonishment. We were used to him slagging his "staff" off, but he usually tried to be minimally polite to members of the public.

'What's up, Digby?' I said. 'Your elegant manners seem to have taken the day off.'

'You know exactly what's up, you blood-sucking cow,' he growled, apparently unaware of the picture his words painted. 'I gave you a raise and cut your hours. You repay me by wagging off, sick. So I have to pay Dulcie overtime. If the Shack goes broke we'll all be out of a job. But do you care? Oh no – you're too sick to work for me, but you carry on with your fucking extra-curricular activities. And then another of your so-called clients boogies in here expecting free drinks and the use of my office. And you expect *"elegant manners"*? Just who the fuck do you think you are?'

I opened my mouth to tell him that this vampire cow was quitting for good, when Carl and Dulcie both got between us.

Dulcie said, 'Hush, Hannah.' At the same time, Carl said, 'I do apologise. It was rude of me. Of course I'd like a mug of coffee and bowl of that delicious looking chili, with crackers, if you have them?'

Obviously it was Carl who had the 'elegant manners'. I'd noticed that right from the first time I met him at the launderette. It was why I'd liked him. Was it why I took his problem on? Were his good manners ultimately responsible for Deena's jealous outburst at the Big Sleep Out? Could that possibly be the cause of her death? Cause and effect. Cause: beautiful manners – effect: a big sleep in the Death Tent? Way, *way* too fanciful – I was slip-sliding with tiredness.

I sat down abruptly on the nearest chair. I stared at Carl. Today he looked older than eighty. His trendy facial hair looked overgrown and he was more stooped. He sat down opposite me. I said, 'Did Mwezi give you a hard time?'

'Apparently,' he began tiredly, 'I was less than frank about my connection with the Rubbish Vigilante, you know, the *whole* Barrymore family – including Deena.'

About half a dozen people, including Digby and Dulcie, were hovering close to the table, looking nosey. I pushed myself back to my feet and turned to Digby.

I said, 'This is confidential. I absolutely *have* to use the office. Carl, pay Digby for your meal. Dulcie, please would you bring the chili through when it's ready?' I turned my back on everyone and walked to the office. I was, I thought, as old and stooped as Carl. My face ached.

A couple of minutes later he came in and sat down.

'Apparently,' he began again, 'you were a little *too* frank about the connection between two rugby players and Deena.'

I sighed in sheer fatigue at his stupidity. 'How am I supposed to know what you want me to say or not say unless you actually tell me more than diddlysquat? What's the matter with you?'

He held his head in his hands and thought about it. After a long pause, during which I could feel my eyelids drooping, he mumbled, 'Embarrassment.'

'How do you spell that?' I asked. 'S-H-A-M-E?'

'Ouch,' he said. 'Look, I'm really sorry I wasn't up-front with you. I just wanted to know for sure who was tipping rubbish down my steps. Of *course* I had my suspicions, but I didn't want to confront the guy without proof. Truth to tell, I didn't want to confront him at all – he's half my age and his sons are twice my size. They'd eat me for breakfast. They probably blamed me for their mother's instability. I just really needed someone else – you – to be able to warn them off, to let them know an outsider was on to them.'

Dulcie chose this moment to come in with his coffee and a steamy bowl of chili. 'No crackers,' she said. 'But I found a packet of breadsticks.' She handed me a mug of strong tea. We thanked her and she left.

Carl made a big deal of tasting his chili. 'Mmm, good,' he said. 'Did you make this?'

'Yes,' I said, crossly.

'You're a great cook,' he said, oblivious.

'No I'm not,' I said. Even in my semi-comatose state I could recognise bullshit when it was thrown at me. 'And flattery doesn't make me believe you more.'

He took two more spoonfuls and then laid his spoon down. 'No, you're right,' he said, sighing. 'This is bland and the breadsticks are stale. Is that what you want to hear?'

'If it's even *close* to what you actually think, then yeah.'

'Look,' he said, 'Mwezi finally got the cousins, Irena and Laura Durham, the owners of the so-called Death Tent, to come clean about whom they spent the night with, and how that came about. You'd already suggested the Barrymore brothers to her. She's putting two and two together and blaming me because she hadn't reached four a lot earlier.'

'Bloody hell,' I said. 'Does she think the brothers topped their own mother?'

'I don't know what she thinks except that she's considering charging me with Obstruction.'

'Well, I hope you're not taking me down with you,' I said.

'Actually, I was hoping you'd put in a good word for me.' He blinked his faded blue eyes sadly.

'What?' I said, incredulous. 'Like, "Give him a break, Chloe, his mum never told him that if a woman comes on to him it isn't absolutely, one hundred percent necessary to shag her? Or that having realised his mistake it wasn't absolutely necessary to keep on seeing her for such a long time she thought it was a kosher relationship? Or that telling women lies just makes more and more trouble. See, Chloe, he's only eighty something – he hasn't had time to learn any of life's basic lessons." Because, Carl, at the moment that's all I can think of to say in your defence.'

'You're angry with me.' He sounded surprised.

'Why not? Your choice of girlfriend – or whatever she was to you, has actually cost her life. If you hadn't picked someone so bat-shit crazy-possessive she wouldn't have been hanging around abusing me at the Big Sleep Out, and what followed wouldn't have followed.'

'You don't know that,' he said weakly.

'Yes, I do. She was the reason her husband was picking on you. You were the reason she was picking on me. And you didn't explain. You didn't give me the information I needed to understand the problem you hired me to solve, or to solve my own problem when she started harassing me.'

'I was lonely,' he said. 'She came on to me like a fan. She said she used one of my old hits as her ringtone.'

'She was a married woman with grownup sons. God's grimy elbows! Why am I still talking to you? Unless Deena made a habit of picking up musicians at small gigs, this would've been a big deal to her.'

'She said she'd fantasised about me for years. I didn't know about her family.'

'You live in the same damn street!' I yelled. 'How could you fail to know she had a family?'

An eighty-year-old git who didn't think about anything except getting his leg over. Gross. But who's to criticise? Haven't I made a mistake or two, or three, or four? Being angry with Carl was a waste of energy. I needed to wind down.

'Was she seeing a doctor or a therapist?' I asked.

He shrugged. 'I didn't think it was my business.'

Sure as shit on a shovel Deena had needed help. I hadn't helped her. But I wasn't in a relationship with her, and I wasn't family – not my business either.

Giving the same answer as Carl made me even more pissed off. And tired.

'I'm sorry,' Carl said. 'I shouldn't have got involved. But she really seemed to want me… *it*. You don't know what it's like being an old man.'

'That's a good exit line,' I said. 'Let's leave it at that, shall we?'

'What will you tell the detective?' He got slowly to his feet, straightening as if all his joints were fighting against him.

I got up too. 'I won't lie for you or about you. I'll tell Mwezi the facts as I know them, and I'll keep all the judgment and speculation to myself.'

'Thank you,' he said with a little bow. He held out his hand.

I took it automatically for a brief shake, but to my surprise he held on.

'I know I've caused you unnecessary trouble,' he said. 'I suppose I value my privacy too highly. But would you, in the not too distant future, let me make it up to you? I'd like to take you to dinner – somewhere nice.'

I almost had to use my free hand to shut my mouth. But Carl was saved from a dragon-hot flaming by Digby who bustled in, saying, 'When you two have quite finished holding hands, I need my office back.'

I snatched my hand back and fled. Carl would've begun an elegantly phrased speech of thanks and apology, but I couldn't bear to hear it. I would've said goodbye to Dulcie but she shoved three packets of sandwiches into my hand and pointed across the Common to where the slender figure of BZee lurked in the tree-line. 'Keep one for yourself,' she hissed. 'I know you haven't had any lunch.'

If she wasn't very careful I'd start thinking of Dulcie as a friend.

BZee and I sat with our backs to a huge horse chestnut tree to eat our purloined lunches. Mine was one of the tuna salads Digby complained I'd over-filled. BZee's were all meat and cheese. Dulcie had learned quickly what he liked best. I thought about Magda and Dulcie. They were both kind-hearted women. Young guys like BZee need kind-hearted women to keep them alive and fed. I noticed that his new jeans needed a wash already. I wasn't going to offer to do his laundry; I don't count myself as a kind-hearted woman. I think of what I do for him as payment for what he does for me. And I wonder where the kind-hearted *men* are in his life.

Yeah, where were they? I wondered where kind-hearted men were in Paulina's life. Or in mine.

BZee interrupted what might easily have become a self-pity fest. He said, 'Got any work for me?'

'Not right now,' I said. 'But you know Tania at the Tea Room?'

'Yeh?'

'Well, if you're free next week she's got something I might be able to use your help with.'

He nodded. 'What about that sad lady in the picture you showed?'

'Don't worry about her,' I said.

Without looking at me, he suddenly said, 'Petra say you should pay me retainers.'

'Oh should I?' I laughed. Another kind-hearted young woman was looking after his interests. 'If someone offers you a job with better pay and conditions, take it. I'm not trying to hold you back.'

He stirred uncomfortably. 'When dogs and other t'ings go missing, I always tell you. Not nobody else. You need help you come to me. But I don't got no job security.'

'Here's the thing,' I began slowly. 'You're under age, BZee. I can't legally employ you. In fact you should be in school. You know that. According to the law I could be prosecuted for "contributing to the delinquency of a minor" by not reporting you to a truant officer or your social worker. This work you do for me *has* to be unofficial and under the table. I give you as much cash as I can afford, and as much food as I can. I don't think I'm exploiting you. But if you, or Petra, think I am, of course you should give me the boot. I'd be very sorry, but you've got to think of yourself first.'

'That's what Petra say.' He nodded emphatically, but he wasn't looking at me.

We both let it ride for a couple of minutes. Then I said, 'BZee, have you noticed anyone following me lately?'

He said, 'Y'mean that bad fucker hurtin' you?' He gestured towards my face but didn't meet my eyes.

'Anyone?' I said, feeling slightly queasy.

He got up suddenly and started walking away.

'BZee?' I said, getting up too.

He walked another five paces before stopping and turning round. 'You angry.' He still wouldn't look me in the eye, so I walked up to him and plonked myself directly in front of him.

'What's happened?' I asked, trying not to sound angry or even anxious.

He turned full circle, craning his neck left and right, front and back.

'What?' I said.

'Someone,' he said at last. 'You say and Petra say, me look to meself, right?'

'Right. So?'

'Rich guy give me hunnerd pounds – whole ton. What me do?'

'You took it, obviously.'

'Yeah. You never give me no ton.'

'I've paid you way more than that over the time we've known each other.'

'You never say I can't work some other job.'

'So why're you being so cagey? What's this "other job", and who gave you such a fat wedge?'

'See, if you give me retainer… '

'No!' I said. 'I can't. I told you. What's this other job?'

BZee stared at the crumpled sandwich wrappings still clutched in his hand. He could've dropped them and left me to pick up after him as he sometimes did when he was feeling lordly.

But he wasn't feeling lordly now. In fact he almost looked like he might cry.

'You,' he said, hanging his head. 'Saw you and me together. You the other job.'

It was no surprise by this time. It was as if I'd known it all along. I wanted to shake him, yell at him, bully him. It wouldn't have got me an inch further forward. Instead I sank to the ground and pulled him down with me so that we were sitting side by side with our backs to another ancient tree. The leaves were turning yellow and beginning to fall. He picked up a leaf and began to delicately remove everything between the veins. I remembered trying to make skeleton leaves when I was a kid a lot younger than him.

He said, 'Magda tell that leaves eat the sun.'

'Poetic truth,' I said. I rested my aching head against the rough bark.

After a while he went on, 'Yurek say he teach me all 'bout growing food.'

'You interested?'

'Hard, hard work,' he said, still occupied with his leaf. 'No dosh.'

'Yeah,' I agreed tiredly. 'But they're good people, I think.'

'Think so too.'

I waited. But BZee's long thin fingers kept on stripping the leaf.

I got my phone out and isolated the screen shot of Paulina. I could feel him looking over my shoulder but I said nothing and didn't hide what I was doing. I sent it to Mark Ferguson with a short message that read: Can you confirm that this is Paulina?

BZee said, 'You find her?'

'No,' I said. 'I don't know where she is, but I spoke to her and took a screen shot.'

'He give you retainers?' BZee asked.

'Who?' I asked, casual as fuck. I didn't even glance in his direction.

He sighed. 'Rich guy. Businessman. Like womens call "silver fox".'

'No,' I said, sighing too. 'No retainer. Did he give you a name?'

'Mark Soprano,' BZee said tonelessly. 'He joking me, I think, lying piece of shit. Say you cheating him. Say you take money from him to find girl, take money from girl *not* to find. See?'

'Yep,' I said. I was thinking that BZee had been with me when I was trawling round the charity shops distributing letters just before the storm. 'Did you tell him where we went the day the storm came?'

'Some,' he admitted. 'Couldn't remember. Said you gone to *all* them cheap-cheap shops in case I left one out.'

'Okay,' I said, because it was.

'Not givin' nothin' back,' he warned. 'He wants to know where you go, what you doin'.'

'Then tell him that yesterday I went to Watford. Today I worked at the Shack and then went home.'

'For true?'

'Yes, for true.'

'You won't nark on me?'

'If you won't then I won't. Deal?'

'Deal.'

I thought he might want to bump knuckles, but he wasn't that corny. I went home. I don't know where he went.

38

Feeling every single bruise, cut and stitch, I took painkillers and showered. Then I dragged on my PJs and crawled into bed.

Whether or not I believed Paulina, I knew for a stone fact that I couldn't trust Mark Ferguson. I didn't know if I was angrier than sad or sadder than angry. He'd actually paid my ally, BZee, to snitch on me.

Without the energy to look at my notes I tried to review what he'd said when we first met. He was the injured party, deserted by a younger wife who'd run off with a chancer who'd probably stolen from her and had certainly stolen from him. He'd rescued Paulina from an abusive brother. The short marriage was over. Three years? Had he actually said they'd been married three years? According to my befuddled calculation, if she'd only just turned sixteen, she'd have been thirteen when she became his wife. So one of them was lying, and my money was most definitely on the man I'd liked to the point of wanting his approval and, oh fuck, yes, wanting his desire. He was, after all, a soon to be single man who was decent enough to feel responsible for a young woman who'd done the dirty on him. What had he said? He wanted to help her any way he could? That she would feel too crushed and humiliated to turn to him? Something like that.

What a hero! I thought, trying to breathe deeply and sleep deeper. I was so tired of being attracted to wrong'uns. If I ever fancied a guy again – which seemed unlikely – I should immediately suspect him of all the sins of sexism, do an instant one-eighty and start running.

That resolution made, I finally dropped off to sleep.

I slept straight through for eleven hours and woke at five the next morning. I texted Digby to say I'd open up and do the morning shift. I was feeling a lot better but I left my phone switched off – there were things I was not yet ready to deal with.

It was a damp and misty morning that smelled like a normal autumn. I slid easily into the rhythm of turning raw foodstuffs into breakfast for the early risers. Some of them asked how I was feeling but no one bothered me.

Digby and Dulcie didn't turn up till after ten-thirty. They were followed almost immediately by Mark Ferguson. I was not surprised.

Digby, who was almost as impressed with him as I'd been, said, 'Take a break Hannah. Use the office.' Turning to the immaculate guy in the enviable suit, he added, 'Mark, good to see you again. Coffee? On the house, of course.'

Mark looked at me and said, 'My goodness, Hannah, I heard you'd been the victim of an assault, but I had no idea how serious it was. Is there anything I can do to help?'

'How kind,' I murmured. 'But no. I'm fine – my face is at the stage where it looks worse than it feels.' I smiled at the devious charmer. I wasn't going to give him even a ghost of a suspicion that anything had changed.

I led the way back to the office adding, 'But I turned my phone off yesterday. I really needed the sleep.'

'Sleep's always the best medicine.' He looked so sympathetic that if this had been the day before yesterday I would have melted like ice-cream on the Costa del Sol.

Digby came in with a tray bearing two mugs of black coffee plus a small jug of milk and some sugar. He was aching to know what Mark's business with me was but as we made it clear we wouldn't start talking until we were alone he left, not quite slamming the door.

Then Mark said, 'Hannah, I can't compliment you enough on your work for me. Yes, I can confirm that the picture you sent is indeed Paulina. Very well done.'

'Thanks,' I said, lowering my eyes modestly. The day before yesterday I would've been fighting back a blush of pleasure.

'Did she seem alright?' he asked. 'What did she say?'

'She accepted the need to provide proof of existence, but she really didn't want to talk to me.'

'I would've thought everyone would want to talk to you,' Mark said. He drank his coffee black with no sugar.

I smiled at the flattery, but didn't answer.

After a pause he said, 'Why do you think she wouldn't speak? You don't suppose, do you, that she was being controlled by someone who was in the room with her? Did you, for instance, see that fellow, Les?'

'No,' I said. 'As far as I know she was alone. Although I have to suppose she borrowed someone's computer to Zoom on.'

'Can you trace it?'

'I can try.' I was alarmed at how fast he came up with that question. 'I was just sent a link. The sender's address was blocked.' When deceiving someone the fewer actual lies you tell, the less likely it is that you'll be nailed. I'd have to be more careful. Quickly, I added, 'You do understand, don't you, that I really don't know where Paulina is. I have to wait for her to get in touch with me. She wouldn't speak to me at all if she didn't want the official documents you are safe-guarding for her. She didn't enumerate; she said you'd know.' I was hoping he'd kept her Estonian papers too but of course I couldn't say that.

'Does she want money?' The question was asked almost hopefully.

'She didn't mention money; just her documents.'

'This is ridiculous.' He was suddenly impatient. 'It's like a hostage negotiation. I'm supposed to obey orders and give her what she's demanding without seeing her and satisfying myself that she's alright and not being manipulated by some nefarious third party.'

'Well,' I began, 'that may not be possible. I haven't found her. Maybe I never will. I've just allowed her to find me. Which she's done. It proves nothing more than that she's alive and she looks healthy. And she's told me what she wants from you. All stuff you asked me to find out.'

'Do you consider the job to be finished? Are you resigning?'

Again I was startled by the abrupt change of direction. I said, 'You pay the bills so you call the shots.'

This seemed to be the right answer. Anxiety – or was it aggression – seemed to slide away to hide behind charm.

Soothed by his apparent control of me, he smiled and said, 'Of course I want you to stay on the case. And I'm open to suggestions.'

'Are you afraid the guy who ripped you off might be back on the scene?'

'I hope not. But Paulina must still be feeling very guilty about all that. I know the bastard was taking her for a gullible fool, but of course her feelings of guilt must make it difficult for her to face me. All I can say is that no one I know seems to have seen hide nor hair of him. But, of course, you're right: at the very least she's shown such faulty judgement that I think I'm justified in having a poor opinion of whomever she might put her trust in.'

'Obviously I don't know what her problem is, and I didn't want to ask – she was already very nervous about me.'

'If this were a normal situation I'd just put her documents in an envelope and post it to her. Or we could meet in a café somewhere and behave like civilised adults.' He shook his head, a picture of innocent puzzlement. 'All this unnecessary drama!'

'Well,' I said, trying to look thoughtful while thinking harsh thoughts about him. 'How do you want to proceed? And what can I do to help?'

He drank his coffee and regarded me thoughtfully over the rim of his mug. He really did look as though he was seeing me, thinking about me. In spite of what I now knew I could feel myself responding, softening.

I waited, hoping I looked more respectful than love-struck. Why is it that I can find even the most sexist, oppressive men attractive? Were they the *only* men I found attractive? What a nauseating thought? But why else had I tried to find a home in the Metropolitan Police? How stupid can a woman get?

Unusually wise, I said nothing. Fortunately my silence was something else that seemed to please him.

Eventually he said, 'I'll take it as given that you would counsel me against a direct approach. It doesn't take a genius to imagine that any attempt by me to impose the condition of a meeting with Paulina would fail.' He paused long enough for me to nod before continuing, 'Yes, definitely contra-indicated.' Then he smiled his beautiful quirky smile. 'Of course I trust you absolutely. Might you agree to continue as the go-between? If we can agree a safe method of delivery of my wife's documents.'

'Okay,' I said. 'Thanks for trusting me.' Something like panic had started interfering with my breathing as soon as he used the word 'trust'. My head was throbbing.

'Good,' he said, apparently not noticing. 'Then we'll just have to wait for Paulina to get in touch again. Of course, if you happen to notice the presence of a third party, or any clue to her whereabouts, I'd expect you to follow up. Or at least tell me. Acceptable?'

'Okay. Then, when I have a list of what she might want to make her feel safe, and you give me a list of what safeguards you need, we'll work something out.'

'Good.' He stood up. 'I'm glad we understand each other. I have the greatest respect for you professionalism.' He left the office and I heard him thanking Digby for his hospitality.

What a smooth talking, double-dyed bastard! I was remembering Carl Barber too – another guy who thought that good manners, charm and a hefty dollop of flattery would turn me into a compliant fool.

Tough talk, I thought. So why do I feel so sad?

Dulcie came in to collect the tray. 'What's up?' she said, wiping the coffee ring I'd left on Digby's desk. 'You look like a plant that needs water. Was the posh bloke mean to you? Digby thinks the sun shines out of his trousers.'

'He wasn't mean.' I straightened and got up. 'I'm just tired, that's all. He seems to expect a lot of me and I'm not sure I can provide what he wants.'

'You can do anything you set your mind to.' She sounded as if she was quoting someone a lot more confidant than herself – someone's mother, maybe. But not mine, of course. And probably not hers either.

'You should go home and get a bit more rest. You need more time, Hannah.'

'She needs to get back to work,' Digby said from the doorway. 'And you need to mind your own business.'

It was Dulcie's turn to wilt. She collected the dirty mugs and scurried away, head down.

'If you don't shape up,' I snarled, 'you'll lose her.'

'Big loss,' he sneered. Then he grinned sourly. 'Nah!' he said. 'She's alright, Dulcie. My hip hurts.' He sometimes had trouble with his left leg and hip.

'As an excuse for being a domineering, exploitative baboon that doesn't go far enough,' I said. 'Tell her about your hip and say you're sorry or you'll lose me too.'

'Ooh, I'm so scared,' he said with his back to me. 'How could I bear to lose you when you've got a leek and bacon quiche to mangle in your usual Master Chef style.'

'Shove off,' I snapped. But I was already starting to peel the leeks.

Situation normal, I thought. Sniping is so much easier than sadness.

39

Sophia Smithson rang while I was walking home. There was a cold wind blowing. I wanted to curl up in my attic room and shut my sore eyes for an hour or two. I nearly switched my phone off but didn't. Why put off the inevitable?

She said, 'My godson paid you good money to find Gina Turner. How can he know you're not cheating him unless he can see her?' She sounded tired too.

I sighed. 'Whether Myles can see her or not isn't up to me, Ms Smithson. It's up to her and her medical advisers. Or does he expect me to drag her, chained to her wheelchair, to his door in order to prove I've done a job for him?' It struck me that this outburst would have been more suited to my oh-so-cautious conversation with Mark Ferguson.

'Of course not.' She huffed. 'That's an extremely stupid exaggeration.'

I ignored this because she was right. Instead, I suggested, 'Wouldn't it be more sensible if you or Myles or both of you together talked to her counsellor. Your Society has vouched for his competence. And who knows, maybe he's already told her that Myles is looking for her. Maybe she wants to see him too. I don't know. All I'm saying is that she's very sick and she should be able to control who sees her that way and who doesn't. There's precious little else she can control in her present condition.'

'I know, I know.' She sounded the way I felt. 'I might be able to talk my godson into some sort of compromise.' She sighed heavily. So did I.

'How about this?' I said. 'May I give Rafael Freshford your number so that he can fix up a video appointment if he thinks it's appropriate? You can fight it out with him?'

'Oh all right,' she replied and rang off.

Rafael wouldn't thank me. Ever. I plodded on.

*

I forgot to turn my phone off, and Chloe Mwezi woke me up an hour after my head touched the pillow.

She said, 'I want to go over certain parts of your statement again. Be at the incident room in forty minutes.'

'Can't we do it on the phone?' I whined. 'I'm in bed.'

There was a silence, so I added, 'If I was still on the job I'd be on sick leave. But there's no sick leave in the catering trade, and I'm exhausted.'

'Alright,' she said crossly. 'But if I'm forced to amend your statement, you will have to come in and sign it no matter how tired you claim to be.'

Bloody cops, I thought, always gotta have the last word.

There was another silence. Then she said, 'Have you checked your social media accounts lately?'

'I haven't had time. What am I looking for?'

She almost whispered, 'Dick-pics. A lot of them. Since the porn posting.'

'Oh fuck,' I said. 'I'm sorry.' I'd had a spate of those after Toxic Tom's shower shots went viral. They're very hard to stop or get rid of. I said, 'The only thing I could do, last time, was to cancel all my accounts and start again from scratch. The hosts didn't do bugger all when I complained. Can't you get any action from the Met?'

'Oh yes,' she said softly. 'I'm constantly being asked where is my sense of humour? That is *such* a great help.'

'Yep,' I said. 'Presumably you know who's organising this?'

'I suspect, of course.' She cleared her throat and got down to business. She went through my statement step by step. Fortunately she wasn't much interested in Carl Barber's evasions. What she concentrated on was why I'd thought the guy who'd hustled Deena away from the takeout hatch was a Barrymore.

'It was just a guess,' I told her.

'A correct guess,' she said. 'You know, of course, that they are fraternal twins. Not identical but quite alike.'

'I didn't know that. At the time I didn't know who the guy was. I thought he was a member of the rugby team that trains on the Common. It was only later that someone mentioned that Deena's two sons played for the team. And I also remembered that the two girls who owned the tent were wearing huge men's sweaters in the morning. So I told you.'

'Yes,' she said. 'And the young women finally confessed that two good-looking guys had persuaded them into another, larger tent. But nothing happened.'

'Of course not,' I said almost laughing. 'They do have mums to answer to.'

'Yes, but interestingly they remember, after they first started talking to the young men, that one of them was being shouted at by an "old woman". It was after that when the boyfriends insisted they come to another tent for a drink.'

'Boyfriends?'

'That was the girls' description. In fact it was a one-night hook-up. They haven't seen the lads since.'

'So?'

'So, unfortunately neither of the young women can remember which of the brothers was being harangued. The brothers are named Will and Walt and, even having spent the night with them, the girls are hazy about which was which. I believe a combination of wine and unidentified pills is responsible.'

'Sounds about right,' I said, remembering the scene, the night, the music, the ever-present stink of weed. Most of all I remembered my sore feet.

'So,' Mwezi said stiffly, 'I must ask you if you can identify which brother pulled Deena Barrymore away from the Sandwich Shack on the night of the Big Sleep Out.'

'Fat chance,' I said without thinking. Then, 'I can try but if they look alike I'll probably be stumped too. I was coping almost single-handed and very, very busy.'

'Nevertheless,' she said in her soft, formal way, 'I would like to be able to say that you will make the attempt.'

'Okay,' I said. I thought I knew what she was up to: she'd failed to get a straight story from a pair of brothers who were colluding about any involvement one of them might've had in their mother's death. She wanted to threaten them with a 'witness' – me – in the old divide and conquer play.

Well, good luck to her. She knew how useless my statement would seem to the Crown Prosecutors, but she wasn't going to take it that far. She was just trying to insert a wedge between Will and Walt. I'd help her as far as I could – without getting myself in the shit, of course.

She needed a big success to cancel the damage done to her by the porn post. And though I really hoped she'd get it, I wasn't going to put money on it – I hadn't survived in a similar swamp. But she was much further up the greasy pole than I'd been. She had way more to lose.

'Thank you,' she said formally as she finished the call. I wondered how much it cost her to be civil to a disgraced constable whose flaky relationship had played a part in her humiliation.

The thought didn't stop me going straight back to sleep.

40

I woke up, hungry, at seven-thirty in the evening. It was almost dusk. Eleanor and Olive were home. The TV sounded faintly from below which meant I couldn't sneak into the kitchen without being heard. I did not want to talk about finding a new place to live. Instead I dressed in sweats and snuck out.

Half a mile down the main road is a cluster of shops, a pub, a tattoo parlour, and The Chippy, my destination of choice. You have to hang around for a while, but they cook their fish fresh, and double-fry the chips.

While I waited, I texted Rafael Freshford, passing on Sophia Smithson's contact numbers. I hesitated for a moment before asking him how he was getting on one-handed. Then I noticed that Les Goodall had rung me fifty minutes ago while I was still sleeping. I rang her back.

She dived immediately into the problems of getting Paulina's papers back from Mark Ferguson without giving away her location. 'Let's break it down,' she said. 'How can we be sure he'll actually give you the right documents?'

'I open whatever packet he gives me, photograph the contents and send the pics to you and Paulina to verify. He's already accepted that if he insists on seeing Paulina it'll be a deal-breaker.'

'He has?' She sounded amazed. 'Paula says... '

'I know,' I interrupted. 'She's right. I've just found out that we have another problem – he's had me under surveillance. I don't know how long for, but... '

'Jesus Christ!' she shouted. 'What a bastard! That's it, the end. We'll have to employ an immigration lawyer and go to the Estonian embassy. Exactly what Paula wants to avoid and the charity can't afford. They can barely afford me. Abused women don't attract anything like the funding needed. I suppose you'll want paying too.'

I let that one slide, although the subject of fees was well on my mind. Just for starters, Mark was *not* paying me to betray him.

After a minute's silence, which Les must've interpreted as offended, she said, 'Look, I'm sorry. But you've no idea what that bloody man did to Paula. And now she can't afford to live, she can't get work, and she's scared all the time – not just of him, but the authorities too.'

I said, 'He's a devious son of a dung beetle, and he has deep pockets – a lethal combination. You advise Paulina whatever way you think best. And I'll give the arse-hole the heave-ho. But don't you talk to me as if I don't know first hand how easy it is for a bloke to ruin a woman's life. Get it?'

I rang off; not in a huff but because I'd just seen BZee sauntering along on the other side of the road hand in hand with Petra, pretending not to see me. I went to the door and shouted his name. He looked up, all surprise. Petra pulled on his hand and, with a show of eagerness, he crossed the road towards me.

'You following me?' I was laughing at him, which should've pissed him off, but didn't.

'Not,' he said, batting his outrageously curly eyelashes at me.

'Fancy a fish supper?' I asked them both.

'Sausage and chips,' he said promptly. 'With gravy.'

Petra's mouth turned down and she let go of BZee's hand.

'*What?*' he said.

'You can't do that,' she said. 'You can't take sausage and chips from her, same time as taking money for ratting on her.'

'But you said,' he retorted.

'Look after yourself, is what I said. Know your value. Didn't say be disloyal to friends.'

'Is your mum a church woman?' I asked.

'Yes,' she said. 'How'd you know?'

'I'm a detective,' I said. Then the guy behind The Chippy counter called my order. While collecting it I paid for sausage, chips and gravy for BZee and fizzy drinks for both of them.

'I'm going home now,' I said. 'I want an early night. Tomorrow I'm on the ten-thirty shift. But before that, or after – I don't know which – I'll probably have to go to the cops to sign a statement about the Big Sleep Out death. Also I might have to drive to Watford again. Got that?'

BZee nodded without meeting my eyes.

Petra looked at the two of us as if we were crazy.

I walked home slowly, eating my fish supper as I went. It tasted as good as it smelled, and it smelled like heaven.

*

Next morning I lay in bed till eight thirty when I heard Eleanor and Olive leave for work. I left forty minutes later. On my way to breakfast I saw, at the T-junction between my road and the main road, a guy outside the betting shop. He was smoking, had his hands in his pockets and was waiting, apparently, for the shop to open. He was oh-so-definitely not looking at me although, by coincidence, he was conveniently placed to keep an eye on my car and my front door. It was almost enough to make me want to drive to Watford if only to give him the wonderful Edgware Road experience.

Sensibly I stopped for a poached egg on toast and a pot of tea at Tania's instead. It was crowded and I had to share a table with an old couple playing cards and trying not to finish their coffee quickly. I didn't mind because Tania was kept too busy to come and talk to me, and I could check my phone at leisure. While I was asleep late last night, Carl Barber rang telling me that Chloe Mwezi had arrested *both* Barrymore brothers and that their father had tied a note blaming him to a brick and flung it through his bedroom window.

There was broken glass all over his bed and a cut above his eye was bleeding.

I didn't know what I was expected to do about that and in fact, for once, Carl didn't ask me to do anything.

Another call I was happy to have missed was from Digby at five in the morning asking me to open up again. Apparently Dulcie had been sick in the night. The next three calls were also from him, yelling at me to pickup and calling me a selfish, lazy, uncaring slug, and finally, saying he'd have to do all the work himself, *as usual.*

When I left Tania's Tea Room I noticed that the guy who'd been outside the betting shop had added a baseball cap to his ensemble, turned his jacket inside out and was now vaping instead of smoking.

I took the longer walk through the Common to the Sandwich Shack and arrived on time to the second. Digby had a face like thunder, but could not legally burst a blood vessel.

Pity, I thought, as the vaping guy sauntered past. Almost as soon as he'd gone I saw BZee lurking in the tree line.

Tag, I thought, grinning sourly, and wondered if Mark hired incompetent people on purpose. Were we easier to buy, charm or control? Certainly he didn't want anyone from his own social background who might gossip about his inability to hang on to his underage wife. But most of all I felt insulted. I was considered too stupid to notice an inept tail. I was supposed to buy his story about wanting the best for Paulina while unwittingly putting her back under his thumb.

That was the last sensible thought I had before Digby, who'd managed to score a load of cut price fusilli, put me to work on a chorizo, pimento and tomato pasta salad for the lunch special. At the same time I had to serve coffees, teas, pastries and the odd brunch burger. He went to the office to do 'admin'. Yeah, yeah, pull the other one – I swear I heard snores coming from behind the locked door. The pile of dirty crockery became mountainous.

Dulcie did not turn up. But BZee, having realised that Digby wasn't on the look-out, came in. I threw a thick ham and cheese baguette together for him and gave him the soft drinks token so that he could help himself.

Before leaving he said, 'Guy following you.'

'Yes,' I said, relieved that he was telling me. 'Who is he?'

'So'jer-boy. On leave. Someone's nephew and such. Got wheels. Follow you to Watford.'

'Thanks,' I said, and cut him a double slice of chocolate cake. He slid away back to his post at the tree-line. He was playing both ends and I had to be thankful for that much. He was too poor to be bought with chocolate cake, and I was too poor to compete with Mark's 'ton'. In any case, as far as I knew, Les Goodall had scratched me off her list of Paulina supporters, in which case Mark would be paying his new little helpers – and me – for sod-all.

Even so, I spent my few free minutes trying to think of a foolproof method for shaking off a tail and delivering Paulina's documents to her without letting Mark know I'd busted him. It was tricky and inevitably my mind went to the movies for inspiration. This didn't really help because now was the digital age and the kidnap movies I'd seen seemed to rely heavily on phone boxes. You could spend a day and a half in London these days looking for one that worked.

I cashed up and closed the Shack at about four-forty-five – a quarter of an hour early because Digby wasn't around to give me shit about it. But I was dead-woman-walking by then.

I was surprised and disappointed at how long it was taking me to bounce back after the attack in the car park. They say that the older you get the longer it takes to recover. I was nearly thirty; maybe old age starts at thirty. That was a pissy thought.

Halfway home Les Goodall rang and instead of taking the call on the hoof I sat down on a bench at the edge of the Common. She said, 'I shouldn't have gone off on one last time we spoke. I sort of panicked. We try so hard here to keep, like, a castle wall around our clients. Paula's vulnerable on so many counts. I couldn't bear the thought that by trying to help her, we were breaching the wall.'

'I know what you mean,' I replied, grinning at BZee who wasn't even trying to hide the fact that he was following me. 'But isn't it better for her if we know what we're up against?'

'We talked a lot about it,' Les said, 'and we decided to continue to trust you. Neither of us wanted to start again with someone else. You're right, it's better to know. Then we can take evasive action. So long as that awful man doesn't know that *we* know you're under surveillance.'

'Yes,' I said. 'A touch of misdirection might be called for. Fortunately he has a poor opinion of my intelligence. Or rather, he's quite convinced, I think, that he's a whole heap cleverer than a bunch of women. Oh, except I've let him think you're a bloke.'

'Not the sort of misdirection I approve of.'

'Well, see, that happened when I hadn't seen you. You signed your emails simply as Les. He assumed his ex-wife was another man's puppet. He doesn't know we've actually had face-to-face contact. And so that's the way I want to leave it. Okay?'

'You're pretty sneaky yourself,' she said, sounding less than admiring.

'You'd better hope so,' I said gloomily. '*He's* paying me, remember? By rights I should tell him what I know about him, and what I've found out about you and Paulina, and give a bunch of money back to him.'

'But he *lied* to you.' She sounded like a school-girl outraged that the world isn't a fair place.

'There's a lot of that going on at the moment.' I was thinking about Carl Barber, and how Mrs Reynolds stitched me up with her husband, Ryan, and how BZee was technically stitching up both me and Mark Ferguson. 'And now *I'm* lying to *him*,' I went on. 'Or rather, failing to tell him the truth. Do you think that's any better?'

'Of course I do,' she said with total certainty. 'It's my job to protect ill-treated women. I do whatever it takes.'

'Well, bully for you,' I said. 'I never know what's true or false till it slaps me in the face.'

'I believe the injuries – physical or emotional.'

I know when I'm beaten. 'Okay. But we need a plan. And you'd better not tell me what Paulina intends to do when she gets her documents back. Don't make me lie more than I have to.'

'But you're taking money from a paedophile. You should give it back.'

'I already paid the rent with it,' I said. I hadn't but, well, I'm a fibber. What can I say? I can't live on what Digby pays me and that's *my* bottom line.

After that we left the moral high ground behind and got down to business, exchanging scenarios until I had something both rational and paranoid enough to take to Mark.

It occurred to me as I shambled the rest of the way home that I hadn't heard anything from Myles or Sophia for a whole day. Maybe that meant that they were making Rafael's life hell instead of mine. I was too achy and weary to care. But I stopped just short of Eleanor and Olive's front door to ring my aunt. She sounded a lot more cheerful. Apparently, if my mother tested Covid-clear tomorrow she could go back to the Bluebells. I asked if she'd heard anything from my brother or father. She said, 'Nattie's still – what's his word – *convalescing* in the Balearics. How very nice for him. I'm supposing he and Kirsty will recover as soon as his mum's back in care and his dad's future has been resolved by someone other than himself.'

'Of course,' I said and we shared a cynical 'humph'. Whoever resolved my father's situation, we both knew it wouldn't be her and it couldn't be me.

41

Back at Eleanor and Olive's house I ate the purloined leftovers of what I'd made for lunch at the Shack. Then I showered and lay down. No sooner had my head touched the pillow than the phone rang.

Rafael Freshford said, 'How're you feeling, Hannah?'

I realised this was the first time anyone had asked me that all day. I felt quite teary – which told me I must be over-tired.

'Okay,' I said. 'You?'

'Okay-ish. Tired. Too full of pain-killers but getting around a bit better than when you saw me. I was so grateful for the lift and the scrambled eggs. I should've texted you.'

'Save your energy.' I said. 'Only do absolute essentials. That's my excuse for not making the bed for three days.'

He laughed. Maybe he thought I was joking, but in fact my bed looked like a dirty laundry basket. He said, 'I just wanted to bring you up to speed about Gina Turner. I've spoken to Myles Emerson and Sophia Smithson; both, as you so accurately described, very intelligent and, in their different ways, utterly relentless.'

'I'm sorry. I'd gone as far as I could go with them – short of actually sicking them onto Gina herself.'

'You did the right thing. As it happens, Gina remembers them both fondly. Where we are at the moment is that she wants to see them but doesn't want them to see her in her present condition. We're talking. She's been disconnected from her past for a long, long time so it's difficult for her.'

I thought about it. 'Well good luck with that. Her brother and sister apparently don't care if she's alive or dead. Harsh. But some families are like that.' Of course I was thinking about my own when I said that. 'In some families,' I went on, 'there actually *has* to be a black sheep to blame for everything.'

'Oh yes,' he said. '*You* must fail so that *I* can feel like a success. You'd never believe how many "black sheep" find their way onto my couch.'

'Or into lock-up,' I added moodily.

'So would you like me to stay in touch?' he asked.

'I'd like to know what happens,' I said, without thinking. Then, 'As a cop I hated not being told how a job I'd been on for weeks ended.'

'You like knowing the end of a story? Maybe it's only *stories* that have proper endings.'

'But real life doesn't – and then you die?'

He laughed again. 'Maybe we both need an early night.'

'Amen to that,' I said. We were both laughing when we finished the call.

I was in bed and just about to turn the phone off when Mark Ferguson rang.

'Any news?' he asked. From the background noise it sounded as if he was ringing from a restaurant or wine bar.

I stifled a yawn. I would have to be very careful. 'I'm glad you rang. I've just had a talk with Paulina.' I almost told him I'd talked to Les, who he still thought was a man. 'I'm writing up my notes while the important points are fresh in my mind. Can we talk tomorrow? It's complicated. I wish I knew why she's so paranoid.'

He sighed. 'I would probably turn out to be the villain of whatever story she's concocted in her head. It's so sad it should end like this – all I ever wanted was to give her a better life. And now, all I want to do is make sure she's alright. It shouldn't be this difficult.'

'I know.' I was trying to sound as sorry for him as he seemed for himself. 'This must be so hard on you. But I have a strong feeling that if we don't play by her rules we'll lose her altogether.'

'Do you think she's being controlled by someone else? This Les person?'

'I simply don't know. Maybe they're just following shelter guidelines.' But I was thinking, 'You sneaky old sod. You bribe my ally, BZee, you pay a squaddy to follow me and you expect me to lead you to Paulina. How can I trust your intentions when your methods stink like a blocked lavvy?

But Mark was saying, 'Can I tempt you away from work for an hour or two at the wine bar? Perhaps, between the two of us and a glass of wine, we could come up with a way of simplifying this labyrinthine process.'

A couple of days ago I would've leaped at the chance. The thought made me blush. I said, 'I wish I could but I think even half a glass would turn me into a babbling fool, and I need to keep my wits sharp. Besides, I'm still a walking bruise. One look at me and babies start crying.'

'Only an idiot would fail to see the fine woman beneath the injuries,' he said gallantly.

Into my head came the memory of my old supervisor saying, simply, 'Bullshit baffles brains', when he thought I was falling for the spiel of someone he knew was a proven scammer.

So I just thanked Mark for the offer and promised to be in touch in the morning.

The morning! With Dulcie off sick and Digby in a permanent strop I'd agreed to open up again. I turned off all my instruments of communication, set the alarm for four-thirty and went to sleep.

*

No one was staking out my car early next morning. It was hardly even light enough to see. If I get enough sleep the night before I quite enjoy the early shift. Nobody hangs around wanting to chat or complain. I just get on with my routine; my customers get on with theirs. I know most of them. Some of them say Good morning. Some of them say Sup? Some just grunt. Mostly I know what they want. There are no surprises. I don't like surprises before my brain has woken up.

So this morning, at eight o'clock sharp, just to make my life peachy-perfect, Toxic Tom turned up with his less than fragrant side-kick, Stoat.

It's one of those universally accepted truths that a woman does not like to meet her ex when she's spattered with griddle grease, her hair smells of bacon, and her face is still decorated with unhealed cuts and bruises. No. The face you *want* to present to your ex would show him how much your life has improved after you dumped him. Fat fricking chance!

I was serving three flat whites and two breakfast rolls when Tom pushed his way to the front of the queue. The queue objected loudly.

'You'll have to forgive them,' I said. 'These "gents" are Metropolitan Police Officers and they never learned any manners.'

'Oh, really?' said one of the Retired Runners who'd been shoved aside. 'Are you here about the murder?'

Someone once told me she'd taught maths at the Catholic School. Her husband, who was just as formidable, chimed in. 'About time you people got your fingers out and we saw some action.'

A third member of the group said, 'That poor woman. It's absolutely shameful – there were scores of witnesses and yet you've done nothing.'

'Stand aside,' I said. 'I'm serving *paying* customers what they've *paid* for. And *you*... ' I'd just noticed Stoat trying the door handle. 'You can't come in until I'm accompanied by a co-worker. It's one of the measures we take to protect ourselves from male violence – the measures we're forced to take because you guys are about as much use as chocolate frying pans.'

'Protect and serve?' said a fourth Retired Runner. 'Protect your own arses and serve yourselves – that'd be a more accurate motto.'

With the whole queue turning against them Tom and Stoat had to move away until the crowd thinned. People Power, I thought, feeling an unaccustomed wave of affection for my clientele.

The other thing I thought was that they had not come on police business. Mwezi, I was almost sure, would never have sent those two to summon me to a line-up or anything official. Also if they were on official business they'd have come in uniform, waving their warrant cards around for all to see.

I was right. As soon as the protective queue vanished Tom was at the hatch and in my face. He said, 'You made a complaint about me. You made an unfounded accusation against me.'

'No I didn't,' I said calmly. I was proud of my neutral, grownup tone.

But Tom wasn't listening. 'I could sue you for defamation of character. In fact I think I will. So will Stoat – right, Stoat?'

'Right,' Stoat said obediently.

I said, 'I have not made an official complaint about you. But you two should already know that if I did, the complaint would *not* be unfounded.'

He still wasn't listening. He said, 'I'll sue you for every penny you got. I'll make sure you get what's coming to you. You can take *that* to the bank.' He turned his back on me and marched away.

'Stoat?' I called before he could follow. 'What the fuck?'

'They're threatening us with a review board about online porn and sexist behaviour,' he said. 'He thinks you'll be called to give evidence. And so do I.' He flipped me the finger and trotted off to catch up with his Führer.

'Up yours too,' I shouted to his retreating back. But apparently he wasn't listening either. So, without any other customers to piss off, I made myself a mug of coffee and sat down with a croissant for company to start the back-page crossword in the local rag.

My break lasted for seven minutes when I was shouted at from the takeout window. I got up and saw, waiting for my attention, an angry man who I recognised as a Rubbish Vigilante with a dead wife and two very large sons. He was alone except for his handsome Dalmatian dog.

'What can I do for you, Mr Barrymore?' I asked, hoping my reluctance didn't show. Then, before he could answer, I turned away and filled the stainless steel dog bowl with clean water and handed it to him through the hatch. This forced him to thank me and postpone whatever blistering verbal assault he clearly had in mind. Doncha just love the middle classes? Sometimes.

'Would you like a coffee on the house?' I asked innocently, hoping to make matters worse for him.

'No I would *not,*' he said emphatically. 'What I *want* is for you to stop accusing my sons of matricide. What I *want* is for you to stop colluding with that adulterous swine, Carl Barber.'

'Whoa!' I said. 'Where's all this coming from?' In spite of my dismay I was impressed. Who uses words like matricide and adulterer these days?

'Both my sons have been charged with murder on your say-so!' he shouted.

'That's ridiculous,' I shouted back. 'Dozens of people saw what happened here. All I said was that your wife was insulting me and a big young man pulled her away. I didn't know who he was but a bunch of others did. I have absolutely zero input to whatever the cops think.' I wasn't being a hundred percent truthful, but I followed up with, 'You're being very unfair. Are you tracking down all the other witnesses?'

'None of this would ever have happened if Carl Bastard hadn't seduced my wife.'

'That has nothing to do with me.'

'And then he was cruelly unfaithful to her with *you.* That's what drove her over the edge.'

'Why doesn't anyone listen to me?' I yelled. 'I told *her* and she didn't listen. And now I'm telling you: there's absolutely zilch between me and Carl. Never was, never will be.'

'So why were you hanging around him?'

'*I wasn't!*'

'You bloody were! She told me a woman young enough to be his granddaughter was hitting on him.'

'This one's on *you!*' I was almost ready to pull my hair out in frustration. 'If you hadn't been tipping rubbish down his steps I'd never even have *heard* of him. And why did you never get Deena some help? She was clearly a penny short of a pound.'

He stared at me, scarlet faced, and then before I could say anything else sympathetic he burst into tears and started hitting his forehead against the counter top.

'Stop that!' I screeched. But he didn't. So I folded a mostly clean dish towel and shoved it between his head and the hard surface. I poured him an Americano adding milk and sugar to the rhythmic thud of self-inflicted brain-damage.

At last I said, 'I'm calling an ambulance and the social services. If you don't want to be sectioned drink your coffee and shut the fuck up.'

They don't even listen to me when I'm trying to save them from Certifiable City. This was why Candice, closely followed by Digby and Dulcie, caught me dumping a glassful of cold water on his bruised noggin.

'Hannah!' Candice cried, shocked.

'Gordon bloody Bennett,' Digby yelled at him. 'If you break my counter I'll kick your arse all the way to The Drain and drown you in duck poop.'

I reached around Mr Barrymore and handed Dulcie the coffee. 'You try,' I said. And to Candice I explained, 'He's having a major wobbler. He's the dead woman's husband.'

They were outside the Shack so they wrestled Barrymore away from the hatch to one of the tables on the forecourt.

Fine, I thought, he's their problem now. Usually I'm not so pleased to see Digby. I busied myself wiping down all the surfaces and washing up, until Candice came over and said, 'He says he doesn't take sugar, and in any case he'd prefer tea, no sugar and just a splash of milk. I think he'll be alright now.'

I made the tea. Digby was standing guard between Barrymore and the hatch. Dulcie was sitting knee to knee with him, saying nothing, and holding his hand.

Candice said, 'You know he's saying you seduced the man who seduced his wife?'

'Yep,' I said tiredly. 'That's what she told him. But the guy he's talking about is over eighty years old. I do have my limit.'

'Don't be too judgemental about old people. They have needs.'

'Okay. But there are plenty of lonely old women. Why does a guy think he's entitled to someone twenty, thirty, even, in my case, fifty years younger than him?'

'Is he rich?'

I laughed. 'I never knew you were so cynical.'

'Where money and loneliness are involved,' she told me, 'one can never be cynical *enough*.'

I handed her the tea, and she said, 'Actually, the colonel and I came to see how you were doing. We also want two lattes and two raisin Danishes, please, to take away.'

'The colonel?' I peered behind her. There was no colonel in sight.

'Speaking of limits,' she said dryly. 'There are some men who think that all emotions are communicable diseases, and that a man's man can die of chronic embarrassment if he comes too close to one.' She took the tea to Barrymore and I got her order together.

The Barrymore interlude was followed quickly by the build-up to the lunch rush and my feet hardly touched the ground till two o'clock. Somewhere in the middle of that, Dulcie told me she was afraid she was pregnant.

'What should I do?' she asked, caught between the hatch and the cash register.

I just had time to say, 'Do whatever's right for *you*,' before throwing a bunch of chicken nuggets on the griddle and burning the inside of my wrist on the deep fat fryer. Sometimes the fast food trade makes police work look like a cakewalk without the cake.

Mark Ferguson rang at about three-thirty while I was walking home. I was so tired I sat on a low wall to take his call. People round here don't like strangers sitting on their walls. Sometimes they come out and shout. I took the risk.

Ferguson said, 'Why is everything taking so long? All we have to do is give my wife an envelope with her documents in it.'

'I don't know what the problem is either. But Paulina doesn't trust me not to tell anyone – you, I suppose – where she is.'

'Paranoia,' he said. 'How can she possibly think I'd do her any harm?'

'I don't know,' I said. 'Maybe, what with losing a baby, she had some sort of nervous crash.' This detail had come from Ferguson; Paulina had never mentioned it, so I didn't know if it was true.

'Maybe,' he said. 'Or maybe someone's influencing her – some left-wing feminist group – or this guy, Les. Can you find out?'

'Not without going back on every assurance I've given her so far. She's only in touch with me because I've told her she can make all the running.'

'Alright,' he said, sounding as if his patience was running out, 'So what have you got so far?'

'So far,' I said, trying to organise my scrambled brain, 'I must video the meeting between you and me. I must get a clear shot of her passport open at her photograph and identity page, and all the other documents you're holding for her.' I thought he might try to get away with just showing me the Maltese documents, and leave the

Estonian ones behind. I went on quickly, 'Similarly, I have to get a readable shot of her birth certificate. She has to see you put everything in an envelope and hand it to me, sealed. Then you must be seen walking away. After that she will give me instructions which will include, apparently, me turning three-sixty every now and then so that she can assess whether or not I'm being followed. My phone has to be open at all times. How does that work for you?'

'Let me think about it,' he said. 'I suppose I'm allowed to negotiate?'

'Why would you want to?' I asked.

'Why wouldn't I?'

I shouldn't have asked the last question. Had I told the man too much, too quickly? Was I making mistakes? Ferguson didn't trust me. He was having me followed. Or he thought I was too stupid to know I was being followed. He was using me to get to Paulina.

Shit – maybe I shouldn't trust her either.

I shook my head. I was too tired to think properly. I needed a couple of days off. I needed to make arrangements with Chloe Mwezi about whatever it was she wanted from me. I needed to clear the decks or everything would go tits up.

I called Mwezi and said, 'Do you still need me to try to identify which of the Barrymore brothers pulled Deena away from the Shack on the night of The Big Sleep Out?'

'Yes, tomorrow,' she said, sounding even tireder than me.

'When?'

'Nine-thirty,' she said and hung up.

I rang Digby. 'I can't come in tomorrow. The police want to re-interview me and I have to attend an identity line-up.'

'Bollocks and buggeration,' he growled. 'Is this about those two giant twats again? You better watch out – Papa Barrymore's one angry little turkey.' Which was rich, coming from him.

On the High Street I stopped at the Garden Café because I didn't think BZee would bother to follow me into a vegetarian establishment. But of course he did. He ordered a baked potato with avocado salsa, same as me. He even ate it.

He said, with his mouth full, 'Rich man want me to nick your phone.'

'Oh yeah?' I said. 'What did you say?'

'I say she copper one time. Not stupidy. He say try anyway.'

I said, 'Do you want me to break your fingers to prove how hard you tried and how not stupid I am?'

He grinned evilly, and we finished our baked spuds in friendly silence.

I said, 'Tonight I plan to stay in, watch telly and go to bed early. I'm still a bit shaky. Tomorrow I have to go to the incident room in Clapham. The inspector's called me in for another interview.'

'For true?' he asked wiping his mouth on his sleeve.

'For true,' I assured him.

'Then?'

'Dunno what then,' I said, weary. 'I need a day off. I told Digby I wasn't working tomorrow.'

'Him boil over.'

'Too bad,' I said. And we left it at that.

Whatever I tell BZee will be fact – I don't want Ferguson to lose faith in him. But obviously I won't tell him everything.

42

I failed to identify which Barrymore brother I'd seen at the Big Sleep Out. They were both over six foot, beefy, soft-mouthed and dim looking. They weren't identical twins, but with the same shape, colouring and expressions I couldn't say anything for certain.

I sat in Chloe Mwezi's office across the desk from her, drinking cop coffee. We were both disappointed but unsurprised.

'Sorry,' I said. 'If we'd done this the day after I might've had a chance. It was worth a shot though.'

She said, 'Even the girls they spent the night with could not be sure with one was which. But they say that the mother came while the four of them were drinking and kissing and listening to the music. They say she was screaming at them, calling them whores and slags. Then she was screaming at her sons, calling them perverts, predators and rapists. People were staring at them so they went to the boy's tent, which was bigger than theirs, for privacy.'

I said, 'But clearly all four of them didn't stay together throughout the night or... '

'That is what wasted so much time,' she said. 'The young women vouched for the boys. They said they had been together all night. They both said it was not just sex – it was love. But when the boys didn't get in touch with them and they realised they did not know for sure which brother had lain with which cousin, they began to feel they were being used for a convenience. So the story changed.'

'What're they saying now?'

'That the mother came to the tent maybe two hours later and started to make a commotion again. The boys were afraid she would wake up other campers. So one of them went out to remonstrate. He came back quite quickly and called the other brother. They begged the young women not to leave. And they came back only a few minutes later, saying they had persuaded their mother to go home.'

'How long were they gone?'

'Long enough,' Chloe said grimly. 'The young women could not say for sure – alcohol and weed were consumed – but long enough for the brothers to drag their mother's body to the tent they knew for certain would be unoccupied.' She stared down at her hands. Her nails were painted with an opalescent varnish. She sighed. 'Mischance,' she said, at last. 'Not murder. Not intentional, I think. I charged them both with murder – a strategy to see if that would scare them into talking to me. It has not yet worked.'

'So now?' I said, sympathising.

'I am waiting to see what the CPS has to say.'

The Crown Prosecution Service would take its sweet time and meanwhile the Incident Room would be quietly dismantled. Evidence would be stored in cardboard boxes along with witness statements, recordings and videos. The Barrymore brothers would probably be charged with manslaughter or something less like failing to report an accident. The girls would have their wrists slapped for withholding evidence and wasting police time. Chloe Mwezi and her team would be seconded to other task forces. Crisis over.

We both sighed and shrugged. So many cases end with a whimper rather than a bang.

After a pause, she said, 'As to the pornography and social media trolling, the event has been logged at the end of a long list of on-going enquiries into sexist abuse and bullying. I will be informed in good time.'

We both wasted a couple of moments looking at the rain spattering onto her tiny barred window.

I said, 'Delete unread – that's what passed for my strategy. I've cancelled all my social media accounts and reopened some of them under a different username and password.'

'Yes,' she said nodding. 'I have been offered an associate professorship in criminology at the University of Nairobi.'

'Wow!' I said, impressed. 'Will you take it?'

She smiled. 'I wonder if there is any place in the world where difficulties of sexism and colourism do not apply. I wonder too how wise I would be to look for such a place in East Africa.'

'Well,' I said, 'such a place doesn't seem to exist in the Metropolitan Police.'

'Not yet,' she said.

'I should live so long,' I said, almost at the same time.

*

On my way home, pissed off by So'jer Boy's inept tailing technique, I leaped onto a bus just before the doors closed. It was heading for Battersea.

I went to the Pump House Gallery in Battersea Park and stood in front of a huge splash of bright colours that was not attracting much attention and returned a call from Ferguson.

'Where are you?' he said. This meant that So'jer Boy had reported losing me. It also meant that BZee had, so far, failed to nick my phone.

'I'm at a gallery,' I told him. 'I spent the last I don't know how long with the police. My head's hurting and I needed somewhere quiet.' Without giving him any opportunity to interrupt with any more questions I went on, 'How quickly can you get Paulina's papers together?'

'When does she want them?'

'Sorry, I don't know. She said that the next time she rang we'd have to move immediately.'

'That's ridiculous,' he blustered. 'I can't rush home to pick up documents at a moment's notice.'

I said, 'Keep them with you.'

'I'm a businessman; I can't afford to be seen as flaky or unreliable. I'll probably have to break up a meeting and rush off somewhere – God knows where.' He sounded aggrieved. 'This isn't like Paulina at all. She's being manipulated.'

'What do you suggest I do?' I asked. I let the silence stretch before adding, 'Is there an alternative? I think time's running out. I've taken a couple of days off work because I'm so nervous. I'm losing money.'

'I can't tolerate the feeling that I'm being jerked around like a dog on a lead.' That sounded angry enough to be the truth.

I said, 'You're the boss. If you want I'll tell Paulina your objections. I'll break off negotiations if those are your instructions.'

'They aren't,' he said. But he was thinking. He went on, 'I wonder what she'd do if I simply backed off and stopped responding.'

'Would you really do that?' I said, sounding shocked. If he dropped his helpful, loving, nice-guy pretence now we'd all be up shit creek.

After a few moments of silence I said, 'I suppose, if she's kosher, she'd throw herself on the British Immigration Authorities' mercy. Or she might contact the Maltese embassy.' I almost dropped the phone. Sweat broke out and trickled down my ribs. I'd so nearly said *'Estonian'*. If *he* knew that *I* knew she was from Estonia and that he'd lied about Malta it'd be all over. I should cut the connection. I was a hair's breadth away from blowing the game. I hurried on, 'Or if someone is, as you suggest, controlling her, it would depend on what they want.'

'Okay,' he said. 'I can imagine what distress exposing her problems to officials might cause her. I don't want that to happen.'

Of course he didn't. As soon as any official knew about her age and origins he'd be in the firing line for trafficking for the purpose of underage sex.

A wave of nausea hit me. If there had been somewhere to sit I'd have sat. Instead I walked towards the exit and fresh air.

'You're the boss,' I repeated queasily. 'Instructions?'

In the last few days, I'd been beaten and injured by a man, and done nothing. I'd been the subject of pornography, and sent dick-pics and obscene messages, probably from serving police officers. These might, at least, have led to charges of Gross Misconduct if I'd reported them through official channels. All I'd done was delete unread. Now, to mollify him, I was telling the abuser of an underage girl that he was the boss. It was, added up, making me physically ill.

I gulped down a lungful of fresh, damp air as Mark Ferguson instructed me to stay in close contact and let him know the minute his wife got in touch again.

Battersea Park was probably what The Common would look like if it was smaller and more strictly regulated – nicer, tidier and safer.

I caught the bus back to The Common and home. There, I stripped the bed, gathered armfuls of dirty clothes and set out for the launderette – stopping only to buy a burn phone at an off-the-High-Street shop called eMenders.

The Clean Machine Launderette was where I'd first met Carl Barber. This time there was no seemingly nice old gent to buy me a pastry and give me a job. Nothing interrupted the hypnotic clunk and rumble of washing machines and dryers. I sat on one plastic chair and put my feet up on another. I went to sleep.

43

It all kicked off at eight forty-five the next morning when Les Goodall rang me to say, 'Today's the day.'

I gave her the number of my burn phone just in case BZee or So'jer boy managed to grab my normal mobile after all. Hers was the only number in the contact list.

I called Ferguson immediately.

'What?' he barked. 'I'm driving to the golf course.'

'Turn round and come back,' I said. 'Today's the day.'

A few explosive expletives later he was on his way to Clapham Junction.

We met at the Artisan Coffee and Bagel stall in the middle of the station mall. He was only just in time, flushed and sweating, clearly uncomfortable and angry.

I switched on to video and filmed him approaching. The camera ran as he put his fine leather document case down on the dirty floor and produced a white envelope. From it he removed two passports open at identity pages. There was also a rather ragged, much folded piece of paper. The writing on everything could have been in Cyrillic or Greek – I couldn't tell.

'They do things differently in Malta,' he explained. 'Understanding European bureaucracy's a nightmare these days.'

I shrugged, making a big deal of focussing my camera on the records of Paulina's birth and identity.

'I wouldn't know – I never go anywhere.'

He seemed relieved.

After a short pause Paulina's voice in my earpiece said, 'That is correct.'

'Okay,' I said to Ferguson, and filmed him putting the documents back in the envelope. No one had asked him to seal the envelope with parcel tape, but that's what he did, making a big show of it and handing it to me. Obviously he didn't want me to examine the contents. I slid it into my canvas satchel and tucked it behind my iPlayer.

'Give him the bobble hat,' Les said.

From my pocket I took a red beanie and held it out to Ferguson. 'You've got to wear this,' I said. 'So that Paulina can see you walk away – and not lose you in the crowd.'

'You're joking!' he spat savagely. 'She's humiliating me. And you're letting her.'

'Don't blame the messenger,' I said, although the red beanie was mine and keeping him in sight in a crowded place had been my idea. 'She needs to know for sure that you're doing this in good faith.'

He snatched the red woolly cap from my hand and jammed it on his head. As an accessory to his sleek golfing ensemble it did indeed make him look idiotic.

'Thank you,' I said quietly. 'Now turn around and walk slowly away.' I pointed to the exit about fifty yards behind him.

As soon as he'd disappeared I turned in a circle so that Les and Paulina could identify any familiar faces. Then I switched the camera off and sprinted to the ticket barrier with my pre-paid travel card already in my hand. I ran, full speed, up stairs and across a bridge to a platform where a train was about to leave. I leaped on, and sat down, panting.

I didn't care where it was going. I'd caught a quick glimpse of BZee lurking near the M&S Food Hall. I hadn't seen So'jer Boy but I'd expected Ferguson, if he really was using me to lead him to Paulina, to have someone on the other side of the ticket barrier too.

I called Les, who said, 'Where are you?'

I was on the Southern Overground to Victoria, I told her, reading the screen at the end of the carriage.

'That's fine,' she said. 'Were you followed?'

'I don't know. There was someone at the station but I'm pretty sure he couldn't have tailed me to this train. I moved very fast. But there might have been someone waiting on the platform side of the barrier. Obviously there were masses of travellers.'

'Okay,' she said. 'Get off at Victoria, leave the station and walk to somewhere quiet. Every time you come to a corner switch to video...'

'I know,' I said, impatiently. I'd just felt the phone vibrate and guessed it must be Mark Ferguson wanting to know where I was too. 'Les, I've got to go. Next time I'll call you on the burn phone.'

I cut the call and saw a missed call from Guess Who. 'Sorry,' I said when he picked up. 'That must've been a bridge or a dead zone.'

'Where the hell are you?' he snapped.

'On a train,' I said. 'Listen, I don't know what's going on or why. I was instructed to sprint to the nearest platform where there was a train about to depart. It didn't seem to matter in what direction. I suppose the intention was to shake off you or anyone you employed. I'm being jerked around while waiting for orders.'

'Never mind that,' he said, 'where's your train going?'

'Victoria.' I told the truth in case he'd actually managed successfully to put a tail on me and already knew where my train was going. I went on, 'We're dealing with extremely suspicious minds here. Please wait till I contact you. If Paulina rings and my phone's engaged she'll guess who I'm talking to and we'll lose her.'

'I'm not so sure about that,' he grumbled. 'She's not very bright.'

'Bright enough,' I said. 'She's got me foxed.'

'Yes,' he said. 'Or whomever she has pulling her strings.' But he rang off, not convinced of my intelligence either.

I knew what to do as soon as I got off the train at Victoria. I made my way through the crowd leaving the station as slippery as a fish swimming upstream. I crossed the road to the corner of Lower Belgrave Street where I stopped, switched on the video and turned three hundred and sixty degrees very slowly. The result was sent to Les. Then I turned left and walked to the corner of Ebury Street where I repeated the procedure. At Eaton Square I walked slowly round all four sides. Then I waited for Les to call me back.

Eaton Square was anything but square. It was a long, narrow oblong with three long, narrow gardens running down the centre. There were benches in the gardens where a bunch of nannies with Rolls Royce prams were sharing a packet of chocolate biscuits while their charges enjoyed what passes for fresh air in central London.

I turned and went around the Square in the opposite direction. No one struck me as suspicious except a delivery man leaving a parcel unattended on an immaculate doorstep.

I was nervous. Les and Paulina were taking too long.

Then Ferguson rang. 'Where the hell are you? Why haven't you reported in?'

'Eaton Square,' I barked back.

'What the hell are you doing there?'

'Waiting.'

'What for?'

'Instructions. Please, *please* don't tie up this phone.' I rang off.

He rang back immediately. 'You're working for me,' he said, 'not her.'

'I'm *trying!*' I said. 'If you think you can do any better, be my guest.'

'Alright!' he said. 'Carry on, but they're pulling my chain, and I really don't like it.' This time it was him who cut the call.

I turned up a side street and walked a hundred yards before whirling around abruptly and going back. Again, I saw nothing to worry me. This in itself was worrying. If dear Mark *had* put someone else on my ass he was a lot better than So'jer Boy or BZee.

I was back in Eaton square when the burn phone rang.

Les said, 'Sorry we took so long. We think there is someone following you. It's a woman, or a trans. She seems to appear in different clothes, colours and hats. So look for someone a little shorter than you, mixed race, who has a slight limp. She has a black and white backpack. Her shoes are trainers. Paulina thinks they're Nikes with two red flashes. The jeans have a designer tear on the left knee.'

'You're good,' I said, impressed.

'Paulina has a very sharp eye, especially for clothes,' Les told me. 'But here's the thing – we didn't see her at Clapham Junction but she turned up at Victoria. Not, apparently, among the crowd that exited the station same time as you. She turns up on your second sweep, then on your fourth. We don't know how she's picking you up so accurately.'

'Oh fuck,' I said. 'Is she on her phone a lot?'

'No,' Les said, 'but she might have a headset like yours. She's never close enough to you to see. What're you thinking?'

'The bastard may have someone tracking my phone.' And if he does, I thought, I'd bet my life I know who it is. And whose fault would that be? Well, actually it would be mine. I'd even sent Mark Sid Nailer's price list when Mark was still Dear Mark who I was trying to awe with my know-how and efficiency.

'What will you do?' Les asked anxiously.

'Turn it off,' I told her. 'We'll be okay. No one knows about the burn phone except you and me.' But I didn't actually know if that would be enough. 'So, if the leak is me, shall we carry on with this?'

'I can't think what else to do,' Les said. 'You have Paula's papers.'

'I could post them to, say, the Estonian embassy or consulate, or whatever, with a note to say they'll be reclaimed by the owner.'

'Insecure.'

'Or find an organisation far out of London who could look after her temporarily?'

'No,' Les said. 'We'd just have the same problem later. In the meantime that bloody man will know you still have the papers. You'll be even more vulnerable.' She paused, then went on, 'Now I'm worried about you too. He's a violent man. You know, don't you, he forced Paula to have an abortion? It nearly finished her.'

'No!' I said. 'He told me she had a miscarriage.'

'Well, he would, wouldn't he?' Les paused again. 'Look, Hannah,' she went on, 'for your own safety, go to a very public place and have a coffee. Paula and I will try to think this through. Okay?'

'Okay,' I said, glad to have something simple to do. It was all too complicated. Why wasn't I working for Les and Paulina? Because I was being paid by Mark Ferguson, who had abused an underage girl. But I mustn't let him know what I knew or he wouldn't trust me anymore. 'Find my ex-wife,' he'd said, 'so that I can make sure she's alright. I admire, like and trust you, Hannah.' And Hannah, of course had fallen for the spiel of a shitty, shifty bull-shitter.

I sat miserably in Costa Coffee in the Victoria Station mall, thinking, Again: my choice of which men to believe was crap. I shouldn't be let out on my own.

But blaming myself was stupid. Did I force Carl to be an evasive coward who deployed courtesy like a deadly weapon? Was it my fault that that Ryan Reynolds was a resentful, violent womaniser? Or that Mark Ferguson was a paedo? And was I to blame that Tom was a sexist bully who didn't love me?

There was a lump in my throat that made it difficult to swallow more coffee. Was I stupid, a victim, or just unlucky? Then I remembered a friend from Police Training saying, 'Apparently, the worst crime of all is to be unlucky.' We'd been studying the case histories of three women jailed for petty theft. All three came from immigrant families and were women of colour, all had been abused, all had spent some time on the game, all had their children taken away from them, and weirdly, all of them were left-handed.

I was just thinking, I'm not *that* unlucky, when the phone rang.

Les said, 'We have a plan.'

'Good,' I said, because sure as shit on a shovel I didn't know what to do next.

'Where are you?'

'Still at Victoria. And in spite of having turned my phone off, I'm pretty sure I've spotted your limping woman.'

'Can't be helped,' Les said. 'What I want you to do is play silly buggers on the underground. Switch platforms, switch trains, but stay underground. And turn your phone off.'

'I can do that.'

'But whatever happens,' Les said, sounding very serious, 'you must be at the front entrance of Kings Cross Station at eleven twenty-five with your burn phone on. Got that?'

'Then what?'

'Hannah,' she began, even more seriously. 'We trust you. Paulina, in fact, has trusted both you and me with her life. *Her life.* But you're compromised. All I can say is that there's a convent up in Leicester.'

'A convent?' I was astounded.

'She needs peace and structure. It's her own choice. I don't think she actually wants to be a nun – it's not the end of the line for her. But I don't expect to see her again.'

'I'm sorry,' I said.

'Don't be,' she said briskly. 'In my business, if I've done my job properly, my clients can get on without me.'

'All the same,' I began.

'All the same.' She cut me off. 'Hadn't you better get on your way?'

So I got on my way, down deep into the labyrinth that is London's tube system. I boarded the Circle Line and circled. I got off, changed platforms, changed from the Circle to the District Line, changed from District to Northern Line, doubled back and forty minutes from the time I started, I got off the Piccadilly Line at Kings Cross thoroughly confused and smelling of something you only find deep under London.

At eleven twenty-five exactly I was outside the front entrance. The phone rang.

Les said, 'Now sprint. Run to the Euston Road – the main road in front of you – turn right and then right again at Pancras Road. The entrance to St Pancras Station is through the arches. When you get there, go to the shops in the main hall. Go! *Now!*'

I ran. I dodged people, luggage, bus queues and half the population of North London. I felt lost and out of breath. And mostly, pissed off because surely there was an easier way of doing this.

Inside St Pancras Station I was confused by contradictory signage – this way to mainline platforms, that way to Eurostar, the other way to the Underground, and the other, other way to buses and taxis. I didn't know what I was supposed to be looking for. And there were too many people, including a huge zigzag queue.

I was feeling like a foreigner who didn't speak the language, sure I'd got something wrong, when I saw someone jumping up and down, waving to me. It was Paulina herself standing in front of a sandwich shop. She looked excited. Her hair was glossy, her makeup perfect and she was wearing a green silk jacket with what looked like hand-carved bone buttons.

'Hannah,' she said, 'you made it. How lovely to see you.'

I was panting too hard to speak, but I had the unreal impression that she thought she'd invited me to a party.

'Just in time,' she chirruped, looking significantly at my satchel.

I opened it and drew out the envelope I hadn't touched since Ferguson handed it over at Clapham Junction. While she was struggling to open it and I was wiping sweat off my face, I looked at her. Although she was tiny and very young, she really didn't seem dressed suitably for a convent.

'What a lovely jacket,' I said, watching her fingers tangle with Mark's parcel tape. She looked down at her sleeve, then up at me, smiling with pleasure.

'Yes,' she breathed. 'It is beautiful. Les gave it to me.'

She finally got the envelope open and I had a horrible moment of doubt that the sodding man, in spite of my vigilance, had managed to switch the contents. But no. What she took from the envelope was what I'd seen him put in.

'Thank you,' she said with a huge smile of relief. 'Now I am free to go.'

'But won't you miss Les?' I asked.

'Who?' She was turning to go. 'Oh, yes, Les. She is so much more to me than an advisor.' And then she darted away and I just had time to realise she was almost the only person to be travelling without luggage. Then I noticed that instead of following the sign to the main line platforms she was making for the Eurostar queue.

'Hey,' I called, 'wrong direction!'

She didn't turn round. She just waved her documents in the air and began threading her way at top speed through the zigzag queue. The other passengers made no objection, letting her jump ahead without complaint. I was just thinking, 'That's very un-British', when I saw, far off at the head of the queue, a woman I thought I recognised. I couldn't see her properly but I was fairly sure she had short, sandy hair and a round pink face.

Les, I thought – Les was holding Paulina's place in the queue for her. But then the *two* of them went through one of the security gates *together*. And disappeared.

Open mouthed, still breathing hard, I looked at the Departures screen and saw that Eurostar non-stop to Paris was now boarding and would leave very shortly.

I just stood there feeling like a total diddlo. I could only mutter 'Convent? My sainted arse!'

All that was left of my unbelievably brief meeting with Paulina was the torn envelope and parcel tape she'd dropped at my feet. I picked it up. That's me – unpaid but useful to the bitter end. And it was a bitter end. I hadn't even managed to take the photo of Paulina receiving her passport that Mark had requested. I'd been out-thought, and under-prepared.

I stood there, jostled by everyone and everyone's luggage. Everyone going every-fucking-where. Except me – caught, paralysed, between two lies.

I realised I should talk to one of the liars right now – bringing him up to date. I turned on my phone, and while I was waiting for it to reconnect I tried to flatten the tangle of paper and parcel tape in my hand. It was just as my phone gave the double buzz that told me it was ready to go, that I felt something small and hard under my thumb. There I found, stuck between parcel tape and paper, a tiny tracking device.

'Perfect.' I said out loud. 'Effing, sodding, crapulously *perfect.*'

I looked up and saw, about twenty feet away, a woman with a black and white backpack and a designer tear on the left knee of her jeans. She wasn't looking at me, but she was even more out of breath than I was. I was starting to walk towards her when my phone rang. I answered it, saying, 'Hang on a minute.' But when I looked for her again the woman was gone, swallowed by the crowd.

'What the bloody hell's going on?' Mark Ferguson shouted into my headset.

44

I hate the Kings Cross-St Pancras part of London. It has no soul of its own, no one seems to live there, it's all transients passing through. And there's nowhere quiet to sit down to have an acrimonious conversation with an enraged man when I want to have my wits about me.

As I walked, I said, 'I can't hear you – it's too noisy, my reception is very patchy.'

As I spoke two police cars shot past followed by an ambulance and a fire truck. All of them had their sirens at full blast.

'Squawk, squawk, squawk,' said Mark Ferguson. I shut him off and went down into the Tube again.

I took the Victoria line straight back to Victoria. No messing around this time. I'd been on a fool's trail, thinking I was shaking off a tail when I switched off my phone and took complicated evasive action. All along, imbecile Hannah was carefully guarding the device by which she was betraying herself.

I'd dumped the tracker and the packaging at the station. The Limping Lady with the torn jeans would find it and report back. But no one needed to know that I'd found it first.

While I was on the train I composed a text to Double Judas Ferguson. I like texts sometimes. You can say stuff without interruption, and you can say what you want to say and delete anything that looks like a mistake.

I wrote, 'Sorry about all transmission breaks. I was sent on a tour of the deep underground. No reception. Paulina was at St Pancras Station. She received her papers safely and gratefully. No time to talk. She was catching Eurostar to Paris. She seemed happy and healthy. Talk when my phone sorts itself out?'

I pressed Send when I was on the Southern Overground on my way back to Clapham Junction. Okay, Central London, I thought, you can stuff your evil-smelling, rackety, claustrophobic Underground labyrinth and keep it exactly where it is – where the sun don't shine.

It was lunchtime when I found myself, with a sigh of relief, back on my home turf. I bought takeout falafel and pita from the Falafel House and went to sit on a bench in The Common. I hadn't had breakfast, I reminded myself, and I'd been jerked from pillar to post all morning. Surely I'd earned a stress-free lunch.

I did not turn my phone on until I'd licked the last crumbs off my greedy fingers. Then I found fifteen missed calls, eleven of which were from Fascist Ferguson. I didn't bother to listen to them; I just tapped his number. As soon as he answered and before he could start shouting, I said, 'Sorry. My phone had no signal underground and it's gone a bit bozeyquat since. But, hey, mission accomplished.'

'What the hell do you mean, "mission accomplished"?' he yelled. 'She's gone to *Paris*. Why, in Gods name, didn't you stop her?'

I let that hang for a moment as if struck dumb, and then I said, slowly and reasonably, 'I don't understand, Mark, why would I stop her?'

That suddenly seemed to register with him. I gave him a second to begin to splutter before cutting in again with, 'Mark, you never once told me you wanted me to stop her going whenever she wanted to go.'

'It's that man,' he yelled. '*Les!* You've allowed that bloody man to control her.'

'But Mark,' I said, soothingly, 'today, for the first time, I spoke to Les in person. She isn't a man. She's Paulina's counsellor. You can't be worried about *her*.'

There was a charged silence. Then he said, much more evenly, 'Excuse me, I've had a difficult morning and there's a lot of new information to process. I'll get back to you soon.' And he cut off.

No shit, Mark, I said to myself. If you want to know about difficult mornings, I'll tell you about mine. I had a lot to process myself. I was on shaky, quaky ground. Who had lied to me? Who had I lied to? Was what I thought I'd done for the greater good of an abused girl, in fact morally all fucked up? What was Les's game? What was Paulina's game? She could have a game of her own, even if she was only sixteen.

Would Ferguson cough up the rest of my fee?

Consequences! Even finding a kidnapped dog had unimagined consequences. Does working for a horrible man make me horrible too? I'd assumed Carl and Mark were good guys. Why? Because they asked me for my help? Why did that little fact cause me to neglect assessing them as *men*?

When I'd asked Mark why he'd employed a one-woman operation who only took cases too small even to merit a call-back from the cops, he said he knew the bosses of the other bigger, better equipped firms in the area. Truth? Yes: given his fear of gossip, certainly. But even more true was the fact that as a one-woman show, I'd be easier to control, easier to fool. I thought he chose me for my strength, but he chose me for my weakness.

While I was walking home depressing the shit out of myself, along came BZee, looking hungry. He was neither a child nor a man, uneducated, uncared for, neither straight nor bent, but an independent survivor. He should be an inspiration to me, but I worried about whether I was I helping or harming him when I bought him the double cheeseburger and double fries he asked for.

We sat on a wall outside the burger bar while he stuffed his face.

'Did you?' he asked when every last scrap of food was gone.

'Did I what?'

'Find her? Girl. Rich man want back.'

'He never told me he wanted her back,' I said. 'Yes, I found her. But she went to Paris. She won't come back. I saw you at Clapham Junction. Is he still paying you?'

'Nah,' he said moodily. 'One time only.' But he gave me his widest grin and added. 'You run like you got chili powder up you bum.'

'Were you supposed to follow me?'

'Yeh, if you stay on foot. Nah, if you catch train. You find guy she two-timin' with?'

'There wasn't a guy.'

'No guy?' He looked surprised. 'For true? Him sure of guy. Told me you selling him out to young guy.'

'He was lying to both of us, BZee,' I said sadly. 'For one hundred percent true, there was no guy. And he's really pissed off with me. Also,' I added, with a bit more grit, '*I'm* really pissed off with *him*. I won't ever work for him again.'

'Me neither,' BZee said. 'Except for one ton, cash up front.'

*

I walked slowly home. Mark did not ring back but there was a text from Les: 'We're sorry we deceived you. Until the last moment we didn't know absolutely that we could trust you. Sorry about that too. And many thanks for all your help. One last favour – please would you delete all texts and emails from me? And also my details from your contact lists. We don't expect MF to give up, and as you once said, I am the weak link. Paula sends love and thanks too. x'

That was all. I was in no mood to be soothed. I deleted that text as soon as I'd read it. Love and thanks, my raging rear-end!

The house was empty. I went upstairs and showered the dirty old labyrinth out of my hair and off my skin. I put on clean, comfy old trackies and lay down.

But I didn't want to think. I was fed up with being lied to, and utterly pissed off with questioning myself. I scrolled through the missed calls and picked Myles as the only one I wanted to call back.

He may be an ache in the aardvark, I reasoned, but that's not his fault and, as far as I know, he's been straight with me.

For a change, Myles wasn't really speeding. He said, 'I spoke to Gina last night. Rafael allowed me twenty minutes on the phone. Everything you told me was right, but I don't want to dwell on that.'

My trashed ego hungered for him to dwell on me being right, but he went on without a pause, 'Hannah, Gina remembered me. She remembered me as sweet, shy and lost. She remembered me being bullied by her father and my mother to behave differently, to erase myself so that I'd fit into the Turner family culture. She watched me try. And that's when she noticed that the family culture was tribal: it didn't want me to fit in. Failure to fit was built into its structure. She told me that my living with them showed her how bent out shape *she* was. So she tried to help me, and she decided, in spite of the disapproval, to follow her own path. Hannah, she remembered me as a bright, hard-working kid who loved her, not as a nuisance everyone wants to avoid.'

'Myles,' I began. But he talked over me. 'And, Hannah, I could remember her as kind and beautiful. I remembered the plays, the pantomime, she'd taken me to. I remembered her as talented and funny. I remembered how great her timing was in comedies, how lovely her voice was when she sang. And, oh Hannah, I remembered her *dancing*. So, she said, I gave her back an identity that wasn't sick, crippled and slurred of speech. We had gifts to give each other.'

He stopped then, and I could hear him blowing his nose. My own eyes were prickling. When I could, I said, 'I'm so glad, Myles. Thanks for telling me.'

'I'll send you a cheque,' he said.

'I'd never discourage you from giving me more money,' I said, 'but you've already paid me quite a lot.'

'And you've given me a lot of time and thought.'

'Any chance it could be cash, off the books?' I said, in case anyone thought I'd gone soft.

I lay back against the head-board feeling weirdly forgiven. It was nice even though I couldn't explain it. The feeling lasted for all of seven minutes when Mark Ferguson rang.

He said, 'Has Paulina been in touch?'

'No,' I said, surprised. 'Did you expect her to?'

'Did you open the envelope I gave you?' He sounded really tense.

'Of course not. You sealed it with a load of parcel tape. She had quite a hard time opening it. Why are you asking?'

'Did she say anything about me?'

'No,' I said, trying to sound more puzzled than I actually was. 'She said, "Thank you," which I think was meant for you. But as I told you, we hardly exchanged a word. She checked her documents and ran to the Eurostar security gate.'

'What did she say about this Les person?'

'Nothing. Les was her counsellor, therapist, advisor – whatever you want to call it. She was helping Paulina, that's all I can swear to. And she isn't a man.'

'Do you think Les is a lesbian?'

'How on earth am I supposed to know that? And so what if she is? Mark…'

'I want you to inform me immediately if either one of them contacts you again.'

'Mark!' I almost shouted, 'you employed me to find out if Paulina was okay, and if she needed your help. She was okay, but she wanted her documents. You agreed to provide them. I agreed to take them to her. I've done everything you required of me, and it was a lot more time-consuming and complicated than I thought it would be. Neither you or Paulina explained why and I'm not asking for an explanation. As far as I'm concerned the job's done, carried out as per your instructions. Shall I invoice you?'

There was a tense silence on the other side of the signal. I almost held my breath. Was I convincing him that I believed his story and his good intentions? Was I hiding my conviction that he was a criminally dangerous creep who was trying to re-assert his will on a frightened teenager?

You could say I wanted to prevent him from employing someone way better equipped and far more competent then me. But actually my most pressing motive was that I wanted my money and I was afraid that he'd withhold it out of spite.

Mark broke the silence by saying, 'Hannah, I must apologise. I think I've been going a little crazy lately. I've been disturbed by the responsibility I feel for a woman I only meant to help. I'm devastated that she should treat me as a threat. You can appreciate that, can't you?'

Yes was the simplest answer, so I gave it.

He went on, 'Maybe the shelter's opinion that all men are potentially violent infected Paulina. You can see that, can't you?'

The only answer I could think of was, 'I get it.'

'I knew you would,' he said softly. 'Of course I'll send you the balance of what I owe. But I don't want to lose you or your know-how and experience, so I was wondering if I might put you on some sort of retainer?'

I felt myself being sucked, willy-nilly, back into his fiction about himself as someone I could admire and fancy. Worse, I *wanted* to be suckered into believing his fiction about me as someone he didn't want to lose.

'That's a great offer,' I said before I could stop myself. I cleared my throat and added, 'But I'm afraid I won't be taking on any more work in the foreseeable future. I have to find new digs, and flat-hunting will take all my time and attention.'

'I might be able to help with that,' he offered. 'Do let me know how you get on.'

I thanked him and we parted, I thought, on good terms.

But I sat on the edge of my bed, going through the conversation in my head – comparing his bullying, demanding approach at the beginning of it with the reasonable, appealing tone at the end. I was confused. Then I thought of how I'd been manipulated and sent on a wild goose chase by Les and Paulina. And they weren't even paying me.

So where did plain fact sit? Had I decided to act on Paulina's behalf because I was *prejudiced* in favour of mistreated women? Well, yeah, probably.

'Oh fuck it,' I said out loud and punched in Sid Nailer's number.

After the usual Hi, How are yous, I asked, 'Did that rich guy, the one with the Alpha Romeo, who I recommended you to, get in touch?'

'Sorry,' he said, a little too vague. 'Remind me.'

'His name's Mark Ferguson.'

'Oh yeah,' Sid said. 'I shoulda thanked you for the connection. Remind me to return the favour.'

'Return it now,' I said. 'Did he by any chance ask you to track *my* phone this morning?'

When he didn't answer straight away, I went on, 'And did you happen to sell him a cute little state-of- the-art tracking device?'

More silence. Then he said cautiously, 'You know I can't break the confidence of a client.'

'Last chance,' I said. 'If the answer's no, keep talking. If the answer's yes, hang up now.'

He hung up on me.

So *that* was where plain fact sat. Sometimes I really need to know.

45

Next day I was back at the Sandwich Shack flipping burgers and chicken nuggets. Apparently the day before, Candice and Magda came in with a bag of oddly shaped vegetables, so today Digby set me to making the first autumn vegetable soup of the season. He'd added a few crusty brown loaves to the baker's order, which meant he thought there was a good chance my soup would sell out.

He was right. Usually there's nothing on the menu that isn't meat-heavy. He thinks vegetarianism is only a fad. But today there was a chill in the air and a north wind blowing.

While I was making soup and Dulcie was cleaning up after the usual protracted breakfast trade Sophia Smithson came in bearing a satisfyingly thick envelope. She plonked herself down at an inside table, demanding latte and a doughnut. As usual she had something to say before she gave me my money. This time she told me to add pearl barley, thyme and parsley to the soup. I told her to mind her own business. But when she was pretending not to watch, I did exactly as she instructed; the result was a lot better than if I hadn't.

When the huge pot was simmering nicely I made her another coffee and a mug of tea for myself.

She said, 'As you know, I don't approve of you, but in this case I have to admit that your judgement was not frightful. My godson seems to have found solace in his renewed friendship with his stepsister, and has enjoyed the first decent night's sleep in months.'

'Glad to hear it,' I said, wiping my hands on my apron and sitting down opposite her. I'd slept like a boulder myself and was therefore more patient than usual.

'Personally,' she said pushing the envelope across the table, 'I think he's been over-generous. But as he assured me you didn't *ask* for more money, I'm prepared to let it go this once.'

I stuffed the money, uncounted, into my back pocket and waited for her next zinger.

She went on, 'And I suppose I should thank you for your introduction to Rafael Freshford. He was knowledgeable, creative and most helpful. I shall be making a donation to the foundation that employs him.' She sipped her coffee before continuing. 'Surprisingly he showed more than a passing interest in you.'

I was surprised too. 'Interest?' I said cautiously.

'He asked me all sorts of questions about you and your situation. Given that I have very little interest in the small amount I know, I was not much use to him. But I thought you should be warned.'

'Thanks,' I said. 'I'm warned.'

She stared at me over the top of her glasses, finished her latte and left without saying goodbye.

Dulcie took her place having first checked that Digby was in the office, out of earshot. She said, 'I'm not pregnant – I came on this morning.' She was pale and puffy around the eyes.

I had the feeling that whatever I said would be wrong so I took a blister pack of ibuprofen from my shirt pocket and offered it to her. She swallowed two tablets with a gulp of my tea.

'I can't go on like this,' she began. But before she could say any more we both saw BZee hovering by the takeout hatch. She leaped up and snagged him two ham and cheese sarnies and a slice of chocolate cheesecake while I used the token to raid the soft drinks machine for his Cokes.

We heard the office door open so we shooed BZee away before Digby could catch us stealing. Dulcie quickly turned on the radio to a Golden Oldies station and continued to clean the kitchen while dancing to Cher singing Love After Love. Digby listened to the lyrics for a few seconds and then switched it off.

Dulcie protested, 'There are no customers to annoy at the moment.'

'Well, it annoys *me*,' he said, 'and I'm the boss.'

'"I really don't think you're strong enough, no",' I sang, taking over where Cher left off.

'"And maybe I'm too good for you, no".' Dulcie went on with the song. She had a nice light voice. She turned the radio on again. 'Besides,' she said, 'there's two of us and only one of you.'

'You're out-voted, Digby,' I said.

'If you two bims think this is a democracy, you've even stupider than you look' he snarled. 'It's an autocracy, and the boss, me, is the autocrat.'

'That's not how Employment Law works,' said a voice from the hatch. It was the weedy mild-mannered old guy who helped out at the Citizens' Advice office on the High street. We all watched Digby march back to the office in a strop.

'A bowl of your soup, please, young lady,' the old geezer said to Dulcie. 'I think I'll sit outside while there's still some warmth in the sun.'

I noticed though that there was precious little sun and he kept his coat buttoned up to the throat while he ate.

That was how the lunch rush started. Digby spent the next two hours sulking in his office, and the radio stayed on. Score for the women.

*

Fifteen minutes before Digby usually cashed up, when Dulcie and I were loading the dish washer and the steriliser, he summoned me to the office telephone.

'Hospital for you,' he said handing me the clunky old fashioned receiver.

'Shit,' I said, thinking it'd be typical of St Georges to release my dad, with his cracked hip and Long Covid, into my care while Nattie was still away on the beach.

But that wasn't it at all. A mellifluous female voice said, 'Hannah Abram? I'm most awfully sorry to inform you that your father, Ezra Abram, passed away this morning.'

'What?' I said, staring at Digby who was waiting impatiently to get his desk back. I sat down heavily in his chair.

It turned out that in the night my father's recovery had come to a snorting halt when his breathing went ape-shit again. He was put back on a ventilator, but he suffered a sudden catastrophic stroke. The crash team failed to resuscitate. And that was that. Finito – quick as a blink his lights went out.

All I wanted to ask was why the Bad News Lady hadn't rung my mobile phone, and how anyone knew to ring the Shack's landline. But I didn't ask and the mystery was never solved.

I texted Nattie, who replied: What do you expect me to do about it? I'm due home tomorrow anyway.

Thanks a bunch, bruv.

I called Aunt Esther who said she'd round up the Rabbi and meet me at the hospital. She knew how to do things properly. So did Dulcie who brought me a mug of strong builders' tea and the last slice of chocolate cheese cake. I felt shock but not sorrow. It was un-nerving. I no longer had a disappointing father; I had a *dead* disappointing father. But there was no sense of loss, except that my questions about why he and my mother had never had time, attention, money or support for me would never, now, be answered. All I had left was a dotty mother who didn't like me. And soon I would be homeless.

I was trying to make myself feel sorry for myself, I thought, in the back of a cab on my way to the hospital. I ought to be feeling something, *anything*. But I wasn't.

It was nearly nine when at last I could crawl upstairs to my little attic room. I turned on phone, iPad and computer searching for something I could think about that wasn't a dead father.

What I found was a missed call from Rafael Freshford, and decided it wasn't too late to ring him back.

I said, 'What's up? How're you getting on?' before he could ask the same question.

'Oh, getting used to being a one-armed bandit,' he said. 'I'm a pain in the arse to my dwindling stock of friends and forming an intimate relationship with the local Uber driver.'

'And you only buy wine in screw-top bottles and you no longer wear shirts with buttons,' I added, beginning to relax.

'You got it.' He sounded as if he'd mastered the screw-top bottle more than once that evening. 'I rang because I wanted to let you know what a success Gina's contact with your Mr Emerson was. Although, if they continue I'll have to set a few unbreakable ground rules.'

'Yep,' I said. 'He's the toy whose batteries never run down.'

'Poor chap,' Rafael added piously.

I burst out laughing, and having started, couldn't stop.

'What's up?' he asked, when he could get a word in.

'Nothing,' I said. 'No, I'm lying. It's been a bitch of a day – my father died this morning and I spent most of the afternoon with a Rabbi making funeral arrangements.'

'Oh fuck,' he said, sounding totally unprofessional. 'And I've heard that Jewish funerals follow death fairly promptly.'

'No hanging around,' I agreed. 'Scoop 'em up and straight into the flowerbed with 'em. Death notice and Save-the-date card comes in the same envelope.'

'No time for grief?' he suggested.

'It's not that,' I said. 'How do you grieve for someone who spent all his love, attention and ambition on his son, and sent his half-educated daughter out to work to help pay for his son's university place?'

'Is that what happened?' Rafael said. 'Stupid question. Of course it is. Well, you might find yourself grieving for the father you never had.'

'I think I've been doing that all my life,' I said, suddenly astonished. 'Thanks, Rafael.'

'What for?'

'Dunno,' I said. 'Insight? Taking what I said seriously.'

'Another stupid question coming up,' he said. 'Would you like me to come to the funeral with you? Or is there a friend or partner to keep you afloat for a couple of hours?'

'But,' I began, even more astonished, 'I only scrambled a few eggs for you.'

'It was more than that,' he said. 'I'm not returning a favour. You were good company. I'm just trying to find a way to see you again without you suspecting that I'm hitting on you.'

'Oh,' I said. Then, in spite of being quite mystified, I added, 'Well, you might have succeeded.'

Why did I say that, I wondered later when I'd taken a couple of minutes to think about it. Wouldn't it have been more in character to say, 'Are you crazy – then what would we find to do for a *second* date?' or, 'Well you'd have to bring a hat and leave the ham sandwiches at home,'? Something tougher or funnier to show that I wasn't taking the offer seriously.

You'd think, wouldn't you, that given my experience with men in the past few weeks, I'd be a tad more wary. You'd think that I'd say to myself, hey, Hannah, you think Rafael's a nice guy? Well, remember your effing record with men you liked to begin with, and run like hell. The only bloke you haven't made a mistake about is

Digby. He's doesn't pretend to be anything other than the arrogant, aggressive, mean, sexist pig he appears to be.

His response, when I told him about my father's death was, 'Sod it, Hannah, I suppose this means you'll want more time off. So why don't I save money and fire you now? You can re-apply after the funeral.'

'If you do that,' Dulcie said, 'I'll go too.' Her chin jutted out although her hands were trembling. She, unlike me, seemed to have learned a thing or two in the last few weeks.

'I don't know why I bother to employ women at all,' he said. 'With you lot it's all periods and headaches, and oh my grandma's sick, and woe is me, my dad just kicked the bucket.'

'Know what, Dick-by?' I said, taking off my apron and throwing it onto his precious desk. 'You were born a short-arse, so before you could walk you learned to climb a ladder just so you could look down on the rest of humanity. Pity you're still up there.' It wasn't one of my best, but here's the thing I like about him: instead of hitting me or canning me, Digby turned his back and walked away laughing.

Much later, as my head at last hit the pillow, I asked myself, Is that my thought for the day – however stinky the situation, always try to walk away laughing? Of course it wasn't the profound kind of thought a short-order PI needed, but it'd have to do for now.

ABOUT THE AUTHOR

LIZA CODY is the award-winning author of many novels and short stories. Her Anna Lee series introduced the professional female private detective to British mystery fiction. It was adapted for television and broadcast in the UK and US. Cody's ground-breaking Bucket Nut Trilogy featured professional wrestler, Eva Wylie. Other novels include Rift, Gimme More, Ballad of a Dead Nobody, Miss Terry, Lady Bag, Crocodiles and Good Intentions (the sequel to Lady Bag) and Gift or Theft. Her novels have been widely translated. In 2019 she won the Radio Bremen Krimipreis.

Cody's short stories have been published in many magazines and anthologies. They are collected in two volumes: Lucky Dip and other stories and My People and other crime stories.

Liza Cody was born in London and most of her work is set there. Her career before she began writing was mostly in the visual arts. Currently she lives in Bath. Her informative website can be found at www.LizaCody.com which includes her occasional blog.

Printed in Great Britain
by Amazon